SALVATION DAY

SALVATION DAY

KALI WALLACE

BERKLEY
New York

BERKLEY
An imprint of Penguin Random House LLC
1745 Broadway, New York, NY 10019

Library of Congress Cataloging-in-Publication Data

Names: Wallace, Kali, author.
Title: Salvation day / Kali Wallace.
Description: First edition. | New York: Berkley, 2019.
Identifiers: LCCN 2018042257 | ISBN 9781984803696 (hardcover) | ISBN 9781984803702 (ebook)
Subjects: | GSAFD: Science fiction.
Classification: LCC PS3623.A4434 S25 2019 | DDC 813/.6—dc23
LC record available at https://lccn.loc.gov/2018042257

First Edition: July 2019

Printed in the United States of America
1 3 5 7 9 10 8 6 4 2

Cover design by Adam Auerbach
Cover photo of stars courtesy of Shutterstock
Book design by Laura K. Corless

For Audrey, who was right about this one

ACKNOWLEDGMENTS

Some books take a slightly more meandering path to existence than others, and I had a lot of help getting this one out into the world. Thank you to my agent, Adriann Ranta Zurhellen, for her tireless work, guidance, and belief in this book even when I was unsure what to do with it. Thanks to my editor Jessica Wade, assistant editor Miranda Hill, and the whole team at Berkley for all of their work and enthusiasm for this dark little space monster. And thank you to Adriana Mather, Shannon Parker, and Leah Thomas for your friendship and support.

Most of all, a million and one thanks to Audrey Coulthurst, who has believed in this book from the beginning and has been a tireless cheerleader every step of the way, even when she had much more important things to do with her time. Thank you for everything, my friend, corpses and all.

SALVATION DAY

SPEC SECURITY—RESTRICTED ARCHIVE REF. #39378832-N
SHIP-TO-SHIP COMMUNICATION TRANSCRIPT (AUDIO)
Source: FIRST SNOW, SPEC TRANSPORT
TimeDate: 15:19:37 01.10.393

FIRST SNOW: Can you confirm the ship's identification?

SCOUT 1: Yes. It's TIGER, Commander. It's from HOUSE OF WISDOM. Lieutenant Naidoo is on tether and approaching the airlock now.

FIRST SNOW: What do you see, Lieutenant?

SCOUT 2: There's no visible damage. Hull appears intact. Control panel is powered and responsive. System says the airlock is functional and the interior is pressurized, but . . .

FIRST SNOW: What is it?

SCOUT 2: There's something on the control panel.

FIRST SNOW: Evidence of sabotage?

SCOUT 2: I think it's blood.

SCOUT 1: Blood? That doesn't make sense. Intel says there was a virus. Bioweapon released by a former crew member. Commander? What aren't they telling us?

FIRST SNOW: I don't know any more than you do at this stage. We'll learn more when the rescue crews reach the primary target. Proceed with caution, Lieutenant.

SCOUT 2: Got it. Moving into airlock—shit, there's more here. Handprints on the control panels, the airlock, the hatch. I'm opening the inner door.

FIRST SNOW: Is there an injured crew member aboard?

SCOUT 2: I don't see anybody—no. Wait. Oh, no. Let me just—

SCOUT 1: Marybelle? What is it?

SCOUT 2: It's a kid. Fuck, it's a little kid.

FIRST SNOW: Can you repeat that? Did you say there's a child?

SCOUT 2: He's strapped into the pilot's seat. He's injured. The blood might be his. Let me just—I need to check. I need to find a pulse.

FIRST SNOW: Do not expose yourself until we are certain there are no biological agents aboard the craft. Do you copy? Do not put yourself at risk.

SCOUT 2: Okay. Okay. He's breathing. He's—oh, sweetheart, it's okay. Don't try to move. I know it hurts. Can you tell me your name? Please don't be afraid.

The Earth was behind me, but I could still feel it. It hadn't yet let me go.

Outside the broad windows of the loading area, the long shaft of Civita Station tethered the port to the ground. As they waited their turn to board the shuttles, the passengers gaped at the Earth, exclaiming with delight as they watched daylight fall upon familiar cities, mountains, curves of seashore. I had looked, once, when we took up our positions. I did not care to look again. A single glance had given me the profound feeling of falling, the gravity of the planet grabbing me back when I was so close to escaping. It was enough that we had left Earth. I did not need to gape openmouthed like these spoiled students now jostling each other for the best view. They could have been squealing schoolchildren rather than honored postgraduate research fellows, so inane was their chatter, so boisterous their excitement. They were supposed to be the best the United Councils of Earth had to offer, but they thought themselves clever for picking out cities as though they were pointing at sweets in a shop.

"Tell me when you spot our target," I murmured. "Anyone?"

There were eight of us in the mission vanguard, four in the

station and four aboard the waiting shuttle. We had assumed our false identities several days ago, long enough to grow accustomed to the uniform and rules of the Space and Exploration Commission, the arm of the Councils that governed space travel and research. So, too, had we grown used to the obsequiousness, the meekness, the smiles, all the playacting required to pass as proud SPEC members. But I was suddenly unsure of how loud I needed to speak for our hidden comms to pick it up. We had never practiced in such a noisy, crowded space.

"Not yet." Panya's voice was a whisper in my ear. She was stationed on the other side of the passenger loading area. Her blond hair was tied back in sleek twin braids. There was not the slightest wrinkle of worry marring her pale white brow. Her uniform fit perfectly, and she wore it naturally, with the blue-and-white SPEC badge gleaming on her upper arm. We had been greeting the Leung research fellows and directing them to their shuttles for over an hour, but Panya's cheerfulness had not flagged.

"Negative," said Dag, and Henke shook his head. They were positioned on either side of the shuttle door, waiting until it was our turn to load up our passengers.

"Stop scowling," I said sharply to Henke, whose expression was creased in a deep frown. "Look like you're happy to be here."

One of the fellows glanced at me. I pressed my lips together and offered her an empty smile. The person I was pretending to be would not be muttering angrily to herself. She would be cheerful, calm, proud of her task and her uniform, never once considering that a career of such mindless servitude was an insult rather than an honor. The student gave me a vague look, then turned away to join her friends. Henke wrangled his sun-scarred face into some semblance of a grin. It looked worse than his scowl, but I didn't scold him again. He disliked obeying me enough as it was. I had learned to choose my battles carefully.

You have to be one of them. A speck of poison in the cancer that is SPEC. That was what Adam had said to me before the mission began. Two months ago, in the cool desert darkness before dawn, he had brushed a strand of hair from my face and touched my cheek. I had shivered with guilt I hoped he saw as pride, with fear I hoped he took for excitement. He was our leader, our savior, and I could not turn away, no matter how certain I was that he had already guessed the secrets I kept from him, the selfish reasons I had for needing this mission to succeed. He had smiled and said, *Inside you will always be my warrior, but on the outside you show them a servant.*

We could not take chances. The Councils and SPEC were watching constantly. If we erred for even a moment, the whole mission would be forfeit. It was one thing to risk arrest and imprisonment for ourselves if we were caught, but it was quite another to endanger Adam and the family. They were too important. Adam was too important. The Councils had been hounding him for years: attacking our compound, poisoning our crops, stealing our family members away, all because they could not abide a free man living as he chose in lands outside their control. They would have no mercy for him if our mission failed. He often said he would choose death over imprisonment if we failed him and our beautiful future was snatched away.

I adjusted my feet slightly in the straps that prevented me from floating free, and I looked over the crowd. Everywhere there were passengers tumbling, shoving each other, somersaulting away, laughing and teasing each other for their inability to move gracefully in microgravity, all of them talking at once. They were being divided into groups and slowly loaded into small shuttles to complete their journey to the Moon. There were more efficient ways to move large groups of people, but those ships were utilitarian, uncomfortable. They wouldn't do for these pampered scholars. The Leung Fellowship was named for one of the founders of the United

Councils of Earth, the leaders who four centuries ago had come together in the aftermath of the Collapse to commit humanity to rebuilding a better world from the ruins of its near destruction. It was that work these fellows were supposed to continue. They had been chosen to spend a term in Armstrong City, and at the end of that time they would participate in the four hundredth anniversary of the First Council. It was meant to prepare them to become scientists and diplomats, engineers and politicians, explorers and artists. They were being honed for the life of "contribution and responsibility" the Councils imposed upon its citizens. They were said to be the Councils' brightest, smartest, and most promising.

And right now they were trying to make each other vomit by whirling around in the microgravity. Long hair whipped, voices shrieked, curse words flew from mouths on showers of spit. I listened for the cruelty in their laughter, watched for the superiority in their eyes. They were young women and men now, joyful and optimistic, but they were training to become our oppressors. If they could see us as we truly were, their bright expressions would harden with disdain. There were limits to what Councils citizens were willing to contribute. Their claims of humane responsibility had borders as impenetrable as the walls that separated their gleaming cities from our sickly wasteland.

A voice boomed over the crowd. "Okay, everybody! Group three, your shuttle is ready! Line up and start boarding!"

The command came from a big man with black skin and gray hair and a voice that carried like thunder. Professor M'Baga was the faculty escort assigned to our shuttle. A theoretical mathematician: soft, elderly, not a threat. He floated his way over to Henke and Dag. He greeted them, shook their hands. They all nodded and grinned and shared a joke about energetic twentysomethings behaving like children. M'Baga admired the Flight Division tattoos on the backs of Dag's hands, clapped his shoulder, and thanked him for his service. Even Henke managed a convincing smile. In that moment I was proud of how well they played their roles.

"Group three! You're boarding now or we're leaving you behind!" M'Baga bellowed.

My pulse quickened as I looked over the crowd. These were our charges, now separating themselves from the others, carefree and unhurried as they moved toward the shuttle loading door. A scuffle broke out when one young woman accidentally kneed a man in the face. The man spluttered in protest and swiped at her, snagging her foot and spinning her away, which sent her barreling into her friends. The woman yelped and kicked awkwardly, caught the man on his jaw. The force of her kick—more accident than intent—shoved him backward into another young man, who caught him around the middle and easily stopped his momentum.

The second man let go of his friend. He turned. My breath caught. I saw him only in profile, but I recognized him instantly.

I had studied his face in photographs so many times I could see him when I closed my eyes. Black hair, brown skin. Eyes so dark they were nearly black. Angular cheekbones, even when he had been a child, more pronounced now. A recording of him roughhousing and laughing with his mother in her workshop had been played countless times on news reports in the months after the *House of Wisdom* incident. My own mother, ashen with shock and grief, her arms wrapped around the twins while they slept, had watched with tears in her eyes, murmuring, *That poor little boy, I can't believe it, that poor little boy.* The other women at the homestead sat with her sometimes, not understanding the depth of her despair. We were at the time newly extracted from the persecution of the Councils and the shadow of my father's supposed crimes, but only Adam knew who we were and what we had left behind. Everybody who joined the family took Adam's name, so my mother ceased to be Mariah Dove and became Mariah Light, for brightness and warmth, for the strength of the desert sun, for the fiery blaze of stars.

The boy on the news reports had never looked sad to me. He had never cried. Not even at his parents' funerals, where he had sat wrapped in a dark blue blanket in a wheelchair, his aunt rigid and silent beside him, a phalanx of security guards encircling them as empty caskets were fed into a meaningless ceremonial fire. The cameras had remained fixed on his face. He had not shed a single tear.

His name was Jaswinder Bhattacharya. He was twenty-two years old, and he was the most famous orphan in the solar system. He was the son of the woman who had designed the engines that drove the fastest spaceships and the man who had solved the root module salt accumulation problem for large-scale microgravity agriculture. Padmavati Bhattacharya, his aunt, was one of the most powerful Councilors in the United Councils of Earth, with a position so elevated few people had any true idea what she did. Bhattacharya himself was an astronomer who studied the life cycle of galaxies, with a focus on the quasars at their centers. It was a rather esoteric and impractical field for the son of people who had done so much to propel modern humanity back into space.

He was the only survivor of the *House of Wisdom* massacre. My father's massacre, or so the world believed.

Ten years ago, four hundred and seventy-seven people had died aboard *House of Wisdom*, victims of a biological attack that had unleashed a fierce and fatal engineered virus known as Zeffir-1 into the ship's atmospheric control system. The system's air filters had been upgraded right before my father left the ship; the virus had struck right after. Captain Ngahere and the Deep Space Archaeology research team had accused him of hoarding data and hiding results for his own personal glorification. And, years before, my father had written a series of papers about Pre-Collapse biological warfare. It was a frail web of circumstantial facts and feeble accusations, none of them proof, but it was all the evidence SPEC and the Councils needed. They never looked for another culprit.

Bhattacharya turned his head. I glanced away quickly—but he was looking past me, through the window to the elegant spine of the space tether, to the Earth below.

I turned to see what he saw. The clouds, the seas, the continents. Cities scarring the landscape. The quicksilver glints of shuttles and transports reflecting the sun. I had not wanted to look, and now I could not look away.

Four hundred years ago, after generations of war, famine, plague, and environmental destruction, a small group of people trapped aboard an orbital weapons platform had unleashed their payload to detonate in the atmosphere. They had meant to destroy Earth, to put it out of its human-inflicted misery, but they failed. Humanity survived. The planet slowly recovered. Governments re-formed, then joined together beneath the umbrella of the Councils. Humans returned to space.

We were supposed to be proud of that. We were supposed to cherish the second chance we had been given. We were supposed to be better now. We were supposed to think it could never happen again. But those of us who had forged our own freedom in Earth's lingering scars knew differently.

Mankind will never change, Adam often said, his favorite opening to our nightly meetings. *So we must make our own fate.*

Somewhere out there, elsewhere above the Earth, our ship *Homestead* was already in orbit, with Adam in command. It was filled to capacity with three hundred men, women, and children—including Anwar and Nadra, my brother and sister. My team and I had been separated from the rest of the family for over a month. They had been smuggled across the border into Councils territory in small groups, slowly, carefully, at great risk to both themselves and the family as a whole, and we had not known they all made it until *Homestead* launched successfully. It was an agonizing and difficult separation. By the end of the day we would be together again.

The hollow feeling in my chest, it was not only from the lack of gravity. It was not only nerves. There was, pressing outward from my lungs, from my throat, from the chambers of my heart, a giddy hope I had never felt before. I would not be going back.

Boudicca's voice came over the shuttle intercom to announce our departure.

"Good morning, passengers," she said brightly. "Welcome aboard *Pilgrim 3* for our journey to Armstrong City. We're honored to have the recipients of the Leung Fellowship and future participants in the Second United Council traveling with us today."

The students were barely listening, but if they had been, they would hear a pilot who was calm and confident, trustworthy to her core. Unlike the rest of us, Boudicca was not playacting an unfamiliar role. She had been a SPEC pilot years before, briefly famous as the pilot of the first ship to attempt rescue after the transport *Breton* crashed on the surface of Mars. Horrified by what she had seen, Boudicca publicly criticized SPEC's response to the disaster; they responded by limiting her flight assignments again and again, putting her on shorter and shorter routes demeaning to her skills and experience. When they finally grounded her, Boudicca had left SPEC rather than accept the insult of becoming an instructor for her replacements. She soon learned there was no room in the Councils for a pilot who was forbidden from flying, so she had given up her Councils citizenship as well, turning her back on them as they had turned their backs on her.

But she had never given up her dream of returning to space.

She had never given up her love of flying. There was excitement in her voice now, beneath the cool professionalism, and no small amount of joy.

"Our flight is going to be a leisurely one," Boudicca went on. "The port at Armstrong is running behind schedule, so SPEC has asked us to spread out the passenger arrivals. Normally we could make this trip in under eight hours, but I'm afraid it'll take a bit longer than that today."

The port was running off schedule because of us: sympathizers to the family, the same anonymous helpers who had smuggled us across the border, had arranged for a complication in permits to slow down traffic at Valle de México Spaceport, which disrupted the flow of lunar traffic. The delay meant that the orbital Tereshkova Shipyard, along with its steady stream of transports carrying supplies for the massive asteroid-bound ice-breaking fleet, would be on the wrong side of the Moon when *Pilgrim 3* was supposed to be landing. We needed the extra time. We needed the distraction.

Boudicca finished: "So sit back, relax, and enjoy the view. If you have any questions, we've got four crew members in the cabin to help you. They'll be serving lunch about halfway through the flight."

Me, Panya, Henke, Dag as the cabin crew. Boudicca and Malachi in the cockpit. Nico and Bao overseeing the engines and cargo. There were enough of us to control our hostages, although they didn't yet know that's what they were: eleven fellows, one professor.

Pilgrim 3 was a small shuttle, with three rows of four seats, split down the middle by an aisle. M'Baga had chosen a seat in the first row on the port side, and next to him was a girl who looked far too young for university. The professor said something and pointed out the window; the girl smiled shyly. A prodigy of sorts, I guessed, and lonely for it. I remembered enough of life in Councils schools to know that if she had friends, she wouldn't be sitting in the first row by the teacher.

Behind M'Baga and the child were a man and a woman in their late twenties or early thirties, older than most of the fellows, holding hands and so wrapped up in each other I doubted they even knew they were in space. Behind them, two young women pointed through the window at familiar landmarks on Earth. Across the aisle, starboard front row, was a short woman with spiky, multicolored hair, and a fat woman with dreadlocks twisted into an elaborate crown. They had fastened their harnesses without having to be told and listened attentively to Panya's safety instructions. Good citizens, obedient, they wouldn't be any trouble. Not so the two young men behind them, who were laughing and showing off. One of them had leered at Panya and said, "I'm so happy you're here to keep us safe."

In the last row on the starboard side sat Bhattacharya and another young man.

The second man was nobody of importance, but I had looked up his history anyway, curious about who might befriend Amita Bhattacharya's son. Baqir Nassar, twenty-one years old, was born in a North American refugee camp during an epidemic of Danzmayr's disease. He had left the desert several years later when his four parents—a complex marriage of two men and two women—finally applied for and gained Councils citizenship, but not before three of his siblings succumbed to the plague. Nassar was permanently scarred by the disease: his left arm had been amputated and replaced by a robotic prosthetic. He did not disguise his metal arm and fingers with synthetic flesh or gloves; the silver gleam caught the light when he gestured.

His scars were all most people would see when they looked at him. He would have to work twice as hard to prove he was worthy of citizenship, of this research fellowship, of a place alongside all the pampered children of the Councils. He would spend his entire life being blamed for the choices his parents had made, for being born in the wrong place, for being ill, for carrying the dust of the desert wasteland in his veins. The United Councils of Earth pretended to care for all of humanity, but their compassion had limits.

I wanted to understand if Nassar felt those limits, or if he pretended he was treated as an equal. I wanted to know what he was doing here. What he hoped to prove. If he knew that it would never be enough.

It was possible, I thought, that my mother had encountered Nassar's family when she worked in the refugee camps during an outbreak. She had volunteered in the borderlands when I was young. That had been her first experience of the desert, the first time she saw how the Councils treated the people who chose to live outside its false security, the first time she tasted that hardship and freedom for herself. She might have held an ailing baby boy in her arms while his mother recovered from childbirth, bringing a small, insignificant life into the world while thousands died around them and the Councils offered nothing but overworked doctors and empty promises. As outbreaks raged and the camps overflowed with the sick and dying, the Councils dragged their feet, refusing to expedite the byzantine citizenship application process, refusing to open the borders, refusing to welcome desperate families, refusing, refusing, refusing. Far removed from the hardship, Councilors and commissioners argued about the risk of a global pandemic, the impact of devoting even the most meager resources to those in need, the danger of opening the gates and letting anybody pass. They may have kept their mutterings about plague-ridden criminals overwhelming their perfect clean cities to private conversations, to whispers behind closed doors, but still they muttered, and my mother heard them, and she never forgot.

Bhattacharya had taken the seat by the window. Nassar was on the aisle. I didn't like that. It made Bhattacharya harder to reach.

"You've got a lot of crew on this flight," M'Baga said.

"Yes," I said shortly. I didn't want to talk to him, but I could not avoid it. Panya was still cajoling the flirting young men into tightening their harnesses. "It's a full crew. We want to keep everybody safe."

"Including two with the engines," M'Baga said.

I silently cursed Nico and Bao for sticking their heads out to watch the passengers come aboard. They were supposed to have stayed hidden.

"They're a teacher and apprentice from the engineering corps. They're only here for training and observation. There's no work being done," I said, hoping our prepared explanation would not make him suspicious. "There's nothing to worry about."

"Oh, I trust it will be a smooth ride," M'Baga said.

"We'll do our best," I said, and I smiled, and I wondered if I would have to kill him before the day was over.

After we had served lunch, about five hours into our journey, I gestured for Dag to come to the front while I went to the back of the passenger cabin. I moved carefully down the short aisle, holding on to the handles on the backs of the seats and hoping nobody noticed how uneasy I was in zero gravity. I wasn't entirely sure how much more time we had, as Boudicca had kept updates to a minimum to avoid drawing attention to our route, but I didn't want to be in the front, far from our target, when the time came.

The shuttle windows to my right showed the Earth, too small and too bright. To my left there was only darkness and stars. Neither view soothed my ratcheting nerves. I took my place at the back and hooked my feet into the straps behind the last row of seats. Beside me, Henke was massive, pale, and grim with menace. I did not tell him to smile now.

I was relieved to be away from Professor M'Baga's searching gaze and pointed questions. Dag was a better choice for the professor's attentions. He had spent years aboard various ships, working his way up from cargo loader to pilot, before he was caught diverting goods to a smuggler and was given a choice: imprisonment or revocation of his Councils citizenship. He had chosen the freedom of the desert. The Flight Service tattoos on his hands were genuine, and he was happy to chat amiably with the professor about flying transport ships to build Halley Station, piloting a gravity slingshot around Venus on his second-ever command, stories we had all heard a dozen times before. There had never been any doubt that Dag yearned to get back into space. That was one reason Adam trusted him so much.

I turned my attention to Bhattacharya and his friend.

"Are you sure you're going to have time to do all that?" Bhattacharya asked. They were talking about what they would be doing during their fellowships in Armstrong City—the same conversation most of the fellows had been having all morning. "That sounds like five projects combined in one."

"Yeah, I know, but it's worth a try, right? It's not like I can replicate a low-gravity hydrological environment on Earth. If I can do this, maybe SPEC will look at my proposal for the Jupiter project." Nassar gestured carelessly, then stilled, looking at his hands before him, pressing the cybernetic one down to the armrest while the other floated above his legs. The contrast between his silver metal fingers on one hand and brown skin on the other was striking. "Okay, that feels weird."

"You get used to it," Bhattacharya said. "It's even weirder on the

Moon, because you keep expecting there to be either Earth gravity or free fall, not somewhere in between."

"Besides," Nassar went on, "at least I'm not basing my entire project on twenty hours of telescope time."

"Twenty-six," Bhattacharya said. "I argued them up."

Nassar rolled his eyes. "So that's what you were doing on that call. What did you do, promise you'd name a black hole after the administrator in thanks?"

"She's already got two black holes, three nebulae, and a galaxy named after her. No, I told her I'd ask my aunt about bringing up the improvements proposal before the end of the year."

I listened to Bhattacharya's words, to the tone of his voice, searching for any waver of fear, but there was none. As far as I knew, he had not been back to space since the *House of Wisdom* massacre. He had never spoken publicly about the attack; his aunt had shielded him from the demands of the public and press. The official line was that he did not remember—but he had been twelve, not an infant. I was only a year older than him, and I remembered those terrifying days so vividly they could never be cleaved from my memory. The Zeffir-1 outbreak on the ship had come only two days after my father was sent away from *House of Wisdom* in disgrace. He had not even arrived home yet; SPEC had been questioning him about the data he was accused of stealing. I remembered it all clearly: the twins asking when Daddy was coming back, strangers charging into the house the night he died, the solemn announcement that the Zeffir-1 vaccine would be distributed globally. My mother yelling at SPEC investigators. Nadra and Anwar crying when we left for the desert. They had been only five and didn't know what was happening. But I had been thirteen, and I understood everything. I could still hear the tiredness in my mother's voice when she said, *There's nowhere else for us to go. They'll never leave us alone.*

Bhattacharya had been old enough to bear witness. His decade-long silence had to be a lie.

"Hey," a man said. "Hey, isn't that—"

I looked up, a prickle of fear shivering over my skin. The unfinished question had come from one of the loud young men in the middle row. Brown hair, olive skin, lanky and tall. The one who had been clumsily flirting with Panya.

In my ear Malachi said, "Oh, shit."

Boudicca's voice was much calmer. "Relax. They were going to notice eventually. Distract them. We have time."

"Should I make the announcement? Give them an excuse?" Malachi asked. I could easily imagine the expression on his face: frantic and strained, his brown eyes wide with worry beneath his curly dark hair. Malachi was copilot because we needed his skills in the cockpit, but I also knew that it was better to keep him hidden, where his inability to veil his worry would not give us away.

But it was too late now. As Boudicca had said, they were going to notice eventually.

"What is that?" the young man asked, and his words fell into a natural lull in the surrounding conversation. Everybody heard him. My heart began to thump faster.

"It's a station," his friend said, leaning over for a better view through the window. "Providence, maybe?"

Providence Station sat at the L1 Lagrange point between the Earth and the Moon. It was home to twenty thousand people and served as the origin port for ships leaving the Earth-Moon system on long-haul journeys. It was massive in size and iconic in shape: a broad ring several kilometers in diameter. It was also a good two hundred thousand kilometers away from where we were headed.

"Don't be stupid," said a woman in the front row, the short one with colorful hair. "It's too small, and it's not a ring."

Panya spoke up brightly. "We can certainly ask the captain to identify it for us, if you like, but right now she's busy following Orbital Control's directives. They've got quite a mess to deal with today."

M'Baga glanced at her, then leaned over to the starboard as far as his harness would allow. "You're right, Ariana. It's not Providence. It's a ship."

"It's huge," said the man in the middle row. "The only ships that big are the new icebreakers, but they aren't done yet. Is it some kind of test flight? It could be an early test flight."

His friend nudged him. "Nobody wants to hear more about your icebreakers."

"I'll pass your question along to the captain," Panya said.

"It's not working," Malachi said over the comm. "They know."

In the front of the cabin, Dag moved to open a storage cabinet; Henke did the same behind me.

M'Baga's brow furrowed. "It's too large to be an icebreaker, even one of the new ones. It almost looks like . . ."

The environment aboard a spacecraft is carefully controlled down to the smallest factor. The mix of oxygen and nitrogen, the permitted concentration of particulates, the temperature, the humidity, even the rate at which air cycles through the vents so that no passenger feels too warm or too cool, too stuffy or too drafty, all of it is determined by the ship's computer, leveled and measured for perfect balance. There was no chance that any passenger aboard *Pilgrim 3* would feel a chill.

But where there were cautious small motions before, now there was stillness. Where there was conversation, silence. The women and men on the port side were leaning and stretching to see the opposite view. Those on the starboard were staring out the windows. They were all looking at the same thing. Panya said something, another soothing reassurance to another volley of questions.

I unhooked my foot from the strap and grabbed a handle on

the wall to pull myself down. I looked over the top of Bhatta-charya's head, past the ghostly shape of his reflection on the window. The voices flowed around me like desert wind. My chest ached. I could not breathe.

It was so close. I could reach across space to touch it.

House of Wisdom had been named for one of the ancient world's great centers of learning, the name a promise of the discoveries and advances that would be made during its explorations through the solar system. Like its namesake, the ship had no equal. At the time of its launch seventeen years ago, it was the largest and fast-est ship in existence, propelled by Amita Bhattacharya's Almora engine—named for the Himalayan town where she had decades ago dreamed up the propulsion system that would secure her leg-acy. *House of Wisdom* was designed to glide through the solar sys-tem as the sail ships of ancient times had crossed Earth's oceans, bringing the bold and curious to places they had never been be-fore. It was meant to be a living laboratory of long-term scientific research and space exploration, an unmatched step forward in modern humankind's reach for the stars. It was the ship that had established the research stations at Europa and Io, intercepted the probe UC33-X when it returned from its centuries in deep space, and rescued the miners of Ceres when a cascading failure had damaged the station's water recycling system. It had traveled the solar system for seven years, and during those years there was not one person on Earth who did not gaze at the sky and imagine themselves aboard the great vessel, soaring among the planets. The day my father was invited to join *House of Wisdom* as part of the team studying the ancient probe UC33-X was the happiest day of his life.

House of Wisdom had once been the pride and joy of the Space and Exploration Commission. Now it was a crypt.

And we were flying toward it on a broad, gentle arc.

In the front row M'Baga reached for his harness.

"We need you to stay in your seat, Professor," Panya said. She was still smiling, but her voice had hitched up a notch, taking on the breathy, little-girl pitch she used when she most wanted to appear nonthreatening. "If the shuttle has to accelerate suddenly, you could be injured."

"Is there something wrong?" M'Baga asked mildly. "We seem to be well off the usual course."

"There's nothing wrong. We're taking a detour, that's all."

But the fellows knew by now that Panya was lying. No ship should pass close enough to *House of Wisdom* to see it with the naked eye. For ten years it had waited in orbit maintained by occasional, automated thruster fire, trailing the Moon on its orbit by some two hundred thousand kilometers, and protected by a ruthless security net of high-powered drones. To discourage daredevils or scavengers from nosing so close that they would put themselves in danger, SPEC maintained a strict no-fly perimeter of fifty thousand kilometers, with severe punishments for even accidental breaches.

"I'd like to speak with the captain," M'Baga said. There was a click as he unclasped his harness.

"This will be fun," Henke said. I glanced at him. He was smiling.

Panya caught my eye over the tops of the seats. I nodded. It was time.

Dag drew a gun from a compartment in the crew area and pointed it at M'Baga. His face carried none of Panya's serenity or Henke's pleasure, nor was there the slightest hesitation in his voice when he said, "You don't need to talk to the captain."

M'Baga stilled, looking from Panya to Dag. "What's going on?"

"You're going to remain in your seat." Panya raised her own weapon; her hands trembled. "Fasten your harness, please."

Henke took two weapons from the rear compartment and pressed one into my hand. We were not carrying the suppression weapons the Councils favored to subdue people using electric shock or sedation. These were projectile weapons designed for use in space. Most of the passengers had probably never seen one before except on news reports or in history books. The Councils saved their violence for those they could not control, not the sheep who submitted to their will.

Nothing has weight in space, but there was a pull to the gun's mass that I could not ignore, and it made my motions awkward. I caught the slightest sneer of disapproval on Henke's broad red face. I ignored it.

"What's going on?" M'Baga said again. He was speaking calmly, deliberately slowing his words, as though we were wild animals and he meant to tame us. "What do you want?"

"Please stay in your seats," Panya said. "We don't want you to get hurt."

"If you tell us what you want, we can help," the professor said.

The passengers gaped at Panya and Dag, all of them transfixed and on the verge of panic. I had not expected fear to mesmerize them so easily. They could not look away as Panya repeated herself, told the professor to stay quiet, told the students to remain seated. She spoke in the same soft way she used to when teaching children on the homestead, and like those children, the passengers were captivated by her voice—save one.

Bhattacharya was not looking at Panya. He was looking at *House of Wisdom*.

There was a spark in the back of my mind, the beginning of something that I might have recognized as doubt, had I considered it at all. But watching and seeing are two different things, and I did not know what it meant that, when faced with armed strangers on what was supposed to be a peaceful trip, nothing inside the shuttle frightened Jaswinder Bhattacharya as much as the ship outside that window.

I heard the click of a harness and snapped my attention to the front of the cabin. M'Baga hadn't moved. There was a collective gasp, the passengers inhaling in fear—

A young man surged from his seat. The one in the middle row, who had been flirting with Panya, who had first spotted *House of Wisdom*. He grabbed the seat in front of him and propelled himself upward with so much force he struck the ceiling with his shoulder and bounced back. Panya and Dag swung their guns toward him. M'Baga took advantage of their distraction to unfasten his harness.

"Panya!" I shouted, but she was already reacting. She turned her weapon to M'Baga again, the muzzle only half a meter from his face.

"Please," she said softly. "Sit down, Professor."

But the young man, that stupid young man, he kicked the window behind him, foot skidding on the smooth surface, and launched himself toward Panya and Dag. He twisted in the air, his arms flung out, grasping clumsily for Dag's weapon. He let out a yell—wordless, pathetic. There was a sharp pop. His head vanished in a pink mist.

My finger released the trigger.

Dag reached out to stop the body on its forward trajectory.

One of the women screamed, and once she started she didn't stop. Her shrieks filled the cabin. Where there was frightened quiet before, now there was only noise. Shouting, screaming, crying, demanding answers and expecting none, a suffocating crush of sound. We were going to lose control of our hostages. They were panicking, and they needed to be cowed.

I pressed my weapon to the head of Bhattacharya's friend.

"Don't move," I said.

Somehow, through the screams, he heard me. I couldn't see his expression; I was looking at Bhattacharya. That face I had studied in news reports and stolen SPEC files so many times, as familiar to me as that of my own brother. He looked at his friend, looked at my gun, looked at me. Above their heads the red mist coalesced into larger droplets, the droplets into globules, coming together like the beginnings of a solar system, gathering around the bits of brain and skull. A molecular cloud forming a star.

"You're going to do what we say," I said to Bhattacharya, my voice just loud enough to carry over the whimpers and pleas, "or I'll kill him too."

The Earth our ancestors left behind was dying. They named this ship *Mournful Evening Song* because they could not see their way through the darkness. But if you can hear this, if humanity survives even now, we want you to know we have found our dawn. Soon we will sink our roots into the soil of a new world. We have nothing but hope in our hearts.

—FRAGMENT 1, *MOURNFUL EVENING SONG* VIA UC33-X

[Archaic Mandarin Chinese [Beijing dialect, circa 200–100 PCE]. Data reconstruction and translation by Gregory Lago, *House of Wisdom*, Deep Space Archaeology.]

JAS

I saw my mother die a thousand times. In nightmares, in unguarded waking moments, in the drug-induced haze following
every surgery and the long, lonely quiet of recovery, I imagined her death as it might have been, as it could have been, and
impossibly as well, methods and means that made no sense and
could never have happened. I imagined a hundred scenarios leading to a hundred more, sometimes peaceful, more often horrific,
the probabilities and potentialities tangling around and around
themselves until they were a storm in my mind, every one true,
every one an agony.

There was surveillance everywhere aboard *House of Wisdom*.
There were cameras in the laboratories, public areas, and corridors. Even in the private living quarters, absent video and audio
recorders, the ship was watching: the medical system monitored
the location and health of every person aboard to constantly assess
who was ill and who was well, who had worked too long and who
was rested enough to call upon in an emergency, a never-ending
churn of calculations and assessments.

On the morning of the fourth of January in year 393 of the
Reconstruction Era, the ship detected the heartbeats of four hun-

dred and seventy-eight people. Four hundred and seventy-eight crew, researchers, staff, and families. Four hundred and seventy-eight thriving and unsuspecting lives, not one of them aware that Dr. Lago's virus had already begun to spread.

Twenty-three hours later, there were none.

Laid out all together on a single image, the pulse lines fell flat like seismographs in the aftermath of a world-shaking quake. For many there was a wild spike of panic as they realized they were infected. Some ended there. Others subsided into an eerie calm with heartbeats so regular they might have been paced by a machine. Their calm might last minutes, hours, but it, too, ended with death. Some died in clusters, groups of ten or fifteen people extinguished all at once. Many died alone.

Somewhere in the mess of flattening lines, my father—

Identification: Roy, Vinod
Position: Chief of Botany and Horticulture
Location: Personal living quarters 7.23-S
Time of death: 17:37:04 01.03.393
Cause of death: Hemorrhagic shock

And hours later, when the signals of the survivors had thinned to a few jangling electric kicks—

Identification: Bhattacharya, Amita
Position: Propulsion Engineer (Research Primary)
Location: Unknown
Time of death: 02:13:56 01.04.393
Cause of death: Unknown

The record of my mother's death was among the last disjointed fragments of data the ship had transmitted before it went dark.

All of this information was sealed by SPEC Security, but if a person were truly determined, and possessed the right connections, those records could be uncovered. My aunt was one such person.

It was just before the start of school when I was fourteen. All summer I had been short-tempered to the point of absurdity, picking fights with everybody, sulking for days in my bedroom with the curtains drawn. Baqir had visited for a couple of weeks, but he had gone home two days ago. We fought before he left—there were shouts, blows exchanged, bloodied lips, and quickly hidden tears—and I was certain when the school year began he would decide that friendship with me wasn't worth the trouble, and I wouldn't be able to blame him. I had said unforgivable things. I couldn't even stand my own company. I woke every morning wanting to crawl out of my skin, went to bed every night hoping I wouldn't wake up in the morning, and through all the hours in between, I felt phantom aches and pains vibrating through my entire body. I would lie in my bed, the house hushed around me, and imagine fissures appearing in my bones one by one, like cracks spreading over a frozen lake. I pictured them as faint lines of sickly yellow light, a spiderweb of fractures spreading through my body, every one of them sparking with the slightest pain as it broke open. I had seen the images from my medical records. Half my bones had broken when my mother's experimental craft accelerated me away from *House of Wisdom*; the pilot's chair had been designed for a full-grown adult in a compression flight suit, not a twelve-year-old child in his pajamas. By the time I was fourteen, the injuries were healing, the constant pain finally reduced to occasional flares, but in dark moments I could feel every wound becoming new again.

It had been a hot day and it promised to be a hot night. The monsoon finally passed from the hills above Dharamsala a week or two before, leaving in its wake a heavy mist that slunk over the lake, cloaking the rhododendrons in a clinging damp veil. It was too warm to open the house to the outside, but my aunt asked the staff to do it anyway. She liked to taste the night around her, un-filtered by the house's enviro controls. We ate dinner at the counter in the kitchen, a simple meal of dal and roti. We did not speak. I picked at my food and stared at the lake. I watched the mist drift above the water and wondered if it would feel good to take a night swim and knew I would not find the energy to do so. The stars were hidden anyway, and the night was no comfort without stars.

"I have something for you," my aunt said.

I was so surprised to hear her speak that I started, bumping my plate into my water glass with a soft clink. "What?"

"You're old enough now," she said.

Padmavati Bhattacharya did not explain herself to anyone, and especially not to me, the nephew she had never wanted to raise. She had told me once that several people came forward after the *House of Wisdom* incident with offers to adopt me. For a time I let myself imagine what my life would have been like if she had let them. To grow up with another family, in the home of people who had seen a broken boy on the news and decided they wanted to surround him with warmth and love. To have siblings, cousins, impostor parents with wringing hands and sad eyes. I imagined a life in which they might have changed my name, taken me somewhere—as though such a place could exist—where I was not a constant reminder of the world's tragedy. Where I could have been somebody other than my dead mother's shattered son.

My aunt had never even met any of those would-be adoptive parents. She told me they only wanted fame and prestige, not a child. She was probably right. Still I wondered.

I waited as she set aside her dinner and turned to the kitchen wallscreen. She had eaten even less than usual. My aunt was a small woman, birdlike in her frame; when my mother was alive, she had dwarfed her older sister so much she could rest her chin on my aunt's head. They would both laugh when she did that, playful, younger than their years. I could not remember when I had last seen my aunt laugh. I could not remember ever thinking her fragile before, but that evening, the two of us in our house by the lake, she looked so very small, and so very old, tired in a way that grayed her brown skin and stooped her normally dancer-straight shoulders. Fear and worry stirred beneath the selfish numbness I had been wallowing in for days. She never rested. She would not tell me if she was unwell.

A list of file names filled the screen.

"What is that?" I asked.

"This," said my aunt, and she sighed on the word, an uncharacteristic pause, "is all of the data received from *House of Wisdom* before the transmissions stopped."

A distant, low buzz filled my ears. My skin went cool and clammy all over. My aunt left me alone in the kitchen. She might have touched my arm as she passed; she was not one for casual gestures of affection. For a long time—minutes, an hour, time stretched and snapped around me, meaningless in its flexibility— I could not bring myself to open even one of those files. I didn't know what to do. I hated that my aunt had given this to me and walked away. She would not have done so unless she wanted me to see something. She never did anything without reason.

Then, without even meaning to, I was looking for my parents.

When I had begun speaking again, months after the attack, I told everybody who asked that I did not remember anything. I had blocked the trauma from my mind. It was all a blur, a nightmare haze. I did not remember. Not the spread of the virus, not the cascade of deaths, not leaving *House of Wisdom*, not drifting in space aboard my mother's ship. I told them I did not remember Dr. Lago and the outrage that gripped the onboard scientists when he was caught hiding data from UC33-X. I told them I did not know how my father had died. They suspected I was lying, but eventually SPEC Intelligence investigators decided that the testimony of a child who could barely speak wasn't likely to provide the answers they wanted.

It was easy to find the surveillance recording of the moment my mother sent me away. I remembered the location precisely: Level 12, Section D. Experimental Propulsion. The workshop where she built her small ships had once been as familiar to me as my own bedroom, but in the recording it looked as alien to me as another planet. There was already a corpse in the workshop, a woman named Linna, a fuel scientist and one of my mother's friends. My mother and I came through the door, floating, not walking; *House of Wisdom* had been in orbit for nearly a month. She pulled me along behind her. My pajamas were damp with my own blood, spilled from my nose, by then sticky and cooling to a ruddy crust, and my mother's blood from the wounds she had sustained protecting me. I had never forgotten how it itched when it flaked from my hands. How it tasted flowing over my lips.

In my aunt's kitchen I stood, walked to the sink, and threw up my dinner. I rinsed my mouth. I returned to the recording.

My mother put me into the first of her experimental ships, the one she had named *Tiger*. There was no audio to accompany the visual record, but I knew I had begged her to come with me. Our hands had smeared blood throughout the craft's small airlock, the cockpit, over the controls and pilot's seat, turning my mother's great engineering achievement into a crime scene. My mother had promised to follow, but she had things to do first. I had been crying when she sealed me inside, alone.

My mother returned to the launch console outside the dock. She gave the launch command. The air vented and the bay doors opened. The docking clamps maneuvered *Tiger* beyond the hull, beyond the reach of the surveillance cameras, and I was gone.

Because I was not properly logged out of the ship's roster, the medical system interpreted that separation as a system error, a curious blip that left me neither dead nor alive in the ship's eyes.

Identification: Bhattacharya, Jaswinder
Position: Minor Child
Location: Auxiliary craft TIGER ME-3
Time of signal loss: 12:53:04 01.03.393
Cause of signal loss: Unknown

When my mother turned to leave her workshop, she looked up at the surveillance camera—a steady long look, her eyes fiery with anger. She said something, lips moving briefly, silently. It might have been *I'm sorry.*

She left her sanctum on Level 12 and vanished.

There was no visual record of her after that. The ship's computer was severely compromised by then—the crew had done it themselves, in fits of hysteria—and the surveillance system was badly malfunctioning. A great deal of information was never recorded, and only a fraction of what was recorded had ever been transmitted to Earth. My mother's heart beat steadily for another hour or so, but she did not appear in the spotty surveillance data. If there were any data at all about where she had gone or what she had done after she sent me away, it was all locked aboard *House of Wisdom*, forever out of reach.

I shut off the screens and sat in the dark for a while. A large beetle had found its way through the insect screens around the house. It was tapping and prodding along the frame of the open door. The fog outside was heavier now; I could not see the lake.

After the massacre, I had nightmares for years about red clouds surrounding me, mist becoming drowning liquid, dancing in the air and light. The shrill, shipwide shriek of the alarm system. Shouting, screaming. Scalpels clutched in hands. Wild eyes filled with panic, going calm, then empty. When a person dies there are seconds when the heart still squeezes, not yet knowing it is time to stop. Human bodies are messy, imperfect things, a tangle of crossed signals and incomplete messages. Blood pumped into microgravity behaves oddly, like a living thing, unbound and restless, drifting, cooling. Never falling.

The beetle changed its mind about coming inside. Turned from the door, scuttled across the patio, vanished into the darkness. The insect screen would catch it on the way out. A snapping silent death: quick.

I had never tried to count how many people I had seen die that day. Their faces blurred into one in my mind, their screams into a single voice. I went to the sink to throw up again, though there was nothing in my stomach but acid.

Then I wrote a message to Baqir. I forgot we were fighting. I forgot that I was certain he would never speak to me again. I didn't have anybody else.

My aunt gave me all the data from the ship.

The response was immediate: INCOMING CALL. My hands were moving without my permission. The buzzing in my head had settled to a muffled numbness.

I answered Baqir's call, and his face appeared on the screen, and he said, "What the *fucking fuck* did she do that for?"

I started to laugh, but I was choking on my own breath, shuddering and shaking, and I could hear him saying, "Hey, hey, Jas, come on, breathe, you can breathe, you're okay," his words running together into a meaningless soothing rumble, the only good thing in a world where a man's life might end with the slash of a knife, a child's skeleton might snap with the burst of a spaceship engine, a mother might vanish with the halt of a heartbeat, and he didn't stop saying it, didn't stop for a second. "You're okay, you can breathe, you're okay."

The woman put her gun to Baqir's head. My mind was a blank white panic.

"You're going to do what we say," she said, "or I'll kill him too."

Baqir was holding himself so still the tendons in his neck stood out like ropes. He looked at me—didn't turn his head, only moved his eyes—and the fear I saw there cut into me.

Salvatore was dead. The dark-haired woman had killed him. His head—gone, like a burst balloon. An hour ago he had been snickering loudly about how many Moon girls he was going to fuck during his fellowship at the Tereshkova Shipyard. Lucian, next to him, had groaned and told him to shut up. They had laughed. Now he was dead.

I had barely looked at the shuttle crew when we came aboard, ignoring my aunt's oft-repeated advice to always, always look beyond the uniform. Look, notice, remember. I had dismissed her concerns as paranoid. People stared at me, but only because I was a morbid curiosity. I never took my aunt's worries seriously.

The blond woman was pale and thin, looked to be in her mid-twenties, but she spoke with a high little-girl voice that seemed more affected than natural. The older of the men, the one with the Flight Service tattoos on his hands, had a shaved head and a bland expression. The other man, the big one at the back of the shuttle, was scowling, his red face wrinkled beneath his flat pale hair. They were all armed.

The woman who had killed Salvatore was in her twenties, with light brown skin, dark brown hair, hazel eyes. She was unremarkable. I had not looked twice at her when we boarded.

"I'll do what you say," I said.

It wasn't a decision at all. I would do anything to keep her from killing Baqir.

Across the aisle Gena's screams had quieted to a high-pitched wheeze. Lucian had started to gasp. It was a horrible sound, those struggling breaths, that growing panic.

Professor M'Baga said to the blond woman, "What do you want? Tell us what you want."

"Please stop talking," she said. Her voice was so calm. She had the same musical, lilting accent as Baqir's, the accent of the North American deserts. "You are all going to do exactly what we say. Please don't make this harder than it has to be."

"Of course," M'Baga said, "but if you'll only tell us—"

The blond woman pushed the muzzle of her gun against his forehead. "You need to stop talking, Professor. Ready, Zahra?"

"You," said the dark-haired woman. Zahra. She was looking at me, but her gun was still aimed at Baqir's head. He had dropped his chin to his chest to shrink away from the muzzle. Our arms were pressed together between the seats. "Bhattacharya. Get up. You're coming with me. And you"—that to Baqir, with a nudge in the back of his head. "You stay here. If your friend doesn't do what we ask, Henke is going to shoot you."

The other man—Henke, she had called him—took her place behind Baqir without question. He grinned and said, "With pleasure."

I unsnapped my harness and put my hands on the armrest to push myself up. Baqir pressed himself into the seat to let me pass, watching with wide, scared eyes. I wanted to tell him not to be afraid. I wanted to tell him I would do what they said and keep him safe. It was what he had been doing for me since we were twelve years old and he had decided to befriend the barely verbal fellow patient in the children's hospital. Me with all my broken bones, him with the disease eating him from the inside. *Don't be afraid,* he had said to me, more times than I could count. *Don't be nervous. You don't have to be scared. It will be okay. I'll protect you.*

I didn't know what they wanted, but my mind was racing. Something from my aunt, that was the only thing that made sense. They wanted to use me to persuade her to do something. They thought SPEC was lying about not having access to *House of Wisdom.* They were separatists or anarchists or militarists who wanted the Councils to vote one way or another, or release a prisoner, or something, *something.* I couldn't wrap my head around what they could possibly expect to get out of this. It wouldn't work. My aunt would not be impressed by their threats.

"Move," Zahra said.

She pointed toward the cockpit. I obeyed without hesitation.

The bald man at the front of the cabin was strapping Salvatore's body to the wall. The man's placid expression was even more unsettling than that of his grinning companion at the back. Salvatore's arms, limp and unbound, floated in front of his chest, reaching blindly, and the man swatted them carelessly when the fingertips brushed his shoulder, with no more thought than a horse might flick away a fly.

Forward of the passenger cabin, the orientation of the ship changed. The arbitrarily designated floor and ceiling ended, replaced by a vertical shaft with a ladder climbing toward a hatch. My hands were sweating as I gripped the rungs. If they wanted me to record a message for my aunt, I would do it. I would not fight them. There was a gun to Baqir's head.

Zahra said something quietly. It sounded like "We're here," and I realized they had been using a private comm system all along.

Another thing I should have noticed—would have noticed, if I had ever taken my aunt's security warnings seriously. The hatch unlocked with a soft clank, then opened.

The first thing I saw was the Earth, a colorful marble, directly ahead. I felt a sudden, dizzying disorientation that passed only when I realized I was looking not through a window but at a panel of six screens, each providing a view of a different angle outside the shuttle. There was Earth, there was the Moon as a small pale disk, and there were three views of darkness and stars—Regulus, Zosma, Denebola, familiar specks of light. Any other time, the views would have dazzled me. My yearning to return to space, to reach farther and farther into the void, had grown steadily over the past ten years. Any other time, I would have marveled. Now I could scarcely breathe.

On the sixth screen was *House of Wisdom*.

From a distance it looked like a skyscraper adrift in space, roughly rectangular, with its drive engines at one end and protective nose shielding at the other. Under acceleration the apparent gravity was oriented along the long axis. It wasn't true that it was the largest ship humankind ever built; the generation ships launched before the Collapse would have dwarfed it several times over. But at a kilometer long it was the largest built in the Reconstruction Era. About one-third of its length was taken up by my mother's Almora propulsion drive and all its associated systems. Just above the drive was the large, square docking bay, a window through the heart of the ship.

The shuttle's pilot was a woman in her forties with white streaks in her red hair. She glanced over her shoulder as we entered, then turned her attention back to the controls. "Five hundred klicks and closing. We're getting pinged with a request."

A request. Five hundred kilometers. The security net.

"That's too close," I said. "You can't—you have to turn away. The security drones, they'll destroy the ship, you have to—"

"Shut him up," the pilot said, without looking at me. There was no anger in her voice, no fear; my warnings might have been gibberish for all the concern she showed. Zahra's gun was already pressed against the small of my back. "You ready?"

The question wasn't for me. It was for the copilot. He was young for a SPEC pilot, maybe midtwenties, with curly brown hair and wary eyes. He grabbed my right wrist and pulled me forward, muttering a quiet apology as he wrenched my arm. He pressed my hand into what looked like a standard rapid-identification unit, the scan-and-verify sort used for basic security. There was a clear glass plate, cool to the touch, and beneath it the five trackers whirred and slid until they lined up under my fingertips, while sensors measured my pulse, my body temperature, the electrical conductivity of my body, confirming that it was a living flesh-and-blood person being identified. The unit pricked one finger with a needle, drawing a microscopic amount of blood.

"Come on," the copilot muttered, looking over the report from the ID unit. "Come on."

"Well?" the pilot said.

"It's processing," he answered, his voice lifting into a question.

That's when I understood what they were trying to do.

"No," I breathed. "It won't work."

The external security system had been developed when *House of Wisdom* was built, but it was kept secret until Dr. Lago's attack forced SPEC to reveal its existence. The most cherished tenets of the Councils, and therefore SPEC, maintained that space was to be open to everybody, free of the warfare and militarism that had brought about the Collapse centuries before. That was written into the Reconstruction Charters four hundred years ago, when the survivors of the Collapse came together to reshape what remained of the world. An armed security system for a research vessel went against everything SPEC was supposed to stand for, even if they claimed it was only experimental, even if they claimed it had only ever been meant for protection.

In the aftermath of the massacre, nobody had even known the security net was active until the first rescue team was killed before their ship could get within a couple hundred kilometers of *House of Wisdom*. The system was made up of a network of fast, agile, high-powered, and well-armed drones that could disable a ship in seconds—and had, twice in the past ten years, before SPEC finally stopped trying to break through.

"It won't work," I said again. I was pleading, but only the copilot spared me a glance. Fear clawed at my throat. We were too close. The drones would attack. This was a passenger shuttle. It had no defenses, no real maneuvering ability. "You're going to get us all killed, don't you understand? You can't—"

"Quiet," Zahra said.

The copilot, his curly brown hair dampened with sweat at the temples, sucked in a startled breath. He tapped frantically at the screen. I couldn't follow what he was doing, but I could guess. He was trying to persuade the security system to accept my genetic identification as a passkey for the quarantine. I was the only person alive whose ID was still in the *House of Wisdom* roster; the nature of my departure would have left an open query in the ship's system. It was possible that a confident hacker could try to persuade the security system that my shipboard identification was enough to allow passage through the security net. SPEC had tried a similar tactic themselves some years ago, but their failure to get it right led to the destruction of a second ship. The loss of one approach team was tragic; the loss of two was reckless. Three would have been unforgivable.

The copilot did not look like a confident hacker. He bit his lower lip, making him look even younger. His hands were shaking. He didn't think he could do this. He *couldn't* do this. Even SPEC hadn't been able to, with all of their knowledge of the *House of Wisdom* system at their disposal. The drones would attack. I wondered what sort of emergency space suits the shuttle had on board, and if we would have time to reach them. What a stupid way to die.

"Well?" the pilot said. She was smiling, but unlike the cruel smile of the big man in the cabin, hers was one of something like excitement. "We're getting pretty fucking close."

"One second," said the copilot. "It's—okay. It's good."

"Then get him out—fuck!" The pilot flinched as an object whirled by the ship outside, flashing from one screen to another so quickly it was impossible to see what it looked like. "What the fuck was that?"

She jabbed at the display, called up a slowed-down recording for a closer look.

It was one of the security drones. The ship's computer gave its distance at closest pass as ten meters.

"What's going on?" the pilot demanded, returning the screen to its live feed. "You said it was good."

The copilot was focused on his controls, his hands moving swiftly, more steadily now.

"Malachi, what's going on?" Zahra said.

"The passkey was accepted." The copilot was Malachi. Another name to remember. "They're not attacking."

"Then what are they doing?" the pilot asked.

The copilot was right: the drones weren't launching an attack. But they were clustering around *Pilgrim 3* in a swarm. Two were joined by two more, and two more, every one of them racing out of the darkness at such a high speed it looked like they were aiming for impact, but stopping suddenly, with a quick, bright flare of reverse thrust. The drones were spheres of absorptive metal about a meter across, with short spines protruding from its surface like spikes. The ends of those spines glowed briefly as the thrusters fired. They looked like eyes, gleaming and metallic and watchful.

"I've never seen drones like this before," Malachi said. "This is some serious dark project shit. Did you know SPEC has weapons that can move like that? Boudicca?" He looked at the pilot when she didn't answer.

"No idea," the pilot said. Boudicca. I was collecting their names one by one, and with it the knowing dread that they would not be saying them aloud if they cared that I heard. "SPEC doesn't build weapons, remember? So they claim. I hope there are no surprises waiting for us."

"There won't be," Zahra said. "And if there are, we'll deal with them."

I pressed my thumb and forefinger together, welcoming the faint distraction of the pinprick pain. None of them were looking at me, but still I schooled my expression. These people would only have gone through so much trouble—hijacking a shuttle, abducting me, hacking the security system—for one reason. They didn't want something from my aunt. They wanted *House of Wisdom*.

"I hope you're right," the pilot said. She tapped on the shipwide communication system. "I know you're all sitting pretty and doing as you're told. You're going to keep doing that as we go into a series of burns. If you try anything, those nice people with guns will shoot you."

"I think they get the picture," Malachi said. He flinched when the pilot glared at him, but he didn't look away.

"Let's make sure they keep getting it," the pilot said. "If this doesn't—" Another alert caught her eye. "Shit."

"What?" Zahra said. "What's wrong?"

"Orbital Control. They're contacting us."

I felt a sudden burst of hope.

"You said they wouldn't notice this soon," Zahra said.

"We don't know what they've noticed," Boudicca said. "Get him out of here—wait, no, let's keep him here, in case we need him. But you keep your mouth shut, or we will kill every single person back there. Got it?"

I nodded numbly. Zahra pressed her gun into the center of my chest. From that close I could see the greenish shards in her brown eyes, the faintest sheen of sweat on her brow, the way her jaw tensed when she swallowed. She parted her lips to say something— another warning, another threat—but the pilot was answering the comm.

"Orbital Control, this is *Pilgrim 3*."

A woman's voice came over the radio. "*Pilgrim 3*, this is *Barcelona*. We have a priority location query from Armstrong Port Control. Their trackers cannot verify your position. Have you ventured off your flight path?"

The hope I'd felt withered. Orbital Control wasn't monitoring the no-fly zone around *House of Wisdom*. They were only trying to find a wayward shuttle that was supposed to be approaching the Moon.

"Negative, *Barcelona*," Boudicca said calmly, without a trace of nerves. I had no doubt that she had been a SPEC pilot in the past. "Flight path maintained."

"Please confirm your position and velocity, *Pilgrim 3*."

"Understood, *Barcelona*. Passenger shuttle *Pilgrim 3* currently located at azimuth 75.5, polar 183.7, radius 367,000 plus 140 kilometers, static velocity 20.45 kilometers per second. We've got Armstrong in our sights and are about to begin deceleration."

There was, of course, no Moon growing ever larger outside the shuttle. We were two hundred thousand kilometers off course, in a strict no-fly zone. If SPEC was scrambling to find us, it would be a while before they looked in the right place.

Say something, I told myself. Zahra's gun was a soft pressure in the center of my chest, but the urge to call out for help was a bitterness at the back of my throat. Say something. Shout when the pilot is speaking. Hope *Barcelona* hears. But it could be hours before SPEC found us, would definitely be hours before they arrived. They would kill me, kill Baqir, kill all the others. They had gotten what they wanted from me. We would be dead before the nearest ship arrived. I could not make a sound. Fear had stitched my lips together, dried my throat, squeezed my lungs so tightly every breath was a struggle.

"Negative, *Pilgrim 3*," said Orbital Control. "Armstrong cannot confirm position. Repeat: Armstrong Port cannot confirm your position."

"I don't understand, *Barcelona*. I've flown this route a hundred times. Our coordinates are accurate."

"Understood, *Pilgrim 3*, but we can't bring you into Armstrong until they've got a fix on your position. There's a lot of traffic today because of the foul-up at Valle de México. Please advance to standard holding in lunar orbital radius of fifteen thousand kilometers and stand by."

"Standing by, *Barcelona*." Boudicca turned off the radio. She looked at me over her shoulder. "There is no help coming for you. The only way you and your friends get out of this is if you do what we say and don't cause any trouble. Is that clear?"

I nodded.

"Get him out of here," she said.

Zahra escorted me back to the passenger cabin, where I took my seat beside Baqir. The scowling blond man, the one Zahra had called Henke, wasn't holding a gun to Baqir's head anymore, but he was watching the cabin carefully, taking in every motion, every sniffle of fear, every whispered word. Baqir met my eyes, twitched his lips in something that might have been, in any other circumstance, a reassuring smile. He always smiled when he was afraid. He had once said it was a survival instinct, like coyotes baring their teeth before a fight, and I had laughed. My hands shook as I tried to fasten my harness. Baqir moved, hesitated, then reached over to do it for me; his metal fingers clicked softly on the clasp.

The shuttle's thrusters fired, filling the cabin with a low rumble.

Baqir cleared his throat and whispered, "What do they want?"

"I don't know," I answered, just as soft. The cabin was leadenly quiet. Even Professor M'Baga had stopped trying to reason with our captors. The blond woman kept her gun trained on him. "They want to get to the ship."

"Why?" Baqir said. "What's there?"

"We only want to be left alone," Zahra said.

Baqir jumped at the sound of her words. But she hadn't raised her voice, nor her weapon, so he turned as far as the harness would allow to look at her.

"What do you mean?" he said.

"Stop fucking talking to them," the big man said. His grin was gone, but there was now a calculating look in his eyes. He wanted us to disobey.

"It does no harm to help them understand," Zahra said. "We have nothing to hide. Our only goal is to break away from the shackles of your Councils and make a life for ourselves among the stars."

She sounded as though she were quoting somebody else, *the shackles of your Councils,* the words rolling off her tongue with the ease of a phrase she had repeated firmly and often. Zahra did not have a North American desert accent like Baqir's, but I was certain she and her people were separatists who chose to live outside the governance of the United Councils. But that didn't tell me who they were, or what they truly wanted, or how to stop them. People fled the Councils to be left alone—not the other way around. The North American wasteland was where they went when they didn't want the responsibilities of citizenship, the burdens of a global society, the rules, the laws, whatever else it was they found distasteful about the Councils. They didn't hijack shuttles to steal ships and risk bringing the whole force of SPEC down on them.

"Are you going to kill us?" Baqir asked and, oh, how I hated him for asking that so baldly, and loved him for speaking aloud what we were all thinking.

"If your masters do what we say, we won't have to," Zahra said. "We'll let you return to them when our own people are safe. After we've claimed our home, nothing you or your oppressors do will concern us."

She spoke the word *home* with a reverence I could not comprehend. She wasn't looking at Baqir or me. She was gazing out the window with an expression of understated wonder, almost joy. She looked happier, more relaxed, when her eyes rested not on her prisoners or her comrades, but on the monstrosity of a ship growing ever larger as the shuttle soared toward it. She did not fear *House of Wisdom*. She stared at it with something a lot like yearning.

I had seen it from this distance before. I had been splattered with blood then, too, and shivering with cold, too short and skinny to sit comfortably in the pilot's seat in my mother's experimental craft. *Tiger* had curved slowly away from *House of Wisdom* at first, the autopilot moving it a safe distance before engaging the full power of the engines. During that slow retreat I had wept, crying for my father, for my mother, overwhelmed by the nightmarish horror of that day. I had been frantic as I watched the ship that had been my childhood home grow smaller and smaller.

Then *Tiger*'s propulsion system had fired up. All I remembered after that was pain.

House of Wisdom looked the same as it had before. Dark, blocky, ugly. Nobody had been this close in ten years.

When my mother had buckled me into the pilot's seat of her experimental ship and programmed the controls, she told me, over and over again, that I would be safe, I would be okay, she was going to get me away. I would be safe. I would be okay. She hadn't been crying; I remembered that clearly. She had been jittery with quick, determined motions, her voice higher than usual, her breath fast. I had asked, *Are you coming with me?*

My mother had only pushed hair damp with sweat and clumped with blood back from my face, kissed my forehead, and straightened the harness over the front of my pajamas. She said, *I've got some things to do first.*

The horrors aboard *House of Wisdom* had been locked away for ten years. On the ship, in lost data, in sealed files, in the memories I never, ever spoke aloud.

And I had just helped open the door.

The ship's velocity abruptly changed. Salvatore's blood broke from its shimmering galaxy and splattered across my face, across Baqir's, across the seats and the walls, over the window, dark and red and specked with bone and brain, obscuring the view.

SPEC SECURITY—RESTRICTED ARCHIVE REF. #39364832-B
SHIP-TO-BROADCAST COMMUNICATION TRANSCRIPT (AUDIO)
Source: HOUSE OF WISDOM, SPEC RESEARCH
TimeDate: 07:21:12 01.04.393

[VERIFIED IDENTIFICATION—HOUSE OF WISDOM, SPEC RESEARCH: Captain Lilian Putnam Ngahere]

HOUSE OF WISDOM: I don't know if these transmissions are going through. The comm system is—it's completely fucked. Pilar hasn't reported back. The computer isn't answering any requests for diagnostics and I—okay. Let me try this.

[10 s elapse. Background noise indicates shipwide medical alarm system is active.]

HOUSE OF WISDOM: This is Captain Lilian Ngahere of the vessel HOUSE OF WISDOM. The time is—fuck, what time is it. It's after 0700. I haven't had a response from Orbital Control since before 0200, but our receiver may be damaged. This is a warning to any and all ships responding to our distress call. There is an unidentified infectious agent afflicting the crew and residents of this vessel. Repeat: the population of this vessel has been exposed to a highly contagious and fatal infectious agent.

[Shipwide medical alarm continues.]

HOUSE OF WISDOM: I don't know how many are dead. The doctors suspect it might be an aggressive viral encephalitis or hemorrhagic fever—or something like that, they were going to test for Marburg-Exo and Zeffir-1 and, another, I can't remember, because of how it's spreading . . . I don't know what the tests showed. I've lost contact with the medical staff. I've lost contact with everybody.

[Shipwide medical alarm continues.]

HOUSE OF WISDOM: It happened so fast. Kichi Akimoto in Deep Space Archaeology was the first. We were supposed to meet today. She wanted to report on the data Gregory tried to steal from UC33-X. It's not important anymore. She's gone. I've never seen her like that. I've never seen anything do that to a person. She was so panicked, and then—then she wasn't. She was so different. Conscious but unresponsive. Did Gregory do this? He told us we would regret sending him away. We would regret separating him from his work. He was so angry, but he never denied it. He said he was hiding the data because we couldn't understand it. He's always been arrogant about his work, but this—I should have reported his threats. I didn't take him seriously. He's a good scientist. I didn't want to . . . It doesn't matter now.

[Shipwide medical alarm continues.]

HOUSE OF WISDOM: I've tried to send the medical analysis in a data burst. I don't know if it's going out. If there is anybody aboard who remains unafflicted, I need your help. This is an unrestricted call for immediate emergency reporting to the bridge. Fuck, I don't know if anybody is listening.

[ARCHIVED BY AUTOMATED COMMUNICATION PRESERVATION SYSTEM]

ZAHRA

Half-illuminated, half-dark, the Earth was framed by the square mouth of the docking bay. It looked so small. Small enough that I could pinch it between my fingers, snag it on the tip of my glove, fling it away to be lost among the stars.

"Zahra!" Dag's voice was muffled, as though carrying over a great distance.

Look, I would say, when this was all over, when I was holding Anwar on one side and Nadra on the other, both of them warm and relaxed and happy. We would have a room of our own, clean and bright with soft blankets and plentiful food, and I would pull them closer to me even as they rolled their eyes and tried to squirm away, and I would say: Look how far away it is. We can't see the desert from here. The tessellated soil above our mother's grave, the windowless punishment shed at the edge of the homestead, the wire fences snagging tumbleweed in the wind, all of it so far beyond reach it was not even a blemish on the face of the planet.

"Zahra! What the hell are you doing?"

Dag was not angry—he was never angry, I did not think him

capable of it. He showed no temper even when he spoke of how he had been stripped of his citizenship for a minor crime, how he had been escorted to the border, how the Councils security forces had laughed as they set him loose in a spring snowstorm. If that did not anger him, then I did not believe anything could. The harshness in his voice now was impatience. We were crossing the space between *Pilgrim 3* and *House of Wisdom*, climbing ten meters along the docking ladder from the shuttle to an airlock hatch. I had not meant to stop.

I had let go of the ladder with one hand, and both of my feet were floating free.

"Put your hand back on the ladder. Zahra. Are you listening to me?"

I knew about space vertigo. I knew about perspective distortion. I knew about the vacuum madness that made people giddy and irrational the first time they stepped into unconfined space. As a child I had sat rapt at my father's side while he told me how excited he was to go into space, how honored he was to have been chosen to work aboard *House of Wisdom*, but also admitting, sheepishly, that he was frightened. What would it be like, he had wondered, to live so long in a place where even the bathrooms were different, where water came in globes rather than glasses, where you could not set your spectacles on your bedside table because they would float away during the night? I had giggled at that, happy to focus on something silly rather than the dwindling days until he departed. I had loved the sound of his voice as much as I hated that he was leaving us.

I grasped three times for the ladder before catching it, frustrated by the clumsy gloves of the emergency space suit.

"Good," Dag said. "Don't let go again."

"Is she okay?" Malachi said. The concern in his voice made my heart squeeze. The close call with the security drones had shaken him. He was too delicate for this mission. I had known it since we chose him, although we never truly had a choice. Nobody else in the family had Malachi's skill with computers. The Councils had been fools to reject him time and time again.

I hadn't meant to frighten him. I had only wanted to know what it felt like to let go. There is no up and down in space, no gravity to preference one direction over another. Dag was several rungs ahead of me, his feet over my head—then suddenly he was below me, and I was toppling headfirst toward the gray ship, disoriented by a wave of vertigo so strong it was like a physical blow.

I gripped the ladder with both hands. Squeezed my eyes closed. Opened them again, and Dag was at the hatch.

"Can you open it?" I asked.

"The airlock has power," Dag said. "Physical seal only."

I swallowed. My throat was dry. The suit's medical monitor expressed mild concern about my heart rate and respiration. "Let's go in."

Dag turned the wheel to disengage the hatch and pulled it open. The chamber beyond was dark but for a cluster of small blinking lights on an interior panel. Dag pulled himself inside. He moved cautiously but gracefully, aiming his helmet light in every direction. Years had passed since Dag was forced out of SPEC, but he had never lost his easy way of moving in space. Seeing that gave me a sharp pang of jealousy.

"Clear," he said.

Dag moved aside to let me enter, then closed the hatch behind us. I went to the interior control panel and tapped to wake it up. I felt a moment's confusion at the letters and numbers that filled the screen.

LCK 0 kPa 0 O2 0 N2 120 K
INT 83 kPa 21 O2 79 N2 263 K

I took a breath. I had prepared for this. Dag and Boudicca and others in the family with space experience had spent months drilling the rest of us, grueling lessons and practices followed by tests in which the slightest wrong answer was punishable by a withheld meal or a public condemnation. I did not get many answers wrong. The consequences were bad, as was the disappointment in Adam's eyes, but what I feared most was the thought that I might not be ready when the time came.

"This interior is pressurized," I said. "It's cold, but it's got air. Eighty-twenty mixture."

"Outer door is closed," Dag said, and I wondered if he was going to announce every step we took, the habit so ingrained in him from his years in space that he couldn't stop it even if he tried.

The computer told me the same thing:

EXT SEAL: ON
INT SEAL: ON

I stared at the screen, momentarily frozen. I didn't know what to do next. I had to know. I could not be forgetting all I had studied already.

"That's the one," Dag said, pointing over my shoulder to the word INGRESS.

The shine of our headlamps cast a glare on the screen, throwing our reflections back to us. I touched the command, and the word INGRESS changed to PRESSURIZING. The chamber filled with a soft hissing sound as air tumbled to fill the vacuum. It grew louder, louder, louder—the numbers on the screen marched upward—then the hiss abruptly stopped.

LCK 83 kPa 21 02 79 N2 258 K

"Airlock is pressurized," Dag said, making a solid fist to state the same thing in gesture. "Two hundred fifty-eight K is cold for an active ship."

I gritted my teeth and tried to ignore him. He was only doing what came naturally to him.

"We're getting another position verification request from Orbital Control," Boudicca said over the radio. "So if you could hurry it up a little, that would be good."

Her impatience, her worry, they seemed so very far away. I turned the wheel on the interior door, felt it loosen and spin, and pushed inward. Some part of me had expected it to stick, to be rusted closed, but *House of Wisdom* had been built to last far longer than ten years in space.

Beyond the hatch was a sea of stars.

I blinked, turned my head, moved my light. The stars winked and turned. It was not empty space, but a cavernous chamber filled with tiny, glinting reflections. One of the stars floated close. I reached. It bumped against my glove and spun away, so I stretched farther and caught it.

It was a shard of glass. Thinner than my finger, clear as crystal.

All of those glinting lights, they were broken pieces of glass floating in the chamber. By opening the door, we had set them turning and glinting, a strange and beautiful dance of air currents and debris. I looked around until I spotted large panes of glass secured to one wall, the whole stack of them shattered where something heavy had struck it in the center. Throughout the cargo bay there were crates and boxes floating free, broken away from the nets and bands meant to hold them in place.

I let go of the shard and sent it spinning back into the darkness. I tracked its motion through the room. The beam from my headlamp danced over the walls, found conduits and panels, cargo secured to the wall with webbing, and a pair of legs.

I let out a startled yelp and released my grip on the handle, then grabbed for it when I realized I wasn't anchored to anything. My body continued to turn, and I wrenched my shoulder trying to stop myself. I kicked at the wall to straighten my arm and caught my feet against the edge of the open hatch.

Malachi's voice came over the radio: "Zahra? What's going on?"

I took a steadying breath, then another. Dag was still in the airlock, his light shining directly at me. Even without seeing his face I knew his expression would be one of stolid disapproval; I should have let him clear the cargo bay before entering.

Carefully, carefully, I turned to look at the wall above the hatch.

"I'm fine." My voice was shaky, so I said it again, more firmly. "I'm fine. I was startled."

"By what?" Malachi asked.

"I'm not sure," I said.

It was a lie. I knew what I had seen.

Boots. Legs. There was somebody above me.

I had thought I was ready for them, the dead who waited for us.

Four hundred and seventy-seven people had died aboard *House of Wisdom*. When I had tried to imagine them, I saw a medical bay filled to capacity, body bags bundled in neat stacks, storage rooms turned to morgues, faces hidden behind white sheets. I had dreamed about walking through gleaming, clean corridors, and all around me there were silent figures wrapped in white, with no features except indistinct shadows where their eyes should be. In my dream, I had reached out to them, to tell them they didn't have to stay aboard the ship anymore, but every one had turned away.

I told no one of the dream. Fear, Adam often said, was more deadly than a virus. We had always known we would have to dispose of the dead to make *House of Wisdom* our home. Panya was planning a ceremony, something mournful and respectful, to prove to the people of Earth that we were not callous criminals.

I pulled myself along the wall, using a line of cargo clamps as a ladder. I was not going to flinch away. We had learned everything we could about the Zeffir-1 virus. We were vaccinated, we were trained, and we had come prepared with supplies for testing the air, cleansing the filtration system, detecting any active traces of the virus that lingered. The Pre-Collapse warlords who created Zeffir-1 had designed it to kill quickly and then spontaneously denature: cruelty and cowardly stealth were their goals. My mind was filled with knowledge about that hateful weapon.

"What is it?" Dag said.

His light grew brighter behind me as he came through the doorway, giving me an overlarge, distorted shadow. I climbed over the crates until I could see the corpse.

She had not finished putting her space suit on. She wore no helmet or gloves, and the legs weren't properly sealed into the boots. Her face was waxy and shriveled. It had been cold and dry inside the ship for ten years. She was mummified. Her straight brown hair floated like a fan around her face.

Her entire torso, her shoulders, her upper arms, they were all stained with blood.

It was such a shocking sight that at first I thought my eyes were deceiving me. It could not be blood. It had to be something else— oil, paint; my mind tripped over the unlikely possibilities. The stains were so dark, the blood so thick. I could not immediately locate her wounds. I had to be wrong. I needed to get closer. I could not make myself move.

A rapid and totally fatal outbreak of Zeffir-1. A known weaponized virus, a savage artifact from humanity's dark past, set upon the ship by a known monster. That was what they had said. Dizziness, fainting, fatigue, internal bleeding that might lead to a bloody nose or bloodshot eyes or massive bruises, but nothing like this. Rapid pulmonary failure. An hour, maybe two, from the onset of symptoms to death, after two days of incubation within the body. Within minutes the victims were too weak to move, much less save themselves. Many fell into comas almost immediately and would not have suffered. That was how *House of Wisdom* was lost. For ten years SPEC had been telling the same story.

This woman had not died in a coma. She had not died quietly.

"Huh," Dag said.

There was no revulsion in his voice, no emotion at all, and for once I was glad for it. I tried to imitate his calm to quash my own growing horror. Nausea churned in my stomach, but I reached for the handholds on the wall. I needed to be closer to the woman's corpse. But I was afraid. I desperately wanted to turn my headlamp away from her bloodied body so that it might vanish into the darkness, and when I looked again, courage regained and nerves steadied, she would be peaceful, bloodless.

"What's going on over there?" Panya said over the radio, her voice laced with concern. "Zahra? Talk to us, sweetie. Is everything okay?"

I licked my lips. "We're making sure the cargo bay is clear."

"Work faster," Boudicca said. "I don't think our friend *Barcelona* is falling for our misdirection."

"But they're not supposed to notice yet," Nico said. I cringed at the whine in his voice. I had not wanted to bring him along, mistrusting his sulking and contrary nature, but Adam had insisted.

"Guess nobody told them that," Boudicca said drily.

"I only meant—"

"For fuck's sake, shut up," Henke snapped.

"Nico, Henke, you're not helping," Panya said, ever the peacemaker. "Let's stay calm."

"It doesn't matter what we planned," I said firmly. "How long until they get here?"

Malachi answered, "Nearest ship I'm reading on this side is one-fifty-two—"

"Did you see that?" Boudicca said sharply.

"No," Malachi said. "See what?" A few seconds of silence. "What did you see?"

"There was a ship there," Boudicca said. "Are you blind?"

"What's going on?" I demanded.

"The nearest ship I can see," Malachi said, his voice slow with doubt, "is a Burro class transport in the MEO-3 shipping zone. Cargo on its way to Providence Station. I doubt it has the fuel to burn up to this orbit, and even if it does it will take ten or twelve hours. Next closest is *Homestead*, and that's a full one-twenty degrees westward."

"There's another one out there," Boudicca said. "It's been hidden."

"What do you mean 'hidden'?" Nico said. His voice rose at the end of the question, squeaking with alarm. "Can ships do that?"

"What I saw—look." Boudicca took a breath, audible over the comm. "We've only got basic navigation here. Our active scanning is for collision avoidance only. For anything farther out, we rely on Orbital Control tracking to locate other ships, and that means we rely on what they're transmitting to us."

I didn't understand until Malachi said, "You think they're hiding something from us?"

"I think they can hide ships from everybody, when they want to," Boudicca said. "I saw a blip on orbital tracking that—it wasn't there, then it was, and it's not there now. Like it's not supposed to be in the position data broadcast, but for a microsecond it slipped through."

"It's possible," Dag put in. "And it is something they would do."

"Liars and deceivers," Panya murmured.

"I don't know," Malachi said.

"Don't be so fucking naive," Henke snapped.

"I'm not. I just don't see it," Malachi said, but his tone was defensive now, wavering in a way I had always hated. He gave in too easily when he wasn't sure of himself. "It's not in the record. Are you sure? How can you be sure?"

"They could have altered the record," Boudicca said, with exaggerated patience. "The position computer takes input from Orbital Control. That's how the tracking system works. You didn't tamper with the tracking system, did you?"

"I didn't touch it," Malachi said. "They would have noticed."

"Why would it show at all, if they're hiding it?" I asked.

"If it's responding to an order, it would have to transmit its position to Orbital Control," Boudicca said. "And in order to do that, it has to connect to the master system. There might be a glitch that lets it show, especially if they aren't using this system often. It's one thing for a ship to be dark when it's still, but once it starts maneuvering, there are a lot more variables."

"Protocol," Dag said, with satisfaction. "They are always predictable."

"There's a dark ship," Boudicca said firmly, "and it began to maneuver as soon as we docked. That's not a coincidence."

We didn't predict this. I looked again toward the dead woman. We should have predicted it. Liars and deceivers. Adam had warned us, long before our mission plans were made real, that the Councils were always watching. Their eyes were everywhere. They were as hungry as buzzards circling a dying man in the desert. *Wherever we go, they will be watching,* he had said once, his words ringing with certainty. Another planting of crops had just failed because of poison in the soil, and Adam paced before us, shouting at the agents he knew to be hiding in the darkness outside our fences. *They will watch us until we leave them behind forever. They will not stop hunting us until they destroy us, or we break away.*

Inside my space suit, my skin prickled uncomfortably. Even here, in this ship so long abandoned, so far from Earth, they would not leave us alone.

I asked, "How long before it reaches us?"

Boudicca exhaled shortly. "If it's where I saw it and they're accelerating from orbital velocity—"

"How long?"

"If it's unmanned, two or three hours. If it's got crew on board, maybe twice that."

Malachi added, "They won't burn higher than 3 or 4 g. Not if they want to stay hidden. The drive thermals would give them away."

"We don't know their propulsion capability," Dag said.

"Is it a gunship?" Nico asked. "Will it attack?"

"SPEC doesn't have gunships," Boudicca said. "That's a myth. Don't be stupid."

"He's not being stupid. He's only worried." Panya, still soothing.

"He's always stupid," Bao said, and Nico spluttered.

"All we know is that it's out there," Malachi said. "We need more information."

"Too risky," Boudicca said.

"Then how do we—"

"Be quiet. All of you," I said.

I was gratified when they obeyed. I could not allow them to fall into squabbling now.

It would be at least another six hours before *Homestead* reached us. That had been an unavoidable part of the plan. It needed to be safely in orbit before we seized *Pilgrim 3*, and the necessary launch window meant that it was not yet anywhere near *House of Wisdom*— but neither was anything else, or so we had believed.

We had to assume the phantom ship was real and coming for us. We had to assume it was powerful and fast. We had three hours, possibly less. Better to assume Boudicca was underestimating than overestimating. Dag was right that we didn't know what this ship was capable of.

They will try to stop us, Adam had said, time and again as we were making our plans, his eyes shining with feverish excitement. *They will use tricks and lies we won't predict. But they won't win. I can see their every move before they make it. I will know every wicked thought before it even enters their minds.*

The hidden ship didn't change our mission. *Homestead* was on its way, and we had to control *House of Wisdom* before it arrived. We needed time to make it ours: to give Malachi a chance to insert his takeover program into the computer system, to test the air filtration system for remnants of the virus, to locate the bridge and fire up the engines, to create a safe place for the family—if not the whole ship, then at least a level or two, enough to welcome them aboard.

We had intended to leave the hostages aboard the shuttle, out of the way and under guard, while we worked. They were our leverage for keeping SPEC away. We still needed that leverage, but we could no longer afford to spare even one or two of our team to remain aboard the shuttle. All hands needed to be working, not babysitting.

Adam had sent me in his place. He trusted me to adapt. To recognize the weapons we had when we needed them most, and deploy them ruthlessly. I had to change the plan. The dried blood on the dead woman's clothing looked like a chasm into which no light could penetrate. I reached up thoughtlessly before remembering that I could not rub my eyes.

I said, "Panya. Henke. Put the passengers into suits."

There was a brief silence.

Panya spoke first, "But Adam said—"

I interrupted her. "Bring Bhattacharya over first. Keep a gun on his friend and he'll do anything you say."

"Zahra," Panya said, "we should talk about this. This isn't Adam's plan."

"I thought we were going to let them go," Malachi said.

"I thought we were going to kill them," said Henke.

And Boudicca asked, "What are you going to do when you get them over there?"

"We're going to use them to keep our people safe." It was so obvious I was annoyed I had to explain it. Adam's will should have been as clear to them as it was to me. "The plan has not changed, but we have less time than we thought. All of us need to be here, preparing for their arrival. That ship may reach us before *Homestead*, but if it does arrive, we will request that they keep their distance, or we start killing their children one by one. And—"

"We can do that now," Henke said. "We should just get rid of—"

"Do *not* interrupt me," I said. "You are not in command of this mission. We are not going to draw the wrath of SPEC until absolutely necessary, nor are we going to get rid of our only insurance against an attack. What we are going to do is work twice as quickly as we planned. We cannot afford to divide our attention."

I made my voice as cold as I could, using the tone I had practiced to make everybody feel as though Adam himself was speaking through me, the force of his wisdom and love ringing from my own tongue. I knew what Henke wanted to do. I knew the dark iron shard he carried around where his heart ought to be. Adam claimed the Councils had broken him, but I suspected that darkness had always been there. He had not been forced to leave the Councils; he chose to leave, willingly and happily, and he only grinned when anybody asked him to explain. He could be useful, however blustery his attitude, however violent his instincts. I was not going to let him seize the control he so dearly desired.

"There is a corpse over here that died . . ." I sought the right words, stamping down my instinct to rail that it was wrong, it was all wrong. "There was violence here. SPEC has kept secrets about what happened during the outbreak. That is why you're going to bring Bhattacharya over first. He is going to tell us what SPEC has kept from the public, and we are going to get to work. Do you understand?"

A long, tense silence stretched.

"Those lying pieces of shit," Boudicca said.

"Adam knew this would happen," I said. "He warned us they were deceivers. Get the hostages and the supplies over here. We are prepared for this. Go meet them, Dag."

The cargo bay darkened as he returned to the airlock, leaving me alone with the corpse. I pulled myself along the wall, closer. Her head was twisted to the side. Her neck had been slashed several times in long gashes, tearing through her skin from beneath her chin to her clavicle. The ruined, ragged flesh allowed glimpses of white bone to show. Through the blood on the outside of her space suit I could see the emblem on the arm: the words *Space and Exploration Commission* around the circle, and in the center the single four-pointed star of *House of Wisdom*. One of the gashes had severed her jugular. She had bled out through the neck.

Her hands were bare—the skin shriveled, cold burned, and papery—and gripped in each was a long shard of blood-caked glass.

A deep grinding noise came from within the wall; Dag was depressurizing the airlock. The others were speaking, discussing the best way to move twelve hostages from the shuttle to the ship, but their voices faded beneath the thump of blood in my ears.

I pushed myself out from the wall to see the name on the suit. *CHIN, M.* There were streaks of dark blood on her name patch.

It had all been a lie. This woman had not died from Zeffir-1. The Councilors, the SPEC investigators, the forensic medical teams, the solemn-faced pathologists and immunologists dragged out of quiet labs to offer their expert opinions, the university colleagues who condemned my father without pause, every single one of them had lied. Padmavati Bhattacharya had lied every time she stood before the Councils and spoke of her sister's death.

And her nephew, that spineless young man who had flinched from my gaze, he had lied too.

I had always known my father was incapable of doing what they said he had done. But it was little comfort in the face of the more immediate concern: We were not prepared for this. The vaccinations, the changes we planned to make to the ship's systems, the tests we had come ready to perform, all of it was designed to protect us against the Zeffir-1 virus. We had no plan for an unknown pathogen that could force a woman to tear herself to shreds with pieces of glass.

Hand over hand, I pulled myself away from the corpse and back down to the airlock. There I hooked my feet into one of the cargo straps, drew my weapon, and waited.

Henke and Malachi brought Bhattacharya to *House of Wisdom*. He was obedient and quiet, offering no protest and revealing nothing of his thoughts. Henke stayed near the airlock to guard the prisoner, while Malachi looked for a functional control panel. He had designed a skeleton key to seize control of the ship's computers. We needed light, power, air, access to every part of the ship. We needed to find the bridge and fire up the flight systems. We needed to scrub the air clean of any remaining virus. Malachi had warned us that it might take several hours, but Adam had laughed at his concerns. Laughed and ruffled his hair and said that

Malachi would not disappoint us. It had not, at the time, sounded like a warning.

"Don't worry about what's out there," I said to him. "Boudicca will handle it."

Malachi glanced toward Bhattacharya. "You know they can hear us. All the suits are on the same frequency."

"It doesn't matter. Are you ready?"

"Always." Malachi smiled, a bit shakily, and he said, "But I could use some help."

For a fleeting moment I saw the boy who had walked out of the desert six years ago, in the purple twilight of a cold winter day. I had been patrolling the edge of the homestead, stomping through the cacti and scrub bushes beyond the wire fence that marked our territory. Thrice in the past fortnight we were awoken in the middle of the night by gunfire and taunting shouts from the desert; Adam had commanded a twenty-four-hour patrol to spot any Councils agents before they got close enough to harm us. Low clouds had blanketed the land, threatening snow. A quiet cough behind me made me spin around, my heart thumping, my gun raised. As the stranger drew nearer I saw that his feet were bare, his clothes little more than rags, his hair long and tangled. He carried nothing. He was no older than my seventeen years and so thin a strong wind could knock him over. When he coughed his entire body quaked.

"I saw the lights," he said, and he spoke with the musical accent of the desert, the one I had been teaching myself to adopt. "Is there a camp near?"

"This is a homestead," I said sternly. "You're trespassing."

He had smiled—bold but warm, a smile that burned through the cold, a smile stronger than my doubts—and he said, "I could really use some help."

I could have killed him that evening in the desert, and nobody would have ever known. I could have turned him away and never thought of him again. That was what the Councils had done, rejecting his application for citizenship so many times he had lost hope. I had invited him into the homestead instead, and only later had I learned what he could do, what he could offer, how he would help us reach our dream. I needed that bold, smiling boy now, not the wavering, doubtful man he had grown to be.

"You cannot fail us," I said.

Malachi's smile faded. I had said the wrong thing.

"Dag will help you," I added quickly. "You'll figure it out."

Dag nodded silently. Together they crossed the chamber toward the control panel by the interior door.

I turned to the prisoner. "Against the wall."

Henke shoved Bhattacharya up to the wall with a hard smack in the center of his chest. Henke was grinning, his teeth a white curve behind the faceplate of his helmet. Either he had overcome his doubts about our change in plans, or a chance to manhandle the captives was enough to lighten his mood.

"You've been lying," I said to Bhattacharya. I didn't raise my weapon; it was threat enough that I was holding it. The widening of Bhattacharya's eyes, that was the flash of fear I wanted to see. "You've been lying all along. The next word out of your mouth is going to be the truth, or I will kill you."

I pointed with my gun to the corpse above the airlock door.

"That was no virus," I said. "What the fuck happened here?"

Bhattacharya and Henke looked, and Henke cursed in surprise. With three headlamps shining on it, the corpse looked smaller, pathetic somehow. No longer a person. A piece of debris.

"Answer her." Henke pressed the muzzle of the gun into Bhattacharya's neck. I had not told him to do that, had not particularly wanted him to, but Henke was a weapon as much as the gun in his hand. It was effective enough.

Bhattacharya cleared his throat. He was still looking at the corpse. "Can you see who she is? She looks—I think I know her."

"Her suit says Chin," I said.

"Oh," he said softly. "She used to babysit me."

Henke snorted a laugh.

"I don't care who she was," I said. "That is not what Zeffir-1 does to people. Was there an attack? Did SPEC Security send a team to subdue the outbreak?"

Bhattacharya started to answer, but stopped abruptly as a red light began to glow around the inner airlock door. A moment later another came on beside it, and another, slowly filling the cargo bay. The light was low, more murky than illuminating, barely enough to cast a dingy red glow over everything. A soft hum rose from somewhere in the walls.

"Low-power dormancy lighting," Malachi explained, although nobody had asked. "It'll have to do until we can get the regular lights on. The environmental controls are still functional, so the power sources are still intact, but I can't access the full system from here." Then he added, quieter, "Sorry. Didn't mean to interrupt."

Now was not the time to scold him, not when he was doing exactly what he was supposed to be doing. I turned back to Bhattacharya. He had not moved, but he was looking at me now, not the corpse.

"That woman didn't die from the virus," I said.

"Yes, she did."

"No. Someone attacked her." I paused. "Or she injured herself. That's not a virus."

"Yes, it is. What happened to her is what happened to all of them. Exactly that." There was a weariness in Bhattacharya's voice that made him seem so much older than his twenty-two years. "SPEC decided it had to be a modified version of Zeffir-1 because that's what doctors here came up with before they died. With how quickly it acted, how it spread, it was their best guess. But what it did to Dr. Chin—that's what it did to everybody."

I looked at Chin's corpse again. Her shriveled hands were caked with blood where the glass shards had sliced into her flesh.

"Explain," I said. "What, exactly, did it do?"

Bhattacharya took a breath. "When they got infected, it was like . . . one minute they were fine, and the next they were out of control. They were hallucinating, having delusions. Seeing things that weren't there. SPEC kept the symptoms classified because they had no idea where Dr. Lago got it. They never found out what kind of laboratory was modifying ancient viruses to do . . . that."

My father's name on his lips was like an electric shock. I did not let myself react.

He was speaking softly, but there was a roughness to his voice that sounded, to me, like the onward edge of tears. "They didn't know who they were. They attacked each other. They attacked themselves. They used any weapon they could. It didn't make people sick. It made them insane. Suicidal and violently insane."

There was a long silence after he finished speaking.

"What kind of pathogen could do that?" Malachi asked. "That's not anything I've ever heard of."

"Me neither," Boudicca put in. "Not even a rumor."

"Fuck, that must've been something to see," Henke said.

Bhattacharya leaned away from him, and I felt the same flash of revulsion. I pushed the feeling aside. I could not be distracted.

"And the vaccine?" I said.

He moved one arm, half a shrug. "It was a precaution in case Lago had planned another attack. SPEC thought it would work, but it's not like they could ever test it with the modified virus. They didn't have a sample."

I needed him to stop saying my father's name. My hand hurt from gripping my weapon so hard, from the folds of the glove creasing painfully against my fingers. We should have known SPEC and the Councils would be so cavalier with human lives.

"This doesn't change anything," I said, the anxious twist in my gut making my words sharp. "We have the ability to purify the air system and test for viral contaminants. We keep our suits on until we can secure parts of the ship. Panya, are more passengers ready?"

"I've got three more waiting," Panya said.

"Bring them over. Nico, Bao, find the bioaerosol testers when you get the next group ready."

Henke left me guarding Bhattacharya to return to the airlock and help Panya with the hostages. I kept my eye on Bhattacharya but turned my attention to what Malachi and Dag were saying.

"We need to find the mainframe," Malachi said. "From there we'll be able to use the skeleton key."

"Try it again," Dag said.

"I *have* tried it again. The systems are isolated. There's a security function in place that can't be deactivated from here. Some kind of override."

"So you can't open the door?"

Malachi made a frustrated noise. "I can open this door, and I can open the next door, and probably all of them, but I have to do it one at a time. That's why I need access to the mainframe. From there I can reset the entire system—including the air scrubbers and medical quarantine."

Bhattacharya tilted his head but said nothing. His expression was hard to read behind the faceplate. I wanted to ask him what he remembered of my father. I had not thought I would get the chance, but perhaps later—I could not worry about that now. I felt the pressure of all we did not know as a ticking clock at the back of my mind. All around us shards of glass tinkled and clinked in the disturbed air.

The airlock cycled again as Henke brought Panya and the hostages inside. The first through the door was Bhattacharya's friend with the prosthetic arm, who immediately went to his side. They were joined by the two women who had been sitting in the front row.

I left Henke and Panya to watch the prisoners and went into the airlock to wait for the next group. I wanted to look down at Earth one more time. I wanted to feel how very far away we were.

When I opened the outer door, the ladder was above, then below, my mind switching the orientation. I gripped a handhold inside the airlock as vertigo washed over me. I would have to get used to it. I *would* get used to it. Adam was fond of saying that humans made a choice to be adaptable or not, and all the failed space missions of the past, especially the generation ships that had sailed into the darkness and fallen silent one by one, they had faltered because they chose to cling to the false comfort of Earth's weighty prison. I was not going to make that mistake. I would adapt. I would make space my home.

Ten meters away the airlock on the shuttle opened, revealing two suited figures in a square of light. One raised an arm to wave, and Nico's voice came over the radio. "Sending the next group across now."

"Did you find the bioaerosol testers?"

"Yeah, but we had to dig for them. I've got the first cargo rack loaded," Nico said. "You first. Get out there. Make sure you hold on tight."

"Oh, no." A woman's voice, barely more than a whisper. "I can't."

"You don't get a choice. Move."

"I can't," the woman moaned. "I can't. I can't. There's so much—it's too much."

"Is that Lilia?" asked another woman.

"Sounds like it. Lilia?" That was Bhattacharya's friend, speaking over the radio from inside. "Lilia, it's okay. Just look at the ladder. Focus on the ladder."

"This is so stupid," Nico said. "I'm going to fucking drag you over there."

"Send a cargo rack across first," I said, annoyed with the woman's cowardice and Nico's stubbornness. "We don't have time for this."

"Fine, fine. Get the fuck out of my way and don't—*fuck*!"

Across the ten meters of space, I saw space-suit-clad legs kicking outward from the airlock door, a flurry of motion, shadows blocking light, a confusion of limbs.

The woman was crying, *"No, no, no!"*

And Nico was raging, "Let go of me, let go, or I will fucking shoot," and over the radio somebody else was shouting at him to not shoot, it sounded like Dag or Henke or both, and Boudicca was demanding to know what the fuck was going on, and for a moment the light from the airlock was blocked, then it reappeared, the woman screamed, then—

It was a quiet sound over the radio, no more than a snap. One, then another. The screaming gave way to whimpering, then silence.

"The fuck did you do?" Boudicca asked.

"She wouldn't—"

Light flashed in the shuttle airlock, and Nico's explanation was lost in a concussion of noise. Somebody screamed, but it sounded so very far away, muffled by the agonizing roar.

Flames exploded from the shuttle airlock, engulfing Nico and the woman in blinding white light. For only a second, through the painful dancing spots in my vision, I saw two figures wrapped in fire spinning away from the shuttle, snagging on the twisted end of the ladder, thrashing wildly, frantically, the material of their space suits melting away, the clinging fire and charred skin beneath—

The shuttle exploded.

It tore itself apart from the inside. Light burned through seams in the metal and punched through the windows of the passenger cabin. The force of the explosion shoved it away from the airlock, crashing into the opposite side of the docking area and tumbling wildly, burning as it tore into the space beyond *House of Wisdom*. Boudicca was shouting over the radio, hers the only voice I could discern in the chaos—then something hurtled across from the shuttle, a flash, a shard, debris—I wasn't fast enough to react, to dodge to the side—it struck me forcefully, shoving me back into the airlock. My entire body felt the pain of impact.

Over the radio there was a wet, gasping gurgle.

A high wheeze.

And silence.

The third field area is the most promising. Densely forested, although the hilltops and clearings have a symmetry to them that does not seem entirely natural. I'm thinking of basalt columns, writ large. You can bet the first thing I do when I get my boots on the ground is find out what's under those hills. I don't know how I'll endure these last seven months to landfall. I don't know how any of us will. We want to stand on the ground. We want to feel the sun on our faces. We want to hear the hum of insects, or whatever ecological analogue this planet has, all around us. We want to breathe air that hasn't been breathed a thousand times before. Seven months. We're counting down.

—FRAGMENT 2, *MOURNFUL EVENING SONG* VIA UC33-X

There was no sound. The suit radios had squealed and crackled, noises so loud they felt like needles in the ears, then a deafening pop—then nothing. Nothing. Only silence.

The red lights in the cargo bay flickered off, on, off again. I saw our captors moving frantically toward the airlock door, gesturing to each other, mouths moving behind their helmets.

Then, as quickly as it had gone, the sound was back, and everybody was shouting.

"You said you shut it down!"

"I did, I did! The system signaled—"

"Zahra!"

"Try them again! You have to try them again."

"Oh no, oh no, oh no . . ."

For one wildly disorienting moment I heard the sound of monsoon rain on a metal roof—it was debris striking the hull of the ship. I kicked away from the wall, dragging Baqir with me, waving frantically for Ariana and Xiomara to follow. If the force of the explosion pushed the shuttle into the ship, we wanted to be as far from the hull breach as possible.

Through the turning, glinting glass, I aimed toward the other side of the cargo bay. I dragged Baqir by his arm, with Ariana and Xiomara hand in hand right behind us. Our captors were still shouting.

"You didn't fucking shut it down! You fucking lied, you have no fucking idea—"

"They can't be gone. They can't be gone."

"Zahra!"

The man called Dag hadn't moved away from the control panel beside the interior door. He wasn't shouting with the others, and his grim silence as he tracked our motion across the bay was unsettling. There was no way we could get past him.

I bumped against the wall a couple of meters from the door, catching a handle to stop myself from bouncing away. Baqir grabbed the same handle, his hand just above mine, and together we caught Ariana and Xiomara. Ariana was crying. The inside of her helmet was dotted with moisture, her breath hitching noisily over the radio. Another rattle of debris struck the hull.

"Boudicca, can you hear us? Do you copy?"

"Please say you can hear us. You can hear us, can't you?"

"Zahra?" That was Malachi, the copilot and hacker. He was on the verge of hysterics. "Zahra, what happened? Tell me you're all right!"

"Quiet." Dag spoke at a normal volume at first, but raised his voice to be heard. "Quiet! All of you. Be quiet."

For a few seconds all I could hear were the impacts on the hull.

"Boudicca, do you copy? Nico, do you copy? Bao? *Pilgrim 3,* please respond."

No answer.

"*Pilgrim 3,* respond."

Nothing.

"Zahra, do you copy?"

"Please," Panya said. "Zahra, honey, please answer us."

"It was those fucking drones." That was the red-faced man they called Henke, the one who moments ago had been guarding us with a gun and a grin. "They came for us. They *fucking* came for us!"

Henke spun around quickly and shoved one of the others into a wall so hard the thunk of the helmet carried over the radio. I couldn't tell who it was through the confusion of slashing headlamps and whirling glass, but I could see that Henke had the muzzle of his gun pressed to the front of the other person's helmet.

"You were supposed to stop them," Henke said. "You didn't stop them."

"Henke, don't!" Panya cried. "He said he shut it down!"

"*Pilgrim 3*, do you copy?"

As long as they were shouting at each other, they weren't paying attention to us. If Dag moved from the door, if I could open the door, we could get away. I knew this ship. It had been ten years, but I sure as fuck knew it better than they did. There were holes in their knowledge, and I could use them. I could find a radio. Contact SPEC. Keep Baqir and the others safe. Hide until rescue came. I couldn't do anything for the people aboard the shuttle. Another piece of debris struck the hull, metal on metal, a horrible sound. We only needed a chance.

"He fucking lied," Henke said again. "You fucking lied!"

Panya shoved herself between them, pushing Henke back. "Stop! Henke. Stop. You are not helping. Stop." She waited until he subsided before she went on. "Malachi, how did—how could that happen?"

"I don't know." There was a tightness in Malachi's voice, as though he was trying very hard not to be sick. "The security system cleared us. The loophole was real. The drones let us through, okay? They let us through. I don't know why they would—I don't know what happened, and I can't—"

He broke off abruptly: there was a low rumble in the walls.

"Oh shit," Xiomara said, her eyes wide. "Is the hull breached?"

For just a second I wondered if she was right, then the rumble changed, dropping in tone, and I recognized the sound. It was the airlock.

After an interminable wait, the repressurization sequence ended and the inner door opened. A suited figure came into the cargo bay, moving stiffly, injured or in pain.

"Zahra!" Panya caught her in an embrace. "What happened? Why weren't you answering?"

Zahra shook her head and pointed to her helmet.

"Wait a second," Malachi said. He turned her around, one hand cradling her shoulder gently. "Let me look at—these fucking emergency suits, they're garbage. The receiver is—there. Can you hear us? Are you hurt?"

"No," Zahra said, but her voice was breathy, unconvincing. "I'm—I'm fine."

"What happened? Why isn't Boudicca answering?"

"It's gone," Zahra said. "The shuttle is gone."

"Gone?" Malachi said, his voice high.

"Those fucking drones," Henke said.

Zahra shook her head. "I don't know. There was an explosion—I didn't see the drones. Boudicca would have seen them. She was watching for them. I didn't see anything." She paused for a breath and pressed one hand to her side. "There was an explosion."

"A missile?" Henke said.

"SPEC doesn't have missiles," Malachi replied, but he sounded unsure. "Do they? Did something hit the shuttle?"

"I don't know," Zahra said. "It looked like—it exploded from the inside."

"Are you sure? It came from inside the shuttle?" Panya asked.

"It's SPEC," said Henke. "Who else could it be? It wasn't an accident."

"Why would SPEC sabotage a passenger shuttle?" Malachi asked. "That doesn't make any sense."

"It's completely fucking insane," Baqir muttered, but quietly, and none of them noticed. They were too stunned. For all their weapons, their plans, their casual violence, for how little they had flinched when Zahra killed Salvatore and how eagerly they had threatened to do the same again and again, not one of them knew what to say to the revelation that somebody was targeting them as surely as they had targeted us.

Henke was insistent. "Who the fuck else could it be?"

"We don't know SPEC doesn't have missiles," Dag said.

I knew perfectly well SPEC didn't have functional space missiles, because I knew my aunt had spent days at a Councilors' closed meeting arguing about future development of a space defense system earlier in the year. But I had no interest in sharing that knowledge, even if they would listen to me.

"They're always watching us," Panya said. Her voice, still soft and little-girl high, was now wet with tears. "You know they're always watching. Adam warned us. I can't believe they're gone, I can't believe—are you sure? Boudicca can't be gone. She can't be. Maybe she just can't hear us?"

"They're all dead?" Ariana said quietly, looking from Xiomara to me. The skullcap of her space suit had pressed her rainbow-colored hair into a fringe across her forehead. "All of them? What the fuck happened?"

It was only a passenger shuttle. It could withstand small collisions from space debris, malfunctions, human error. It was not built to survive an explosion from within.

"We have to go out to check," Henke said.

"Too dangerous," Dag replied. "There's too much debris."

"We have to—"

"Quiet," Zahra said. "Just . . . be quiet. I need to think."

In the brief pause that followed, Baqir touched my elbow, inclined his head toward the way out. But Dag was still blocking the door, and he was still watching us. I shook my head minutely: Wait.

Finally, Zahra said, "We can't help them now. We have our mission. We have to make this ship safe for *Homestead*."

It was Baqir who asked, "What's *Homestead*?"

Five headlamps turned toward us.

"Shut the fuck up," Henke said.

"No, it's okay," Zahra said. "We have nothing to hide. *Homestead* is a passenger vessel bringing the members of our family here to join us. There are three hundred people aboard, including many children."

"Three hundred people is a family?" Xiomara asked.

And Ariana said, "Why would you bring them *here*?"

I couldn't say anything at all. A sickly understanding knotted my stomach.

We only want to be left alone, Zahra had said, when Baqir had asked what they wanted. Not demands, not a ransom, not a list of political goals. They wanted to be left alone.

There were separatist groups and communities all over the world who, for whatever reason, did not wish to join the United Councils of Earth. Usually they retreated into the North American deserts or pieced together nomadic islands in the Pacific, forming small enclaves of their own design, with their own governments and their own rules. They wanted nothing from the Councils, they claimed, except a chance to live as they pleased. For most that was enough.

But not for all. Others looked to the sky and wondered why only Councils citizens could dream of frontiers beyond Earth.

It was a yearning I understood. I knew what it felt like to turn toward the stars because it was easier to gaze into unknowable darkness than to look at the painful wreckage of the life that surrounds you. I knew what it meant to take the knot of hopes and hurts and fears from inside and hurl it into deep space, across voids and galaxies, through dust and light. There were persistent rumors of some group or another plotting to seize a Martian habitat dome or a mining colony in the asteroid belt. My aunt always found those plots amusing; none had ever amounted to anything and, she believed, none ever would. SPEC had absolute control over space travel, and only Councils citizens were permitted aboard SPEC ships.

My aunt had never told me about any separatist group attempting to overtake a spaceship, but it did not seem likely these were the first people to have tried. Before the Collapse thousands of people had decided that Earth was no place for them, looked to the stars, and sailed into the dark. Only one of them had ever sent back any evidence of having reached its destination, the ship *Mournful Evening Song*, which had returned a single, lonely, unmanned probe after hundreds of years of resounding silence. But still people dreamed, and surely they dreamed outside the Councils as much as within them. *House of Wisdom* was a massive ship designed to be self-sustaining for an indefinite period of time. It could support hundreds of people. And it was, for all intents and purposes, abandoned.

They weren't seizing *House of Wisdom* to achieve a political goal. They were seizing it because they wanted to stay, and there were three hundred people coming to join them.

I pressed my lips together and breathed steadily. I could stop them. I could contact SPEC and the other ship could be diverted. I only needed to get away.

"Zahra is right," Dag was saying. Their discussion had gone around in circles. "We have our mission. We have to get control of the ship."

"And to do that we need to access the computing mainframe," Malachi pointed out. "I wish we didn't, but I can't work around it. We need it to access the primary systems before we can even begin to make this place safe."

"Where is it? How do we get there?" Zahra asked.

"Slowly," Malachi said. "All the interior doors and interlevel access points were locked down during the medical quarantine. It could take hours."

Sometimes, in quiet moments, I could still hear the calm computerized voice advising people to shelter in place. Await medical help. Remain calm. It had been futile from the start. The virus had spread too far and too fast before anybody even knew it was aboard.

"It doesn't have to," I said.

Headlamps swung to look at me.

"What?" Malachi said. "What are you talking about?"

"I can get you there faster."

"We can't trust him," Panya said.

Baqir said, "Jas? What are you doing?"

"Explain," Zahra said.

I said, "You don't have to get through every level between here and there. You just have to get to the agricultural labs. They're connected across the bottom three levels, and their internal security is a different system."

"You don't even know where we're going," Henke said.

"The entrance to the computer core is on Level 4," I said. "Starboard side. I lived here for eight years."

"How do you know you can get through that way?" Zahra asked.

Malachi answered before I could: "They were his father's labs."

No, I thought, with a pang of grief, they had been so much more than labs. They were my father's pride and joy, his warm and welcoming gardens, sanctuaries of greenery and life. He had fought for every square meter of green space as *House of Wisdom* was being built because, he had always said, the crew will need food and air, but they will need beauty, too, and peace, and the quiet of a cool dewy dawn.

I did not want to see what had become of my father's passion and brilliance, but it would get us closer to where I wanted to be. To where I could leave our captors behind. Radio for help and get Baqir and Xiomara and Ariana off this ship. I didn't know Xiomara and Ariana well, only those small pieces of information exchanged during stilted cocktail parties as our fellowships began. Xiomara was a biomedical engineer working on long-term human stasis. Ariana was an artist already somewhat famous for high-profile protest art; she had introduced herself to Baqir by telling him that she sympathized so much with the plight of the North American refugees and asking if he wanted to hear about her planned exhibition for the Second Council. That was all I knew of them. Whether they would stay calm or panic, follow my lead or obey our captors, trust me or take their own risks, I had no idea. I only knew I had to get them off this ship.

"I know the way," I insisted.

"Why would you help us?" Zahra asked.

"I'm not helping you," I said, with absolute truth. "I just don't want to die here."

Zahra looked at me for a long moment, her expression hidden by the blinding beam of her headlamp. "Very well. Show us."

The dead were everywhere.

In my nightmares I had always seen them as they were on the day of the massacre: screaming, clawing at imaginary enemies, flushed with panic, damp with sweat, chins smeared with spittle, and so much blood, all the blood hot and red, every spray and smear creating an obstacle my mother went to great lengths to avoid. When the medical staff stopped making announcements and nobody knew what to do, those who avoided infection quickly determined that blood, not air, was the most likely carrier. With people injuring themselves so savagely, so violently, there was plenty of blood.

All that blood was now dried to dark stains, nearly black in the low red light. The corpses were waxy and pale, shriveled beyond recognition. More than once I felt a shiver of unease, a wash of unreality, that I should be here, again, moving through my nightmares. More than once I closed my eyes and tried to will myself away: to Armstrong City, where we were meant to be been joining a welcoming reception for the Leung fellows; to the Takashi Lunar Telescope array, where I had twenty-six hours of time booked to gaze at the ancient, redshifted blaze of galaxies from billions of years ago; to safety, to light, to anywhere, anywhere at all, but here. The silence around us was complete.

Our passage through the cargo sublevels was slow. Malachi could open some of the doors but not others; his hacking skills, it seemed, were not infallible. At first our captors spoke a lot, arguing about their mission, their plan, the supplies they had lost on the shuttle, the three hundred people heading toward us. They seemed to believe there was a hidden SPEC ship stalking them from the darkness of space, and I could not tell if their fear was valid or delusional. They grew quieter with every corpse we encountered. I wanted to throw my arms wide and shout at them: Is this what you expected? This darkness filled with death, this massive crypt of shriveled and mummified memories, is this what you wanted? Is this the home you imagined for your children? I didn't ask. I did not care to hear their answers.

As captives we said little. The others followed my example. Henke and Dag kept their weapons in hand, and I was not going to risk angering them. I trusted neither Dag's calm adherence to a parody of SPEC routine nor Henke's frustrated snarls. A man who barely reacted to the explosion of a shuttle and the death of his comrades was as bad as one whose reaction swung from delight to rage without obvious cause.

I led the group to the nearest security hatch between the cargo sublevels and Level 0. The hatch was propped open by the body of a young woman, her arms reaching toward us from the apparent ceiling. Her face was turned to the wall; I couldn't see if I knew her. Only when Dag shouldered the hatch open did we discover that her left leg had been severed just above the knee. Another dead woman, a couple of meters away, held a large powered clamping tool, the sort used to move cargo. Her I recognized: she was the ship's lead boatswain. Between the teeth of the clamp were the remains of the first woman's leg.

"How could a virus do this?" Panya said, whispering hoarsely. "How could anybody do this?"

Nobody answered. After that, even our captors stopped talking.

There was another corpse in the corridor outside the entrance to the nearest of my father's laboratories. He was surrounded by a nest of metal scraps and tools, as though he had tried to barricade himself inside a makeshift cage. He rotated slowly, slowly, caught in a gentle vortex of air. There were clumps of dried blood suspended in a spiral around him like a dancer's ribbons. He had slashed his arms several times, great long gashes from elbow to wrist. I didn't know him. There was scarcely room to squeeze by the cage of metal he had built around himself. I went first, Zahra right behind me, and the others followed one by one with a series of grunts and frustrated noises, and a sharp curse from Ariana when she snagged the sleeve of her space suit and had to pry it free.

"*Fuck.*" Ariana jerked her arm. "That was stupid."

"Are you okay?" Xiomara asked.

"She's fine," Henke said. "Stop wasting time."

"But she—"

"The suits are self-mending. Keep moving."

"I am fine," Ariana said quietly. "Really."

At the end of the corridor, beyond the dead man and his cage, was a closed door.

AGRICULTURAL RESEARCH 2
CLIMATE CONTROL ZONE

There was a spray of dried blood over the sign.

My throat was dry, my mouth tacky with thirst. I touched the control panel, which was, thankfully, clear of blood. At my touch, the words MEDICAL QUARANTINE IN EFFECT appeared in bright red. I unclipped the seal on my right wrist and tugged the glove off. The air was bitterly cold. When I pressed my hand to the center of the screen, a halo of frost formed around my sweat-damp fingers. It was so much colder than a still-functional ship ought to have been. I counted slowly to ten, then removed my hand.

"What are you doing?" Malachi said, looking over my shoulder. "It's not prompting—what is that?"

The screen went dark. There was a pause—I was holding my breath—then the electronic lock within the door disengaged with a quiet click. I put my glove back on and closed the seal, then reached for the handle to pull the door open. Trapped air breathed outward. The agricultural levels were always kept under positive pressure to protect them from contaminants.

"How did you do that?" Malachi studied the screen by the door, still dark, before giving me a look that was half-baffled, half-accusing. "Why didn't you open the other doors?"

"It wouldn't work on the other doors," I said.

"Why did it work here?"

I hated him for asking, and I hated the way he asked, as though he wanted me to confide in him. All I said was, "My dad set it up that way."

There was no trick to it. There was only my father's kindness, and the sad way he had smiled the third time I was caught skipping lessons to explore the maintenance tunnels that honeycombed the ship. *I know it gets boring for you when your mum and I are working all the time, but it's not safe for you to go poking around in places nobody expects a kid to be,* he had said, his arm hooked over my shoulder. I had only shrugged. That was the whole point: if I spent my time sneaking around places where I was allowed to be, it wouldn't count as sneaking. Dad had looked down at me and laughed, and he had said, *How about we give you a way to explore that's less likely to get you chewed up by a faulty filtration system?*

He had only wanted to give his lonely, wandering son something to do. I had no intention of explaining that to Malachi or the others. They had no right to those memories.

I held the door and welcomed them into my father's world. Here there were no living quarters, no workshops, no flight operations. The sprawling labyrinth of the agricultural zone had once been filled with greenery and life: food crops in long rows, nitrogen-fixing plants in carefully placed patches, flowers and fruit vines, trees and grasses, epiphytes and ferns in every orientation, all growing beneath the carefully regulated artificial sunlight.

The door opened into a long corridor, flanked on either side by glass walls. The red lights rose to welcome us, but the growing rooms behind the walls remained dark. Our reflections on the glass were ghosts of murky red punctuated by careless flashes of white. Moving through that corridor, there was a nervous jolt of fear every time somebody saw a motion they did not expect, then turned, breath caught and blood racing, to find it was only their own helmet-blank visage looking back at them.

There were no dead in that long corridor. The researchers must have evacuated to other parts of the ship. Zahra moved ahead of me; I did not stop her. There were no wrong turns for her to make until we reached the garden.

At the end of the long passage, the ship opened into a large, round atrium. In the center was a fountain. The water was enclosed in an elegant tangle of transparent pipes, with algae and aquatic plants filtering the water as it flowed. The water was stagnant now, and the algae and seaweed in the pipes had long since died.

Zahra reached the atrium first. The light from her headlamp bloomed to fill the space as she looked up, and she gasped.

"What is it?" Panya asked.

Zahra did not answer. The rest of us were only a few meters behind. I joined her at the edge of the garden. It had been beautiful once, a quiet green place of leaves and mist, wrapped on every side by vines and flowers, grasses and ferns, with a winding path for strolling when the ship was under acceleration, seats and alcoves for quiet relaxation, soft full-spectrum light giving the appearance of gentle sunlight that brightened and faded with the schedule of a natural day.

There was no green anymore. The plants had all died and withered, their leaves turned to crisp paper, their stalks blackened and brittle. There was no light. There were only the dead.

Arms frozen around each other in a grotesque sculpture, waxy and pale among the branches and leaves. Faces, barely human anymore, staring blankly into the darkness. I tried to count the bodies. Twenty, thirty, forty. My mind stuttered. Vines and tendrils of once-vibrant plants had continued to grow after the humans had died, wrapping around them, drawing them into a dry, crumbling substrate. Leaves had grown into hair. Flowers had bloomed and died where eyes and mouths ought to have been. Hands reached, feet dangled, and faces, so many faces, yawned in the peculiar distortion of desiccation. The corpses had shriveled to brown, frost-burned husks.

They looked as though they would crumble to dust at the slightest touch. I curled my fingers at my sides.

Zahra cleared her throat. For a second I imagined that the rasp of her breath over the radio was faster, edging toward panic, but she controlled it quickly. "They didn't . . . it doesn't seem like . . ."

"What? What's going on?" Malachi said, coming up to join us. He looked up at the garden. "For fuck's sake. What are you—*fuck*. Why are there so many of them here?"

"They didn't die like the others," Zahra said. "Look."

She was right. There were no marks of violence on these bodies. No torn skin or flesh, no clothing stained with blood, no wounds at all. By the fountain there were two women clinging to each other, heads tilted together, eyes closed.

A shape moved beside me and I started. It was Panya. "Oh, that's awful. Why didn't they call for help? Didn't anybody know they were here?"

"This looks more like what Zeffir-1 is supposed to do," Malachi said. "Doesn't it? Did the virus affect them differently?"

I had no answer for him. I had seen only the mindless violence of Lago's virus. Nothing I remembered, and nothing in the records from *House of Wisdom*, explained the presence of so many here who died quietly, slowly enough that they could cling together in their final moments. Whether or not they were infected, I could guess why they had come here. My father's work had brought life into space, where no life should thrive—and that meant breathable air, naturally cleansed, even if all of the machines that normally chugged and churned around them fell silent.

"They were waiting for rescue," I said. "They thought they could survive here."

"But—no, that only makes sense if the ventilation system shut down?" Malachi said, then shook his head quickly. "Of course it would have been. The virus was airborne. That would have been the first thing they tried, if the quarantines failed."

I didn't correct him, although I knew the virus had not been airborne, no matter what SPEC believed, or let the public believe. I would have contracted it if it were, as I had spent days breathing the same air as everyone who fell ill, across multiple levels of the ship. I trusted my mother's conclusions in those final frantic hours more than I trusted the distant determination of SPEC.

"But the ventilation isn't shut down now. The air mix in here is the same as everywhere else we've been," Malachi added, more quietly. "I don't know. I could be wrong."

"How frightening that must have been." Panya was on the edge of tears.

"We're wasting time," Zahra said. "We're going up?"

"Yes," I said. "All the way."

She kicked away from the wall—with too much force, I knew that even as she moved—and caught herself on the pipes of the fountain in the center of the atrium. She swung around to awkwardly arrest her own motion, righted herself, and began to pull upward.

There was a nudge at my back: Dag, urging me to follow.

In a tangled thicket beneath the first arched bridge was a man I knew. I recognized him from the bold, dark tattoos that covered his face and neck. His name was Ulan. He had been one of my mother's engineers, the one who developed materials strong enough to withstand the forces exerted by her experimental engines. I remembered him most by the booming quality of his laugh, the strength of his hands, the way he would spin me around and fling me across the workshop while I shrieked with laughter and my mother rolled her eyes in annoyance. He had little sisters and brothers and nieces and nephews on Earth, all living aboard one of the floating cities in the Pacific that had been admitted into the Councils when Ulan was a child. His mother used to send him recorded messages of the entire family grinning and waving and shouting hello. I had been so jealous of them—it looked so fun, to be there on the sea surrounded by friends and family, so different from the life aboard *House of Wisdom*, where there were few children, and my parents rarely had time to play with me.

I had never wondered how Ulan died. I had never thought about him at all.

"Move," said Dag. "Keep going."

His voice was gruff, but I thought I heard, for only a moment, the slightest hint of something almost like pity. I reached ahead, found a metal rail to grasp, pulled myself past Ulan. I wanted to say his name aloud—to tell somebody, anybody, that he had been a person I knew, that he had a family who had loved him and missed him. I could not make a sound.

On the other side of the bridge, I followed Zahra upward, upward, while the others trailed behind. When the girls reached the bridge, Ariana shrieked at the sight of Ulan's face tangled in the gray leaves, and that shout hit me like a blow to the chest. I heard her scream, and echoed with it I heard all the others, the screams and pleas and desperate, gurgling gasps that filled my nightmares.

I closed my eyes, but it didn't help. Ulan's face was there, even in the darkness. I could not move. They had screamed, the infected and the dying. They had screamed as panic ripped through every person aboard, shouted and cursed and thrashed, clawing at their own skin and scrabbling for phantoms moving through their bodies. I had never forgotten, but I had always been able to push them down, to muffle them, if not ever truly silence them. Voices over the radio joined with the chorus from the past. I couldn't move. I couldn't open my eyes. I would only see them again, all the dead, their faces shriveled and inhuman.

"—the fuck is he doing?" Henke, angry.

"Is he having some kind of fit?" Panya, concerned.

"We don't have time for this." Zahra, ever in a hurry.

I wanted to tell them I could hear them just fine. Every word throbbed in my skull like a hammer blow. They needn't speak so loudly. It was too much, too many layers of fear and pain. The thorns of panic tore at the inside of my throat, the walls of my chest. The voices blended together into an unintelligible roar.

Then: a pressure on my arm.

"Jas," Baqir said. "Jas, hey, come on."

He gripped my elbow, slid his hand up my arm and around my shoulder, pulling me into a sidelong embrace.

"You've got to breathe. You're going to pass out."

"The suit," I started to say, but my voice hitched, choking on the words. My vision blurred with tears. I raised my hand to wipe them away but tapped uselessly against the helmet instead. "Suit won't let me."

"Let's not test it, okay?" Baqir said. He kept one arm around me, pressed his other hand to my chest; through his glove and my suit I could feel the metallic lines of his prosthetic fingers. "You need to breathe."

I leaned my head toward him. Our helmets tapped together. "I *am* breathing."

"You need to breathe and *not talk*," he said.

His voice was so serious, so concerned, I sniffled and tried to do as he said, inhaling and exhaling. There was motion around me, and through the blur of tears I saw the others moving upward, upward. There were three levels to go.

Finally, Baqir said, "You okay now?"

"Do you remember," I said, "that time you asked me what I was so afraid of all the time?"

He rubbed my arm lightly. "Yeah?"

Of course he remembered; I hadn't thought he would forget. It was at the beginning of our second year of upper school. Our first year we had been assigned different roommates—new students were encouraged to expand their social horizons—but for the second we got to choose. I had no other friends, so my choice was obvious, but I had worried all summer Baqir might want to live with somebody else. But he never mentioned it, never brought up the possibility, and by the time the school year began, I was both thrilled and terrified—thrilled that we would be together all the time, terrified for the same reason, because by that point, fourteen years old, I had certainly figured out that the way I felt about Baqir was not the way he felt about me. I was sure he would notice that I sometimes lingered too long watching him while he bent over his schoolwork or when he stretched after waking in the morning. He would notice, and he wouldn't be cruel about it, that wasn't his nature, but as soon as he understood, something would break between us, something irreparable, and everything would change. I carried that fear with me during the first days of that school year.

Then I woke one morning to find Baqir already awake, sitting on the edge of his bed with his elbows on his knees, watching me. My heart leapt into my throat. He was going to tell me that he wanted to move to another room. He wasn't comfortable sharing with me. He was sorry but he just couldn't. I was so sure of what he would say.

But what he said instead was that he'd noticed I was having nightmares, and he wanted to know what it was that frightened me so much in my dreams. His own worst dreams, he said, were of being back in the refugee camp at the edge of the wasteland, lying in a cot beside his sick sister and not knowing if she would survive the night, knowing only that his parents wept every day because the children weren't getting better, and being so afraid he wouldn't notice her dying that he couldn't breathe. He had never told me that before, but he told me then in a quiet, sad voice. He wanted to help. He knew what it was like to be afraid of the past. He didn't like seeing me so scared.

I knew that morning that the love I had for him wasn't going away. Not then, not ever. I resigned myself to a thousand small joys and heartbreaks every day because he didn't feel the same way, and it wasn't going to change.

The answer I had given him then, three years ago, was honest but incomplete.

I knew they were all listening. There was no privacy in the linked radios. The whispers we shared in that dead place were for everyone, but in that moment I didn't care.

I said, "This."

Baqir lifted one eyebrow, an expression that under normal circumstances would make my heart skip. "This?"

"This is what I'm afraid of all the time," I said. "I don't want to be back here."

His dark eyes regarded me thoughtfully from behind his helmet. He had never asked me to fill in the blanks of what had happened aboard *House of Wisdom*. He had known there were lacunae in what the public knew and what I shared, but he never demanded those secrets from me, just as I never asked for the childhood he had spent living in a refugee camp in the desert. We had always been so very careful of the separate horrors of our past, so mindful of the most jagged edges of memory. If he had pushed, I probably would have caved, but resented him for it, and he would have been so eaten up with guilt we might not have come back from that.

"We'll get out of this," Baqir said. "We will."

The panic had mostly passed, leaving in its wake a shivery, cold fear I did not know how to banish. I gently squeezed Baqir's hand on my chest to tell him it was okay to let go. He did so, slowly. I yearned for the pressure of his arm around me the moment it was gone. I wanted to answer his reassurance, to tell him that I had a plan. But the others were listening, and we had a long way to go.

SPEC RESEARCH—PRIMARY EDUCATION OUTREACH #98832-V
PUBLIC COMMUNICATION TRANSCRIPT (AUDIO/VIDEO)
Source: HOUSE OF WISDOM, SPEC RESEARCH
TimeDate: 10:01:34 07.14.392

TITLE: Voices from the Past—Deep Space Archaeology on HOUSE OF WISDOM

[CHIN, M. and LAGO, G. are standing together in a large, bright laboratory. Visible in the background is the tail end of UC33-X.]

CHIN: Good morning, everyone! My name is Dr. Ming-shu Chin, and this is my friend Dr. Gregory Lago. We're scientists here on the research ship HOUSE OF WISDOM. I'm a geologist, and Dr. Lago is an archaeologist.

LAGO: You might be wondering why a geologist and an archaeologist would bother coming into space. After all, there isn't any dirt for us to dig around in up here. Look, our hands are clean! Not a speck.

CHIN: But there is a lot we can learn in space, especially if we work together. What we're learning right now is part of a story that began a very long time ago. Hundreds of years ago, people built very large ships to travel into space. They were looking for other planets that might be like Earth. They were hoping to find new places to live.

LAGO: We don't know what became of most of those ships. They stopped sending messages back to Earth centuries ago. Space is very big, and space travel is very dangerous. But we do know where one of them ended up.

[CHIN and LAGO approach UC33-X.]

LAGO: You're probably wondering what this thing is, and I don't blame you. When astronomers first spotted it, they didn't know either. They named it Unidentified Craft 33-X, which is a silly name, but it seems to have stuck. The astronomers didn't even see it like we normally think of seeing things. They heard it instead, because it was sending out a radio signal. Have a listen.

[A woman's voice speaks briefly in an archaic language.]

LAGO: If you listen carefully, you can probably recognize most of the words. The woman in this message is speaking a language we now call Archaic Mandarin Chinese, which is an old version of the same Chinese language you may be learning in school, along with your other language lessons. She recorded her words a very long time ago, very far away, and sent them back to us on this probe so we could hear them.

CHIN: We don't know that woman's name, but we know she lived aboard a ship called MOURNFUL EVENING SONG, which left Earth hundreds of years ago. She sent this spacecraft back to Earth to let us know about MOURNFUL EVENING SONG's long journey. But there's a problem. This little craft has been traveling through space for a very long time, through deep cold and powerful radiation and unpredictable magnetic fields. The data in this probe's computers are very old and very badly damaged. That's where my friend Dr. Lago comes in.

LAGO: Space archaeologists may not have dirt and ruins to dig around in, but that doesn't mean we don't have artifacts to study. To hear what the people who recorded these messages wanted to tell us, we have to understand the very old technology they were using as well as all the ways the message has been damaged by its time in space. We have a lot of special techniques for piecing together old data like this and listening to what they had to say.

CHIN: What is she saying, Dr. Lago?

LAGO: That's a good question. Let's play it again, only this time we'll play the restored and repaired version.

[A woman's voice speaks briefly in an archaic language.]

LAGO: What she's saying is that the people aboard MOURNFUL EVENING SONG found a planet they wanted to explore.

CHIN: That's astonishing!

LAGO: It is, and now it's your turn to shine. Dr. Chin is what we call a planetary geologist. Planets and moons are her specialty.

CHIN: We don't know yet how far this probe has traveled or what secrets it holds inside, but we do know what direction it came from. We can point our telescopes in the right direction to look for the planet MOURNFUL EVENING SONG might have found. From that we can learn a great deal about planets outside our solar system—and about what ancient humans were looking for when they launched their ships to find them.

LAGO: A long time ago, when the United Councils of Earth were brand-new, the founder Leung Ma-Lin said, "The past is a mirror, and only by examining it can we examine ourselves." That is the lesson both geologists and archaeologists must remember every day.

CHIN: In the rest of this lesson, Dr. Lago and I are going to share with you what we hope to learn about this mysterious, distant world.

ZAHRA

The impossible stench of death followed us through the ship. I had not yet taken a single breath from the interior of *House of Wisdom*; the space suit was sealed. But I could smell it nonetheless: the vegetable rot of the gardens, the septic stink of human decay, the acrid iron taint of blood. I could taste it on my tongue.

I had not suffered the explosion directly; the wall of the airlock and position of the shuttle meant I had absorbed only a fraction of the possible force. But my back and shoulders ached with a deep pain that spiked sharply when I moved the wrong way. My head throbbed, and when I turned I could feel the pressure of the helmet against the knots and bumps. The pain that threatened to turn to nausea with every careless move.

I had never liked Nico. He was brash and cruel and had spent his entire life in the desert. I had wanted to choose somebody steadier for the mission, somebody better able to masquerade as a Councils citizen; Adam had not let me. But Nico had not deserved to die like that, wreathed in flame that peeled the space suit from his skin, screaming. Bao, who only ever did what Nico did first. The frightened woman who could not bear to leave the shuttle.

None of them deserved that. Boudicca, who had endured such tragedy before she left SPEC, who had never stopped dreaming of returning to space, she had not deserved to die like that.

I had thought I hated the Councils and SPEC as much as I could, but it was nothing compared to what I felt now. I had been naive. I knew they could murder their citizens to protect their secrets, as they had murdered my father, but I had not thought they would slaughter their own cherished young women and men.

I felt callous for letting a less tragic but more pressing concern push my anger and grief aside, but I could not ignore that all of our supplies had been lost as well. Our tools, our medical testing units, food and water, everything we had brought on the shuttle for our initial exploration of *House of Wisdom*, it was all destroyed. We had nothing but our weapons, our suits, and Malachi's skeleton key.

"This is it," Bhattacharya said. He stopped in front of a closed door: SYSTEMS CORE A-04. "But I can't open this one."

He had recovered from the panic that overtook him in the garden, but his cowardice had seeped into the others like a sickness. They spoke little. They had not once tried to get away, nor balked at our commands. Henke was frightened and trying to hide it; he wanted them to give him an excuse to lash out. I could hear it in the way he directed them, see it in the way he shoved a bit too hard, snarled a bit too loud, never holstered his weapon. I let him bully and bluster. I was afraid that if he stopped, the silence would overwhelm us.

Malachi tapped the door's control panel. The now-familiar MEDICAL QUARANTINE IN EFFECT glowed red on the screen. He attached his skeleton key and got to work. He was growing more practiced at bypassing the locks, although some still defeated him. His gestures were quick and nervous. But he had not failed us. He had never failed us, not once since he walked out of the desert six years ago, so lost and alone after being turned away from the border so many times. I needed to remember that, to tamp down the impatience. He would not fail us.

The warning vanished. The door opened, and the dormancy lights filled the room beyond. I was growing to hate those lights and the bleak red stain they cast over everything.

The mainframe control center was a C-shaped room that curved around a large, cylindrical chamber about ten meters in diameter. Behind the transparent wall, the ship's computing core stretched into the levels above and below. The machines flickered with pinprick lights of blue, white, red, and green. There was a slight hum in the air. After so much darkness, so much quiet, those signs of activity were reassuring. The ship had been waiting for us. It needed only to be awoken.

"I don't like how cold it is," Malachi said. "The computing core is still functional. It should be warm in here."

"I noticed that too," Dag said.

"The whole ship is cold," Panya pointed out. "It's been abandoned for ten years."

"I know, but the machinery—"

"Don't get distracted," I said. "Start with the radio."

Malachi hesitated before answering, "On it."

There were four dead in the room. Two women, two men, all seated at computer terminals. They wore SPEC uniforms. They were, like all the others, mummified to brown husks. Like the bodies in the garden, they bore no obvious external injuries. There had been no violence here.

To Henke I said, "Get these out of the way."

He grunted wordlessly and dragged the corpses to the far side of the room, where he pushed their faces into the wall. I watched him for a moment, then turned to the hostages. I did not draw my weapon, but I did put my hand on the holster and hoped it looked like a subtle threat rather than a nervous gesture.

"You said the virus made everybody violent," I said to Bhatta-charya. "But at this point we've seen more corpses who died with-out wounds than with them." I had no idea if that was true; I had not been counting. But I didn't care. He was still lying to us, and I was tired of it. I was tired of opening every door and rounding every corner to discover more lies. "Did these people suffocate too? Like the ones in the garden?"

"I don't know," he said. "I have no idea."

"Why didn't they evacuate? If they were still thinking clearly, why didn't they escape?"

"I don't know," he said again. "Maybe they couldn't."

"You were here during the outbreak." I tried to keep my voice calm, to hide the frustration and fear I was feeling, had been feel-ing since I first came into the ship. "Did you see anybody die like this? Without injuries?"

"No," he said, but there was a crack in the middle of the word. He was silent for a moment. I wished I could better read his expres-sion behind the faceplate. I could not tell if he was trying to re-member or trying to lie. "But I wasn't here at the end. I didn't see everything. And . . ."

"What?"

"In her last transmission, Captain Ngahere said there were two stages of the infection. Panic, then calm. So it's possible, I guess. I don't know."

I had listened to Captain Ngahere's final transmission a hun-dred times or more, sinking into every fearful hitch in her voice, every pause, every sigh. I had carried the wail of the ship's medical alarms into my dreams. "She didn't say that."

"Yes, she did. In the full transmission, she says that."

"We've heard the full transmission."

Bhattacharya shook his head. "The one released to the public was incomplete."

"We've heard more than what was made public," I said. Even as I said it, doubt wormed into my mind. "Malachi. Tell him."

Malachi glanced up from the workstation. "We know more than the public, yes, but it's always been possible that we don't know everything. You know that. I warned Adam."

Malachi had been clear from the start that if SPEC suspected even for a second that an outside hacker was mining their restricted files, the whole plan would fail. Adam had never been concerned. The coup of discovering the loophole in the security drones was our greatest triumph—that information was so carefully guarded we assumed we had stripped bare all of SPEC's biggest lies.

But we had not known the true nature of the virus. We may not have known the full extent of Captain Ngahere's final words. My mind spun with the dizzying possibilities of everything else we might not know.

"I don't know what you heard, but Captain Ngahere talked about the two stages of the virus in her last transmission," Bhattacharya said. "The same one where she said it might be Zeffir-1 and Dr. Lago was probably responsible."

"He's lying again," Henke said. He was grinning. It was the grin of a feral dog, more threat than amusement, the same way he had grinned when Adam first brought him to the homestead and introduced him as a man devoted to a new beginning. "We don't need to listen to this asshole."

"Um." Malachi cleared his throat. "The radio is functional."

I spun to face him. "Can we contact *Homestead*?"

"If I can make sure it's encrypted . . . There. Okay. *Homestead*, this is *House of Wisdom*. Do you copy?"

A noise came over the space suit radio, a click and two low beeps directly in my ear. Malachi watched incomprehensible data scroll over the screen and tapped out a few commands. He didn't seem concerned.

"None of you are going to say a word," Henke told the hostages. They nodded mutely, eyes on his weapon.

"I repeat: *Homestead*, this is *House of Wisdom*. Do you copy?"

Another click, another beep, and a man said, "*House of Wisdom*, this is *Homestead*. We hear you loud and clear."

Panya let out a relieved laugh, and Malachi grinned. That was Orvar, captain of *Homestead*.

"Good to hear your voice, Captain," Malachi said.

"What the hell is going on over there? We picked up a distress signal from *Pilgrim 3*, and Orbital Control is lit up with emergency transmissions."

Malachi looked up at me. I leaned forward, then stopped, feeling foolish. I didn't need to speak into the terminal. I only needed to speak.

"*Pilgrim 3* is gone," I said.

Orvar was quiet for a long moment. "Is that you, Zahra? What did you say?"

"The shuttle is gone. There was an explosion. It's been destroyed." I swallowed. I could not allow my voice to break. There would be time to grieve later. "We lost Boudicca, Nico, and Bao, and several hostages."

"Fuck me," Orvar said. "How could that—*fuck*. How did that happen? The security drones?"

"The drones didn't attack. We don't know what happened. The explosion might have come from inside the shuttle."

"It may have been a missile," Dag said. "We don't know it came from inside."

"Nobody knew that shuttle was ours until today. Nobody knew our destination," Orvar said.

"I know, but they must have found out," I said, trying so very hard not to sound like a child insisting the adults listen to her.

"The explosion tore the . . ." I had to pause for a breath. "It took the shuttle apart, and it came from the inside."

"A missile is still more likely," Dag said.

I did not need Dag contradicting me in front of everybody. I had seen the explosion. He hadn't. But now was not the time to scold him. "We haven't had any contact with Boudicca or the others since. They're gone."

"Fuck." Over the radio I could hear Orvar taking deep breaths. His voice a bit muffled, he said, "Go find Adam. He needs to hear this." Speaking to me again, he went on, "Are the rest of you okay? Were any of you hurt?"

My head was still throbbing, and my entire body ached from the force of the impact. It would be so much easier if we had the medical supplies from the shuttle—but I couldn't think like that. I was only bruised, not broken. I had suffered worse. It was not important.

I said, "The rest of us are unharmed. We have four hostages, including Councilor Bhattacharya's nephew. We brought them over before the explosion."

"Thank the ancestors for that," Orvar said. "Better than losing all of them. How did this happen? How did they find out?"

Malachi said, "Boudicca was sure SPEC has a dark ship in orbit. We couldn't confirm its presence or location, but you should be on watch for it until we can get our radar up and do a complete survey. If it's there, it's close. The security drones will keep them away for a while, but we have to shut the system down to let *Homestead* approach, and we have to do it soon."

A low whistle from Orvar. "We knew the bastards might have a trick like that, but attacking the shuttle . . . fuck. *Fuck.* I never thought they would kill their own kids to stop us." His voice hitched on the word *kids.* Orvar had children of his own, but he had not seen them in a very long time. When he left the Councils to live in the desert, his wife and children had remained behind. That was years ago, long before I was born, before the Councils had closed the border even to former citizens seeking a temporary visit, when those who left still believed they could see their families from time to time. That, like everything else the Councils did, had been a lie. Every time he had tried to return to them, whether for a visit or to stay, he was denied. Orvar's children would be grown now. I had never asked him why he left in the first place, but it scarcely mattered. There was no reason good enough to justify the Councils denying a man the chance to watch his children grow.

"None of us thought they would do that," I said. "We should have known better."

"We won't make that mistake again," Panya said, her voice soft and shaky. "Never again."

"There's more. It's about the virus," I said.

"Just a moment—Adam is here. We've got *House of Wisdom*, sir."

Orvar spoke quietly for a few moments, relaying to Adam what I had just told him. A shiver of nerves passed over my skin. We had lost so much, and I did not know how Adam would respond. Both profound sadness and fiery rage would be justified. I had not seen him in about a month, not since we had left the family to embed ourselves into SPEC under our false identities. I did not know how to brace for his mercurial temperament when I could not read his face and voice and whims every day.

"Zahra," Adam said, and I tensed. He spoke my name with an exhaled breath, like the swoop of a hawk that had spotted its prey. "Listen to me. Boudicca knew the danger when she chose this mission. She would have thought it worth it, for a chance to bring our family to freedom. She knew her sacrifice would not be in vain."

What Boudicca had wanted was to fly again, after having been forced to give it up so long ago. She had wanted to push aside the tragedies of her past and return to space. She had known this mission, our dream, was dangerous. But anticipating danger and going happily into death were two very different things. She had only wanted to fly.

Now was not the time to argue with Adam and open myself to his anger and recriminations. I said, "I have to tell you about the virus."

"Ah, yes," said Adam, chuckling softly. "Dr. Lago's infamous virus. It has always fascinated you."

He put a sly emphasis on my father's name. I had to ignore it. I had to make him understand this wasn't about me or my father. "It isn't what we thought. The symptoms don't match Zeffir-1, so we can't trust the vaccine to work."

"Zahra." In Adam's voice I heard a familiar note of exasperation, the same one I heard every time I doubted, every time I hesitated, every time I questioned the path we had set ourselves upon. It made me feel like a small child, and I cringed. "Zahra, my dear, you would have us tremble in fear like the cowards who abandoned that ship to space? You would have the memory of a single Councils-brainwashed madman keep us from our new home?"

I was glad Adam could not see my face, but I wished I could see his. I knew every cadence of his voice, from his gentlest kindness to his most towering anger, but at that moment, separated by a vast gulf of space, I could not tell what he was thinking. He had kept my family's secret for ten years. Even when my mother died, he did not reveal to anyone that she had once been Mariah Dove, wife to Gregory Lago. But more and more as we prepared to leave Earth, Adam had brought it up in moments when we were alone, talking quietly by the fire or poring over SPEC data, or alluded to it when we were among others, his mouth twisting in a smile as he watched me squirm with discomfort. I knew he had been testing me, but I did not know why. He was testing me now.

My stomach was knotted, my jaw so tense my head began to throb anew. I took a breath before I spoke.

"There was a great deal of violence during the outbreak," I said. "The virus drove them mad. They slaughtered each other."

"They were cowardly and cruel in the hour of their greatest test."

"I think it's more than that. I think the virus drove them mad. We need to make sure it's safe," I insisted. "We lost our viral testing equipment in the explosion. You can't bring anybody aboard until we know for sure."

I knew at once it was the wrong thing to say. I knew from Panya's sharp inhale, from Malachi's startled glance. We all knew better than to tell Adam *you can't*. But there were ten people dead, the shuttle destroyed, and SPEC stalking our presence with a ship we could not see, and *House of Wisdom* was nothing like the glittering ark of our dreams. It would not be safe until we banished every last reminder of the massacre.

"Adam, listen to me," I said quickly. "I only mean we might need to keep everybody aboard *Homestead* for a—"

"Nothing has changed," Adam said coldly. "You have your orders."

"But we need more time—"

"Are you doubting us? Are you questioning the dream that has carried us this far? We have been chased like *dogs* from the Earth, and you allow doubt to infect you now?"

"No. No, Adam. The dream is true. The ship will be ours. I have no doubt."

My words were a lie. I had nothing but doubts, and no clear view of the hours and days to come. Everything had changed. None of the plans we had so eagerly shaped on the ground applied anymore. If the explosion wasn't enough, if the unknown identity of the virus wasn't enough, I didn't know how to make Adam understand. I looked around helplessly. Malachi's eyes were wide and frightened, and Adam never listened to him anyway. Panya would not look at me. Dag was, as ever, placid and unreadable. Henke was still grinning at the hostages. Nobody would speak to support me and counter Adam. Even aboard *House of Wisdom*, there was nothing they feared more than Adam's anger.

"Tell me what you are going to do, Zahra," Adam said.

There was only one answer I could give. "We'll make the ship safe. We'll be ready by the time *Homestead* gets here."

"Everybody understands," Adam said. His voice softened fractionally, and I felt sickly and cold. "Everybody is ready for hard work. But we cannot begin that work if you fail."

"I won't. We won't."

It was as though he didn't hear me. "The consequences will be terrible if you fail. For all of us. So terrible. We must carry this burden. We cannot go back."

My throat was tight and aching. "I know. Are the—"

Are the twins okay? The question was there, on the tip of my tongue, but I dared not ask. It was better to keep Anwar and Nadra far from Adam's mind when he was angry with me. Some days he praised me for caring for them so deeply; other times he raged because it was forbidden to love anybody, even children, more than we loved him.

"Is the family well?" I asked.

"We have encountered no complications," Adam said. "There is the matter of the vessel Malachi believes he saw. We must keep them at bay."

"I know," I said. "I have four hostages."

"The Bhattacharya boy is among them?"

"Yes. He is. We can use him—"

"We will use him to warn SPEC to keep their distance."

I pressed my lips together. It was easier to let Adam claim ideas for his own when he was suggesting what I had planned to do anyway.

He went on, "I will assure Councilor Bhattacharya that if they do not stay away, we shall consider her nephew's life forfeit. That will keep them occupied for a while."

There was a quiet sound over the radio, a gasp of fear. From the corner of my eye I saw Henke raise his weapon. I had forgotten the hostages were listening. I should never have let them listen. They had been so quiet I had fallen into the rhythm of a private conversation. It was the mistake of an amateur, a child. I felt sick with shame.

"I can't wait for you to join us," I said. I tried to sound eager, but in truth I wanted Adam to take command so the burden of every decision was no longer on my shoulders. He wore the mantle of leadership so easily, and I so poorly.

"Do your duty, Zahra," he said. "You cannot fail me now."

"I won't."

"Our fate is in your hands," he said.

I strained to hear reassurance in his voice, to hear any hint of warmth, to let myself be bolstered by Adam's belief in me. But his tone was cold. There was no comfort to be had, only warning.

Orvar said, "He's left the bridge. He's spending a lot of time soothing the family."

I blinked rapidly and struggled to control my breathing. "Is there something wrong?" I asked.

"Only cramped quarters, stale food, and bad tempers." There was an unconvincing lightness in Orvar's words. "We've endured worse. Knowing that you've made it to *House of Wisdom* will lift everybody's spirits. But it will help even more when we get word you've got the ship under your control."

"We'll work as fast as we can," Malachi said. "Keep an eye on what Orbital Control is doing, okay? Until we get the system fully functional, I'm not comfortable with sending or receiving any open transmissions."

"Understood," Orvar said. "Best of luck."

Malachi tapped the comm screen to break contact, then looked up at me. "I didn't want to worry them, but I honestly have no idea how long it will take me to get the skeleton key into the computer system, and even less of an idea how long it will take to clear even one level of the virus."

I touched his shoulder. That was not what I wanted to hear, but Malachi needed to focus. "Do what you can. *Homestead* is safe for now."

"Okay. Right. I can start with lifting the medical quarantine, so we can get around the ship faster."

"Do that." I nodded quickly. I should have thought of that. I would have thought of that, if I did not have Adam's words still ringing in my ears. The survival of the family rested on my shoulders. I had accepted that burden when I accepted this mission. But my body ached, and with every passing minute I could feel the SPEC shadow ship drawing closer. Did they have missiles? Was there more than one ship? Did they care who they harmed in their desire to stop us? Adam believed Councilor Bhattacharya could stay their hand to save her nephew, but I was not so sure.

I moved away to let Malachi work. Before we left Earth, I had imagined our first hours aboard *House of Wisdom* would be filled with ceaseless toil and vital industry, all the welcome tasks of waking a ten-years-abandoned ship from its long quiescence. The work was part of the dream. We were not afraid of the labor before us. We never had been. So many people in the Councils worked their entire lives for the benefit of people they would never know, places they would never see. Adam often reminded us that life in a desert homestead was harder, yes, but it was more honest. When we tilled the land, we knew who would eat the food that grew from it. When we dug a foundation, we knew who would live in the house built over it. It was supposed to be the same aboard *House of Wisdom*. We were ready to work, for ourselves and for our families, if only we could.

I had never once imagined we would not even be able to open the doors on our own, or turn on the lights, or raise the temperature above freezing.

The hostages were pressed against the outer wall of the control room, exactly where Henke had directed them to stand. I looked them over one by one and wished I knew how dangerous they could be. Both women met my eyes with angry glares before looking away. Nassar was watching Malachi work. Bhattacharya was looking right at me.

"Who was that man?" he asked mildly, as though we hadn't been discussing his death.

"Shut up," Henke said. "You don't need to—"

Panya interrupted him. "His name is Adam Light. He is our leader. He is the one who protected us when your masters tormented us in the desert. He is the one who has lifted us from the oppression of the earthbound liars and deceivers you serve."

"What the fuck does that even mean?" one of the women said. The short one with the colorful hair, the one who had been crying before.

And the other woman, the fat one, muttered, "Who we *serve*?"

"Where do you come from?" the first woman asked. "From the wasteland?"

"The *wasteland*?" Panya said, whirling to face her. She moved too fast and had to catch herself with one hand on a console. "Is that what you think of us? We're nothing more than waste, because we do not subject ourselves to a life under the heel of your Councils?"

"No, but you are from the North American desert, aren't you?" the woman said. "You've got the same accent as Baqir."

"The Inyo desert," Nassar said. "Right? The northern part?"

"You don't know anything about us," Panya said.

There was anger in her voice, but also sadness, a sadness so familiar it tugged at my heart. Panya had lived her entire life in the desert, moving from one encampment to another, one community to the next, never finding a home until she met Adam. She had worked her fingers bloody to build the homestead, and she had wept when it became clear we could not stay. She knew better than most what it was to dream so hard for a better life that the dream became an enduring ache in the center of your chest.

"Then tell us," Nassar said. "Who are you? What do you want?"

"Don't pretend you care for us, simply because you have dust in your veins," Panya said. On her pretty face a sneer was little more than a crease, like a single cloud marring a summer day. "You left the desert. You surrendered your freedom to become one of them, even though they will never see you as more than a desert rat. You don't understand anything. We know we're no more than *waste* to you and all the other spoiled Councils brats. But that man—our Adam of Light—he is greater than all of your leaders, greater than all of your citizens. He is bolder and braver than any person you have ever known. Do not think for one second we will let you get in his way."

There was pride in her voice, ringing as clear as a bell, but I did not like the way she smiled. We did not want to push the hostages into a place beyond fear. We needed them to be obedient, not reckless.

"We're not trying to get in your way," Bhattacharya said. "We'll do what you say. Do you need me to record a message for my aunt? Do you want me to tell her to make SPEC stay away? I'll do it. Just tell me what to do."

There was something unnerving about the way he stared at me as he spoke. I had the foolish urge to snap at him, tell him to avert his eyes. I didn't know if it would help or hurt to have Councilor Bhattacharya receive a message from her nephew. I could not risk undermining whatever Adam would say in his own contact with SPEC and the Councils.

"Not yet," I said. "And until we have use for you, you are to stay quiet."

"Okay. We can do that." But Bhattacharya was still looking at me as though he were trying to see what lay beneath my skin.

I turned away from him to speak to Dag. "We need to secure—"

"Ow." One of the women spoke suddenly, but I did not know which one it was until she moved one gloved hand to touch her opposite arm. It was the short woman, the one who had called the desert a wasteland. She pressed her fingers into her forearm.

"Are you hurt?" the other woman asked.

"No. It just feels weird."

"Weird how?"

"It's feels like . . ." The first woman shook her head. "I don't know. Just weird."

"Did you hurt yourself?" Nassar said. "When you tore your suit?"

"It sealed over." The woman plucked at the tight material of the space suit. "It was only a tiny puncture. But I think there's something in here."

The other woman reached for her hand. "So take your glove off—"

"Get away from her." Bhattacharya's voice was stern and sharp, so unlike the soft tone he had been using before.

"But she's hurt—Jas, what the fuck?"

Bhattacharya grabbed his friend by the arm and pulled him away from the women, shoving him backward toward the far end of the room. The friend flailed and grasped, stopping his momentum only when he caught the back of a chair. Bhattacharya took hold of the other woman next and pushed her away as well.

Henke swung his weapon back and forth, aiming for one, then the other. "For fuck's sake, I told you to stay still!"

The woman slapped at Bhattacharya's hands, but she only managed to spin herself around so that she was grasping for something to hold. "Stop that! What are you doing? I'm just trying to help Ariana."

"Stay away from her," Bhattacharya said.

"I really think there's something in my suit," the short woman— Ariana—said. She began to slap and tug at her own arm, twisting around and around as she grew more frantic. The suit was pressurized and taut; she couldn't get a handle on the slick fabric. "There's something in there! What the fuck? Help me get it out!"

"Henke, Dag. Restrain her," I said. They approached the woman with their weapons drawn. "Malachi, keep an eye on the others."

He hesitated, then rose from his chair, fumbling his gun from its holster.

"Ari, calm down so we can help you," the other woman said. She was trying to push away from Bhattacharya, but he held tight to her wrist. "Jas, let me go. We have to help her."

"We can't," Bhattacharya said. "She's infected."

There was a short silence, no longer than the space between one heartbeat and the next.

"What? How is that possible?" Malachi said, his voice rising sharply with alarm.

"She tore her suit," Bhattacharya said. "That's how it got in."

"It was only a pinprick," Panya said doubtfully.

"He's lying," Henke declared. "He's trying to bullshit us again. The virus is airborne."

"We don't know for sure how it spreads," Malachi said.

"I swear, there's something in my suit. I can feel it, okay? You have to help me!" Ariana was grasping at her arm again and again, turning in a circle. Then her eyes widened suddenly, and she fell silent with a quick, sharp intake of breath.

"Ariana?" the other woman said. "What's wrong?"

Ariana's answer was a ragged whisper. *"It's moving."*

"She's hallucinating," Dag said. He pushed away from the machine console, one hand on the crew chairs to guide him, floating toward the girl. "Help me grab her."

Henke rolled his eyes, but he holstered his gun and moved toward Ariana.

"Ari, there's nothing there," Nassar said. "It's making you think there's something there, but there isn't. Don't hurt her. Please, she's sick. Don't—"

"Get it out!" Ariana shouted. With both hands she unsnapped the clamps on her helmet and broke the seal. She pulled it off and sent it spinning away from her, then grabbed at the neck of her suit, tugging frantically at the collar. There were tears on her cheeks and snot glistening at the end of her nose, and her hair was stringy with sweat. "Get it out! Get it out, it's moving, it's here, I can feel it! *Get it out!*"

"Henke! Dag!" I snapped. "Stop fucking around!"

Henke caught Ariana's arm and yanked her toward him, trying to seize both of her wrists behind her back. But before he could, Ariana shrieked and began batting at his arm and shoulder and face with her free hand. Dag reached for her flailing arm, but she kicked out with both legs and struck him square in the chest. He caught himself on a chair and pushed himself back toward her and Henke. Together they got her under control, Henke holding both arms behind her, and Dag catching her feet. She arched her back and kicked a few more times, making tight, scared animal noises. She was breathing heavily and shivering as the cold sapped her strength. A fine sheen of frost formed on her sweat-damp hair.

"You're going to stop making a fuss now," Henke said. "Okay?"

Ariana dropped her chin to her chest. The muscles of her arms were tense, the tendons in her neck standing out. Her jaw clenched and unclenched. Her breath was quick and ragged. I could not see her face.

"Okay," she said. Her voice was flat, all the hysteria drained away. "Okay."

Dag let go of her feet, and a second later Henke released her wrists to grab her upper arm. "You're going to do what we say, okay?"

Ariana relaxed into his grip. "Okay," she said.

Then, moving so swiftly I could barely track her motion, she spun around and lunged into Henke.

"Shit!" he shouted, bending away as she struck his helmet.

Ariana ducked when he grabbed for her, down and to the left, dodging under one of his arms, the motion so smooth it was as though she had practiced it a thousand times.

When she spun away from him, she had his gun. She had plucked it from his holster.

She leveled it at him and said, "You're going to stop making a fuss now."

And she fired.

The bullet hit him square in the chest. It penetrated his suit and exploded with a wet, gruesome sound: the bones of his rib cage cracking outward, his lungs sucking in, a wheeze of shock. He flew backward and struck the glass wall of the computer core with a thump. He blinked rapidly behind his faceplate. A red flood spread from the gaping cavern of his chest.

Firing the gun had sent Ariana backward, too, but she used the momentum to propel herself gracefully toward the door. She hit the control panel without pausing and grabbed the frame to pull herself into the corridor. She hit the panel on the outside, and the door slid shut.

It happened so fast. A matter of seconds.

"She's fucking playing us," Dag said, and he went after her at once, without waiting for a response. Panya followed only a second later. They both had their weapons drawn for the chase. Malachi launched himself across the room to Henke, but already it was obvious there was nothing he could do.

Their shouts blended together, an ear-stinging cacophony, and I could not move. Henke's chest had been exploded from the inside. That's what the guns were designed to do. Stop the target, but don't pass through. Don't endanger the hull of the ship. She had moved so quickly, so gracefully, after panic that had seemed so very real. Henke was dead.

"Malachi," I said, too softly.

I turned slowly, looking over the room, casting my headlamp into every corner. My heart was thumping, my blood racing. A roar filled my mind. In the corridor, Panya and Dag were arguing about which way to go.

"She's been planning this," Dag said. "It was a trick. She has an escape route."

They had lost the woman already. Their shadows moved in the low red light, bending through the door in a distorted dance.

"She must be a SPEC infiltrator," Panya said. There was uncertainty in her voice, but not as much as I expected, and it faded as she went on, convincing herself as she sought to convince Dag. "She must be. It was all an act. She isn't who she claims to be. She sabotaged the shuttle."

I choked back a sudden laugh, although there was nothing

funny about it. A trick. An *infiltrator*. It was a ridiculous idea. She was a postgraduate student. The names and backgrounds of all the Leung fellows were public knowledge. There was no way she could be SPEC—but I knew nothing about her, nothing about her background. If her fear had been an act, it was a convincing one. She was not the one I had expected to try to flee.

My heart thumping rapidly, I looked around again.

There were no side rooms. There were no floor or ceiling hatches. The door to the corridor was on one side. The door to the computer core was on the other—closed now.

We had not checked if it was locked.

Not a trick. A distraction.

"Panya!" I shouted. "Dag! Shut the fuck up!"

The silence was abrupt. I heard the rasp of Malachi's breathing. I recognized the way he sniffed, inhaled, exhaled, sniffed again.

"They're gone," I said. I was going to throw up. I couldn't breathe. Henke's blood was forming larger and larger globules in the air.

Panya appeared in the doorway. "What?"

"Quiet," I said.

There: a sharp breath.

A crackle. A click. Silence. The space suit radios had switched off.

The hostages were gone.

[data corruption] keep everybody in our tents, but nobody is saying why [data corruption] only two from the archaeology field team came back. They lost the others in the ruins when [data corruption] I should go see if they need volunteers for the search party. They haven't even begun to map the complex. They'll need the aerial data. I keep looking at it, wondering if we could have [data corruption] The medical shelter is all lit up. Nobody's getting much sleep. We all need sleep. We all [data corruption]

—FRAGMENT 3, *MOURNFUL EVENING SONG* VIA UC33-X

Xiomara was yelling through her helmet. She was right behind me, following so close I kicked her twice, but with
the radios off her voice was muffled. I looked back only to
be certain she and Baqir were following. I didn't stop.

We had to get far enough from the computing core that our
captors couldn't follow. They were chasing Ariana. I listened to
their arguments and accusations long enough to learn they
thought she was an embedded SPEC agent, or causing a distraction
to help us escape, or any number of other outlandish possibilities,
but I knew the truth. I had seen that desperate flailing and scratching before, the frantic shedding of a protective suit, the instantaneous snap from confused to distraught. I had heard those panicked
pleas before. The hallucinations always began the same way. There
was something inside. There was something moving. The echoes
of those cries had never faded from my memory. Ariana was infected.

I led Xiomara and Baqir farther into the hidden maze between
levels. I had kicked up to the door to a computing access room on
Level 5, wrested it open, then passed it by for a maintenance tun-

nel between Levels 5 and 6. Let them think we fled into Level 5. Let them waste time searching. I knew this ship. We could get away.

Ariana was infected.

It shouldn't be possible, but I had no doubts. Lago's virus was supposed to be a modification of Zeffir-1, a biological weapon designed to denature after its host died. Infect quickly, kill quickly, vanish quickly. But SPEC's conclusions had been wrong. The hallucinations, the panicked outburst, the sudden lash of violence, even the swift, eerie calm to follow—it was all the same. The virus, whatever it was, was still here.

That cage of metal tools we had squeezed by, where Ariana pricked herself. There must have been sharp points bloodied by an infected victim. All it had taken was a scratch. Dried blood was still blood. The virus had found a new home in Ariana's bloodstream, and it was flourishing again.

The maintenance tunnels that had been endlessly exciting when I was a kid were significantly more claustrophobic now. The space between each level was about two meters high, most of which was taken up with machinery and conduits, wiring and ducts, filters and heaters and coolers, water filtration and antistatic and demagnetization systems. The machines were labeled with codes of numbers and letters. L6 for the level. S for the ship's starboard side. Arrows, numbers, symbols. I had memorized the code as a child. I had been so proud of myself for sneaking through places I was not meant to be.

I stopped at a junction and moved to the side so Xiomara and Baqir could join me. I checked the suit's environmental readout:

98 kPa 5.7 C 80/20 12% humidity

Still cold, but warmer than the ship's corridors and rooms.

I lifted a hand to keep them quiet, held my breath, and switched on the radio.

". . . did she go?" Dag.

"We'll find her." Zahra. "She's not important right now."

"You don't know what she could be doing."

"She can't escape. She can't access the radios. What can she do?"

They had lost Ariana.

"Please, everybody, *please*. We can't fight each other." Panya.

"We'll recapture the hostages later. It will be trivial when we get control of the ship and its surveillance systems." Zahra again. "Malachi?"

"I told you. I can't do that here." Malachi.

"You said you would be able to."

"I know. I'm sorry, I know, but I can't. We have to get to the bridge."

They were still at the mainframe on Level 4. They had failed to hack into the ship's computer.

I turned off the radio and exhaled slowly, then reached up to take off my helmet.

Baqir grabbed my wrist. His voice was muffled by his faceplate, but his words were clear enough: "What the fuck are you doing?"

"It's okay," I said. "It's warmer here."

"It's not safe!"

"The virus isn't airborne," I said. "It's passed through blood contact only."

"How do you know?"

"My mother figured it out, and some of the others, before they died. She watched how people got sick. There was always violent physical contact. And I was never infected, even though I was breathing the same air as everybody else." My breath was misting in the cold, pushing small clouds between us. "It was never in the air, okay? I didn't say anything because *they* don't know, and I wanted to find out what else they've missed."

Baqir looked at me for a long moment, then opened his helmet seal and pulled it off. "Then why the fuck did SPEC let everybody think it was airborne?"

"I don't know. I was unconscious in a hospital bed when word got out it was Zeffir-1. By the time anybody asked me, they'd already distributed the vaccine. Lago was already dead. I guess they didn't think it was worth backtracking on their claims and letting everybody know they had no fucking idea what happened here."

Xiomara snapped her helmet off. "I don't fucking care what SPEC did or didn't do. We need to help Ariana!"

It was what she had been shouting for several minutes, only now the words were loud enough to make me wince. "We can't."

"We shouldn't have left her. We have to—"

"We can't," I said again. "There's nothing we can do. It's too late."

"You don't know that! You just said nobody has any fucking idea what happened here!"

"Don't shout," Baqir hissed. "They'll hear us."

"I don't care! Can we get—" Xiomara's voice broke, and her face screwed up with the effort of keeping the tears at bay. "We can get help. If we can get her to a doctor . . ."

"It's already too late," I said.

"Fuck you," Xiomara spat. She shoved me with both hands. "I am not giving up. I am not going to fucking let her die."

I let her push me. I understood why she was angry. But I also knew there was nothing we could do.

"You knew about this. You could have said something," she said.

"Don't be stupid," Baqir said. He grabbed her arm to yank her back. "Like these people would listen."

"Not to *them*," Xiomara said. "Before! To everybody! You knew what it was like here. Why didn't you tell anyone? Fuck SPEC. You could have told the public."

"Really? Would that have helped? Would anybody have believed me, if SPEC was denying it?" I asked. "If I'd gone against the Councils and SPEC and told everyone that no, actually, Dr. Lago didn't send up the *nice* kind of virus that just lets people die in their sleep, he sent the *bad* kind, the kind that made them go so fucking crazy they hacked their own limbs off trying to cut out invisible bugs? Tell them that the reason SPEC wouldn't release the transmissions was because all they showed was a massacre? That I didn't feel much like talking about it because I'd just watched my father carve himself up with a kitchen knife? And all of that happened because somebody who was their *friend,* who came over for *fucking dinner* and told jokes and they all laughed and the whole fucking time he was thinking about how to murder them to prove a point? Do you really think that would have stopped these—these—"

"Jas," Baqir said.

I shut my mouth. Looked down. Rubbed my hand over my face. The feel of the grimy, cold space suit made my skin crawl. I opened the seals and tugged off the gloves, let them dangle like severed hands on the ends of my sleeves. I ran both hands through my hair and tried to breathe steadily. Tried, but it was so hard. I felt as though my entire chest was spasming and seizing. The air was so fucking cold. I couldn't panic. Not now.

When I finally looked up, Xiomara was wiping tears from her eyes.

"I got this," she said. "But I don't know how to use it."

For the first time I saw that she was not empty-handed. She was holding a small black object with prongs on the end. It was a suppression weapon, the sort SPEC Security used to shock or sedate targets. Baqir and I stared.

"Where the fuck did you find that?" he asked.

She shrugged. "It was in a console by the—you know. The crew. I didn't even know SPEC crew were allowed to be armed. I took it. I don't know if it still works."

"You can check the charge with—that button, there," Baqir said, pointing.

Xiomara turned the weapon, then simply handed it over to him.

"It's charged," he said after a moment, studying the weapon thoughtfully. "The charging node must have had power. It won't last long in this cold, but at least now we have something?"

He tried to hand it back to Xiomara, but she shook her head, so he tucked it into the collar of his space suit, where the battery would stay warm.

"We have to check our suits," I said. "Any puncture. Any tear. We have to be sure. Before we do anything else."

"Okay," Baqir said quietly. "We'll check each other."

We found no tears or signs of self-sealing. None of us had felt any prick, jab, or scrape. We looked, then we looked again, the three of us in an awkward, waiting silence. We found nothing to indicate our suits had been breached or our skin broken.

Finally I said, "I can get us off this ship, but we have to get to my mother's lab."

"Why there?" Baqir asked. "There are evac airlocks on every level, aren't there?"

"They're locked down—that's part of the medical quarantine. And if they haven't shut down the security drones, we would be vulnerable in evac suits. But Mum's workshop isn't locked, and there are two more experimental ships. We can use one of them to get away."

"What about the security drones?" Baqir asked. "If they attacked the shuttle . . ."

"Mum's ships can outfly the drones. It's always pissed SPEC off, that the engines fast enough to beat the security web are stuck inside of it."

"We can't leave Ariana behind," Xiomara said. "They'll kill her when they find her again."

"Xi," I said softly. "She's already gone. Nobody survives the virus. Not once it's in them."

Xiomara shook her head, swiping tears away still. "You don't know that. You don't even know what it *is*. You can't know that."

I started to say something, but Baqir shook his head minutely to stop me. To Xiomara he said, "Think about it. If there is some way to help her, what's the best way to do it? She was firing at us too. She didn't recognize us. She could be anywhere on the ship. Doesn't it make more sense to call for help? SPEC can send a whole medical team. They can put her in quarantine and get her real help. You heard what those people said. There's already a ship close, and probably more on the way. The shuttle sent out a distress signal."

Xiomara ran her hand over her mouth. "What the *fuck* happened to the shuttle? Do we really think it could have been shot by a missile? Or was it the drones?"

"SPEC doesn't have missiles," I said. "And I don't just mean officially. They really don't. My aunt and a bunch of other Councilors have been shutting down space-based weapons research for years."

"You wouldn't need a space-based weapon to sabotage a shuttle," Baqir pointed out. "That one lady seemed pretty certain it exploded from the inside."

"So she says," Xiomara said. "Shit. This is so fucked up. We need to call for help."

Baqir said, "Jas? Is there a radio we can get to?"

"There must be." Xiomara jutted her chin stubbornly as though she was expecting me to argue. "We have to tell them everything we know, so they're prepared when they get here."

I nodded. "Yeah. There is. But I don't know if we can even access the system."

"Where is it?" Baqir asked.

"We have to try," Xiomara said.

We were close. Somewhere inside, beneath all the scar tissue and denial, I had known we were close. I had explored this route between levels hundreds of times. It had been my playhouse, my secret fort, my territory.

Level 7. Starboard. Room 23. My childhood home. The quarters where my parents had raised me. Where we'd played silly games after dinner, where they'd argued about whether to send me back to Earth for school, where my father taught me to read and my mother gave me broken bits of machinery to take apart. Where we had lived for eight years. Together, a family, and happy, most days.

Where my father had died, and still remained.

The code on the door had never changed. Every time *House of Wisdom*'s security staff sent around a reminder to change the passcodes on personal quarters, my mother had laughed and said any new combination would slip through my father's mind like water through a net. There was no need to worry. The ship was safe. Everybody ignored the reminders anyway.

I had not forgotten: 2-9-9-7-9-2-4-5-8. My fingers shook as I tapped it in. 299,792,458 meters per second. The speed of light in a vacuum.

There was no medical quarantine preventing our access. Malachi must have been able to turn it off—and he had turned it off shipwide, not only on the levels they were moving through. He should have been able to trap both us and Ariana wherever he wanted, corral us like animals, but he hadn't thought to do so.

The door opened. The room was dark. I fumbled for the panel

to switch on the lights. They came on dim, more than half the fixtures remaining dark, but at least the glow wasn't red. The faint hiss of the environmental controls surrounded us: the air was circulating and warming from its stale deep freeze. That was another thing Malachi had claimed he had not been able to fix.

I removed my helmet again, then my gloves, mindful of every surface I touched. There was an arc of blood on the wall beside the closed bathroom door, a smear over the handle, fingerprints smudged across the latch. I remembered lunging for that door, screaming when my mother pulled me away.

On one wall Mother's favorite sweater was tucked into a net. On another were drawings of my father's: delicate botanical sketches of the beautiful plants he grew in his laboratories. The tablet I had used for my lessons was tucked neatly beneath a band on the table to keep it from floating free. I had been reading about the life cycle of stars when I last used it, captivated by how such simple equations laid out in so many clean lines could represent the roiling, raging blaze of our sun. Gravitational contraction. Nuclear fusion of hydrogen into first deuterium, then helium. When the hydrogen is gone, another phase of contraction, then expansion, and the contradiction of a star both drawing in on itself and surging outward to form a red giant had filled me with so many questions I'd made a list to present to my mother when she got home. So many evenings Dad and I spent here alone while Mum was working late. I carried my mother's name, and like her, my interests had me gazing toward the stars, but I had always gotten along better with my father. I didn't feel like an idiot around him. He and his plants were calmer, quieter, easier to approach than my mother with her engines and theories. He had promised to take me to the sequoia groves in North America when we returned to Earth. The largest trees on the planet, he had explained in a voice hushed with awe, showing me pictures of towering giants with specks of people made as insignificant as gnats beside them.

The terminal that connected our quarters to the ship's computer system had not been folded away. I touched the screen, and the terminal whirred softly, waking with a pale blue glow. The air was warming already, lessening the sting of the cold. A ship's interior should never be that cold. My mother had always said heat, not cold, was the engineer's true challenge. A ship produced heat in abundance, and every joule was difficult to shed in the vacuum. My nose was running and my ears ached. I rubbed my hands together and brought the communication commands up onscreen.

For a moment the interface was utterly indecipherable to me. It had been too long. Standard protocol for outward communication was to record the message and pass it to the ship's central comm, which would compress it for inclusion in a scheduled data burst. That wasn't necessary when the ship was in orbit around Earth, but communications had remained regulated to avoid overwhelming Orbital Control's relays and satellites. I couldn't remember what I was supposed to do. Every minute I wasted, the more danger we were in. I kept thinking about the panic in Ariana's voice as she swatted at her own arm. The casual way the man on the radio had talked about killing me to persuade SPEC to stay away. The way Zahra had stared at House of Wisdom from the shuttle as though it held the answer to every question.

Everything I tried came up with the same response: ACTION PROHIBITED. I couldn't get into the open transmission system. I couldn't send an emergency or distress signal. I couldn't even record a message to transmit via a private file transfer. ACTION PROHIBITED. Whatever Malachi had done to get the radio in the mainframe control room to work, it had not opened all the comm systems.

Baqir bumped into my shoulder, caught the edge of the terminal to stop himself.

"Drink," he said. "We can't get dehydrated."

He had found tubes of nutrient beverages in the kitchen. He tossed one to Xiomara and one to me. I remembered the flavor well: sweet orange, with a foul chemical aftertaste lingering on the tongue. It was what my father would make me drink when I was sick, or give to my mother when she had been working too long without stopping for a meal. The memories as much as the bitterness made me gag, but I forced myself to swallow. Baqir was right: we couldn't get dehydrated. Our shuttle lunch had been a long time ago.

"What's wrong?" he asked, looking at the screen over my shoulder.

"I can't send anything," I said. "This is all I get."

Again: ACTION PROHIBITED.

"Fuck," Xiomara said. "Can we do anything about that?"

"I don't think so. Not from here."

"Let me try."

I moved aside; they were both more adept at computer systems than I was. They huddled over the terminal for a few minutes, but all they could get out of the system was the information that outbound messages were prohibited by order of a command override that had been issued by Captain Ngahere on the date 01.04.393.

When the outbreak was still happening, something had first disrupted, then completely ended, outgoing transmissions from *House of Wisdom*. SPEC and Orbital Control had always assumed it was because of system damage or a cascading error due to the medical quarantine interacting with any number of unpredictable, uncontrolled shipboard actions. But what the system was telling us now was that the final silence had been intentional. Captain Ngahere had shut down shipwide communications, and she had done it on purpose.

"How do we shut down a command override?" Baqir asked.

Xiomara was frowning at the screen. "Why *is* there a command override? Why would the captain do that?"

"Maybe to stop people from causing too much damage? If they were delusional and hallucinating, it may have been the only way she knew how to keep the systems protected."

I shook my head, although I had no idea if Baqir was right or not. We had no way of knowing what Captain Ngahere had been thinking at the end.

"Look," Xiomara said, indicating the screen. "The ship's still accepting incoming messages. I wonder if we can . . . There's an active transmission."

Baqir leaned over to look. "Is that SPEC? What are they saying?"

Xiomara opened the radio channel. The voice of Adam Light boomed from the terminal.

". . . as though you expect us to tuck our tails and flee! As though we are as cowardly and weak as you are! But we aren't. *We are not weak.* Every man on this ship is a thousand times stronger than your Councils servants in their uniforms, spitting empty threats at us, hoping to use our love for our family against us. But we won't let you. *We will not let you.*"

"Not SPEC, I guess," Baqir said quietly.

"You ask for surrender and offer nothing but a life of drudgery in return. We will not toil our lives away to feed your pampered children. We will not surrender our freedom to enslave ourselves to your goals! We will not send our families to become insects in your anthill of empty industry! *We reject your offer!*" There was the low roar of a cheer; he had to be speaking before a large group aboard *Homestead*. "You cannot imagine our strength! You cannot accept that we would rather *die* than surrender to the cruel yoke you call responsibility! You will not indoctrinate our children! You will not put the seeds of rot into their minds! Our wives and our children will not fall into your hands!"

"He's disgusting," Xiomara said. She had sucked her own beverage tube flat already. "Wives and children? Does he think he's a warlord from the Collapse?"

More cheers, wild and raucous. I lowered the volume. Adam Light continued with more of the same. No surrender. No capitulation. Courage. Cheers.

"They must be in contact with SPEC," I said. "He wouldn't be refusing to surrender if nobody had asked him to surrender."

"You don't know that," Xiomara said. "We don't know anything about these people. We have no idea what they want. That story about wanting a place to live is bullshit. Nobody would come *here* for a place to live. They must want something else. Nobody's that insane."

"I don't think they're lying about that," Baqir said, "and I don't think they're insane."

His voice was quiet, but I knew from the way he was deliberately not looking at Xiomara that the feeling behind the words was anything but calm.

"You can't be *defending* them," Xiomara said. "They're murderers!"

"I'm not defending them. I just don't think they're lying about what they want."

"But listen to him! If these people want to go to space that badly, why don't they just become citizens like everybody else?"

"It's not that easy," Baqir said.

"It's not that fucking *hard* of a choice to make. The Councils don't allow *slavery*. They don't indoctrinate anyone. You don't really think that, do you?" Xiomara looked at Baqir, her expression baffled and angry. "You should be more grateful than anyone for what the Councils provide."

My breath caught, and Xiomara seemed to realize what she had said as soon as the words were out.

"Grateful?" Baqir said. I knew that tone of carefully cultivated mildness. I had known it since we were twelve years old, the first year we met, two outcasts in a children's hospital with far more anger and hurt than sense.

"I don't mean—"

"You're right, I guess," he went on, still speaking so softly, not looking at Xiomara at all. "I know I would be dead if my parents hadn't become Councils citizens. I also know that it took ten years for their application to go through."

Xiomara blinked. "Ten years?"

"And I know that my brother and sister both died in the refugee camp while we were waiting."

"I didn't . . ." Xiomara trailed off. Her eyes were wide. "But . . . families with kids, during the outbreaks, they were—"

"Supposed to go to the front of the application line," Baqir said. "I know that too. But then one of my grandmothers got caught stealing medicine from a camp doctor when my sister was sick, so the whole family was considered a criminal risk until her probation was up. She stole *medicine* for a *baby*." For the first time, Baqir's voice rose with a crack of anger. "And for that they put her on the same list as the fucking murderers and rapists and terrorists they'd shunted out to the wasteland to get rid of them. The whole family, even though my parents hadn't stolen anything. So, no, Xi, it's not that fucking easy. It's never been that easy."

Xiomara stared at Baqir without saying a word. I knew the shock she was feeling. She didn't know him well. During their brief acquaintance, she had only ever seen the mask he wore to hide his anger, the one that was so stunningly effective few ever saw beyond it. He wore it when anybody mentioned what a drain North American refugees were on Councils resources, needing so much support, so much education, so much training, so much special care before they could become citizens who could offer meaningful contributions to the global society. He wore it when self-important professors muttered about the danger of letting an unassimilated separatist boy into a Councils school and spoke to him slowly, warily, as though they were afraid he might turn into a snarling animal without warning. When students in our secondary school accused Baqir of starting every fight, when teachers had taken me aside and told me gently that I was doing myself no favors by letting Baqir copy my schoolwork—and never believed me that the reverse was always true, as Baqir was both smarter than me and harder working, and I was the one who would lash out at the least provocation. When the Leung Fellowship administrators interviewed him three times more than they'd interviewed me, and when I asked him what they'd wanted to talk about, he had only given me a crooked smile and told me not to worry, he'd make the cut, because they needed a refugee scholar to make their program look well-rounded. Through it all Baqir perfected that carefully bland mask, the face of somebody who was not angry, was not bothered, was not hurt, was not any of the things I knew him to be when he was unguarded.

Xiomara could not imagine any life on Earth so terrible that even an abandoned slaughterhouse in space was better. She had never had to imagine it—nor had I, for all the horrors in my past. In moments when Baqir's mask dropped away and the anger shone through as bright and terrible as any supernova, I kept quiet. I let him rage. There was nothing I could say. I could not imagine the traumas of his childhood any more than he could imagine mine— or had been able to, before we came to *House of Wisdom*. He no doubt had a much better idea of what filled my nightmares now.

But of the three of us, only Baqir knew what was driving our captors, because his life had once been no different from theirs.

"And just so we're clear," Baqir said, the calm returning with eerie alacrity, "I agree that that man is probably a fucking monster. And the people who brought us here are murderers. But I don't think they're lying about wanting a safe home, far from Earth. And nobody outside the Councils has any other way of getting into space."

Xiomara hesitated, then nodded. "Okay, but why—"

A loud thump interrupted her. We all jumped, whirled around in panic, our eyes looking to the closed door to the corridor.

"Is it locked?" Xiomara whispered.

There was another thump. It didn't come from the main door. It came from the bathroom.

Dad, I thought, with a child's panicked desperation.

I didn't realize I had spoken aloud until Xiomara said, "What? In *there*?"

It was the sound of something hard hitting the inside of the door. A hard clank on impact, the faintest whisper of a scrape as it drew away.

I stared at the door. Closed, these ten years, a door that had slammed again and again in my memories, waking me from sleep in a cold sweat of terror that I might find myself here again—

There had been a knife in my father's hand.

A knife in his hand and a cut in his arm and blood soaking through his clothes. His eyes wide. His voice high and terrified. My mother had slapped him—watching from my bedroom doorway, I had gasped in shock. My parents were never violent. They had never hit me or each other, not once in my entire life. But that day Mum had slapped Dad, and for a second, the briefest, cruelest second, my father's senses returned. The babbling stopped, and he looked at my mother, looked at me. He inhaled—as if to speak, but it was only a gasp, a breath. Without a single word, he had fled into the bathroom. He took the knife with him.

Identification: Roy, Vinod
Position: Chief of Botany and Horticulture
Location: Personal living quarters 7.23-S
Time of death: 17:37:04 01.03.393
Cause of death: Hemorrhagic shock

The bathroom door rattled again. Something hard dragged over its interior surface.

"What the fuck is that?" Xiomara's voice was rising, rising, a shout that stung my ears. "How can there be somebody in here?"

"Jas," Baqir said. "It can't be."

"Can't be what?" Xiomara said.

"I know," I said, or meant to say, but the words did not make it past my lips.

There was something in the bathroom. It thumped against the door again, again. A faint cracking sound followed, like ice breaking.

"Go," Baqir said. He yanked at my arm, shoved Xiomara toward the main door. "Go, go, get the fuck out of here!"

We scrambled across the room, clumsy and jostling each other in our panic. Xiomara hit the panel to slide the door open, then whirled around. "My helmet!" But her momentum was wrong, she turned too quickly and kept spinning, arms grasping for the door frame but failing to catch it.

"I'll get it," I said, pushing her through the door, and Baqir right after her.

There was another thump from the bathroom. The door shook, and as I watched, frozen in momentary terror, it began to slide open. My heart was racing and my mind was a constant refrain of *no no no,* but a part of me, the small shameful child hidden beneath the fear, was pleading: *It might be.*

Ten years. It was *not possible.* The door was grinding open. Fingers pressed through the widening gap, fingers shriveled and dark, stiff, unable to curl around the edge of the door. Moving with agonizing slowness, the door opened a few centimeters, a few more. I saw the edge of a sleeve, the jut of a wrist. The hand twisted, and the motion tore at the flesh with a soft, wet noise, like meat halfway thawed.

More of the arm emerged. Along the forearm were three deep gashes caked with dried blood, the skin and fat and muscle frozen but slowly thawing. It was my father's arm. I had watched from the doorway to my bedroom as he made the first frightened cut, shouting frantically, *Get it out, get it out, it's in my veins, Amita, help me get it out get it out get it out.* He had fallen quiet only when my mother slapped him. He had fumbled to shut the door, his hands bloodied and clumsy. Only when he fell silent did I hear the screams from outside our quarters. He made no sound as he opened his own veins. He had known what he was doing.

There was a hand on my elbow. All I could hear was the thump of the impossible knock, the rasp of the opening door. Baqir pulled me into the corridor and took Xiomara's helmet from my hands. The cold was shocking; I hadn't realized how much the quarters had warmed.

The rattle of the bathroom door stopped abruptly. I turned to look through the open doorway, hope and fear and nausea twisting together in my gut. I could still see the narrow gap into the bathroom, the smudged stains of my father's bloody fingerprints, and the frozen hand, now unmoving. I watched it without blinking, my eyes stinging with cold and tears, willing the fingers to bend, and terrified they would. There was no sound in the corridor except our fast, ragged breaths.

Then Xiomara gasped. *"Ariana."*

I spun around, swinging my helmet and headlamp as I turned. Ariana rounded a corner down the corridor, her space suit brilliantly pale in the crossing beams of light. Her short hair was stiff with ice, and there was a layer of frost over her exposed skin. She did not blink. There were frozen crystals on her eyelashes.

"Ariana," Xiomara said again. "Are you okay?"

Ariana still had Henke's gun, but it dangled uselessly by her side, as though she had forgotten she was holding it.

"Ari, say something." Xiomara started to move forward, but Baqir stopped her. "Ariana? Say something."

"How did she find us?" Baqir said. He was holding on to both of us now, one hand on my wrist and the other on hers. "If she followed us, they could have too."

The bathroom door rattled. Ariana turned her head sharply to look directly at the wall. She stared intently for a long moment, as though she could see through the barrier to the noise beyond. Then she moved her hand, the one that wasn't holding the gun, raised it in front of her body and curled her fingers, grasping at something in the air. She turned her wrist and moved her hand to the side—

I felt a thunderclap of understanding.

She was miming opening the door.

She was doing what the thing in the bathroom would be doing, if its flesh were pliable rather than half-frozen. She pushed the invisible door to the side; the noises from the bathroom echoed her motion. She tilted her head, watching.

"Ari?" Xiomara said, her voice ragged with fear. "Can't you hear me?"

Ariana's face was utterly devoid of emotion. It was as though the muscles that lifted smiles and turned frowns and furrowed brows had frozen in place, and there was nothing but a veneer of skin, empty of input from her brain. Her mouth was open and slack.

"Ariana, please, say something. You're sick, okay? We can help you. We have to." Xiomara looked at me and Baqir. "Please, she's not attacking anybody right now. She's not hurting herself. She's calm. We can help her."

The hope in Xiomara's voice carved a fissure in my chest. Every instinct in my body, every memory I carried, they were telling me to turn and run. Ariana's stillness would not protect us from terrible, bloody, deadly violence. But those instincts knocked up against the truth of what Xiomara was saying: Ariana was not attacking. She had followed us here. This was, perhaps, the second phase of the virus, the one I had never witnessed. I had only seen them go mad, lash out, harm themselves and others in delusional fits. I had not seen them follow people through a dark ship to float silently, eerily in a corridor. Xiomara might be right. Ariana had passed through the panicked, violent onset of the infection without dying. We might be able to save her.

Then she spoke.

"Vinod, what are you doing with that knife?" Ariana said.

"What?" Xiomara said, startled. "What did she say?"

I could not answer. The blood in my veins had gone cold.

There was no recording of my father's death. There was no visual or audio surveillance in the personal quarters. There had been no witnesses to my father's final moments aside from my mother and me.

Ariana spoke again: "Vinod, what are you doing with that knife?"

My mother's final words to my father. The question she had asked right before she slapped him. Right before he closed himself in the bathroom and died.

I had never told anybody. Not my aunt, not the investigators, not Baqir, not anybody. It was an echo from the past that had always been mine and mine alone, breathed now on a cloud of mist from Ariana's slack mouth and expressionless face.

"Vinod, what are you doing with that knife?" Ariana said.

There was no inflection in her tone, nor the least emotion. "Go back to your room. Jas. Go back to your room. Jas."

Nausea roiled through me, and with it a black wave of rage. She had no right to speak my mother's words.

There was another rattle from inside the quarters. My father's arm was reaching through the gap, stiff and bent at an awkward angle, the shoulder shoving ineffectually against the door, but reaching still, like a puppet jerking on tangled strings. Xiomara made a small noise in her throat. Baqir's grip on my wrist tightened. I looked back at Ariana.

The light from Xiomara's headlamp was still fixed on Ariana's face, which was paled by the thin layer of frost over her light brown skin. Ariana grimaced—but it wasn't a grimace, her expression wasn't changing at all. There was a ripple in her skin, a line of frost melting across her left cheek, a subtle undulation moving toward her temple.

Just before Ariana turned and fled into the darkness, leaving us without a sound, with barely a glance, the ripple vanished into her hairline. Something narrow and fast was moving beneath her skin.

UCE SECURITY COMMISSION—RESTRICTED ARCHIVE REF. #R3459322-C32
CONFIDENTIAL WITNESS STATEMENT TRANSCRIPT (AUDIO)
Source: SPECIAL INVESTIGATIVE COMMISSION FOR THE HOUSE OF WISDOM
   INCIDENT
TimeDate: 09:00:00 01.22.393

[VERIFIED IDENTIFICATION—SPECIAL INVESTIGATIVE COMMISSION: See
transcript section c03.2]

LEAD COUNCILOR: Please state your name and position for the record.

WITNESS: Alfonso Dietrich, security officer first class for the Unified North
   American Transportation Commission.

LEAD COUNCILOR: Do you affirm that during the course of this testimony you
   shall speak the whole truth as you know it and offer no intentionally misleading statements to the Special Investigative Commission?

WITNESS: Yes, I do.

LEAD COUNCILOR: Then we will begin. Please tell us about the events on
   Platform 2 of Fremont Station in East Presidio Bay on the night of January 17.

WITNESS: My shift began at 1700 on that day, and I began a foot patrol of
   Fremont Station at approximately 1745.

SECOND COUNCILOR: Did you undertake your patrol alone?

WITNESS: Yes, although I remained in radio contact with fellow officers.
   Heightened security protocols require thirty-minute check-in intervals.

SECOND COUNCILOR: Were you armed with a firearm or a suppression
   weapon?

WITNESS: No, of course not.

SECOND COUNCILOR: Not even under heightened security protocols?

WITNESS: I know you think we must all be in fear for our lives that close to the border, but it's not like that. Presidio Bay is a safe place. Our purpose is to help people, not scare them.

THIRD COUNCILOR: We understand. Please continue, Officer Dietrich.

WITNESS: At approximately 1930, a woman approached me at the entrance to Platform 2 to report a man in need of assistance. She thought he might be a refugee newly granted citizenship. She was concerned that he needed medical attention, as he appeared unwell to her.

SECOND COUNCILOR: Did you summon your fellow officers for help?

WITNESS: What? No, of course not. The witness reported a man in need of aid. I went to render aid. The platform was mostly empty, and it was easy to locate the man. He was alone.

LEAD COUNCILOR: Did you recognize him?

WITNESS: Not at first. He was wearing a hooded jacket, as it was raining heavily that night. He was hunched over, holding his head in his hands. He did not appear to be armed and had no parcels or bags with him. I approached and asked if he needed help.

SECOND COUNCILOR: Now did you recognize him?

WITNESS: Yes. That is the point at which I made a positive identification of Gregory Lago. I didn't address him by name, but I don't think he was surprised to be recognized. I asked him again if he needed assistance, and he said, "It will be too late. I did everything wrong. I did it all wrong."

THIRD COUNCILOR: I beg your pardon, Officer Dietrich, but are you sure about that? Dr. Lago stated to you that it will be too late? Not that it was already too late?

WITNESS: Yes. I am sure of it. I asked him what he meant, and he said, "I thought they wouldn't understand." I told him we could find somebody who understood. I told him his wife and his kids wanted him to come home. I shouldn't have said that.

LEAD COUNCILOR: Why not? Isn't that standard de-escalation protocol?

WITNESS: It is, but when I mentioned his family, Dr. Lago jumped to his feet. He was visibly distressed. He said, "It's too late. I've already failed them.

I was so arrogant. I've failed everybody. Tell them I'm sorry." Then he ran for the tracks.

LEAD COUNCILOR: In your opinion, was his goal to flee or self-terminate?

WITNESS: The latter, Councilor. He knew the train was coming. He waited until just the right moment to jump.

ZAHRA

L evel 5. A dead family huddled by the sealed hatch of an evacuation airlock, father and mother and infant child, without any sign of infection or injury.

Level 6. A man whose face had been torn to shreds, and the broken piece of metal he'd used still clutched in his mummified fingers. It was the rung of a ladder; he had wrenched it from the wall to rip his own flesh away.

We had left Henke's corpse behind. My suit was stained with his blood: a spray across the faceplate of my helmet, long streaks across my arms and chest. Dag and Panya were convinced Ariana's hysteria had been a ruse to give the others a chance to escape. Malachi offered no opinion.

I was not so sure. I did not think Bhattacharya had been feigning the fear in his voice when he said she was infected. I did not think she had been pretending panic. And, most of all, I did not think dismissing infection as a possibility would serve us. We had to be careful. Every prickle, every itch on my skin sent a spike of fear through me.

We were heading toward the ship's bridge. It was, Malachi said, the only way to get control of the ship, to break through the command override that had locked all the systems. It wasn't supposed to be this way. We had planned for years, detailing every aspect of the mission, considering every possibility. It wasn't fair. There was so much we hadn't known.

Level 7. Two men dead in a gallery of windows looking out to the stars. One's face was a mass of bruises and lacerations. He had been beaten to a pulp by the other man, whose hand still gripped his hair in a frozen fist. Dried blood and bits of bone and brain were splattered over the windows, the seating, the control panels, the abstract sculpture affixed to the center of the room.

Henke. Bao. Nico. Boudicca. I had failed them. The shuttle was gone. The hostages were gone. We had no control over this ship, *Homestead* was unprotected, SPEC was coming, and somewhere in the darkness was a girl with Henke's gun. Maybe she was a SPEC agent. Maybe she had been lucky. Maybe she was infected by a rage-inducing virus. Whatever the case, I had failed. There was a sickly acid churn in my stomach. Fairness was for children and fools. I was not a child anymore, and I should have known better than to let the hostages make me a fool. I would not make that mistake twice.

Level 8, and I heard my mother's voice.

I stopped with one hand on the wall. The beams of the headlamps behind me cast my shadow as a long, distorted thing, stretching into darkness.

Look here, my mother had said, tracing her finger along the image of *House of Wisdom* on our kitchen wallscreen. She had been speaking normally, but in my memories she whispered as softly as the turn of autumn leaves, *This is where Daddy is going to be for a while. He'll be doing important work.*

"Zahra?" Malachi said. "What is it?"

I started moving again, pulling myself hand over hand along the broad corridor, following the signs toward the next interlevel hatch. We had spoken little since leaving the computing core. We could not turn off the radios, lest the hostages make a mistake and reveal their position to us, but neither did we want to provide any information to them, should they be listening. There wasn't much to say anyway. We needed to get to the bridge on Level 10, and we needed to do it quickly. I felt a weak sort of relief that our plan offered little room for argument.

The corridors of Level 8 were broad and straight. There were no living quarters here, no recreation spaces, no gardens. Beyond those well-spaced doors were research laboratories, each labeled by a small, neat sign.

PLANETARY NAVIGATION. ORBITAL COMPUTATION. MINERAL RESOURCE ASSESSMENT.

As a child I had imagined passing through this corridor a thousand times, when I had wanted to join my father for the adventure of living in space. Later, after he was gone, and my mother as well, I had once again walked this corridor in my mind, planning what I would say to Nadra and Anwar about the father they scarcely remembered and the mother they had only known after she was crushed by grief.

MICROGRAVITY COMBUSTION. CELESTIAL MECHANICS. EXPLORATORY ROBOTICS.

We had no time to spare, but we were right here.

DEEP SPACE ARCHAEOLOGY.

I grabbed a handle on the wall.

We were *right here.*

"Zahra?" Panya said. "Is something wrong?"

"We don't have time for this," Malachi said, reading the sign over my shoulder.

I was losing him. I had known it since we left the computing core. Dag remained as silent and stalwart as ever, and the soft concern in Panya's voice never wavered, but Malachi's fear had been sharpening with every level, and with it was an anger I did not recognize. Malachi did not carry rage in his heart like so many in the family. Even when he had been newly arrived at the homestead, his feet blistered and lips cracked from his long, lonely wander through the desert, his spirit dulled by the repeated humiliations inflicted upon him by the Councils citizenship process that promised so much and delivered so little, even then he had been smiling, grateful for a respite, open with his thanks. The smiles, the gratitude, the openness, it was all gone now. *House of Wisdom* had crushed it out of him.

"This is where the outbreak started," I said. "Open the door."

Malachi did not move to obey. "Why? Adam said—"

"Adam isn't here," I said. "Open the door."

Behind the faceplate Malachi's expression was unreadable.

"Everything we know about the virus has proved to be a lie," I said, speaking as calmly as I could. "I am tired of the lies. We have to find out what we can. If there's nothing here, we won't stay. Panya and Dag will go ahead and find the route to the next level."

"Of course we will," Panya said. "It won't take long."

She nodded at Dag, and they continued down the corridor.

"Open the door," I said for the third time.

Finally, Malachi obeyed. I watched the stiff line of his shoulders as he worked to bypass the medical quarantine, and I tried to find words to reassure him, to bring him back to hope, although I had none to spare.

I said nothing. The door opened. Malachi moved to the side to let me through.

The dark room beyond slowly filled with low red light, casting our dim reflections back at us from a wall of windows. Facing the windows was a long row of workstations. There were no bodies.

I turned my headlamp off to see the room beyond the glass. A second later, Malachi did the same.

The chamber was a large cube, and in the center of that cube, mounted on three sturdy metal supports, was UC33-X.

The name Unidentified Craft 33-X had been bestowed upon the probe when the space telescope at Phobos spotted it soaring gently toward Earth in year 385 of the Reconstruction Era. It had arrived at the edge of the solar system with no warning. There had been panic when SPEC scientists realized it had come from deep space. Panic, but also wonder. Some people were relieved, others disappointed, when scientists confirmed the probe had been constructed by human hands aboard an ancient ship called *Mournful Evening Song*. I remembered sitting in a circle in my grade school classroom as the teacher read to us a child-friendly story about the Pre-Collapse generation ships. How brave those ancient humans had been, how noble, to flee an ailing planet for the stars, and how exciting it was to receive this message from their journey. Both the teacher and the picture book had conveniently left out the uglier truths: that the generation ships had been for only the privileged and elite, that none of those ships had ever come back, that it was widely believed they had all failed within a couple of decades of launching.

My father had been thrilled by the arrival of UC33-X. To him, it was a gift. He had devoted his life to studying Pre-Collapse space travel, picking through ruins of shipyards, skeletons of dead satellites, fragments of records, echoes of transmissions, all the different ways an archaeologist peering across a catastrophic divide in human history might learn about what had passed. He idolized the founders of the Councils who had survived the Collapse, and to him UC33-X was proof that at least some of the humans who had fled Earth had not only survived, but they had also cared enough about the world they had left behind to send part of themselves back as a message. My father had come to *House of Wisdom* to recover and decipher that message, corrupted as it was by centuries in the harsh environment of space, and learn what he could about the people who had sent it.

SPEC claimed my father had been concealing data and results from his fellow scientists. They said he had grown selfish with the prospect of making a grand discovery and sabotaged the research of others to keep the glory for himself. They said that when he was caught and dismissed from the ship, he was so furious he massacred the ship's entire population in revenge—a plot he must have held in reserve for months or years, perhaps since his long-ago research on Pre-Collapse biological weapons, just waiting for the right target. They said he had always been unstable. They apologized for not realizing it sooner.

They did not care that my father loved humanity so much he spent his life searching for proof of its survival in deep space. They did not care that he loved the Councils, too, because he saw them as proof that humanity could do better than it had before. That humankind could drive itself and the Earth to the brink of destruction, look upon the ruins of their violence, and choose to rebuild a wiser, kinder world had always been, to him, a source of pride and reason for optimism. The Councils, with their accusations, cared nothing for the truth about who Gregory Lago was.

Certainty about my father's innocence had carried me for ten years, driving me even when all else seemed hopeless. But now, faced with the dim red lights casting ghosts on a wall of glass, I needed more. Somebody had released the virus aboard *House of Wisdom*, and they started in this laboratory.

"I want to see their logs from right before they got sick," I said.

Malachi was moving toward the workstations before I finished speaking. I pulled myself up to the glass wall for a better look into the laboratory.

UC33-X was seven meters long from nose to tail, cylindrical in shape except for a blunted cone at the nose and slight flare at the tail, with very few protrusions or instrumentation on the outside. The solar sails that had carried it so swiftly through space had been removed, leaving the probe naked and slender. The scientists had been dissecting it. There were panels open on the side, its instrumentation revealed, its inner guts of wire and metal visible. A workbench and its stool were positioned next to an exposed section on the top of the probe; a strap of tools tethered to the workbench floated like a vine adorned with spikes.

They had brought UC33-X aboard *House of Wisdom* about eight months before the outbreak, after years of tracking its progress from the outer edge of the solar system toward the sun. During those eight months, as the ship returned to Earth, my father and the other archaeologists had studied, cataloged, measured, and assessed every aspect of the probe, analyzing its materials and integrity, never allowing themselves to rush, never giving in to the urge to crack it open too soon and risk damaging what it contained. They had only breached its hull a month or two before the outbreak. My father had been so excited, grinning widely in the recorded message he sent to us, so happy with the progress he and his colleagues were making.

"I can open the interior door," Malachi said.

He was watching me, his gaze fixed on where my hands rested on the glass. I pushed away quickly, embarrassed to have been caught gaping.

"Do it," I said.

There was a soft mechanical click and the door eased open. I pushed toward the probe, but I misjudged my angle and had to bump into it to stop. I felt a wild pang of guilt—it was too precious to jostle; my father would be aghast. The probe's hull was slick; my gloves slipped over the surface. I crept along centimeter by centimeter, pulling myself toward the workstation and tools.

Only when I reached the terminal did I notice the bodies.

One was adrift on the other side of UC33-X. She wore a plain jumpsuit with the *House of Wisdom* patch. Her hair, white and long, floated around her head. She had crossed her arms over her chest, and she lay in the air parallel to the probe. Her feet were bare, as were her hands. She might have been sleeping peacefully, if it weren't for the mummified dryness of her skin. The desiccation and white hair gave her the look of a very old woman. There was no name on her jumpsuit, but I recognized her. Dr. Mariska Summers, another archaeologist. She had been my father's friend since they were students together. There were no visible wounds, no obvious weapons. She bore no signs of violence.

Not so the second corpse. That one, a man, had been strapped to the opposite wall with a cargo tie. The valve of a gas canister had been jammed into his mouth. His face was parched and burnt. His lips, stretched around the canister valve, were blackened and cracked.

"I don't like this," Malachi said. "What the fuck is that—is that liquid helium? What happened here?"

After encountering so many dead, passing through so many cold, dark crypts, the restful quiescence of this white-haired woman, of those who had huddled in the garden, of the crew of the computing core, was every bit as unsettling as the violent deaths. I had grown almost numb to the brutalized corpses everywhere—almost—but I could not stop staring at Dr. Summers with her arms crossed peacefully over her chest, and the man who had died so horribly just beyond.

Malachi's voice in my ear: "I found the last entry recorded into the system. It's a personal log from an M. Summers."

The screen on the workstation flickered. The blue vanished, replaced at once by the face of Dr. Summers. She looked younger than I had expected; her light brown skin was creased only in laugh lines around her eyes and mouth. Her eyes were bloodshot, and there were tears on her cheeks. She took a breath before speaking.

"I might well be the last one left." Her voice was thin, soft, her accent southern hemisphere Oceania. "I haven't heard anything for over an hour. It's quiet outside. The captain hasn't answered since she initiated the medical quarantine. I told her what happened with Saul. I didn't want to hurt him. He attacked me, and I tried to incapacitate him. He wouldn't stop moving. I didn't know what else to do. I told the captain everything. I take full responsibility for his death. I am so sorry for his children. Tell them I am so very, very sorry. That was—" A glance down and to the left. "Seventy-three minutes ago. By the time you find this, you'll likely know what's happening out there. You'll certainly know more than I do. But I want you to know—whoever finds this—I want you to know that we weren't careless."

I glanced at Malachi through the glass, but he was watching his own screen.

"We weren't careless," Dr. Summers repeated. "We took every precaution we knew to take. We knew better than to trust that the people of *Mournful Evening Song* were benevolent. So many humans before the Collapse were violent, selfish creatures. We searched for even the tiniest sign of viral or bacterial contamination—human or alien—before we took the probe on board. We didn't find anything. We began to believe they had not meant us harm. We learned everything we could at every step before we proceeded to the next one. We didn't ignore Gregory's theories, no matter what he says."

My heart skipped at the sound of my father's name.

"I know he's angry with us. But he didn't trust us—worse, he didn't think we were clever enough to follow where he led. Hubris was always his flaw. He should have let us all work together. We did listen to him, but we didn't have all the information."

Dr. Summers didn't sound angry with him, or frightened of him. She didn't sound as though she blamed him at all. She pinched the bridge of her nose.

"Gregory, I wish you had, for once in your bloody life, risked a share of the glory. I wish you had trusted us." Here Dr. Summers looked directly at the camera. Her eyes, a deep soft brown, filled with tears. "Do you remember that week we spent diving at Pio-piotahi when we were students? You found the wreck of that old twenty-first-century rocket. It was marked on the wrong spot on the maps, so you thought it was an unknown wreck, one nobody had found yet? You were so disappointed when we realized it was the same one others had explored a thousand times before."

Dr. Summers stopped again to clear her throat. She looked to her right and extended her arm. She reached beyond the range of the camera, but I knew she was touching the probe.

"That night after we explored that sunken rocket, we were sitting on the boat under the stars—do you remember? It was an unremarkable night, I suppose, and so many years ago, but it was beautiful. The sky was so clear, the stars so bright, and all of us were talking like we always did, students who thought we knew everything. You were going on about your lost ships . . . Even then that was all you ever wanted to talk about." Dr. Summers pressed her lips together, inhaled through her nose and let the breath out again, and on the exhale it was damp, ragged, with barely suppressed sobs. "You were talking about the people from before the Collapse, and how it was amazing they had ever gotten into space at all, with all the times they had blown themselves up trying, with how obsessed they were with gathering wealth and waging wars and killing one another for the stupidest of reasons. So much hatred, so much cruelty, and so many failures, all across the world. All their broken ships and rockets scattered around like so many toys underfoot. Just another part of the mess they left for us to clean up.

"And you said—you said even knowing they were so bad at everything except killing each other and poisoning the world, even knowing that, you hoped some of those idiots survived out there in the black. You wanted that for them, even knowing what they had done.

"Gregory," Dr. Summers said, leaning forward, her white hair flowing around her. "I don't know when you lost trust in us. But I hope you remember that night out on the water, and when it comes time for you to tell them what's happened here, you—"

A loud siren wailed. I jumped and looked around before realizing it was on the recording. Dr. Summers looked down at the screen. The siren wailed again, and white lights pulsed brightly around her. Her shoulders slumped.

"Oh," she said quietly, in the momentary space between sirens. "I didn't recognize that. I've only heard it—"

Another earsplitting wail.

"—in drills. But it says right here: fire suppression. I guess she—"

And another, painful in the ears.

"—to me after all. This might at least slow them down."

Dr. Summers waited for the siren, but it did not sound again. In its place came a low hissing. Behind her the white emergency lights stopped pulsing to shine steadily. She looked up and around, every plane of her face, every line of her body signaling defeat. "If this is Lilian's doing, I hope you remember her as a hero, not a murderer. Please forgive her. Please forgive us all."

She reached forward, then paused, looked at the camera again. For a moment her lips parted as though she was going to say more, but in the end she only shook her head and said, "End recording."

The screen went black.

Z ahra," Malachi said.

"Wait," I said.

I needed to think. Dr. Summers had known my father and his work. She had considered him a lifelong friend, somebody she cherished. She had not blamed him for the massacre.

Because she did not think the virus had come from Earth.

"Play it again," I said. "Did you hear what she said?"

"Zahra." Malachi's voice was strained and uncharacteristically high. I turned.

Dag and Panya had joined Malachi in the outer room. Through the glass they were lit by the red glow of the dormancy lights, three shapes beyond the ghost of my own reflection.

"Panya, Dag, you have to hear this. It's about the virus. Malachi, play the log again."

Malachi was looking right at me, but he said nothing.

"Come on," Panya said, and Malachi flinched. "Up. You're going in to join her."

Only when he rose from the chair at the console did I see that Panya had the muzzle of her weapon pressed against his back. Dag's weapon was drawn, too, resting easily at his side. I looked from one gun to the other.

"What are you doing?" I asked stupidly.

Dag reached out and slid Malachi's gun from its holster. I remembered my own weapon too late. I was slow to draw it, and clumsy. I didn't know where to point it.

"Please don't be angry with me, Zahra," Panya said. "It's not your fault."

"What—"

"It's not," she said, as though I was arguing with her. "You're too soft and too uncertain. I tried to warn Adam, but he wanted to give you a chance. Go in, Malachi. He wanted to give both of you a chance."

Malachi pulled himself toward the door, but slowly, deliberately stalling. "Panya, you—"

"Shut up," Dag said. He took Malachi's skeleton key from the terminal. "Get in there."

"Tell me what's wrong," I pleaded, my mind racing. "Tell me what you want. I know the mission has gone wrong, but we can fix it. We still have time."

"We are going to fix it," Panya said, her voice soft with pity and regret. "We are, Zahra. Not you. We will be ready when Adam arrives. We will fix the damage you have done. We will restore hope to him and to the family. Give your gun to Dag."

I adjusted my grip on the weapon. I didn't know what to do. I didn't want to hurt Panya and Dag. They were my friends—my family. They were scared and confused and frustrated, but they were still family. I couldn't hurt them. I kept seeing the boy on the shuttle, the one I had killed, how his head had vanished in a cloud of blood. I had killed him without a thought, as though he wasn't a person at all. I couldn't do that to Panya. She had taught me how to survive in the desert, selflessly imparting wisdom she had known her entire life. She was the one who had comforted me when Mama died, who had told me how to avoid angering Adam when I fell from his favor, who had lifted her hand and her voice in support when others argued against letting me lead this mission.

Panya pressed her weapon to the back of Malachi's head. Her voice was damp with tears. "Zahra. Don't make this difficult."

"Panya, please don't. Don't hurt Malachi. Help me fix this."

"You should not have brought the hostages over here," Dag said. There was no apology in his voice, no pity, but neither was there anger. He spoke as though it was the plainest fact. "If you had left them where Adam commanded, Henke would be alive, and there would not be an armed girl loose on the ship. And now you are getting distracted by unimportant things."

"It's not unimportant," I said quickly. "You have to listen—"

"You are too inexperienced for this command," Dag said. "Adam was blinded by his affection for you. He made a mistake."

Malachi said, "You're right. Zahra wasn't ready for this. But you still need our help. You still need—"

"And you," Dag said, "have failed every step of the way. We should have the ship by now. It should have been ours hours ago."

"He's been *trying*," I said, confused. "You've seen it! He's told you why—"

"Zahra," Panya said. "Zahra, sweet girl, do not make me kill him. Give your gun to Dag."

I braced myself on the workstation and tossed my gun toward Dag. It glided easily through the air, turning slowly. I saw Malachi twitch—the beginning of a motion, indecisive—but he stilled again. Dag caught the weapon and holstered it.

"Now, both of you," Dag said. "Suits off."

"What?" I said.

"You heard me. Take off your suits."

"But—"

"We can't have you following us," Panya said apologetically. "Please let's not argue anymore. We have work to do. There's so much work to do. We need you to stay here, where you'll be safe."

"We'll be infected," I said, horror making my voice high. "We can't."

"It's not safe here," Malachi protested. "This is where the virus—"

Panya pushed his head forward with her gun. "I said I don't want to argue anymore."

Malachi's hands were moving at his sides, his head swaying

minutely: he was looking around, he was going to do something, he was going to try to get away, and if he did, Panya would fire. He might not believe her, but I knew she was not bluffing. Panya was always sincere. I could not let Malachi die because of my mistakes.

I released the seal of my helmet and tugged it off. The bitterly cold air was like a slap in the face. Beneath the outer suit, the thin fabric of the SPEC uniform was soaked through with my sweat. I began shivering at once. I felt naked and vulnerable, stripped down to the stolen uniform with nothing on my hands, nothing on my head, only socks on my feet. Malachi followed my lead, shedding his emergency suit as well.

Dag gathered up the suits and helmets and boots. Panya took one of the helmets from him and aimed the open neck toward us.

"I wish you had not forced me to be the one to decide your punishment, Zahra," Panya said. Her voice carried through the helmet's speaker, small and distorted. "I never wanted to carry this burden. I know it will pain me for a long time."

Dag shut the door to the laboratory as they left. The lock engaged with a solid metallic thunk that made me jump. I spun toward Malachi. His eyes were wide, his gaze darting and quick, and he was looking all around the room, at all the controls, all the panels, every corner and wall. His breath misted a cloud with every exhale. I wanted to apologize. I could not speak. I hated to breathe, hated to think I might be drawing the virus into my lungs. My jaw ached with the effort of keeping my teeth from chattering.

On the other side of the window, Panya and Dag spoke to each other in the dim red light. Dag gestured, and Panya hesitated, then nodded. Dag tapped a few commands into the panel.

The light in the laboratory faded abruptly, deep dormancy red giving way to darkness. When the light returned, the outer room was empty and the door to the corridor was closed. They had left us.

Malachi said, "We should—"

Before he could say what we should do, an alarm wailed, so loud I winced and slapped my hands over my ears. The careless motion sent me into a slow spin. I flung one hand out to stop myself and caught one of the probe's metal support struts. The red light gave way to a brilliant, blinding white. There was a brief silence.

I asked, "What is that?"

The alarm shrieked again, like needles pressing into our ears. When it stopped that time, my ears were ringing, and Malachi's voice was murky when he spoke. Even so, I understood his words.

"Fire suppression," he said. "It's venting the oxygen."

In the silence that followed came a soft, steady hiss. It was the same sound that had followed the same wailing alarm on Dr. Summers's last log entry. The same bright light.

They meant to suffocate us. Malachi was already moving. He spun around and kicked himself toward the door.

"There has to be a fail-safe," he said. "It can't—"

The alarm screamed.

"—in case somebody's trapped," he finished.

He tapped frantically at the panel by the door, but the door remained stubbornly locked. The alarm screamed again. It had been so long since I'd seen him in bright light; he looked tense and exhausted.

"Help me!" he shouted.

I searched the workstation, the instruments, the array of computers lining the walls. Help him, help him—but I had no idea what a fail-safe mechanism would look like. This was not a test of loyalty. This was not punishment. They would not return. How quickly they had made the decision. How quickly they had left.

"Zahra!" Malachi shouted, after the alarm sounded again. "Zahra, snap the fuck out of it and help me."

I looked up quickly, turning my head so fast it sent a wave of dizziness over me. I had never heard Malachi sound like that before, so angry and sharp. There was no waver in his voice, none of his usual quavering uncertainty. I blinked once and nodded. The cold, the thinning air, they were taking their toll, but I had to concentrate. I pushed away from the support strut and caught myself on the workstation screen—the metal was so painfully cold it burned my skin—and twisted myself up, grabbing for the open panel on the probe. I kicked up from the stool for momentum and launched myself to the other side of the probe.

I caught Dr. Summers's corpse about the middle. As we floated toward the far wall of the laboratory, I began searching through the pockets of her jumpsuit. In the first I found a gold ring, half of a protein bar, a couple of small screws. In the other, only a pocketknife, not quite ten centimeters long. I let out a growl of frustration. We needed a way out. We needed more time. The hissing had grown louder. I winced, trying to turn away from it, but there was no escape. There was a ventilation panel high on the wall, right over the head of the other corpse.

And on the panel's edge a neat label: INTAKE/OUTGO.

I grabbed Dr. Summers's arm and kicked up from the floor, dragging her cold-stiffened body with me, using the dead man's shoulder as a step. He was infected, he was infected, the thought was a drumbeat in my mind, but I needed the boost. I was growing light-headed, and every piercing shriek of the alarm was like a knife in my ears. I kicked too hard and floated right by the vent to hit the ceiling. Dr. Summers's white hair was a cloud of dandelion puff around me. I coughed as strands drifted to my mouth, flinched away from its feather-soft touch on my skin. Her face was close to mine, close enough that I could see every wrinkle around her eyes, every hair of her eyelashes.

She jerked away, and I yelped, the noise lost beneath another wail of the alarm, but it was only Malachi tugging her down. He had figured out what I was trying to do. Together we positioned her body over the air evacuation vent.

"It won't stop it completely," Malachi said, gasping on every word.

I knew that. I only wanted more time. My mind was racing, my thoughts punctured by the siren, by fierce awareness of every breath, by the aching, clawing cold. The glass wall might be breakable, but we had nothing to break it with. There was only the one door.

One door. A single human-sized door.

I looked at Malachi. "How did they get it in here?"

The alarm shrieked over his answer, but he grabbed my hand and pulled me toward the floor, catching a support strut with his free hand. Urgency made his motions more focused, chasing away the doubt that normally accompanied his every choice.

"There's space between the levels," he explained. "Find the panel that opens."

We traced the edges of the floor panels with our fingertips, but we could not pry anything loose. The cold made my fingers feel fat and numb, and my vision was beginning to blur. I found four small screws holding one panel in place. I pointed, and Malachi nodded—we were too short of breath to waste words.

I pushed myself back up to the workstation. We needed a tool. A screwdriver, or anything that could be used as one. I fumbled with the strap of tools, not bothering to search through them, just tugged the entire collection down to the floor again. The room swam around me, and my head throbbed with crescendoing pain. I began coughing—rough and dry, an uncontrollable urge—and in spite of the cold, a sweat broke out all over my skin. I struck my head on the hull of the probe when I misjudged the distance, but the sound of the impact was muffled beneath the siren and the cotton-stuffed feeling in my ears. Malachi was a blurry shape before me, moving with underwater slowness as he searched through the tools.

He found an electric screwdriver, but the cold had long ago killed the battery, so he had to turn it manually. When he got the first screw loosened he moved on to the next, and I took over with my cold, clumsy hands, turning each screw the rest of the way, tugging them out and leaving them to drift. When all four had been loosened, Malachi tried to jam the screwdriver head into the seam, but it was too wide. He cursed in frustration. Every breath he sucked in was shallow and desperate.

I searched through the tools again, looking for something thin enough to pry, wasting precious seconds before I remembered Dr. Summers's pocketknife. I kicked up to her to retrieve it, kicked down again, and snapped it open. I sliced my palm in my hurry, but the quick-hot sting was only a small pain among so many other agonies. I jammed the short blade into the seam, as careful as I could be, terrified of breaking the thin little blade.

It took only the slightest nudge. The pressure on the other side of the panel was still normal; that air was pressing into our suffocating chamber. The seal broke and the panel lifted.

Beneath the panel there were only wires, tubes, and a red handle with no label.

"What do we do?" I said in the brief silence between sirens.

There was no answer. Malachi's eyes were open, but he was staring blankly, unseeing, his entire body shuddering with useless breaths. I reached for the red handle and tugged. After a few wasteful, fruitless, angry pulls, I realized it rotated. It was a manual crank.

I turned the handle as fast as I could. My grip was slick with the blood from where I had cut myself, and at first nothing seemed to be happening—then I felt a warm breeze flowing upward from the control compartment.

There was a gasp—not me, not Malachi, but mechanical—and a larger panel began to sink into the floor. Rushing air hissed all around it, shoving through the gaps and flowing over my blood-slick hand, warmer than the air around us. I wanted nothing more than to lean my face down to that tiny crack and suck at it, but I didn't stop. I turned the crank until the floor panel dropped and moved to the side, centimeter by centimeter, at first moving so slowly I could scarcely see it change, then in great gaps—my mind was stuttering, blacking out and snapping to—and a hole opened. The space beneath the floor was dark.

"Malachi," I said. His eyes were still open, but he didn't react. "Malachi! We can get out!"

He blinked vaguely and twitched one hand, moved his lips as though to speak, but the word came out as an unintelligible mumble. I grabbed him by the shoulders and shoved him down, headfirst, through the half-meter hole in the floor. It was harder than I expected to push him against the flow of air, but I was able to maneuver him far enough to make room for me to follow.

The air coursed around me like a strong wind as I tugged myself into the hole and pushed Malachi's legs aside. He groaned and said my name, and my heart stuttered with relief to hear it. I fumbled for the crank again, turned it closed as frantically as I had opened it, blocking the light but also the air rushing out. The hiss grew to a higher pitch when there was only a sliver of light left, and I turned the crank the last few rotations.

And it was quiet, and it was dark.

I let go of the crank, fumbled in the dark for one of the handholds.

"Zahra?" Malachi said. His voice was still slurring, weak, and he coughed on the exhale. "I don't want to, um, alarm you. But I can't see."

I couldn't help myself: I laughed. It hurt, laughing as my lungs filled again with air, as oxygen flowed through my blood, and the feeling of clammy cold returned to my skin, with the pain in my hand and the bitter metallic taste of every breath. The air was stale.

"Zahra?" Malachi said again.

"Yeah," I said. "I can't see either. There's no light."

"There's—oh, shit." A clank as something hit metal with a dull thunk. I hoped it wasn't his head. "We're in the maintenance tunnels?"

"I guess so," I said. "I don't suppose you know how to get us out?"

"Uh," he said. "Not exactly."

I started to laugh again, but it turned ragged, rough, and I slammed my mouth shut before it could turn into a sob. I was not going to cry. My head, my heart, every pulse of blood through my veins, they all ached with my failures, and I was not going to cry.

I reached down, down, feeling blindly until I found Malachi's hand. After a second he squeezed mine in answer. I closed my eyes, and we stayed there, breathing that bitter, precious air, clinging to each other in the darkness.

Nothing helps. They're in so much pain. Another group escaped custody and fled into the ruins. Every time we think we have [data corruption] the people up in the ship don't know what to do with the samples we sent to them. It's not safe for them to come down, and it's not safe for us to return. I always knew I'd die here, but not like this. Not this soon. I was supposed to have decades. We were supposed to have a lifetime.

—FRAGMENT 4, *MOURNFUL EVENING SONG* VIA UC33-X

And she was gone. In the fraction of a second between the ripple beneath her skin and our gasps of shock, Ariana had whirled away and propelled herself down the corridor.

"*Wait!*" I shouted. Driven more by wild instinct than logical thought, I followed.

She was outrageously, impossibly fast. She moved as though she had lived in space her entire life, kicking from one wall to angle off another, gliding so smoothly it was difficult to see how she anticipated each necessary motion and planned each action and reaction. She didn't look back. If she heard us shouting, she chose not to react.

My heart was pounding, my mind racing. My mother's words from Ariana's mouth. The rattle and thump of the bathroom door. It wasn't him. It couldn't be him. That terrible grasping hand.

The thing beneath her skin.

I wasn't as fast as Ariana, being ten years out of practice, but I was faster than Baqir and Xiomara. Soon their shouts were well behind me. I didn't stop. She had spoken my mother's words. I was not going to lose her.

I held my helmet in one hand, the headlamp lighting every turn. My breath formed whirling clouds in the cold. The hallways burrowing through Level 7 were short, rarely straight, interrupted by common areas and alcoves: the shipbuilders' attempt at softening the engineered precision of living spaces. What had made the hallways fun to play in as a child made them frustrating now. I caught the edge of a doorway to change direction, kicked with both feet to propel myself around a bend. A few meters ahead the passage opened into a large chamber.

Ariana had paused in the doorway. She was a silhouette in the low red light. Her rainbow hair shone in stiff streaks of light and dark. Unmoving, her back to me, she did not turn. I stopped only a couple of meters behind her.

Beyond Ariana, visible over her right shoulder, was the Earth.

It was one of my father's gardens. A large, round chamber on the side of Level 7, with windows facing outward like a great eye, it had once been home to cascades of ivy, flowering vines in living braids, delicate epiphytes embracing sturdier branches, and shadowy alcoves of trellises shaded by broad leaves. Small benches looked out toward the stars, tucked away in what should have been a riot of greenery and color, misty air and endless twilight, a place for quiet and contemplation.

My father had liked to come here after supper, when the ship was settling into its evening routine. If my mother was still working—and she was, most nights—I would accompany him. He taught me about pruning the vines to encourage healthier blossoms, clipping away the old to make room for the new, gently guiding the plants into a living work of art. I had never been as interested as he wanted. The stars beyond the windows always drew my attention.

Now, like everything else, the garden was dead. The vines were dull and crisp, the leaves crumpled by an unending winter. Even in the cold I could smell a faint decay.

I felt an unexpected rush of anger, remembering the warmth of my father's hand on mine, the cool metal of the clippers in my grip, the clean snap of a stem cut through, and how beautiful this chamber had been, how joyful my father's manner when he tended it. There were scientists aboard the ship who called him a gardener in a mocking tone, but he always laughed as though they meant to compliment him. He believed there was no shame in being a gardener in space, where every living thing had to be protected and cherished. There was no shame in teaching life to flourish where before there was only darkness.

Ariana pushed herself through the doorway and drifted slowly toward the center window. She lifted both hands to stop herself. Halos of condensation surrounded her fingers like ghostly gloves. Silent, still, unaware of me so close behind her, she stared at Earth. From this distance it was small enough to hide behind an outstretched hand.

Countless times I had gazed out that very window, in that very pose, a child staring at wonders both familiar and incomprehensible. During the eight years we lived aboard *House of Wisdom*, the ship had carried us throughout the solar system. Through that window I had watched Mars pass as a dusty red marble, Ceres as a dark rock lit from within by the sprawling mining colony, Europa with its frozen face pockmarked by research bases. I could still feel the slick sensation of the glass-mimicking window on my fingertips. I could still hear my father's voice as he speculated about what the universe might hold beyond our sun and its satellites, and how he envied me that I might live to travel so far, that I would surely discover wonders of my own when I was older.

"Where did they go?" Xiomara's voice carried through the corridors.

"Just up ahead," Baqir said. "I think this way?"

"Are you sure? It could be—"

"Here," I said. I did not shout.

They were coming closer, but Ariana showed no sign of having heard them. She was gazing at Earth, rapt, her bare fingers flexed against the window. I could not see her face, only the mist of her breath. I heard the tap of boots on the wall behind me.

"What are you doing? Why did you stop?" Xiomara asked in a hoarse whisper. Then her voice rose in surprise. "Ariana? Ari! Are you okay?" She tried to push by me, shoving angrily at my arm. "Let me go to her. We need to help her. She recognized you."

"No, she didn't. That wasn't—"

"What is wrong with you? You heard her! Ariana!" Xiomara ducked under my arm and pushed away from the garden entrance. I grabbed after her, but she had given herself enough momentum to move out of reach. Baqir caught my arm before I could go after her; the grip of his metal prosthetic hand was cold and strong.

"Don't," he said. "Don't get close to her."

Xiomara thumped against the window a couple of meters to the left of Ariana. "Ari, can you hear me? Are you okay?"

For a long moment, there was no reaction. I held my breath, terrified of stirring Ariana into another violent frenzy. None of the people infected during the massacre had been like this. They had been delusional, violent, out of control. They had screamed, shouted, begged for help, attacked friends and colleagues, slashed their own limbs to pieces. If this was the calm Captain Ngahere had witnessed, it was far more eerie than I had ever imagined.

Then, Ariana turned.

Baqir sucked in a breath and let go of my arm. I heard the tap of his metal fingers on the doorway and glanced to the side; he was bracing himself with one hand to raise the suppression weapon Xiomara had taken when we made our escape.

"Ariana," Xiomara said quietly. "Can you hear me?"

After another brief, agonizing silence, Ariana spoke. But it was not an answer. It was a rapid-fire stream of words in another language.

Xiomara blinked in surprise. "What? What did she say? What language is that?"

Ariana spoke again. Her tone was flat, the words without inflection, but there was something recognizable in what she was saying. It was like the words of a familiar song spoken without their tune, inviting the mind to fall into the rhythm but jarring the ear by resisting.

"Ari, I don't understand," Xiomara said, pleading. She extended a hand toward Ariana, withdrew it again, trembling with fear. "What are you saying? Can't you understand me?"

"It sounds like some dialect of Chinese," Baqir said. "But it's atonal. It's all wrong."

My chest was tight, and blood thrummed in my ears. "It's Archaic Chinese," I said.

"The fuck? Ariana doesn't speak Archaic Chinese. She can only barely hold a conversation in modern Chinese."

But I was certain now. "It's the message from *Mournful Evening Song*."

I had listened to those words more times than I could count. *The Earth our ancestors left behind was dying.* The woman who sent her voice across light-years aboard UC33-X had spoken with an accent nobody recognized, in an oddly stiff dialect not spoken on Earth for hundreds of years. *Soon we will sink our roots into the soil of a new world.* Retrieving that data and restoring that long-traveled greeting would have been Dr. Gregory Lago's legacy, if not for the virus. *We have nothing but hope in our hearts.*

"Ari? What's going on? Why are you saying that?" Xiomara reached out again, jerked her hand back abruptly when Ariana stared at her outstretched fingers. "Sorry. Sorry. Can't you just say something? Can't you—"

Ariana spun around—one hand on the window, one foot braced against the base—and lunged. She moved so fast Xiomara had no time to react. Fingers splayed, hand outstretched, Ariana reached for her face, caught the collar of her suit instead. She pulled Xiomara closer—Baqir pushed by me—Xiomara screamed and flailed, striking at Ariana, but it didn't have any effect. Ariana didn't loosen her hold. She was pulling Xiomara toward her, fingers curled into claws and whipping toward her face, and I couldn't move, I couldn't breathe, I couldn't think anything except, *again again it's happening again,* and in seconds Xiomara would be infected, she would be writhing and panicking and tearing at her own skin—

There was a loud snap. Ariana jerked and, for an instant, froze. She began to tremble with powerful, full-body convulsions that seized every muscle.

Xiomara shoved her away with both feet on her midsection, twisting her collar from Ariana's grasp. Ariana turned, no longer in control of her motions, and I saw the electroshock darts of the suppression weapon gleaming in her arm.

Baqir did not lower the weapon. He turned it slightly to check the charge, aimed it again, and kept it fixed on Ariana. The trembles continued, her arms and legs twitching, her face contorting—and it was not only the spasms distorting her face, but a ripple, that swift, pulsating presence of the thing that had invaded her body, shivering through her neck, along the side of her face, weakening until there was no more movement beneath her skin. Ariana shook as small seizures rolled through her body. Her eyes were open but unseeing, her mouth clamped shut, her breath hitching loudly.

I pushed myself from the doorway to grab Xiomara and tug her away from Ariana.

"Did she break your skin?" I asked, looking her over frantically. "Did she scrape you? Did any of her blood touch you? Her spit?"

Xiomara shook her head but didn't fight me. She sucked in a wet breath and wiped the tears from her eyes. "I don't—I don't think so?"

She lifted her chin, turned her head this way and that. Only her face was exposed, as she was still wearing her gloves. I did not see any marks or scrapes.

"What did you do?" Xiomara asked Baqir. "How did you even—how do you even know how to use one of those things? Is she hurt?"

Baqir looked down at the weapon in his hand. "The shock setting hurts like a fucker, but it doesn't do any permanent damage."

"How do you—" Xiomara stopped herself, shook her head. She pushed me away. "I'm fine. She didn't even touch my skin, only my suit. We have to get help. She can't hurt us right now. We have to help her."

I was watching Ariana. The weapon should not have rendered her unconscious, but she gave no indication that she was aware of what was going on. But she wasn't attacking anymore either.

So close to the window, with Earth to my left and the dead garden to my right, I had a moment of dizzying, disorienting vertigo, as though I was suspended for only a moment before tumbling into space, falling toward that bright and distant and impossible marble of blue and green. Could it be so simple? It didn't seem possible. The uninfected would have tried to stun the infected during the outbreak. I had not seen it myself, nor were there records in the data Aunt Padmavati had given me, but sup-pression weapons were the only weapons aboard. Somebody would have tried—surely somebody would have tried. It had not been enough to stop the outbreak.

But Xiomara was right: with Ariana incapacitated, even tempo-rarily, we might have a chance to help her. We had only one in-fected person, not hundreds. I didn't know what to do. I couldn't stop thinking about the words she had parroted to us, her voice so empty of intonation it was as though she was making sounds that had no meaning to her.

"She's still in there," Xiomara said. "Jas. She recognized you."

"I don't think she did," I said.

"She did say your name," Baqir pointed out.

I shook my head. "No. That's not what that was."

"Well, it wasn't all fucking Archaic Chinese," Xiomara snapped. "Maybe she was still—hallucinating, or something, but she was talking to us, she saw you and—"

"No. She wasn't. She didn't."

"You don't *know*—"

"Yes, I do," I said, cutting Xiomara off firmly. "I know because what she said were the exact same words my parents said right before my father died. The last time they spoke to each other."

I looked at Xiomara, at Baqir, both of them silent, and willed them to understand.

"There's no recording of those words. I've never told anybody. Not the investigators. Not the doctors. Not my aunt. Not you." I looked at Baqir. "I never told *anybody*. But Ariana repeated them exactly."

"She said something about a knife," Baqir said quietly.

Our breath was creating clouds of mist, tinted red by the dor-mancy lights. Ariana drifted, the toe of one boot rustling over a dried and frostbitten cluster of leaves.

"I was in my room," I said. "I didn't know anything was really wrong yet. I knew people were getting sick, but not . . . like that. They thought it was a chemical leak in the research labs or something. There was no quarantine yet. My dad had come back to stay with me, and when Mum came home . . . that's what she said. She said, 'Vinod . . .'" My voice cracked on my father's name. " 'Vinod, what are you doing with that knife?' I went out to see what was going on, and she told me to go back to my room."

I rubbed my hand through my hair, knocking loose shards of frozen sweat. I didn't want to remember the fear on my mother's face, the dawning horror on my father's in the brief moments of clarity before the panic took him.

"He was infected," I said, "but he was aware enough to know he was infected. He closed himself in the bathroom. We didn't see what happened. But we could hear it."

The struggled breathing, the thumping. A quiet gurgle. He had not cried out.

"How could a virus do that?" Baqir asked. "Or—whatever it did to Ariana?"

Xiomara shook her head, sending shivers of motion through her frost-edged dreadlocks. "We have to stop thinking of it as a virus. We saw it moving through Ariana. That's not a virus." Her tears were drying up, her voice growing stronger. "The doctors and SPEC got it wrong. It's big enough to be seen through the skin, and it grows quickly from the point of infection, and it's at least partly mechanical. It's some kind of bioengineered parasite."

"If it's even bio-anything," Baqir said. "It could be entirely mechanical. If there was some sort of transceiver or radio—"

"It could have recorded my parents' words," I said.

Xiomara nodded thoughtfully. "There are neuromedical devices that are triggered by changes in body temperature and chemistry. Something like that—when it got into Ariana, if it sensed the right conditions, it would wake from a dormant state and begin functioning again. It might have detected a signal from the other one, the one in . . ." She winced as she looked at me. "The one in your father. We warmed up the room, gave it favorable conditions again. Temperature might be the trigger for activity. The device in Ariana knew it was waking. That's why she followed us there."

"Fuck," Baqir said. "They were never hallucinating. None of them."

"It would have to have very high-level nerve control. Brain systems and autonomic functions. Voluntary functions, too, if it can take over and make the hosts move and speak. Is that even possible? Does technology like that exist? You must know something about the research into communication between brain and machine," Xiomara said to Baqir.

"A little," he conceded, which I knew was a massive understatement. He was flexing the fingers of his metal hand, frowning in thought. After a moment he said, "It's not impossible. But most neural engineering is on interfaces that work the other way around—getting signals from the brain to control external devices. The research on signaling the other way . . . nothing I've ever heard of can even get close to using an engineered device to control higher brain functions. Things like making muscles twitch, controlling spasms, anything that's a straightforward electrical effect, that's easy. But speech and decision-making and mimicry . . . I don't know. I've never heard of it."

"And after death?" I said.

Baqir touched my arm. "I don't know. It might be—what we saw in Ariana was big enough to *see*. It might grow large enough for crude motor manipulation, even without any neural input. Or life signs."

"We have to assume it's possible," Xiomara said. She lifted her hand to her neck, and I tensed—looked for any sign of motion, for any squirm of discomfort—but she was only adjusting the suit's collar. She saw me staring and moved her hand away. "If it's a biomechanical parasite, we can help Ari. Somebody can take it out."

Ariana groaned. It was a small sound, more breath than voice, but unmistakable. At her sides her hands uncurled from their clawlike rigidity. She groaned again, rolled her head from side to side, worked her lips as though preparing to speak.

Her eyes snapped open.

"Oh," she said. "Oh, no. I thought it was a dream."

A riana blinked. She hadn't been blinking before, and now she did so rapidly, then hissed and rubbed frantically at her eyes. She shuddered when she looked at her hands, grimy with dirt, stiff with cold. She did not stop blinking.

"Ari?" Xiomara said. Her voice was breathy with banked hope. "Are you okay?"

Ariana looked at her through newly damp eyes. "Is it . . . what . . ." She looked at Baqir, at me, at the dead garden around us and the Earth so small through the windows. "It wasn't a dream. Was it?"

She sounded like herself. Ariana's normal speaking voice was rather high and strident, with a strong Rio accent. All of that inflection had been flattened before, when she was speaking words not her own.

"No," Xiomara said. There were tears gathering in her eyes, and her face was screwed up with the effort of staying calm. "It wasn't. Are you okay? Are you hurt?"

Ariana looked at her hands again. Then she burst into tears.

Xiomara lunged forward, hurry making her clumsy, and threw her arms around Ariana, bumping both of them into the round window. They bounced back, and Baqir stopped them with a hand on Xiomara's shoulder, arrested their motion as they clung together.

Ariana was weeping with short, gasping sobs, her breath hitching as she said, *"Oh no, oh no, oh no,"* over and over again.

"It's okay," Xiomara murmured. "It's okay."

When she lifted her gaze to glare at me over the top of Ariana's head, I knew exactly what she was saying: This was Ariana. I was wrong. She could be saved.

They could have all been saved, if only we had known.

Four hundred and seventy-seven people. My father. My mother. A low tremor built somewhere at the back of my mind. I was afraid if I opened my mouth to speak, I would vomit, or scream. I pulled myself away from Ariana. I wanted her to be okay, but I did not want to be near her. I had never felt so cold.

"Ariana, what happened?" Baqir said quietly. He was looking at me as he spoke. He had seen my short, clumsy retreat. "Can you tell us what happened?"

Ariana took in a few shuddering breaths before she lifted her face from Xiomara's shoulder. She wiped the tears from her eyes, grimacing at the feel of her gritty hands on her face. "I don't know. I don't know what—I couldn't stop it. I could *feel* it but I couldn't . . ."

"Start when you first noticed something wrong," Baqir said. "You snagged your suit?"

Ariana looked down at her left hand. "Only a little. It was barely even a scratch. I didn't think . . . It didn't feel like anything, and then it did. I wasn't hallucinating." She looked up sharply and glared at me. "There really was something there. I could feel it moving under my skin. At first it was small but . . . it grew. I was not imagining it."

I couldn't say anything. It was as though there was a hand clamped around my throat.

"All I could think about was getting it out of me," Ariana went on, her voice growing stronger. "It was like—it was like I was fine one moment, and the next I couldn't think of anything except getting it out. I've never been that scared. I couldn't think of anything else. I thought my heart was going to arrest."

Xiomara said, "We think it must be a biomechanical parasite. That could be what Dr. Lago had on board instead of a virus. That's our best theory."

"Maybe," Ariana said. "All I know is that it—it changed. Like somebody hit a switch. I was still afraid, but I couldn't do anything. I was awake, but I couldn't move my own hands, I couldn't turn my head, I couldn't do *anything*. It was like I was trapped inside my own body and . . ." She trailed off, her breath hitching. Xiomara rubbed her shoulder soothingly. "I couldn't stop it. There wasn't anything I could do to stop it from doing what it wanted to do."

"That's awful," Xiomara whispered.

"What do you mean, 'wanted'?" I asked, and Ariana started. I said, more gently, "You said 'what it wanted to do.' What do you mean?"

"I meant . . . Oh, fuck, I don't know how else to describe it." Ariana's words were ragged still, and her hands trembled as she clutched at Xiomara's arm. "It was—it *was* like that. Like this switch came on and—and there was just this overwhelming feeling of inevitability."

"Did you hear a command?" Baqir asked.

"No, no, I didn't hear anything. I wasn't even really understanding words, when everybody was talking."

"But you spoke," Xiomara pointed out. "You spoke to us."

Ariana shook her head. "I didn't. *It* did. It was like . . . input and output. That's what it felt like. I don't know how to explain it. My mouth was moving and sounds were coming out, but it was all just noise. Fuck. *Fuck.* How can I not even know what I said? It felt like I was making sounds because those sounds went in that order. And moving because those motions went in that order. Then there was suddenly *something.* Something else. More input. A reason to change direction."

Baqir glanced at me. "We think we accidentally woke one of the other—machines, whatever they are. That could be what you heard."

"How did you end up here?" Xiomara asked. "Is this where it was telling you to go?"

Ariana looked quickly toward the window, looked away again, as though something about seeing Earth there, so fragile and far away, was unbearable to her. "I don't know. I don't know why it came here. I don't know *why* it does anything. There are no *reasons.* There are only impulses. Impulses I can't control."

"But what does it *want*?" Xiomara said.

"You mean, what do the people who designed it want," Baqir said. "Isn't that the real question? Whoever was working with Dr. Lago, or whoever he stole it from, whoever created this thing, they did so for a reason."

How quickly we had begun referencing the will of this *thing* we had seen rippling beneath Ariana's skin. We had shifted from viewing it as a senseless pathogen to speaking of it as a sentient creature with wants and desires of its own. But it was a designed thing. A built thing. A thing created for a purpose. It could slither into a woman's mind and take away her control of her own body, her language, her will, but it did so because somebody had designed it that way. It was impossible to comprehend, that so much violence, so much blood and fear, could have been in service of a goal, unless that goal was mayhem.

Baqir let out a frustrated breath. "If it's even supposed to do anything. This could be a test. Dr. Lago could have stolen something unfinished, or something that was supposed to be monitored or controlled. It could be malfunctioning. We don't know."

Ariana's expression was thoughtful. "It was just like . . . you know how when you're worried about something, something you can't avoid, and it keeps running through your head over and over again, every single step you take to get there? It was like that. Everything it made me do was like a step toward the end."

"What was at the end?" I asked.

"I don't know," Ariana said, but she glanced toward Earth again. "It wasn't like I was *thinking* anything. It was just . . . like a fractal, sort of, but it was everywhere around me, and there was this circle near the middle that felt like—I don't know. It was pulling me in. I can't explain it. It was—I don't even remember moving through most of the ship, because that's the only thing that made sense. Get to the circle. Why the fuck could it control me so easily if I couldn't even figure out what it *wants*?"

"It had an advantage," Baqir said. "Trial and error with hundreds of people."

"We don't know that," Xiomara said. "We don't know anything for sure, which is why we need help. Jas knows how to get us off the ship. And surely SPEC must be getting closer by now."

But I was thinking about the shape of *House of Wisdom*. The levels, the laboratories, the corridors and maintenance tunnels. I had once known the schematics by heart. The division of space on every level and the hidden places between. I saw the maintenance tunnels, the vast, breathing breadth of my father's agricultural labs, the cozy living quarters, the cool distant bay of my mother's workshop.

There was one large circle in the ship. A bull's-eye at its heart.

"I think—" I began, and they all looked at me. I cleared my throat. "I think it wanted you to get to the bridge."

W̲e made our way to the bridge as quickly as we could, checking the location of our captors every few minutes. Before we left the garden they were on Level 8, in the Deep Space Archaeology lab, and by the time we reached Level 10, Panya and Dag were arguing about whether to try to open a locked passage on Level 9 or search for another. We had beat them.

The bridge was as cold as the rest of the ship, but the light was different, the low dormancy red mingling with quick flashes of blue, steady glowing green, pulsing bright white. A faint hum surrounded us.

There was a famous photograph of Captain Ngahere, taken not long after she assumed command of *House of Wisdom*. In it she was standing on the center of the bridge, right in front of what appeared to be a giant window looking down upon the red face of Mars. She was turned halfway away from the view, shown in profile, her expression pensive. There was nobody else in the frame, although there must have been half a dozen bridge crew just out of sight. She looked to be alone, and quiet, and so very serious. Exactly the sort of person you wanted to be your commander. It wasn't a true window, that wall-spanning view of Mars behind her. The bridge was at the center of the ship, a protected nerve center well away from the vulnerable hull, and the only views it had to the outside were transmitted via camera and sensor to a series of screens. Even so, the majority of seats and workstations on the open half of the bridge, including the captain's chair, were oriented in a half circle facing one direction, like an audience in a theater. People always want to feel like they're moving toward something.

It was considered another example of Captain Ngahere's heroism, that even at the end of everything, she had thought to ensure

House of Wisdom would remain safely in orbit, to protect Earth and the Moon and the orbital stations, everything that might be endangered should the ship tumble into a long, slow free fall. The bridge was where she had made those last, desperate choices, and where she had died. She had not died alone.

"What the fuck," Baqir said. His words, though not spoken loudly, broke into the quiet like the crack of a whip. "What the *fuck.*"

There were at least twenty bodies on the bridge. More than we had seen gathered in any one place since my father's garden. They were not scattered around, torn by violence, or huddling together in fear, but sitting at their stations. Strapped neatly into their chairs. Hands resting on terminals. Eyes open, all staring toward the screen before them.

They were as shriveled and dry as all the other corpses we had found, but there was no sign that they had been fighting or fleeing or cowering. There were no indications they had been aware of the fate that was to overtake them.

"It looks like they died flying the ship," Xiomara said.

Baqir added, "They don't look wounded."

Not at first glance. Not in comparison to the savage, deadly wounds we had seen elsewhere. But as I looked over the dead, looked beyond the eerie strangeness of how orderly they were at their final stations, I noticed smaller details. Sleeves pushed up and forearms raked with scratches. Collars torn open. A dried line of blood from one ear, another from a nose. Small, thin fingers stained reddish-brown, now resting on a control panel. I stared at those hands for several seconds before I realized what I was seeing.

She wasn't a member of the bridge crew. She was a child.

The wrinkles of her dried-up face were misleading. I knew her. Her name was Jessamyn. She had been twelve years old when she died; we had shared lessons and tutors for years. I had never liked her, and she had not liked me, but there had been nobody else our age aboard the ship. We had endured each other's presence as something less than friends, but more than strangers or classmates. She hated living in space. She wanted to care for the megafauna of Earth, the elephants and giraffes and tigers brought back from the brink of extinction following the Collapse, and there was no place for animals aboard a spaceship.

She had died sitting at the navigation terminal. Beside her was a man I recognized as one of the ship's food scientists. I couldn't remember his name. He had worked with my father sometimes, tweaking breeds of tomato and spinach, arguing over the viability of carrots. He had no more business being on the bridge than Jessamyn.

"They shouldn't be here," I said. "They're not bridge crew."

Baqir understood immediately. "So they are infected. And this is . . ."

"What it wanted them to do," I finished. "Come here. Fly the ship."

If it could make Ariana attack a man twice her size, steal his weapon, kill him; draw her through a ship she had never been aboard before as though she knew it by heart; open doors, open hatches, evade capture; store and communicate memories from ten years ago and movements from now; isolate the ship during the initial outbreak; disrupt the data transfers—if it could do all that, if it could *learn* all of that from its hosts—flying the ship was not so different.

"What's that?" Xiomara said. She and Ariana had moved to the other side of the bridge. They approached a long glass wall.

"The officers' meeting room," I said, my attention still on Jessamyn and the others. The parasite was a small thing, small enough to pass through a pinprick of broken skin, small enough to operate on the level of neurons and electrical impulses. It needed hosts to interact with the larger world.

"There's somebody in here," Ariana said.

"There are two of them." Xiomara paused, then said, in a very different voice, *"Jas."*

I pulled my way chair by chair across the bridge. The faces of the dead blurred together. I felt as though the cold had seeped so far into my limbs that my bones were turning to ice, and if I moved too quickly, if I moved carelessly, they would shatter again as I had long feared they would. I could not turn away. Xiomara's and Ariana's breath had clouded the glass wall of the officers' room. Xiomara wiped the fog away.

Captain Ngahere had died in her seat at the head of the table. There was a tablet before her, floating just out of reach of her desiccated fingertips.

And beside her, in the chair normally reserved for the first officer, was my mother.

INTERNAL COMMUNICATION ARCHIVE REF. [UNKNOWN/CORRUPTED]
Source: HOUSE OF WISDOM, SPEC RESEARCH
TimeDate: 11:01:37 01.04.393

BRIDGE: It's been quiet for some time now. They've gone quiet. They were making a lot of noise earlier. Not the screams, but words. They were saying—it sounded like—

ENGINEERING 12-009: The words of the dead.

BRIDGE: Who is that? Where are you?

ENGINEERING 12-009: It's me, Lilian. It's Amita.

BRIDGE: For fuck's sake. Where are you? Are you—it really is you?

ENGINEERING 12-009: I haven't been infected. There's nothing inside of me.

BRIDGE: Thank fuck for that. Is Vinod with you?

ENGINEERING 12-009: He's dead.

BRIDGE: And your little boy? Is he—

ENGINEERING 12-009: I think I may have just killed him.

BRIDGE: Amita? What do you mean?

ENGINEERING 12-009: I had to get him away, get him out as fast as I could. He wouldn't leave until I promised to come after. The evac system is locked down, so I sent him away on TIGER. We haven't properly damped its acceleration system. I might have killed him.

BRIDGE: You're in your dry dock? You have access to your vessels? You have to get away. You have to tell them what's happened here.

ENGINEERING 12-009: What has happened here, Captain? Whatever would I tell them? Have we achieved the greatest dream of humankind, that hope that stretches all the way to before the Collapse?

BRIDGE: You have to warn—

ENGINEERING 12-009: Or have we walked right up to that dream only to find it was only ever a mirage all along? Do they seem intelligent to you? Can you see them?

BRIDGE: I'm looking at them right now. They've overtaken the bridge. Josef's little girl is there. Jessamyn. She's at the navigation control.

ENGINEERING 12-009: We're under thrust. I can feel it.

BRIDGE: Yes. They've altered the course. I don't think they're very good at flying. Give it a few hours and this won't be a sustainable orbit.

ENGINEERING 12-009: Have they also seized the environmental control system?

BRIDGE: No. They haven't touched it. All they care about is propulsion and navigation.

ENGINEERING 12-009: Calculate a course for an indefinite stable orbit.

BRIDGE: I don't have control of the ship, Amita.

ENGINEERING 12-009: I know. I know. Calculate it anyway.

BRIDGE: Why? What good will that do?

ENGINEERING 12-009: I'm coming to you. I'll explain when I get there.

[ARCHIVED BY AUTOMATED COMMUNICATION PRESERVATION SYSTEM]

We breathed in the darkness, Malachi and I.

The alarm still blared on the other side of the hatch, but it was muffled now. The cold, stale air was the sweetest I had ever tasted. Malachi made a sound like the beginning of a word, then broke into a long coughing fit. I squeezed his hand, offering silent reassurance, though not yet daring to speak. His cough was terrible but familiar—the same sound he had made on the day we met, the day he came out of the desert, a stranger in the winter twilight, asking for help as though he already knew what my answer would be. The uncertainty had come later, after we had walked the hard-packed path from the perimeter to the heart of the homestead. The stammering, the averted eyes, the hesitation before every decision, that had only come when he faced Adam for the first time and began to tell his story. How hard he had worked to learn, to excel, to become useful. How many times he had tried to convince the Councils to grant him citizenship. How every rejection was another wound, until he bore so many he had layers of scars around his heart. He had been ashamed until he realized we did not blame him for the fickle cruelty of the Councils. Adam wanted the wretches and wanderers the Councils had no use for: there had been no doubt he would take Malachi in.

I remembered all of this, and more, as we recovered in the darkness. He had been with us so long I had forgotten how easily he had slipped into the homestead and the family. Malachi threatened nobody, least of all Adam. The only person he had ever frightened was me, in that cold purple twilight, when my doubts and my gun were no match for his smile.

"We need light," Malachi said. His breath was warm on my cheek. "Can I just—I need to reach around you."

I pressed myself against the metal ladder. He reached past me, accidentally bumped my face with his elbow, whispered a quiet apology. I heard the wheeze in his lungs, the creak of the ladder. I imagined, even, that I could hear his heartbeat.

"Ah. Here we go."

A blue glow pierced the darkness. Malachi had found a control panel.

"You could have gone with them," I said.

The words were a rasp of air, but loud enough to startle him into looking at me. Although his skin was soft brown in sunlight, now he looked sickly and pale. His curly brown hair was damp and plastered to his head. His lips were chapped and cracked.

"What?" he said.

"You should have gone with them. You could have convinced them. They need you."

"Zahra," Malachi said. He took in a breath, let it out slowly. "They tried to kill us."

"They're only doing what they think is right. What they think Adam would want."

"Which is it?"

"Which is what?"

"Are they doing what they think is right, or are they doing

what they think Adam would want? Do you really think they're the same thing?"

"They're only thinking of the mission."

"Why the fuck are you defending them? After what they just did? *They tried to kill you.*"

I stared at Malachi, stunned by his manner as much as by his words. In profile, half-illuminated by the light from the control panel, his mouth was twisted into a scowl, his jaw tight, his neck rigid.

"I'm not—"

I closed my mouth. Took a breath. Let it out. I had a thousand answers, and none. They were family. We were meant to work toward a common goal, a shared future of peace and strength. I had broken that covenant with my failure—

Or they had, with their betrayal.

"I'm only—I don't know. I need to think," I said.

Malachi scowled at the control panel for a couple of seconds, then jabbed his finger. The maintenance shaft filled with low red light. I wondered if that awful red would ever bleed from my eyes, or if it would forever stain the rest of my life.

"We need to get out of here." Malachi pushed away from me and moved down the ladder, past the larger rollers that would move the floor of the chamber above. Dark tunnels stretched in three directions, each lined with tubes and ducts and pipes in a tangle of junctions and bends; the fourth was blocked by a heavy steel door labeled INTRASHIP TRANSPORT. That must have been how they brought the probe into the laboratory. Wherever it led, it was closed to us now.

Malachi looked down the open passages. "There will be a hatch somewhere along here. It shouldn't be far."

"Malachi. Stop." I grabbed at his foot, flinched when he kicked free. "Wait."

"We can't stay here."

"I know, I know, but . . . what did you mean?"

"About what?"

"About Adam. About Panya and Dag and what they're doing."

He turned to look at me. "What do you want me to say? You know this isn't right, Zahra. None of this is right. They've gotten everything wrong from the start."

My heart was pounding so hard I could feel it in my throat. "We haven't gotten everything wrong," I said, but weakly, barely a protest. "I don't know why you're saying that."

Malachi exhaled sharply. "Yes, you do. You don't need me to explain anything. You're perfectly capable of thinking for yourself. You don't need Adam to tell you what to think, and you don't need me to explain to you how fucked up it is that they've stuck you in this situation."

They. Them. He should have been saying *we.*

"They haven't *stuck* me anywhere," I said. I was shivering, and my body ached with the effort of holding still. "I chose to be here. I wanted to be here. I'm not stupid. I accepted this responsibility because Adam asked it of me."

"Asked?" Malachi said.

Yes, I thought, then: no.

A wisp-gentle reversal: no.

I could not allow the lie to blossom, not even inside the privacy of my own mind. Adam did not ask us to do as he wished: He commanded, proclaimed, decreed. He administered punishment if we could not see his wisdom. He turned his back on those who did not agree. He had not asked me to lead this mission. He had told me that I would, and smiled when I accepted with pride. His command had aligned so perfectly with what I wanted—the only way I knew to clear my father's name—that I had ignored my doubts, dismissed the protests from older and more experienced members of the family, let Adam's certainty wash over all the concerns like a flash flood scouring a desert arroyo. That was how it had always been. That was how it had to be, because Adam was so much more than any of us. His knowledge and his wisdom would protect us, even if we did not understand how. That was the tenet that had held the family together through so much hardship. That was the truth that had made our star-reaching dreams possible. Whatever challenges the future offered, Adam would protect us.

But he hadn't. He hadn't known what danger we faced aboard *House of Wisdom*. He had told us time and again, at every stage of planning, in response to every doubt raised, every question asked, that he knew the Councils better than they knew themselves, and there was no secret they could hide from him. But they had hidden the truth of what Bhattacharya had witnessed. They had hidden the truth of how closely *House of Wisdom* was watched. They had hidden the truth of what the virus did to its victims.

I had been silent too long. Malachi sighed. "I don't think you're stupid, and I don't think this is all your fault."

My heart fluttered painfully. "But it *is*. I didn't know SPEC was going to attack the shuttle. I should have. Boudicca and Nico and Bao would still be alive if only I had realized the danger."

Malachi looked at me for a long moment, his eyes dark and tired. "Do you really think SPEC would do that?"

"But—you said it wasn't the security net. Was it? Did you—"

"The security system let us through. It wasn't the drones." Malachi touched my arm. I looked down at his hand. His fingers were barely warm, but compared to the aching cold around us, his touch felt like a flame. "Zahra. Think about it. Take a breath and really think about it."

I did as he said, and I tried, oh, I tried, but my mind was too full. I heard the screams of the woman who had died before she could cross to the ship. The quick red pop of a man's head vanishing at the pull of a trigger. Boudicca's laugh when she knew she was going into space again. Nico's screams as the terrible, voracious fire roiled from Pilgrim 3. My back and ribs had been hurting for so long the pain had become a part of me, inseparable from my skin and my blood.

The man I killed was devoured by the explosion. What a dirty thing it was, to feel relief that another crime had covered my own.

"I don't know what you're getting at," I said. I was so tired. "Tell me what you mean."

"SPEC does not have missiles and—"

"We don't know that," I said. "They have secret weapons. The security grid was secret until they had to reveal it."

"Okay, but even if they do, your first instinct was that the explosion had come from inside the shuttle. Inside, not outside. That's what you said before Dag argued otherwise. You were the only one who saw it. You know what you saw." Malachi spoke patiently, like a teacher guiding a reluctant student. "Do you think SPEC would sabotage a passenger shuttle? If they wanted to stop us, why not do it at Civita? Do you really think they would endanger the passengers? A group of researchers? Including a famous man with a powerful aunt absolutely guaranteed to launch a thorough investigation into anything that happens? Why would SPEC or the Councils do that?"

I knew what I should say: There is no limit to the violence they will inflict upon the world. One of Adam's favorite ways to close a meeting was to drop his voice to a low and ominous level, force us to lean in to hear him murmur, *They will sacrifice their own children. Their own mothers. Their own freedom. Do not underestimate them. Do not ever forget, not once, not ever, that they will trade blood for power.* I had believed him absolutely. They had destroyed my father and my family, and they had gotten away with it for ten years. My mother had died never seeing my father's name cleared. And mine was only one family—what had happened to us could happen to anybody, any time the Councils wished, for there were no checks on their power. That was why we had to leave. That was why we needed *House of Wisdom*. The force of Adam's certainty, the righteous fire shining from behind his eyes, the anger he felt toward those who had done us wrong, did not leave room for doubt.

Malachi was watching me intently. If Adam were asking the question, I would know it was a test, a way of rooting out weakness before the doubts and fears spread like gangrene. But I didn't know how Malachi wanted me to answer. If SPEC had not attacked the shuttle—

Nico had prepared some of our cargo and was trying to wrangle the frightened woman onto the ladder. They fought. He had threatened her with his weapon—and he had fired, at least twice. Perhaps more. I couldn't remember how many shots I had heard. Boudicca had shouted at him, but her admonition had been cut short by the explosion. Fire had rolled from the hatch. Nico. The woman. The cargo.

"There were no explosives in our cargo," I said, but it was a question, not an answer.

"There weren't supposed to be. But you didn't load the crates, and neither did I. Neither did Nico and Bao. Dag and Henke did that."

Dag would have loaded anything Adam told him to load, and Henke would have been happy to include more weapons. Nico wouldn't have known. He had always been careless, but even so he wouldn't have fired a projectile explosive into our cargo if he had known it would be deadly. Dag and Henke could not have meant to risk the precious lives of our family. We needed Boudicca. We needed Nico and Bao. Nobody was expendable. It had to have been an accident.

"But why?" I said. "We don't need explosives. We need—needed supplies. And why hasn't Dag said anything?"

"I don't think the explosives were for us."

I thought we were going to kill them, Henke had said.

"Adam never intended to release the hostages," Malachi said.

I shook my head, wanting to deny it. But it was all too easy to see Adam's plan. He would have sent the shuttle away. He would have invited SPEC to fetch their students. He would have smiled when the rescue ship was close enough, and he would have smiled when the explosion consumed both vessels. He would have called it a lesson more merciful than what they deserved.

"But the woman who killed Henke," I said desperately. "How could she do that? She's supposed to be a student, but she—she could be . . ."

"I think Bhattacharya was telling the truth. I think she was infected somehow, when she tore her suit and scraped herself. It made her delusional, made her lash out. She got lucky with Henke. He was careless."

Henke had been confident, grinning, looking for a fight. He had been twice her size. He had not thought she was a threat.

"Zahra," Malachi said, "we can't stay here. We have to keep moving."

He sounded as tired as I felt. I wanted to close my eyes and rest, the two of us alone in the darkness, sleep until the cold drained away and the ache in my head was gone and the sour taste of fear had faded from my throat. I couldn't remember the last time I had tried to choose right and wrong for myself. I felt cold and hollow, as papery as the savaged corpses. Nadra and Anwar were on their way. I had promised them safety. I had promised them peace. We were supposed to be together here, and happy.

But our dream of a new life, of freedom and beauty unshackled in the stars, it had been dead before we left the ground. I understood now the fear I had seen on Bhattacharya's face aboard the shuttle, and the horror in his voice when Ariana began to panic. He had known what we were too arrogant to see. *House of Wisdom* was not a sanctuary. It was an abyss. It had taken nearly five hundred lives already. If we brought the family here, it would swallow three hundred more.

On the door was a sign: SATELLITE INTERFEROMETRY. Malachi chose that laboratory because, he said, it would have a dedicated data transmission link. I didn't ask how he knew. The room was clean and empty, as though the scientists had simply gone home for the night.

While Malachi got the radio working, I fumbled through the storage lockers until I found a bulky knit sweater and a jacket with the *House of Wisdom* patch on the sleeve. The jacket fit Malachi; the sweater was too big on me. Neither provided much insulation.

"I've got the comms," Malachi said. "And it looks like—shit."

"What?"

"Incoming transmissions. Listen."

A woman's voice crackled from the speakers. "This is SPEC Orbital Control vessel *Pangong*, addressing the persons who have illegally entered the vessel *House of Wisdom*."

"Is that the dark ship? How close are they?" I asked.

Malachi shook his head. "I don't know."

"Your presence aboard *House of Wisdom* endangers both yourselves and your hostages. Open a channel of communication immediately so we may discuss the safe return of the hostages and continued safety of the ship *Homestead*. This is SPEC Orbital Control vessel *Pangong*, addressing the persons who have illegally entered the vessel *House of Wisdom* . . ."

The woman's voice droned so calmly she might have been a machine, but the words filled me with dread. Adam would hear a threat, no matter how mildly she spoke. To him, the message was proof that he had been right all along. They had always been after us. They would never leave us alone. The family would be frightened, the children crying, Adam raging. She ought not to have mentioned *Homestead*'s safety. That would only tell them they had none.

Malachi said, "There's a reply. Sent about an hour ago."

An hour. We had been out of contact so long. I nodded minutely.

"You dare call us criminals?" Adam's voice boomed from the speakers so loudly I jumped. "You dare accuse *us* of endangering our children? We have lived our entire lives beneath the boots of your oppression, and you speak to us of your laws? Save your breath and your condescension. We have no need for your lies. We have broken free of the chains you use to bind us. We have achieved the frontier you would deny us. We are prepared to make great sacrifices to keep our freedom. There is no fate worse than surrendering to be your prisoners again."

A fragile hope, so small I had barely acknowledged it, splintered.

"Are you prepared to sacrifice your children to enslave us? Are you?" Adam spat out the question derisively; even without seeing his face, I knew his expression would be twisted with scorn. "Go and ask your masters. Ask them how many of their beloved children have to die. Ask them which we ought to kill first."

The message ended. My heart was hammering in my throat. Tens of thousands of kilometers of empty space between us, and I feared Adam's anger as though he were right beside me.

"We need to talk to them." I swallowed painfully. "We have to make him understand it's too dangerous to come here."

Malachi didn't move. "You want to contact *Homestead*?"

There was something in his voice that made me look at him. "They can't come here. You know that. You haven't been able to shut off the security web yet, and even if you could—"

"I know." The words were soft, but there was something in Malachi's voice that tightened the knot of fear in my throat. "But, Zahra . . ."

"You don't think they'll listen," I said.

"I don't think Adam listens to anybody when they're telling him something he doesn't want to hear. Zahra, he's ranting about being *enslaved*. He's not rational. I don't think the drones will deter him, and I don't think the virus will either."

"He's only . . ." Only what? It was so hard to know anymore where Adam's hyperbole ended and his true beliefs began. I had never cared before, when his hatred of the Councils was driving us to achieve a dream that should have been impossible. When I had thought he was saving the family, and my brother and sister, not endangering them.

"We need to contact *Pangong*," Malachi said. "We have to tell them what's going on."

I stared at him. "You want to contact SPEC before we talk to Adam?"

"Adam won't listen."

"Maybe not, but he's not the one piloting *Homestead*. Orvar will listen. He won't want to endanger the family. He wants to keep everybody safe."

Malachi turned to the control panel. "Okay. We can try. Do you want visual?"

"Yes." It would be better for them to see my face. My mouth was dry, my head aching, my entire body sore from the bruises I knew must be purpling my skin. One look was all Orvar would need to understand how dire our situation was. "Go on."

It took only a few seconds for the encrypted transmission to go through, but it felt like an eternity before Orvar's face appeared on the terminal. His expression was grim, his hair wild, his flight suit loosened at the collar. There was a cacophony of noise around him.

"Where the hell have you been? SPEC is tracking us. The dark ship Boudicca saw is real," Orvar said.

"We know," Malachi said. "We've heard their warning."

"Tell me you've got good news."

"I need to talk to Adam," I said.

A hush fell over the bridge of *Homestead*. Orvar's eyes narrowed. Two young men appeared behind him, leaning down to peer at the terminal. My skin prickled with unease.

"Where's Dag? Henke?" Orvar asked.

"Henke is dead," I said. "One of the hostages killed him. I need to talk to Adam immediately."

Orvar nodded at one of the young men, who grimaced but obeyed. He looked so very young, and so very scared, as he turned to leave the bridge.

"How far away is the SPEC ship?" Malachi asked.

"Quarter million klicks," Orvar said grimly. "They're not hiding anymore. A bit less. Can't you see it?"

"We're having trouble getting the systems online," Malachi said.

"I don't like the sound of that. He isn't going to . . ." Orvar glanced over his shoulder. "It's Zahra again."

"Zahra!"

My heart stuttered—I made a small sound of surprise—and I was reaching for the screen without thinking. That was not Adam's voice. Malachi caught my hand before I could do anything to disrupt the transmission, and for one irrational second I hated him for it, for pulling me away from them.

Anwar appeared first. In the months since I had last seen them, the twins had passed their fifteenth birthday. Anwar had grown even taller, and his black hair was too long, drifting around his face in unruly curls. His boyish limbs were even thinner than they had been. He smiled, but it was a wary, muted smile. He raised a hand in awkward greeting.

"Hey, Zahra," said my brother, his voice so much more like a man's than I recalled. He glanced to the side, a question plain on his face, as though he was awaiting instruction for what to say. There was no reason for him to be on the bridge. The children were meant to be safe in the passenger cabins.

A second later Nadra came into view. With her was Adam. He had his arm hooked around her skinny shoulders. He was smiling. Nadra was not. He pushed her to stand behind Orvar; she hunched her shoulders and let herself be steered.

"Zahra, tell us the good news!" Adam said. "We've been waiting far too long."

His voice was bright, his tone cheerful, but there was a manic light in his eyes. I did not like the way Nadra was leaning away from him. I did not like the way she glanced at the comm, then looked away quickly, as though she could not bear to see me. I ached to reach across space and hug her, to pull her away from Adam and tease her into smiling. We could not make a home together aboard *House of Wisdom*, but anywhere, anywhere would be better than being apart.

I reached for Malachi's hand and tried to draw comfort from his warmth. I looked straight into the camera. "I don't have good news for you, Adam. Everything I have to tell you is bad."

Adam's eyes narrowed. Nadra flinched as he dug his fingers into her shoulder.

He said, "We are depending on you, Zahra. Tell me what has happened."

"You can't come here," I said. "*House of Wisdom* is too dangerous. We can't make it safe. Henke is dead, and we have no protection against the virus. One of the hostages is infected, she got infected through a scrape, not from the air. All it took was the slightest contact. The people here didn't just get sick—it's so much worse than that. It wasn't an outbreak, Adam. It was a massacre."

He was gripping Nadra's shoulder so hard his fingers pressed indentations in her sleeve. "Zahra, my girl, you are hysterical. You don't know what you're saying. Where is Panya? Where is Dag?"

"I am not hysterical," I said. "We've found information SPEC never had, a log recording from one of the scientists before she died. The virus isn't Zeffir-1. It never was. It is not safe here. We can't bring children to this place."

"Can you even hear the hateful things you are saying?" Adam demanded, his voice rising with alarm. "You pretend to care about keeping them *safe*? As though turning them over to the oppressors is safe? As though offering ourselves up for capture is safe? You are speaking from fear and cowardice."

"I'm *not*," I said. "I'm telling you what we've found. I'm telling you we cannot make a home here. We can't even turn on the lights, Adam. We have no way of turning off the security web. We got the shuttle through because we had the right genetic signature, but the drones will attack *Homestead*. They might be powerful enough to completely disable it. And even if we could—everyone aboard died by terrible violence. Everything SPEC told us about the virus was a lie. The girl was infected through a scratch. She killed Henke and fled, and now she's out there somewhere in the ship. We can't find her because we can't *do* anything. Do you understand what I'm saying? She went mad from a single scratch." I took a shaky breath. I was holding Malachi's hand so tightly it had to hurt, but he did not pull away. "Please listen to me. Please. *You can't come here.*"

The other members of the bridge crew had left their stations to gather around Adam, their expressions ranging from disbelief to naked fear. Anwar was staring at me, and Nadra had finally lifted her eyes from the floor.

"Adam, you trusted Zahra to make this judgment," Malachi said. "Listen to her."

"You would have us give up on our dreams when we are so close," Adam said.

"I would have us *survive*," I retorted.

"You would destroy everything I have worked for."

"I don't want us to go mad and slaughter each other like—"

"You would send your brother and sister to the prisons of the oppressors without a thought. That is what you are doing. Are we no more than animals to you, Zahra? Have you grown power mad in your time away from me?"

"Adam," Orvar said hesitantly. He glanced over his shoulder. "If the virus is still a threat—".

"It is," Malachi said. "It is absolutely a threat."

"You are cowards," Adam spat, his face contorting with anger. "You are weak, foolish cowards. You have betrayed me even worse than the liars and deceivers. They are cruel, but you are so much worse, because you let me believe you would help me."

"Adam, take a minute to think about it. We need time to figure out our plan," Orvar said.

"*There is no time!*" Adam roared. Nadra ducked away from him and turned into Anwar's arms; she hid her face against his shoulder. "I have *given* your orders and *you will follow them*."

"I know we were supposed to break free," I said, but I was speaking to Orvar now, not Adam. My voice was raw, my entire body trembling. I needed him to hear me. "We were supposed to find a home. But this isn't it. This ship is a death trap. Orvar. Please. You can't bring them here."

"It's a terrible thing," Orvar said, and he sounded so tired, so much older than he had ever seemed before, "to let yourself dream of something better after you thought you'd forgotten how." He glanced down and tapped something on his terminal. "This is the captain speaking." His voice trembled. "We'll be initiating a low-g course correction burn in−"

There was a loud crack, like a bone breaking. Orvar's head snapped to the side with an eruption of blood. Anwar screamed, and the bridge crew was shouting, scrambling against each other, shoving away from the terminal.

The shot had blown off half of Orvar's face. His remaining brown eye stared blankly from the ruin of blood and shattered bone.

Adam pushed Orvar's body aside and looked into the camera. I had not even seen the weapon in his hand. His pale eyes were blazing and wild. Blood and bits of skull and brain had splattered across his face. Spit flew from his lips as he spoke.

"You disgust me. You are traitors. You have chosen death. You have chosen betrayal. You are as weak as your father, Zahra, and the blood on your hands will be so much greater than any of his pathetic crimes. Everything that happens now is your fault. You have destroyed everything."

"No!" I found my voice again. "Please, Adam, Adam, listen, you have to listen to me, you have to−"

He had ended the transmission.

[data corruption] keep thinking of an old song the aunties used to sing in the nursery, right after the captain announced we had a date for landfall. Everybody was celebrating, laughing, throwing parties, making plans. It's been stuck in my head and I can't shake it. Hope and joy in the forests ahead. Hope and joy on the plains. Hope and joy. They had no idea what was waiting for [data corruption] so long since I've slept. They've gone quiet. That's worse than the screams. With the screams at least I knew [data corruption]

—FRAGMENT 5, *MOURNFUL EVENING SONG* VIA UC33-X

JAS

I have few memories of my life before *House of Wisdom*, but this is one: a clear, quiet night shortly before we left, at my aunt's lake house in the hills above Dharamsala, sitting by my mother on the dock as cool air tickled my skin and stars glinted overhead.

"Where is it?" I had asked, wanting to see the ship that would be our home.

My mother's arm was warm around my shoulders; her long hair tickled my cheek. Her voice was full of joy. "You can't see it from here. It's too far away. But it's up there. It's ready for us."

Our journey seemed to me little more than a holiday. I was four years old and baffled by all the manic energy and urgency that had gripped my parents in those final days of preparation. I asked how long we were going to stay.

Mum laughed and said, "It's going to be a long, long time. But I bet that as soon as we're up there, you won't want to come back at all. We're going to have so many adventures. There's so much to see. Just you wait."

She kissed my cheek. I squirmed in her arms. I did not know if I ought to laugh too.

"Oh, Jas," she said, "I'm so excited to get up there I could float away."

I had imagined my mother's death a thousand times, but never like this.

They looked so calm in the officers' room. Side by side, my mother and the captain, as though they had sat down for a routine briefing and never rose again.

I had always believed that she must have died much the same as my father: overcome with panic, tearing her own skin. A spray of blood. Thick screams. My mother, who did everything deliberately and thoughtfully, made mindless with fear.

I reached for the door. Xiomara grabbed for my hand, and Baqir said, "Jas, wait." I ignored them. At my touch, the panel flashed green and the door slid open. I passed through and bumped into the foot of the table.

I had not been in this room before, had only glimpsed it from the outside the one time I visited the bridge. There had been a ceremony or celebration of some sort; all of the chief science staff were invited. My mother had spent the hour talking to other engineers about an upcoming propulsion test, but my father, having no interest in their engineering chatter, had instead gazed at the massive screens that showed the view outside. We were passing Jupiter. The true view of the planet was from much farther away, but on the bridge screens it was magnified and glorious. Its red eye, endlessly whirling, had been as big as my father's head. I was eight or nine, just old enough to feel a pang of embarrassment at the childlike wonder on his face, not old enough to keep from staring as well.

Baqir followed me into the officers' room. It was so quiet I could hear him swallow as he considered his words. "They don't look infected," he said.

I nodded mutely, but how could we know for sure? The infected on the bridge had died sitting calmly at their stations.

"Look." He pointed across the table. "Can we find out what they were doing?"

The tablet at the captain's fingertips had a red light slowly pulsing on and off: it was still connected to the ship's power. It was the heavy-duty kind my mother and her engineers had used in her workshop, shielded against temperature extremes and changing atmospheric conditions, made to withstand being bumped and knocked and tossed about. My mind was skipping, like a data transmission with corrupted bytes, and I thought: She brought it here. I thought: That's hers. I thought: Why didn't she come after me?

I thought: She promised. She promised to follow.

I pulled myself around the table and grabbed the tablet. Baqir was at my shoulder, while Ariana and Xiomara watched from the doorway. The only blood in this room was staining my mother's jumpsuit; the tablet was clean. Still I was wary. Every time I looked at Ariana, I searched for the rippling motion beneath her skin, and I caught myself looking for it in Xiomara's face as well, in Baqir's, in my own bare hands. I turned the tablet on.

My mother's face looked out at me. Her black hair was pulled back into a messy knot. There were smudges of exhaustion under her eyes. Her mouth was slightly open, drawing breath or forming a word. It was a frozen image from a log entry. There was a time and date stamp in one corner, a location signifier in the other: 12:35:19 01.04.393. HOUSE OF WISDOM, SPEC RESEARCH.

I keyed the entry to the beginning and played it. The image changed to one showing both Mum and Captain Ngahere. They were seated in the same chairs in which they had died. The captain spoke first.

"This is Captain Lilian Putnam Ngahere of *House of Wisdom*." She cleared her throat. "If you have received this message, you may already know what has happened. We are recording this not to excuse what we are about to do, but to explain how we came to the conclusion that it was necessary. We don't know if we'll be able to transmit it."

Mum shifted in her seat and looked directly at the camera. The torn edge of her collar brushed her cheek. "We assume you are investigating the aftermath of what has happened over the past twenty-four hours. We will tell you what we can. Right now, we have the ship quarantined behind its security web. It is too dangerous to attempt a rescue mission."

To see my mother's face again, to hear her voice, it was like a nova in the center of my chest, a racing pain radiating outward through the long-healed fractures in my bones. She sounded so much like herself, and not like herself at all. Absent was all of the enthusiasm she had carried into her work, the razor-sharp intellect approaching smug superiority, the fervor with which she had argued, the teasing laughter she had reserved for my father and aunt and her closest friends. She was drained of all spark. She sounded defeated.

Captain Ngahere said, "*House of Wisdom* has been attacked by a person or persons unknown. The method of this attack appears to be a blood-borne, neuroengineered pathogen or device capable of complete neurological control over targeted individuals. We don't know the source or the purpose. Most of the infected succumb immediately, many from self-inflicted wounds suffered during an initial stage of infection. Others pursue actions meant to deliberately infect others. But others . . . once the unknown agent has successfully subdued them, this is what it does."

The captain turned the tablet to give the camera a view of the bridge. The screens were lit up with maps and navigation information, feedback from the ship's systems and engines. There seemed to be rather more than a healthy number of flashing red warnings on every display.

And all along the curved banks of terminals there were people at work. None of the crew were speaking. None of them were so much as glancing at their neighbors. None of them turned their heads or looked around at all. Only their hands moved, skating lightning-quick over panels and screens. Every one of them performed their task without glancing down.

It was confirmation of what we had already suspected, but it was still a deeply unsettling sight. There was Jessamyn, twelve years old, with her hands skittering over the navigation controls as though she had flown the ship a hundred times before. Her mouth was slightly open, giving her a fixed expression of surprise. She did not blink.

"We don't know who is controlling them or why," Captain Ngahere said. "We have established that if one of them is disabled, the others pick up the task without any visible communication. We've tried to isolate them, to incapacitate them, to stop them. So far we've failed."

My mother took the tablet from the captain. Her hand grew large, momentarily blocking the view, as she tapped a command. "They don't seem to care that we can watch them. They don't care that we're here at all, not now that they have control of the ship. So we can see what they're doing."

Her image was replaced by a navigation display, a dizzying array of lines and colors and shapes. I tried to make sense of it, feeling the once-familiar sensation of being too slow to follow where my mother's mind was leading.

"The hostile force is altering the ship's navigation constraints.

They have disabled the collision-avoidance mechanism. They have reduced the atmospheric correction to zero. They have removed all of the acceleration dampers. I don't know how they did any of this, but I know the result. They have, in short, disabled every automated and manual component of the ship's drive system that protects it from a planetary collision. They are going to crash the ship into Earth."

"No," I whispered, as though Mum could hear me.

There was a pause, and in the silence Ariana said, her voice hollow, "I thought it was admiring the view."

"We haven't been able to regain control of the ship's navigation and drive systems," Captain Ngahere said. "Every time we try, they catch up. There's no delay between our removing one hostile individual and another taking their place. We haven't been able to disrupt their communication."

"We have one last thing to try," said my mother. "We will attempt to incapacitate the hostile force for long enough to put the ship in a stable orbit."

"Beginning atmospheric quarantine protocol," the captain said.

They were isolating the air in small sections throughout the ship—but they had known the parasite was transferred through blood, not air. I stared at the screen, trying to understand.

My mother took a breath. "Ready with new course calculation. It's going to try to reset the navigation every two seconds. It will get through. Once they aren't stopping it . . . it will get through."

"Okay." Captain Ngahere paused, then looked at my mother. "Okay. Shipwide fire suppression protocol."

"Oh, no," Baqir murmured. On the recording, an alarm began to sound.

The fire suppression protocol meant oxygen would be replaced by carbon dioxide in some places, argon in others. It was meant to deprive a burning fire of fuel. It was meant to be used sparingly, in closed sections, when fires were raging out of control, only after everybody had been safely evacuated.

The crew at the mainframe. The crowd in the garden. The people throughout the ship who had escaped infection. They had remained at their posts or found secure places to cling together in hope. They had been waiting for rescue.

My mother and the captain had found a way to turn the ship's own systems into a weapon against the parasite. But to use it they had to suffocate everybody on board.

"It's done," the captain said. She spoke quietly, as though the effort of expelling those final words defeated her. She looked at my mother, then reached out to take her hand. Their fingers twined together.

"I wish there was another way," my mother said. "Please forgive us."

The log entry ended. Once again her face was frozen in a still image. Eyes clear, mouth open, dark hair in wisps. My heart was pounding so hard I could feel it in my throat.

Ariana was the first to break the silence. "That's what it was trying to make me do? Get right back to where they left off when they . . ."

"This ship is a kilometer long," Xiomara said. "Even if it broke up in the atmosphere, no matter where it crashed, the impact would be catastrophic. Hundreds of thousands of people would die. There would be mass extinctions. It would be . . . it would be a second Collapse."

It was too awful to contemplate, and too easy to imagine. It was part of the answer that had been missing for ten years—and the rest might also be within reach. The screen on the tablet had gone dark.

"We have to get this to SPEC. This and everything else from after the data transfers stopped. They need to know." I looked at the others, hoping they understood. I knew I was asking a lot, stalling our escape. "Then we can leave."

To my relief, nobody protested. They got to work instead.

"We can get a system dump of all the system commands and actions from that day," Baqir said. "If the systems were still compiling summaries, it shouldn't take too long."

Xiomara turned to a console. "I can get the medical info."

"Maybe that will help them get this fucking thing out of me." Ariana offered a brave, trembling smile. "I like that idea. Let's give them everything we can. I'll find the personal logs and messages."

I had not even thought about what the personal logs might contain. How many people might have recorded final messages for their loved ones, how many tears and goodbyes, how many last words spoken in fear and despair. I did not tell Ariana not to do it, because I knew she was right, but part of me wanted to stop her. The families had suffered enough. The dead were dead, and their voices should not be dragged from this crypt, for no solace or comfort would come from hearing what they had suffered at the end. I said nothing. It was not my decision to make. I had my mother's final message, though it was not directed at me. I had my father's final words echoing in my mind. Others deserved the same, even if it brought them no peace.

"What I don't understand is, who would want to do something like this?" Ariana said suddenly. "What possible reason could they have?"

"I know SPEC had reasons for blaming Dr. Lago, but they don't make much sense anymore," Xiomara said. "This doesn't look like revenge that got out of hand."

"Unless there was something way more fucked up than data theft going on," Baqir said. "Can we—"

"Find the data he was hiding? Yeah, I'll look for it," I said.

Only two fragments of recovered and restored data from

UC33-X had been released to the public before the massacre. The rest, the parts of the data Lago had hidden from his colleagues and worked on in secret, had been held back pending the results of the investigation into his actions. But only two days had passed between his dismissal from the ship and the massacre, and Lago died by suicide only a few days after that.

In the archive I found five additional restored fragments that had never been made public. They were short passages, no more than a couple hundred words each. I read them quickly one by one.

Then I read them again, more slowly.

"Fuck," Baqir breathed, reading over my shoulder. "This is about the planet they found."

"We already know they found a planet," Xiomara said.

"We didn't know there was an archaeological excavation."

Xiomara started to reply, then turned to look at us. "But that means—"

"It means they found the ruins of an alien civilization."

For a moment, none of us spoke. The claustrophobic closeness of the ship faded away, and with it the dead, the persistent red light, the blood.

Before the Collapse, as the world descended into chaos and darkness, those with the means had identified planets like Earth and aimed their generation ships toward them, hoping to find a home unspoiled by what humanity had done to Earth. But the ships had fallen silent one by one, and the dream of finding life on another planet had faded away. The people who survived the Collapse had focused on rebuilding civilization on Earth. There was a famous quotation from Leung Ma-Lin carved above the entrance to every Councils building across the globe, said to be the words she spoke when opening the First Council four hundred years ago: "First, we heal our home and ourselves."

But as humankind soared back into the stars, we began to look again. It was still the dream that filled the dark spaces in the sky when people gazed upward and wondered. Dr. Lago's recovery of these messages would have marked him as the father of one of humankind's greatest discoveries. He had kept them from his colleagues because he wanted all the acclaim for himself. Such a petty, human thing to do, in the face of such knowledge.

Mournful Evening Song had traveled to a planet that had once been home to an alien civilization. And they sent UC33-X back not as a greeting, but as a warning, because what they found there had destroyed them.

W e left the bridge. The cold, dark hallway curved out of sight in both directions. I turned to the left and grabbed a handle on the wall, trying to remember the fastest way to Level 12. The bridge had been full of ambient noise, the persistent hum of a functioning ship, but beyond its walls the unnatural silence returned. I was reaching for the next handhold when I saw a flicker of light ahead.

I held out my arm to warn the others. The flicker steadied into a beam. I hadn't listened for our captors before we left the bridge. My helmet and its radio were hooked uselessly to my belt. Stupidly, *stupidly,* I had forgotten about them.

A voice carried down the corridor: "Did you hear that?"

Panya. Not muffled or echoing through a microphone. She had taken off her helmet.

There was no answer, only the soft sound of gloves scraping over the walls: somebody was using friction to stop themselves. The beam of light stilled. I pressed myself close to the inner wall of the curved hallway and gestured for the others to do the same.

"I heard something," Panya said. She was speaking in a loud whisper, but the words carried. "Didn't you?"

"Quiet." That was Dag, the bald, unsmiling one whose face seemed carved from stone. "I'll check it out. Wait here."

I didn't hear Zahra or Malachi. The light ahead moved, and the shadow of a person stretched around the corridor. I gestured urgently, motioning for the others to turn and head in the other direction. Baqir had been bringing up the rear; he was at the head of the line now. When he reached the door to the bridge, he glanced back at me, inclining his head with a silent question. I waved for him to keep going. Xiomara was right behind him. Ariana followed, but the sleeve of her space suit caught on the handhold; she jerked her arm in frustration. I reached out to pry the snagged material free. She looked at me, then looked down at her hand, bending her fingers into a fist for a moment. I wanted to ask her if she was hurt, but I didn't dare speak. I nudged her onward. Baqir and Xiomara had already disappeared around the curve in the hallway.

We passed the entrance to the bridge as the light behind us grew brighter.

Then, from ahead, Xiomara's voice came clearly: "Hey, don't—"

She was cut off by a wordless shout of surprise. Ariana kicked away from the wall, arrowing herself toward the shouts. I was right behind her. Shadows danced wildly in the low red light.

Baqir shouted, "Let me go!" I rounded the bend in the hallway just in time to see Dag grab him by the arm. Dag had come around the opposite direction, moving swiftly and silently while we fled Panya and her light.

Baqir struck at the man's face, at his torso, at the hand that was holding his weapon, but Dag dodged the blows easily. He swung Baqir around by his prosthetic arm, and Baqir screamed. I heard something creak, heard something crack, then Dag released him, and Baqir slammed into the wall. The horrible whimper he made on impact was so much worse than the scream had been. I couldn't see his face. He curled into an instinctive ball, not even trying to grab a handhold or right himself. I pushed over to him, but I had no more than touched his back before he let out another cry of pain.

Xiomara launched herself at Dag feetfirst, her boots aiming directly for his head, and Ariana flung herself forward to grab his arm. He dodged to the side, and Xiomara hit his shoulder, deflecting herself into a sideways spin; he caught her ankle and whipped her away from him. She struck the wall with a loud grunt, then flailed for the nearest handhold. Dag hit Ariana across the face, sending her spinning away easily. Momentarily stunned by the blow, with her nose and lip bleeding, she floated past me and right into Panya, who had come around behind us.

Panya grabbed Ariana by the neck, catching her beneath the chin. Ariana twisted to the side and bit Panya's hand, hard enough that Panya let out a surprised shout.

"Stop." Dag's voice was a calm rumble. "All of you. Stop."

He had caught Xiomara again; his gun was pressed to the back of her head. Panya still had a grip on Ariana's throat. I clung to the wall with one hand, too afraid to move away from Baqir, not daring to leave him insensible with pain. His artificial arm floated at an unnatural angle from his side. He was breathing heavily, sucking in ragged breaths and forcing them out again, every one accompanied by a faint groan.

"We have a lot of work to do," Panya said calmly. She shoved Ariana away and aimed her gun. "Into the bridge, all of you."

[data corruption] supposed to be an invitation. Come to our paradise. A world humanity hasn't ruined. Come see the beauty we've discovered. We were such fucking fools. The people who lived here, whoever they were, whatever they were, they were in love with beauty. You can see it in everything they did. This must have been a beautiful planet, once. But we weren't the first to find it.

—FRAGMENT 6, *MOURNFUL EVENING SONG* VIA UC33-X

Get them back." I slapped at the terminal. Anwar's screams still rang in my ears. "Get them back!"

"Zahra." Malachi reached for my hand.

I shook him off. "We need to talk to them. We have to make them understand."

"He won't listen," Malachi said. "Zahra. He's not going to listen."

I didn't want him to be right. I could not have failed so badly that there was no way to fix it. Adam had flown into rages before. He had made irrational and dangerous decisions. It was our responsibility to ease the hurt, to protect him from the petty cruelties of life so that he might lead us—or so he had always claimed. The punishment for failing was swift and great. When the lashes were counted, when the banished were driven away, we told ourselves the transgressors deserved it. Only the disloyal failed to do what Adam needed them to do.

There was a hard knot in my chest, right between my lungs. I had done everything Adam asked of me. But our dream was built on a lie. Nothing Adam could do, no speech he could give, no punishment he could render, would change that.

"We have to do *something*," I said. The words scraped my throat, and tears stung my eyes.

"We'll contact SPEC," Malachi said. There was no hesitation in his voice, not the least hint of doubt. "We'll contact that ship that's been waiting."

"Why would SPEC help us?" I said, incredulous. "That's not what they do. They'll throw us in prison. They'll tear the family apart. You know that. You're not thinking clearly."

"We need help." His voice was calm and unyielding, his expression solemn, but as he spoke my skin prickled.

"What do you mean, waiting?" I asked. "Waiting for what? Waiting for *us*?"

"Zahra. We don't have much time."

"Do you think they knew we were coming here? But they could have stopped us at Civita Station if they . . . You said that." My voice faltered, dropping to a hoarse whisper. "You just said that. If they wanted to stop us, they could have."

"Zahra," Malachi said quietly.

I needed him to stop saying my name. "How did they know we were coming here? Did you tell them? Did you go to them? Is that how you were able to get through the security net? What did they promise you?" My voice was rising, my hands shaking, anger washing over me like a storm. He didn't deny it. He didn't even look surprised by the accusation, and that was the worst reaction I could have imagined. "Do you hate us that much?"

"I don't hate you," Malachi said.

"Don't fucking lie to me. You betrayed us. What did they offer you? Did they offer to make you a citizen? Was that your price for betraying Adam? Betraying us?"

"Zahra. That's not what happened. I came from SPEC."

I stared at him. "What?"

"I've been a Councils citizen since I was a child."

"But you . . . you came to us."

"I found the homestead because I was looking for it. That was my assignment."

I could barely speak. "I don't believe you."

But I did, and I could not even manage disdain enough to hide the crushing feeling of dismay. He was a SPEC agent. He had been a traitor all along. The stories he had told about applying for citizenship, being turned away at the border, giving up hope, they were lies. I had thought he was my friend.

"Why?" I asked. "Why would you do that? Did they send you for Adam?"

Malachi shook his head. "I wasn't looking for Adam. My mission had nothing to do with him. The Councils don't care about him. They've never cared about him. There are men like him all over the desert, building wretched little kingdoms that collapse as soon as they're made. He was never a target. Do you understand what I'm saying, Zahra? SPEC has never been interested in Adam or his followers."

"But the raids. The sicknesses. The disappearances."

All the times Adam had claimed we had to stay one step ahead of the Councils to survive their schemes. All the times he insisted our crops had failed because they were poisoning our fields. Every single time we lost members of our family and Adam said they had been stolen away by the Councils, taken to interrogation chambers deep beneath a secret base, tortured for our secrets. All the drills, the patrols, the preparation for midnight raids, the punishments dealt to anybody who compromised our safety and security.

Malachi's voice was full of pity. "He's always been very good at convincing the family that you need him."

"I don't believe you," I said again.

But I had never seen the Councils soldiers surrounding our

homestead; I had only heard the sirens and Adam's exhortations to stand strong. I had never tasted poison in our food or water; I had only learned how hard it was to scrape a living from the ailing desert wasteland. I had never seen any family members dragged away by Councils agents. I had only ever seen them walk away, and never return.

It had all been a lie. We were never in any danger. Our only prison had been the fevered paranoia of Adam's mind. Our greatest weakness was how easily we believed him.

"Then what were you looking for?" I asked. "What does SPEC want from us?"

"I was looking for you. Your family."

I could not breathe.

"My mission was to locate Gregory Lago's widow. Mariah Dove."

It had been so long since I had heard my mother's name spoken aloud.

"SPEC Intel believed she had to know something about her husband's actions. We needed to know who he had been working with and how he acquired a Pre-Collapse biological weapon that was supposed to be locked away in a secure archive. Dr. Dove had done immunological research. She visited several laboratories in her career."

"Danzmayr's disease," I said weakly. "That's what she studied. She was looking for a cure. She hated that the Councils didn't devote the necessary resources to it because it only affected North Americans. She never knew anything about what happened here. But they didn't believe her. They hounded her at the hospital, everywhere she went."

"I know," Malachi said.

"They never left us alone. That's why she took us to the desert."

"I know." He cleared his throat. "By the time we confirmed she didn't know anything, we had already learned about Adam's plan.

The orders were to observe and report. To see how far it would go. Not to interfere."

"Your orders."

He said nothing.

"You keep saying *we*. But it was you. You were spying on us."

"Zahra," he said. I had never heard my name like that, a wound torn open.

Six years ago a dirty, bedraggled, starvation-thin young man had walked out of the desert, and it had been no accident. He had not stumbled upon our homestead because it was the only source of warmth and light for miles. He had not scuffed his bare feet on the rocks behind me because I was the least threatening guard; he had been looking for me all along. I had brought him to meet Adam and my family. We had listened, rapt, to his stories of hardship and humiliation at the hands of the Councils. My mother had given him a mug of hot tea and smiled when he thanked her. She always tried to bring comfort to those who needed it.

"How long have you worked for them?" I asked.

"Nine years."

Something inside me crumpled, the last ashy log of a fire falling to dust. He was older than he looked. They would have chosen him because he was so nonthreatening, with his brown eyes and curly hair, his kind smile.

My vision blurred with tears. "Why didn't you stop us? Why did you let us come here, if you knew what it was like?"

"Zahra," Malachi said. He moved his hand, as though to reach for mine, but did not. "I didn't know it was like this. I swear to you, we didn't know. I had no idea there were secrets SPEC was keeping even from its own people."

"Somebody must have known. The people you work for? None of them knew?"

"The mission was to observe and report," Malachi said. "And retrieve data."

"Retrieve—you mean from the ship. Have you been doing that?"

For the briefest second, Malachi's lips twitched with a wry smile. "I was until Panya took my skeleton key."

If what Malachi was saying was true, we had been nothing more than a means by which SPEC Intelligence could sneak an agent aboard—a mission the Councils had been refusing to authorize for ten years.

"You're not even supposed to be here," I said. "Officially. Are you?"

Malachi's smile was gone. "You know what? I have no fucking idea. I know what my handler thinks I should know. And until we got to this place, I thought that he'd told me everything. But now . . ." He exhaled sharply, his breath a thin white cloud. "There are people in SPEC who have wanted to come back to *House of Wisdom* for years. I guess somebody got tired of waiting."

The worst of it, I thought, was that I had once believed I could tell when he was lying. But he had been lying to me for six years—and to people far more suspicious than me. He had convinced Boudicca, who had been a SPEC pilot herself. He had convinced Adam, who saw spies and traitors in every shadow. He had convinced all of us.

"My mother never knew anything," I said. "And my father did not kill anybody. Your whole mission was pointless before it even began."

"I know that now," he said. "And I will make sure everybody knows it. I will make sure the whole world knows it. I promise you, Zahra, I will see that they learn the truth. But we can't do that alone. I'm contacting *Pangong*. Captain Chavannes will help."

He was not asking for agreement. "*Pangong*, this is *House of Wis-*

dom. Captain Chavannes, do you copy?" He adjusted something and tried again. "*Pangong*, this is *House of Wisdom*. Do you copy? I don't understand. The radio is functional, but the transmission is blocked by a new command code—shit."

A low hum rose from the walls and machines around us. I felt it as much as I heard it, a vibration born in my bones, at the base of my throat, behind my eyes. I looked around frantically, but Malachi's attention was fixed on the terminal.

"Shit," he said again. He tapped in a series of commands, but nothing happened. "Shit shit *shit!*"

"What is it? What's that sound?" I asked.

"It's the ship," Malachi said. "It's waking up. Panya and Dag are on the bridge."

My stomach twisted. "They have control of the ship?"

"Not yet," Malachi said with an expression that was almost a smile, or a grimace. "My skeleton key can only get them so far. We have to stop them before they get farther."

The ring corridor around the ship's bridge was lit with bright white light. I had thought the low dormancy red was bad, giving the ship a dingy look no matter where we went, but with the glaring emergency lights on, *House of Wisdom* looked even more like a derelict. There were splatters of blood with no attendant corpses, handprint smears along the wall, discarded tools floating in corners, doors scratched, panels smashed, wires exposed.

To say that Malachi and I had a plan would be more generous than we deserved. All we knew was that we had to get onto the bridge. We could not risk allowing Panya and Dag to control this ship and welcome *Homestead* to *House of Wisdom*.

"Get over there. Move."

I stopped at the sound of Dag's voice from up ahead. His words were firm, with a trace of impatience.

The answer came from a woman: "Okay, okay. We're going."

I felt only a small pang of surprise. They had found the hostages. I pulled myself along the curved wall until I saw the entrance to the bridge. Malachi was right behind me. I had no idea what he was thinking. I didn't know who he was, now that he had shed his false persona. I didn't even know if Malachi was his real name. He nodded, urging me through the door.

It was not Panya or Dag who noticed me first. It was the woman who had killed Henke. The one who had taken his weapon and fled. Ariana.

"What is she doing here?" Malachi said, his voice ringing with the same surprise I felt.

Panya and Dag both turned to face us. Dag was guarding the hostages, his weapon raised.

Panya was seated at a terminal. When she looked up, her expression brightened. "Oh! I am so glad to see you!"

I stared at her in disbelief. "You're glad to see us?"

"What is she doing here?" Malachi said again, pointing at Ariana. "She's infected. She can't be here."

She didn't look infected. She looked scared, and a bit angry, but perfectly in control. She no longer had Henke's gun. She and the other hostages had their backs to a glass wall on the far side of the bridge. Bhattacharya's friend, Nassar, was badly hurt; his prosthetic arm had been twisted at a horrible angle, and there was blood from his shoulder soaking the collar of his shirt.

Behind the glass wall there were ten, fifteen, twenty corpses, all shoved haphazardly into a room too small to hold them. It was a puzzle-tangle of limbs and faces. I could not bear to look at it. I could not look away.

Panya laughed. "Don't be so gullible. She was never infected. It was a ruse to help them escape."

"It wasn't," Ariana said. "We've already told them. I was infected."

"We know. We've learned more about the virus," Malachi said.

"We can show you," I said, aware of the desperate whine in my voice. "There's a message from one of the scientists. Panya, Dag, please listen. She's infected. It was in the blood. It's always been in the blood."

"She seems fine to me," Dag said.

"Because we incapacitated the parasite," Bhattacharya said. "We don't know if it's permanent."

"Convenient, isn't it?" Panya said. She held up a black weapon—not a gun, but a nonlethal suppression weapon, not something we had brought aboard. "They claim to have used this. But these are all over the ship and they didn't help anybody before, did they? Come here, Malachi. We need your help."

"We're not going to help you," I said, incredulous. "You tried to kill us!"

Before he could answer, Panya sent the suppression weapon spinning away across the bridge and took her gun from her holster. She pointed it at me. "Zahra, you're being hysterical. You know that transgressions against the good of the family must be punished. Malachi will turn off the security web so *Homestead* can approach safely."

I was so angry I was trembling. "But if they can incapacitate the—did you call it a parasite? Not a virus?"

"They're talking nonsense," Dag said. "Don't listen to them."

"We are not!" Xiomara said. "For fuck's sake, listen to us!"

A parasite, I thought. Dr. Summers had not known. But she had believed it was a weapon, sent back by *Mournful Evening Song*. A parasite could be a weapon as easily as a virus.

Panya gestured impatiently. "Malachi, don't make me ask again."

"What do you want?"

"Security drones first. Then you're going to fly the ship."

He glanced at me as he shouldered past, a lightning-quick look I could not read, and moved toward Panya's terminal and reached over her shoulder. She grabbed his wrist and twisted herself out of her chair, turning to face him. She held his wrist so tightly he flinched; the tips of her nails broke his skin, and droplets of blood welled around her grimy, clenching fingers. There was a bite mark on Panya's hand, a neat half-moon of punctured skin. I wondered which of the hostages had done that.

"You will do exactly what I tell you and nothing else," Panya said. "Do you understand? Please don't make this difficult for us."

Malachi tried to pull his arm away. Panya only dug in harder.

"Do you understand?"

"I understand," he said. "Let go of me."

Panya tilted her head to one side, the same way she always did when she was trying to intimidate somebody. When I was younger, I had found that look crushing, to know I had disappointed her so badly, but now I saw only an empty coldness. The calm I had always taken for serenity seemed to me now to be the same calm of a snake before it struck.

She let go of Malachi's wrist. He slid into the seat and set to work, calling up report after report, switching between displays, moving so fast it was impossible to tell if he was following Panya's directive or not. He couldn't be. He was a SPEC agent. He had to be working for his own agenda, not hers. But I didn't know enough to be certain—nor, I hoped, did Panya.

"Tell me about the parasite," I said to Bhattacharya. "How did you kill it?"

"Stop humoring them, Zahra," Panya said idly.

"Electric shock." Bhattacharya glanced at Ariana as he spoke, but she said nothing. She was looking steadily at Dag, her gaze focused on his weapon. Bhattacharya went on, "It's biomechanical. We think the shock shorted it out."

"We found out by accident," Xiomara said.

They had gotten away, then they had been caught again, and now there was a room of corpses at their backs and a weapon aimed at their heads. I could not tell if they were lying. I could not guess what reason they might have. I knew, in their place, I would say anything to placate my captors, and this did not seem to be placating Panya.

"Dag, make them stop talking," Panya said. She nudged Malachi's shoulder with her weapon. "Well? Can you restart the rest of the systems?"

"As far as I can tell, the ship's engines are functioning normally." Malachi didn't look away from the screens, didn't look at any of us. "There are a lot of systems failure alerts, but nothing critical. Nothing to keep the ship from traveling. Is that what you wanted to know?"

She leaned over his shoulder, arm braced on the terminal to hold herself in place. "Our vision has not changed, Malachi, even if you and Zahra have lost sight of it. Our duty is clear. We will rendezvous with *Homestead*. Shut down the security web."

A moment of quiet, then Malachi said, "Done. It will take a few minutes for the drones to return to their hull docks, but the web is disabled."

"Contact them now."

Malachi hesitated. "Orvar is dead. I don't know who—"

There was a crack as she slapped his cheek. "Do not stall. Contact *Homestead*."

Malachi touched his face where she had hit him, then reached for the terminal. He stilled with his hand centimeters above the surface.

"Panya," he said softly.

He grabbed her wrist. She looked down. There was something moving beneath her skin. It looked like a small, round stone pressing up from the inside, rolling along her forearm toward her elbow.

There was a moment of stillness—a second in which nobody breathed—then everybody was moving at once.

Dag swung his weapon away from the hostages toward Panya without the slightest hesitation. Malachi twisted Panya around, jamming her arm up behind her back and slamming her face down onto the communications panel. The force of the blow was enough to stun Panya for a moment; she released the gun from her other hand. I darted forward to grab it. Panya shrieked and kicked at Malachi, trying to fight and flail.

"Let me go! What the fuck are you doing? *Let me go!*"

Malachi held her tight. "You're infected."

A look of pure shock overtook her face. "I am not!"

"Panya. Listen to me!"

Then Dag was beside him, taking hold of her other arm, dragging her away from the terminal. She was screaming and thrashing, spluttering with fear as she shouted, "Let me go! Dag, don't believe him! Help me!"

For a second, only a second, Dag hesitated. It was enough. Panya wrenched one arm free and swung at him, but she missed Dag and struck Malachi's cheek instead. Dag grabbed her arm and tried to wrestle it back behind her. As she cursed and fought, spittle pinked with blood sprayed from a bitten tongue or split lip. Malachi spared a second to wipe his face before reaching for her again.

"No!"

The shout rang across the bridge. It was Bhattacharya, with Xiomara echoing the word a moment later, but before I could even react, Ariana slammed into Malachi from the side. She caught a chair and turned to launch herself toward Malachi again. Her expression was slack, her mouth slightly open, her eyes unblinking.

The woman was gone. The virus—parasite—whatever it was—had returned.

Ariana's shoulder struck Malachi in the center of his chest, knocking him away from Panya. He twisted swiftly and grabbed for her, hands raking over her short hair and face, seeking leverage to hoist her away.

"Don't hurt her!" Xiomara screamed.

"The shock weapon," Bhattacharya said. "Use the fucking shock weapon!"

Dag wrestled Panya away from Malachi and Ariana with one hand, reaching with the other for the suppression weapon tucked into his belt. He had Panya's arm twisted behind her back, and she was shouting at him to stop, to let her go, but Dag ignored her. Her gun was warm in my hand. I didn't know who to aim it at. The other suppression weapon, the one Panya had shown us, was across the bridge, spinning toward the ceiling.

Ariana broke free of Malachi's grasp and reached for his neck with both hands. Dag raised his arm, and there was a loud snap. Ariana jerked, her entire body tense. A spiderweb of blue light rolled through her, just beneath the skin.

For a second—long enough for Malachi to shove her away, no longer—she was completely, utterly still. Her eyes wide, her mouth open, the eerie blue light fading, every limb stiff and motionless.

"It worked." Panya was breathing heavily. "It worked. Let me—"

Ariana whirled around so quickly she became a blur of motion. She raked her hands across Malachi's face and took hold of his ear, moving even more swiftly than she had been before.

Dag fired the shock weapon again, but this time it had no effect on Ariana aside from the briefest flutter of blue light. Her face was still blank; she didn't even blink as Malachi struck at her face, grabbed her wrist, trying to break her hold on him.

"Are you going to stop making a fuss now," Ariana said flatly. "Are you going to stop making a fuss now. Are you going to stop making a fuss now."

"No," Xiomara said, breathless. *"No."*

Ariana and Malachi turned and turned in a circle, neither one breaking free, neither letting go. When Ariana's back was to me, without thinking, without letting myself reconsider, I lifted the gun, and I fired. The shot spun me backward; I hit a console with such force it sent waves of pain through my battered back and legs. Malachi and Ariana moved at that same moment, still locked together in a desperate struggle, and the shot missed Ariana by centimeters. Panya screamed as the projectile sliced across her upper arm. Behind her an eruption of red blossomed on Dag's chest.

The projectile exploded on impact. It tore Dag's arm from his shoulder and propelled him backward through the open door of the glass room, dragging Panya with him. A cloud of his blood enveloped them as they bumped into the floating tangle of corpses.

Malachi caught Ariana's jaw with a lucky blow that shoved her away from him. He grabbed the nearest chair, twisted to give himself leverage, and kicked her solidly in the back before she could recover. The force of the kick pushed her through the doorway; she thumped into Panya and Dag.

Dag's heart still pumped blood from his wound, but weakly, weakly, and there was no light of awareness in his expression. Panya, trapped between them, her screams now fallen to whimpers, tried to push Ariana away.

Ariana grabbed her by both wrists. "Are you going to stop making a fuss now," she said.

Panya spit in her face and kicked at her legs. "I'm not infected! Get her off me! Get her off me! *Zahra! Help me!*"

But even as she was screaming and fighting, splattered with Dag's blood and bleeding slowly from the wound on her arm, there was a ripple of movement on the curve of her shoulder, along the line of her collarbone. The small bead elongated to a short, squirming line.

Malachi moved toward the panel to shut the door, wiping a spray of blood from his face.

"Malachi," I said, my voice shaking. I raised the gun.

He looked at me. "What? Zahra, what are you—"

"You're covered with her blood."

"I know, I know, but you need help."

"She broke the skin on your arm. She spit in your face."

"I *know*," he said again, more urgently. "We need time. I can—"

Panya screamed. She thrashed at Dag's body, her arms whipping through the cloud of his blood, and she was screaming, screaming, and somehow through her screams I could make out what she was saying: *"It's coming out, oh fuck, it's coming out!"*

From the wound on her arm, a silver tendril reached into the air. It was thin and flexible, gleaming with a metallic shine beneath the glistening red blood. It looked like a wire, but it moved like a living thing, a reaching, *searching* thing, twisting and bending as it slithered from the bloody scrape on Panya's upper arm.

Another one joined it, sliding from the mess of blood and skin, slowly, as though it was nosing its way into unknown territory. They could have been threads or hairs, they were so fine, so uniform, but they moved with purpose. Surrounded by so much blood, by so much death, they seemed so tiny, so slender. Their silver bodies caught the light as they bent and turned.

Another thread rippled beneath Panya's skin, racing along

her neck and jaw, over her fine cheekbones and toward her eyes. Her screams cut off with a strangled gasp. Her eyes widened—something silver and bright flicked across the blue—then her entire face went slack.

I moved without thinking, kicking toward the door—I had to close it, had to stop *them* from escaping that room—but Malachi was closer than me, and faster. He spun himself through the door, caught the frame to turn and grab the inside panel. He punched in a command. Panya and Ariana watched him expressionlessly, with no indication they comprehended what he was doing.

"Are you going to stop making a fuss now," Panya said, and Ariana echoed her a second later, their words just offset from being in unison. "Are you going to stop making a fuss now."

Panya launched herself at Malachi, surprising him with a solid blow to the back. There was a loud thump as his head struck the glass wall, but he recovered quickly to shove her away.

"You have to contact SPEC," he said, dodging Panya's grasping hands. "Zahra!"

"Are you going to stop making a fuss now," Panya said, raking her fingers along Malachi's arm and shoulders, clawing and grasping. There was no expression on her face. The silver worms that had crawled from her arm were wriggling back in, the ends of their tails whipping as they burrowed into her veins. "Are you going to stop making a fuss now. Are you going to—"

Malachi pulled Panya's head back by the hair and slammed it into the wall. Then he did it again, and again, hitting Panya's head into the glass until she stopped fighting. Her face—her beautiful face, her fine cheekbones, her sky-blue eyes—it was all a mess of blood from her split lip and gushing nose. Malachi shoved her away and kicked over to the door again, dodging Ariana's attempt to grab him, and jabbed hurriedly at the panel.

There was a metallic clank as the door closed and locked. He tapped a series of commands, then smashed his fist into the control panel just as Ariana was reaching for his neck.

"Zahra! You have to contact SPEC. The security web is off. They can come get you. Do you understand?" He ducked away from Ariana again, reaching for the shock weapon still clenched in Dag's hand.

"I—yes!" I answered, but I was shaking my head. "The radio— is it—"

"They'll be trying to contact us," he said. "The ship is yours now."

"But they won't—"

"Make them listen," he said. He fired the suppression weapon at Ariana, but once again it had no effect. She grabbed his free arm and pulled him toward her, not even flinching as he kicked her solidly in the abdomen. "You have to tell them about what's here."

"I know," I said. A single silver thread had emerged from the bloody wreck of Panya's face. It twisted and curved, dancing through the clumps of blood.

"No, listen to me, you can't let them . . . You. Bhattacharya." Malachi thumped his hand on the glass wall. "Don't let them cover this up. Any of it. Tell your aunt everything. Do you understand?"

Bhattacharya nodded shortly. "Yes."

"Don't let them make you lie like they did before," Malachi said.

Bhattacharya nodded again.

"Zahra."

I swallowed. I was still holding the gun, and my hand was sweaty, my fingers aching with tension. I could fire at the glass. I could get him out. Maybe it wasn't too late. A bigger shock, help from doctors, from somebody, maybe—

"Zahra, I'm so sorry. Make sure they know the truth. You deserve that. I never meant—"

He stopped suddenly. One hand clutched instinctively at his neck. His lips moved, but there was no sound emerging except a hoarse rasp. His eyes went wide and he looked around quickly, one arm still anchored by Ariana's unbreakable grip. He kicked the wall to give himself momentum, reaching with one hand for the gun at Dag's belt. In the blink of an eye, he turned it on Ariana and fired. Her chest ruptured in a ragged wet burst.

Then, just as quickly, Malachi turned the weapon on himself. One second the muzzle was pressed to the bottom of his chin. The next his head was gone.

After the crack of the shot, the only sound that came from the glass room was the gurgling, wheezing rasp from what was left of Panya's ruined face. All around them, in a slow, elegant dance, silver worms twisted and twisted in clouds of blood.

The hostages were silent, stunned. Nassar had his uninjured hand clamped over his mouth. Xiomara was at the wall, hands pressed to the surface, mist surrounding her fingers where warm skin met cold glass.

"She's gone," Bhattacharya said quietly.

"I know."

"It's only the—"

"I know," Xiomara said. Her breath fogged the glass. "I fucking hate those things."

Three strangers, and a gun. I looked down at the weapon in my hand. It was identical to the one I had used to kill the man on the shuttle. SPEC Security use only, highly restricted, these weapons and their ammunition had been difficult to acquire, in some ways harder than the false identities that got us aboard Civita Station and *Pilgrim 3*. SPEC wanted people to want to go to space; they did not want anybody to go armed. Before today I had never killed anybody. I could tell myself that I had never meant to, but I had no strength left for the kind of slithering lies that had carried me for so long. I had always known people might die. I had simply told myself they were less important than our dream. We had all repeated it, around and around all of our plans and plots, nodding at ever more vehement exhortations until every doubt was quashed.

They were all gone. Everybody I had chosen for this mission, everybody I had brought to this hateful place, they were all dead. We had failed to claim the ship, *Homestead* was still heading into danger, and I was alone with three strangers who had no reason to listen to anything I had to say, and every reason to hate me.

All I had were the words of Dr. Summers in the laboratory. Proof that my father had not done what the Councils claimed he had done. I could clear his name. I could restore the memory of who he had been to the world, and to Nadra and Anwar. But I could not do it alone. The world would not listen to me, not after all I had done.

I looked at Bhattacharya, trying to see the broken boy who had not cried at his parents' funerals in this dirty and exhausted man. It was hard to remember why those images of him had once filled me with such rage.

I passed the gun from one hand to the other and flexed the fingers that had been gripping it so tightly. They noticed the motion, my former hostages, and all three reacted. Bhattacharya moved himself in front of his injured friend. Xiomara scowled deeply as she turned to face me.

"Oh, fuck you," she said tiredly. "Haven't you done enough?"

I turned the gun to grasp it by the muzzle, and I held it out to Bhattacharya. He didn't move.

"The virus—parasite—it came from UC33-X."

Bhattacharya said, "We know." He was watching me closely.

"We found a log entry from Dr. Summers in the lab where it— where it was released. She tried to tell them. Everybody. She left a message."

"Why do you care?" Xiomara said. "What do you want?"

She sounded scornful, as though she could not believe I could provide an answer. But what else was there left to want? Everything I had yearned for, a home that was a sanctuary, a place in the stars, a window where I could look upon the universe with Nadra and Anwar beside me and know they were well, it was impossible, it had always been impossible, a barren dream with no more chance of lasting than a desert thunderstorm, every violent crack of thunder fading even as it reverberated from the flanks of the mountains.

"I only want people to know the truth," I said. "And to stop *Homestead* from coming here. That's all."

Finally, carefully, Bhattacharya reached to take the weapon from my hand.

The silver threads danced, gleaming with blood, slow, searching, reaching out from their dead hosts. The motion of one thread was tugging Ariana's arm and making her fingers bend. Another made the muscles in Panya's cheek twitch. The parasites moving through each body looked, on the outside, like puppet strings tugging from the inside.

I didn't know what to do with the gun, so I tucked it into my belt.

"We could kill you right now," Xiomara said to Zahra.

"Xi," Baqir said. His voice was weak, barely more than breath. He needed medical help, more than we could provide, and soon.

Xiomara looked at me, looked at Zahra, then said, "If you do a single thing to fuck us over . . ."

"I won't," Zahra said.

"What was that guy talking about, don't let them cover it up?" Xiomara asked.

"Malachi was . . ." Zahra swallowed. "He was a SPEC agent. I didn't know until today."

"That's not possible," Xiomara said. "SPEC wouldn't have let this happen. They would have stopped you."

They weren't looking at the dead anymore, but I could not stop staring. Thin lines rippled beneath their skin, moving like shadows along Malachi's arms, under the rainbow spikes of Ariana's hair, along the curve of Panya's neck. It was easy to see now what had been moving my father's body behind the bathroom door, and why it had been so much clumsier than Ariana when she was under the parasite's control. There was no life there, no thought, no sentience. There was only that elegant silver worm trying to manipulate the clumsy husk of its dead host.

"They didn't want to stop them," I said.

I tore my eyes away from the dead to find the living staring at me.

"SPEC has wanted to come back here for years, but the Councils keep shutting down any proposal for another attempt," I explained. "Maybe some people decided to try anyway."

"What do you mean? In secret?" Xiomara said.

"I don't know. It's possible."

"Malachi thought it was too," Zahra said.

I was trying to think about it as Aunt Padmavati would think about it, looking at every angle, every shadowy gap between what was known in secret and what the public believed. There were factions within SPEC, as there were in any sprawling governing commission, and among them were those who certainly believed that another mission was worth the risk. They had been thwarted many times by the Councilors, like my aunt, who did not want *House of Wisdom* to claim even one more life.

I would never have suspected the nervous young man with the curly hair and brown eyes of being a SPEC Intel agent—but if I had, he would not have made it this far. I moved over to the comm where Malachi had been working, slid into the chair, and hooked my feet to hold myself in place.

"What are you doing?" Xiomara asked, following me.

"Calling for help. We have to get away from here."

"Can we use the evacuation suits now?" Xiomara asked.

"We need to contact SPEC first, to warn them."

"What was it called—*Pangong*?" Baqir asked, his voice thready with pain. It was hard to see how much damage Dag had done, as removing his suit for a better look might do more harm, but the jut of his shoulder beneath the space suit was all wrong, angular and seeping blood where the prosthetic ended.

"Stop moving," I said. "You'll hurt yourself worse."

I looked over the display, trying to make sense of what I was seeing. I blinked quickly and rubbed my eyes. Malachi had been telling the truth. The ship was ours. There were no more command overrides, no more quarantine protocols. The radio was functional and waiting.

I opened a channel. "Um, *Pangong*, this is *House of Wisdom*. Can you hear us? Can anybody hear us? This is *House of Wisdom*."

The response was instantaneous. A woman in a SPEC uniform appeared on the display at the front of the room, her brown face looming larger than life. Compared to *House of Wisdom*, the bridge of *Pangong* was so clean and bright it seemed unreal, like what a child would imagine a spaceship to be. The woman had a crown of braids and captain's star on her collar. Her uniform was crisp, her expression alert.

"We hear you, *House of Wisdom*," she said. "This is Captain Chavannes of *Pangong*. You're Jaswinder Bhattacharya, aren't you?"

I felt sick with relief. "Yes, I am."

"Are you safe? What's your status?"

"We're safe for now," I said, hoping it was true. With every movement, I felt itches on my skin, tickles on the back of my neck, but I had no abrasions, no injuries, nothing crawling beneath my skin.

"You're not alone?" Chavannes asked.

"There are four of us." I hesitated, then added, "The SPEC agent is gone."

I could not read her face as she processed that information.

"We were only recently aware of the agent's presence with the hostile group," she said. I could not tell if she was lying. "Do any of the hostile individuals still present a threat?"

"No. I want to talk to my aunt."

"The hostiles have been neutralized?"

"Yes. Let me talk to my aunt."

"You need to stay calm, Mr. Bhattacharya," Captain Chavannes said. "Can you tell me what happened?"

"I'll tell my aunt," I said. "I know you can contact her."

The captain nodded curtly. Still, I could not read her expression. "Of course. Lieutenant, locate Councilor Bhattacharya. Please tell me what you can."

"Have you heard from the ship called *Homestead*? Are they still headed here?"

"We've lost communication with *Homestead* for the moment. We are attempting to reestablish contact, but we have reason to believe they have heard our warnings and altered their plans. The vessel has been making course adjustments for some time. As of now their rear propulsion system is still firing."

"Are they coming here? They're not decelerating?" I asked.

"They do not appear to have begun a deceleration burn yet," Captain Chavannes said. "The new trajectory remains undetermined as long as they are making adjustments, but the changes indicate they do not intend to approach *House of Wisdom*. Mr. Bhattacharya, please be assured: We are going to get you out of there. We are preparing a team to bring you home. Do you understand?"

Oh, I understood. I wanted to nod and tell her to hurry and trust that they would come, and they would listen when they did, and the rescue crew would heroically take us away. We would land in Armstrong City. We would tell our stories. We would resume our lives, our research. The quasars I was studying had burned with brilliant fire billions of years ago, and it would be easy, so easy, to once again cast my mind and my focus into that distant past again, across the darkness of space, clinging to pinpricks of light so ancient and so far away that nothing could touch them. Not memory, not pain, not fear. It would be easy.

But others would come to *House of Wisdom* after our rescue. They would not be able to stay away, not with what we had learned of the parasite and where it had come from. They would be careful. They would wear protective suits and work in sealed labs and follow every protocol.

I felt the squirming itch on the back of my neck again.

They might keep the laboratory a few degrees too warm. They might shatter a glass vial. Slice a finger. It might be an accident.

They might want to know what would happen.

They might believe they could limit the danger.

I wish there was another way, my mother had said.

Captain Chavannes turned away from the camera, speaking to a member of her bridge crew. I heard something about a diplomatic vessel, an emergency launch. When she faced me again, she said, "We have Councilor Bhattacharya now. She is aboard a diplomatic vessel headed to Armstrong."

There was a blink on the screen, and there was Aunt Padmavati.

I had seen my aunt upset before. I had seen her exhausted, unwell, uneasy in ways she had hidden from the rest of the world. But I had never seen her look so old and weary as she did now. She wore a brilliant green and gold sari, one she reserved for when she wanted to be most intimidating, and all of her jewelry was in place, but her white-streaked black hair was escaping from its braids in wild wisps, and there were dark circles under her eyes. She reached toward the camera as though we could touch across the great distance. Her hand was trembling.

"You're hurt," she said.

"I'm fine," I said. My voice was shaking, and I was too tired to hide it. "Aunt Padmavati, you have to listen to me. You can't let them come here."

"Captain Chavannes will prevent *Homestead*—"

"Not just *Homestead. Pangong.* SPEC. Anybody. You can't let them come here. You have to stop them."

"Jas," said my aunt, and inside my chest my heart cracked. She never called me by my nickname. I had always assumed she thought it childish. "What are you talking about?"

"It's not a virus. It's not a disease at all. It's a biomechanical parasite. It can self-replicate. It infected one of us from just a scratch. It took over her—made her do things she had no control over. Mum and Captain Ngahere knew. They left a message."

"Amita left a message?" she said, her voice faint.

"She did." But not for you, and not for me, I thought, unable to say the words aloud. Mum's message, like her work, like her life, had been for a much greater purpose. "We'll bring it to you. There's data, too, the data that didn't make it into the last burst. But the rescue teams and everybody else—you have to stop them. They don't know what they're coming into. It's not safe."

My aunt was quiet for a moment. "You know that what you're telling me won't dissuade SPEC. They have been wanting to return to *House of Wisdom* for years. There are a lot of people who have been waiting a long time for answers."

"I know. I know." They would want to return even more when they found out what Dr. Lago had learned from UC33-X. "But can't you at least get them to wait? Until we can tell them what we've seen? We'll bring them answers, but it's too dangerous to come here."

Another pause, then she nodded. "I will do what I can."

My aunt did not make promises she could not keep.

Captain Chavannes broke into our conversation. "*Homestead* seems to have ceased its trajectory corrections. The lateral thrusters haven't fired in several minutes. The ship is now on a course for Providence Station. The crew has indicated they intend to surrender to security personnel when they arrive."

Quietly, so quietly there was no way it would carry over the radio, Zahra inhaled a short, sharp breath.

"Are you able to make your way to the main docking area of *House of Wisdom*?" Captain Chavannes asked. "Our assessment tells us that's the safest place for us to extend a sealed passage between the ships, but if you aren't able to get there—"

"No," I said. "We're not going to wait that long."

"There are evacuation suits aboard, but you would be adrift for several hours."

And that would only give SPEC a reason to come to us. "We're taking my mother's experimental small craft away from here."

Captain Chavannes's eyes widened; it was the strongest reaction I had seen from her. "Absolutely not. That is not safe. You cannot—"

"We can, and we will," I said. "We are not waiting here any longer than we have to. And when you pick us up, you're going to put us in full quarantine. No exposure to anybody until we're sure we're not infected."

"Mr. Bhattacharya, if that's—"

"It is absolutely necessary. See you soon, Aunt Padmavati. Please make them listen."

I ended the transmission before my aunt could see the tears in my eyes. The display changed to *House of Wisdom*'s location in orbit, with *Pangong*, *Homestead*, Providence Station. The Moon. Earth. It all looked so small on the screen.

For a long moment, nobody spoke.

Then Baqir said, "Will they listen to her?"

I rubbed my face. "She'll have a better chance of convincing them to stay away if we get out of here. My mother's workshop is on Level 12. It's not far."

There was blood smeared on the door. A handprint with a long trail: somebody had slapped a bloody hand on the wall before being dragged or pulled away. It was brown, dried nearly to dust. I avoided it carefully.

Slowly, as though waking from a deep slumber, the lights came on. My mother's workshop was a massive chamber on the starboard side of the ship. It spanned two levels, large enough to house three of my mother's small experimental vessels side by side. Numerous catwalks surrounded and crossed the space, with ladders and handholds on all sides to facilitate work in zero gravity.

The two remaining ships loomed above us, pinned like butterflies in a display, struts and braces holding them in place. They were nearly identical in outward appearance, both to each other and to *Tiger*, which my mother had put me on ten years ago. I couldn't remember how they differed beneath the surface; I wasn't sure my mother had ever told me. By the time I was twelve, she had mostly given up hope that I would follow in her footsteps.

To the right was a corpse with her arms slashed to ribbons, her throat cut, and so much blood staining her jumpsuit that the fabric appeared brown rather than white. Linna, a fuel scientist, who had in life had a big, hearty laugh and a bawdy sense of humor. She must have had the same idea as my mother, to flee using an experimental ship, only for her it had been too late. The parasite was already inside her. She bled to death after trying to carve it out with a scrap of metal from the recycling system.

I pushed myself to the nearest workstation and tapped the screen to pull up the ten-year-old flight schedule. *Tiger* was on the calendar for a drive efficiency test the day after the outbreak. Two days later, *Brahmin* was scheduled for a navigation test. *Jackal* was not on the schedule at all. It was flagged for environmental system repairs: air filters, thermometers, high-g couch positioning.

I found the *Brahmin* information. The test was to have three stages: journey outward, hold and reposition, return on command. The flight path would take the ship near the radio station at the L2 Lagrange point. I pressed my fingers to my aching head; grainy, dragging exhaustion was muddling my thoughts. It had to be good enough. I didn't know how to change the ship's course, but they could abort the flight midway through, during the repositioning test.

"Okay." I took a breath; the cold burned my throat. "Xi, Baqir, you're getting in that ship."

Xiomara looked toward the ship, but Baqir was watching me. "What about you?"

"We're going in the other one," I said. "But I'm launching you first."

I kicked my way over to *Brahmin* and let myself inside. The small cockpit was at once breathtakingly familiar and painfully disorienting. I found the control panel and called up the preflight sequences. Turn on the lights. Raise the temperature. Filter the air. Test the reactive cushioning in the seats.

Xiomara could make her own way, but Baqir needed help. I ducked my head under his good arm to hook it around my neck. I was careful to hold on to his waist, avoiding the damaged shoulder, but it seemed like every motion, no matter how small, caused him more pain. He no longer stifled the whimpers and gasps. I didn't know if this would be safer for him than the evacuation suits, but I knew it would get him into a doctor's care faster.

Xiomara settled into the pilot's seat; she had tucked the tablet containing Mum's message and the storage device with the ship's data into a secure compartment. I maneuvered Baqir into the navigator's chair behind her. He hissed when his wrecked shoulder touched the cushion.

"I'm sorry," I murmured. "I'm sorry, but I have to—it's worse if you're not sitting right."

"I know," he said through gritted teeth. "*Fuck.* I know. You made me look at your X-rays, remember? You fucking show-off."

"Shut up," I said, laughing a little. "I was twelve. And you thought it was cool."

There was no way to adjust the five-point harness so that it did not pressure his broken shoulder, no way to arrange his damaged artificial arm so that it did not pull on the wounded flesh and bones. I tightened the harness as much as I dared. Baqir clenched his teeth and closed his eyes. It would be kinder, I thought, if he passed out.

"You're coming after us, right?" Baqir said. His eyes were still closed, his voice a ragged whisper.

"Yeah," I said.

I reached out to touch his face, to brush his sweat-damp hair back from his forehead. He leaned his head into my hand. His skin was clammy, far too cool. I couldn't stop looking at him. The line of his jaw, his thick dark eyebrows, the thin scar on his chin from our first year at secondary school, when some swaggering upper-classman had shoved him down the school stairs. He had been defending me from some insult or another; all the petty cruelties had blurred together. Baqir had given himself the task of jumping between my cowering fears and the blows thrown by the world, and I had never thanked him for that, never told him how that day, when he lunged at that hulking teen and went sprawling onto the ground and jumped to his feet again with blood pouring from his nose and lips and his grin angry and fierce as he charged again, we might have been friends already, but never before had he so easily cracked through the numb cold that had enveloped me since my mother sent me away from *House of Wisdom*. It had been one of many ominous signs of a thunderous oncoming thaw, but I hadn't known it then. All I had known was that this mad bleeding boy with a wasteland accent was laughing with blood on his mouth, and it felt like the first time in an eternity anybody had looked at me and smiled.

I brushed my thumb over his temple. There was blood splattered there, softened by his sweat. His eyes were still closed, my hand still cupping the side of his face. I kissed him.

It was barely a brush of lips. He let out a small, surprised gasp. I backed away quickly. Baqir's eyes were open now, wide, his lips parted. I thought he might say something, so I moved out of reach. He reached up with his uninjured hand, then stopped with an abrupt hiss of pain. He dropped his head back against the seat, and without thinking I kissed him again, this time on his clammy forehead.

"It's going to hurt a lot when the ship's under acceleration," I said. "I'm sorry."

A beat of silence, then Baqir exhaled something like a laugh. "It already hurts a lot."

"I'm sorry," I said again.

"You're coming right after us?"

"Yeah. Make sure they quarantine you. Just to be sure."

"Promise me again."

There were thorns in my throat, pressing outward.

"I promise," I said.

I had been lying for half of my life. By now it came naturally to me.

I secured the door to *Brahmin* from the outside, then returned to the control room. Zahra was waiting. She could have fled, but where would she go? There was nothing in *House of Wisdom* except death.

I had watched my mother launch experimental flights before, but I was only able to replicate her steps because most of the procedure was automated. The first step was to depressurize the dry dock; the second was to open the doors and maneuver the ship outside. My hand was shaking as I sent the commands. The doors slid open with a rumble I felt in my teeth, and the docking clamps began to unfold and extend, nimbly carrying *Brahmin* through the square opening.

"I really hope you know what you're doing," Xiomara said over the radio, "because I only just realized how completely fucking insane this is."

"It'll be fine," I told her.

The arms of the docking clamps were fully extended. *Brahmin* looked so small, framed by the massive open doors and the darkness of space. My heart was racing. The maneuvering thrusters fired—over the radio Xiomara relayed what the ship was telling her, all systems normal—and the clamps released. The craft moved away from the ship, so slowly at first it did not seem to be moving at all, but then it was turning, the side thrusters firing as it found its course and calculated its trajectory. It was beyond the view in moments. The doors closed.

"See you on the other side," Xiomara said.

"Yeah," I said. "Soon."

I turned off the radio.

Zahra had not spoken a single word since we arrived in the dry dock. But now she looked at me and said, "You lied to them."

On the navigation screen, I watched *Brahmin* sail farther and farther away from *House of Wisdom*. I hoped they would be safe. I needed them to be safe. I could still feel the worrying coolness of Baqir's skin.

"We're not going to follow, are we?" Zahra said.

I kept my eyes on the screen. I had thought I would be able to tell when *Brahmin*'s main thrusters engaged, but the ship's acceleration was smooth. Mum would have made sure it was smooth. Xiomara and Baqir had the message from her and the captain. My aunt would understand the danger and do everything she could to persuade SPEC to stay away.

But my aunt's power had limits.

"No," I said. "There's something I have to do first."

Her only reaction was to nod, and I knew then that I was right: there was something she had not told us. Something that had remained hidden in Malachi's final words to her, in that catch of her breath when Captain Chavannes spoke about *Homestead*'s surrender.

"What did your friend mean when he told you to make sure they know the truth?" I asked. I turned to her and saw the minute flinch on the word *friend*. "He said you deserved that. What did he mean?"

"He was talking about my father," she said.

"Your father?" It was not the answer I was expecting.

"The whole world believes my father is a monster, but he didn't do what they said," Zahra said. "It isn't about what I deserve. It's about what he deserves. His memory. He deserves to be remembered for the work he did, not for the crimes he didn't commit. My brother and sister deserve to know he was a good man."

It took me a second to understand. "Dr. Lago was your father?"

"Yes."

Dr. Lago had been a smiling and jovial man with a round face, laughing eyes, and soft shoulders. I had known he had a family on Earth, because everybody who had family on Earth spoke about missing them, but I had given them no thought until afterward. Only then had I learned that his wife was an epidemiologist who took her children and vanished into the North American desert after his death. My aunt had told me that the Councils were trying to locate Mariah Dove, but she thought they ought to be left alone. No children deserved to suffer for what their father had done.

"He didn't release the parasite," Zahra said. "Dr. Summers said—in the message we found, she said it wasn't his fault. It came from the probe. They took every precaution, but something escaped when they opened it up. She thought the people from *Mournful Evening Song* had sent it back to Earth on purpose."

This must have been a beautiful planet, once, the woman in the messages had said. *But we weren't the first to find it.*

I shook my head. "They didn't send it. Not on purpose. It found them. That's what's in the messages from UC33-X. They found an alien civilization that had been destroyed."

"Alien?" Zahra said, surprised. "That's in the messages?"

"The ones that were never released. It sounds like they were exploring it when they began to get infected. I don't think the woman who launched the probe meant to send it to Earth. I think she meant to warn us."

In keeping the recovered fragments to himself, Lago had also kept that warning from his colleagues. They might have proceeded differently if they had heard the whole of what the messages had to say. Or they might not have changed a thing, except that everybody would know it was not a virus, and he would not have been blamed.

The distinction between machine and weapon was one of intent, and if what Ariana had understood was accurate, if what my mother and Captain Ngahere had deduced was true, this parasite's goal was to cause destruction. They had understood its danger in terms of the impact of a kilometer-long ship crashing into Earth. But even without the crash, it would be catastrophic for the parasite to get loose on Earth. It would be a pandemic. It would, in fact, be an invasion, because something or somebody—so far away the distance was inconceivable, perhaps so long ago the light by which they worked might exist only as a ghost star in Earth's sky—somebody had created this thing, and set it free.

It was a discovery the likes of which humanity had never made before. I knew that. I knew it, and there was a part of me that could still feel how exciting it was, how very much it mattered. That part of me that believed my parents had died doing important work, that believed exploring the stars and stretching the reach of humankind into space was a noble and necessary goal. Yesterday I would have happily argued that the search for life and civilization elsewhere in the galaxy outweighed any danger. Maybe it should. Maybe that was the bolder choice. But everywhere on this ship there was a weapon that had, over the space of a single day, made the people of *House of Wisdom* attack their own bodies with violence and fear, had made my father take his own life with a knife from our kitchen, had turned my mother from an engineer into an architect of mass murder.

On the screen, *Brahmin* sailed farther and farther away. I turned to Zahra.

"Those things—the parasites—they want to crash the ship into Earth."

"What?"

"That's the information Xiomara and Baqir are taking to my aunt. Ten years ago, when the parasite had control of the ship, it had a collision course set. My mum and the captain stopped it."

"But that would be . . ." She faltered. "Why would it do that?"

"I don't know," I said. "I don't care about its reasons. I know you hate Earth. But I can't let this thing get anywhere near it. You can help or not. Just don't try to stop me."

For a long moment we looked at each other, both of us dirty and bedraggled and shaking with exhaustion. I no longer had any sense of how long I had been awake. Zahra crossed her arms over her chest and shivered, looking absurdly young in the too-large knit sweater, her black hair flying free of its plaits.

She said, "I'll help. I need to talk to *Homestead*."

She turned from the terminal and headed for the door.

The dead had stilled in our absence. The worms drifted among the corpses, delicate as filaments, without any obvious motion. The alien parasites—it was hard to think of them like that, as things from another world, created by inhuman hands. They were quiet, but I knew better than to think they were destroyed. They were only waiting.

"Radio is here," Bhattacharya said. His voice was rough, and he was doing everything he could not to look at the glass-walled room. When I hesitated, my hands hovering uncertainly, he reached out and opened the channel for me. "You can talk to *Homestead*, if they're listening."

I slid into the chair and swallowed, trying to gather moisture in my desert-dry throat. The large displays at the front of the bridge still showed the navigation chart: an array of lights and symbols, words and numbers, bewildering in its complexity. I hadn't thought I would have to do any of this without Malachi or Boudicca or the others. I had never even been in open space, untethered from Earth, until today.

"*Homestead*, this is *House of Wisdom*. This is Zahra. Is anybody listening?"

There was no answer. Beside me, Bhattacharya listened to radio traffic across all frequencies. Orbital Control was tracking the ship with Bhattacharya's friends and was preparing a transport to intersect them. *Pangong* was trying to contact us again. They were trying to contact *Homestead* too.

Homestead wasn't answering.

"Please," I said, trying again. "*Homestead*, this is *House of Wisdom*. Can you hear me? Is there anybody there?"

Nothing. I tried again. Nothing. Fear curdled in my gut. I tried to think of rational reasons for their silence. Adam could have forbidden the bridge crew from answering hails from me or anybody. There could be nobody on the bridge—but why would they abandon it, if they were making course adjustments to approach Providence? Images of what might be happening aboard the ship flashed through my mind.

I slid back from the console and looked at Bhattacharya. I wanted to know what he was planning. He would not have lied to his friends and sent them away unless it was something he did not think they or SPEC would condone.

"You want to stop the parasite," I said.

"Right." He nodded absently; he was still listening to the radio chatter. "But first I need to figure out how. And I've got no fucking idea."

"What did your mother and the captain do before?"

"Vented the air and suffocated the parasite's hosts, which gave the captain a chance to set the command override so they could alter the course to a stable orbit."

I stared at him. "Suffocated the—"

"The hosts. And everybody else on board. Each section has a system for venting the air for fire suppression." He was speaking quietly, with a heavy tiredness that dragged on every word, but without shock, without horror, only a bleak sort of acceptance. "It replaces the oxygen with carbon dioxide or a nonreactive gas. They set them to all engage at the same time. The system eventually reset and recovered, so we have air now, but it took long enough that nobody could survive."

All over the ship there had been people who did not die violently. In the garden, in the mainframe, in corridors and doorways, alcoves and labs. That was the alarm Dr. Summers had heard while recording her final message. She had known what was coming.

"Does SPEC know?" I asked.

Bhattacharya looked at me then, really looked at me. "No," he said. "Are you serious? They have no fucking idea. They think it's a virus, not a—whatever it is. Not something from space."

"I don't know what they know," I reminded him, "because everything they've made public has been a lie."

He shrugged slightly. "Well, they don't know this. They don't have the full message from the probe. The research team was supposed to be reviewing the fragments Dr. Lago had kept from them."

That meant Dr. Summers, Dr. Chin, maybe others. Summers had known UC33-X set something free aboard *House of Wisdom*. More than that, she had known it had to be destroyed. She had killed the man in the Deep Space Archaeology lab. He had been infected, he attacked her, and Dr. Summers killed him in self-defense. The first try didn't work, she had said. For the second she used a canister of liquid gas.

"Venting the air wasn't enough," I said. "They had to make it cold too."

"Oh, fuck," Bhattacharya said. He sat forward suddenly, almost pushing himself out of his chair. "*Fuck.* Yeah. That's right. That's why it's so bloody cold aboard."

"But space is always cold," I said, my voice rising uncertainly.

"Yes, but spaceships aren't, and something this big has a lot of trouble shedding heat in the vacuum. It should be warm in here. It should have been fucking obvious from the second we came on board."

It had been to Malachi, to Dag, both of whom had remarked on the temperature. They had known something was wrong. I hadn't listened. I had not wanted to be distracted.

Bhattacharya ran his hands through his hair. "But the cold didn't work either. All it did was put the parasite in a dormant state. It's traveled through space for who knows how long. It probably likes the cold."

"At least fifty light-years," I said. "That's what my father thought. Why don't you want SPEC to help?" He didn't answer right away. "Bhattacharya. Why don't you ask them for help? Why are you still here?"

"Jas," he said.

"What?"

"You might as well call me Jas."

"Oh. Okay."

Jas exhaled slowly. "I'm not telling them because they won't agree to what I want to do."

"What's that?"

"Kill it," he said simply. "I want to kill it. Every trace of it. It's the first sign of advanced alien life that humanity has ever discovered, and I want to fucking kill it."

He sounded so tired, so resigned, it took a second for the full impact of what he was saying to sink in. I had not thought of it like that. I had seen it only as a threat to be eliminated. Not contact from an alien civilization. Not proof of advanced alien life. Not the thrilling, brilliant grail for which humankind had been searching for centuries. Humankind was not alone in the universe. We had proof. I hadn't thought of it like that at all.

But I should have. I would have, if I had been thinking about what I'd learned in the Councils schools, or at my father's side. My father would have been first in line to argue that proof of alien life, however destructive, should be preserved, studied, cherished. There was a part of me, the part that still ached with grief, that wanted to take his position, to argue as he would have argued, to speak up for the sacred nature of curiosity, the never-ending joy of discovery.

But from the corner of my eye I could still see the blood and mangled corpses. I could still hear Panya's screams and Malachi's final words. I felt no revulsion about what Jas wanted to do. I understood why he did not want to place that choice in anybody else's hands.

In my mind I retraced the route we had taken from the docks to the bridge, how long the journey had felt, how darkly it stretched behind me. The parasite was everywhere. There had been corpses all the way. Gathered in forlorn groups and scattered in lonely ones and twos, bodies ravaged by their self-inflicted wounds, every one of them desiccated into husks.

"If cold doesn't kill them," I said slowly, "maybe heat would?"

He thought for a moment before answering. "The electric shock did affect it. It wasn't permanent, and it didn't work the second time, but it is conductive . . . Heat would increase the electrical resistance of its metal parts. Who the fuck knows what it's made out of, but if it's designed to travel through space, high temps might make it malleable or even melt it?"

"Where are the incinerators on the ship?" I asked.

Not far, it turned out. There was a medical laboratory on Level 9, just below the bridge. Inside the laboratory, floating beside a refrigerator with a smashed door and dozens of shattered vials, was a woman with long gashes on her arms and three syringes sticking out of her shoulder.

She was obviously infected. Jas was still wearing his space suit and gloves, but I had to search through the lab until I found a bio-hazard suit in a storage closet. I put it on quickly, thankful for both the protection and the warmth, then went to help him drag the woman's corpse over to the waste processing unit.

It was much like the waste disposal units at my mother's old hospital, the only difference being its intake had been adapted for zero gravity. I opened the hatch, and Jas fed the corpse into the unit headfirst, wincing when the syringes in her arm snagged on the side and broke free. I caught them before they floated away, and pushed them into the intake after the woman. I shut the hatch and sealed it.

One touch of the evac command and the machinery rumbled. There was a loud whoosh as the unit drew the corpse into the incinerator. The interior monitoring system blinked on.

One of my mother's students used to let me watch her dispose of their experimental waste when I visited their laboratory. The jet of flames would engulf everything inside, shriveling it to ash and sweeping it away. The student had explained that the cameras were for safety, but all I had ever cared about was what they let me see.

I had not thought about that woman or those visits to the hospital in years. Most of my memories of my mother at work were in the desert, her thankless toil against hunger and sickness and injury. But that had not been all there was to her. She had believed in discovery once too.

This unit was not designed for waste as large as a woman's body. She was jammed awkwardly into the narrow space, and all we could see on the screen was the curve of her shoulder, the twisted reach of one arm, the top of her head. The thermal image glowed brighter as the cycle began and the internal temperature increased.

The woman's hand twitched. I started, even though I ought to have expected it. The parasite inside of her was emerging from dormancy.

"She tried to sedate herself," Jas said suddenly. "Twice. That was two of the syringes. I recognized the drugs. The third was to stop her heart."

Would I feel it, I wondered, if there was a worm inside me? Surely I would—Ariana had felt it, although we had dismissed it as a hallucination. But I could not help but wonder if the parasite might be learning to hide itself better. It had learned to control a human body, to fly a human ship, to use human language. It had learned to withstand an electric shock. It might even now be biding its time inside me, weaving thin, grasping threads into the fibers of my spine.

A gleam of silver appeared between the woman's fingers. The parasite wriggled from her corpse slowly, searchingly. On the thermal image display it was the same temperature as the air, utterly invisible, but the camera showed it clearly, bending this way and that, so slender and delicate, like a snake tasting its surroundings.

Suddenly, with a muffled roar, there was fire. It rolled from the far end of the chamber, swamping the thermal imaging. I had thought the parasite might twitch or whip back and forth, try to flee or escape, but even when the flames engulfed it, it scarcely seemed to notice. The metal glowed red-hot, then broke into red beads that pulled apart and disintegrated.

It was working. The fire was destroying the parasite.

We watched in silence. It seemed to take a very long time, to reduce what had been a human to a fine white ash, but according to the disposal unit, fewer than twenty minutes had passed.

Twenty minutes. Four hundred and seventy-seven bodies, and not all would be as easy to access and move as this one had been. And even if we could destroy every single body before SPEC arrived, we could not cleanse the blood from every surface. It was impossible. We could not make the ship safe. The parasite would find a way. The outbreak would begin anew on the Moon, or Earth, or Providence, wherever it found itself again in favorable conditions.

Rather than stopping the thought where it began, I let myself imagine it. A SPEC agent forgetting, for one single moment, the danger. The parasite hiding inside him until it could overtake him and his team. A ship of infected SPEC crew landing at Armstrong City or docking at one of the orbital stations. The wounded, the ill, the dead and mourned, they would be carried on stretchers or sealed in biohazard bags, and they would be taken away to hospitals or morgues. They would be passed into the hands of loving doctors and curious scientists like my mother had once been. And the silver worms would slither from host to host, unseen. The parasites would replicate themselves, create children upon children to whip through countless bodies, scratching and squiggling and itching their way through doctors, nurses, mourners, politicians, and researchers, writhing beneath the skin. The infected would not know, at first, what fate awaited them. Their discomfort would turn to panic, their panic to violence. Surely the parasite's capacity for replication was not endless—it needed material, it needed energy—but it might find all of that, somehow, as it spread. It would pass from patient to doctor, doctor to family, family to the rest of the world. Within weeks, days, a pandemic of blood and screams and helpless fear would overcome all attempts to halt it.

One by one the cities of Earth would fall silent. They would become crypts, dusty with the remains of the forgotten dead, who would number so many their names could not be counted even if anybody remained to count them. Wind would echo through the canyons of tall buildings, through windows edged with teeth of glass, through fences of shivering wire and walls of crumbling brick, and when it broke free of the cities the mournful wind would race over deserts now empty of barefooted boys limping toward lights that glowed like a promise on the horizon. And the world, the Earth that had endured thousands of years of civilizations rising and falling, whose people had driven it to the edge of destruction and clawed their way back, would be nothing more than a curiosity for some alien explorers to find in a thousand years, ten thousand, more, when the night sky was a graveyard of satellites slowly, slowly, slowly crashing into the atmosphere.

"I don't hate Earth," I said.

Jas was still watching the screen, searching for any sign the parasite had withstood the fire. "What?"

"I don't hate Earth," I said, and that time it sounded less like a question. "What you said earlier. You're wrong about that. That's not why I came here."

"Then why did you?" Jas said.

"For my father. I told you. To prove he wasn't a killer. And for the twins. I thought they could have a better life here. Life in the deserts isn't easy, and it's even harder to find a way out. Coming here, following Adam, that was our way."

Finally he turned from the screen to meet my eyes. "But you weren't born there. Your parents were Councils citizens."

I swallowed; my throat was dry and sore. "Do you know my mother was a doctor? She was a wonderful doctor. All she ever wanted to do was help people, to make them well. She hated that the Councils would refuse citizenship to people who needed help. She hated that just being unlucky enough to be born in a poisoned wasteland could be a death sentence, if your family didn't get moved through the application process fast enough. She hated that people are always being told to just get in line, follow the rules, wait your turn, as though that would make their children well and bring their loved ones back. She saw how cruel that was. Helping people is all she ever did."

And that was what she had done, even after we went to the desert. The homestead was a quicksand trap for the lost and ailing. The children always needed their scrapes bandaged and their bruises kissed. The work never ceased. And every night, every single night, while the rest of us looked upward and dreamed, my mother soothed the ill, tended the wounded, comforted the dying. I had not understood it before, how rooted she was on the ground, but I remembered how sad her smile had been when those who had been to space and yearned to return told their stories, embellishing what the darkness had to offer, spinning its dangers into beauty. My mother never shared her own stories. She only worked while Dag was telling eager young daredevils about his slingshot around Venus, while Orvar was remembering the first time he had sailed so far that Earth was nothing but a speck in the distance, while Boudicca was speaking quietly about the exhilaration of racing above Mars, so close to the surface there was an ever-present danger of clipping a mountaintop.

The rewards, Boudicca had said, outweigh the dangers, in the end.

I had an idea.

When we returned to the bridge, I asked, "Do you know about the crash of the *Breton*?"

"The one that crashed on Mars?" Jas returned to the navigation console and pulled himself into one of the chairs. He tapped the radio on again to hear what Orbital Control was saying. "I remember learning about it in school. Why?"

"Boudicca—the pilot on the shuttle. The woman with the red hair." It hurt to say her name and remember the confident rasp of her voice as she told her own truths around the fire at the center of the homestead. "When *Breton* crashed, she was the pilot of the first ship to respond to the distress signal. She told me that when they got to the crash site and inside the wreck, they couldn't even find the crew. The bodies. SPEC told the families the conditions were too dangerous to retrieve the bodies, but really they were so badly burned most of them were just—dust. Debris."

"We didn't learn that in school," Jas said. "But it makes sense. It was a horrible accident."

And, prior to *House of Wisdom*, it was the single greatest loss of human life in space since the Collapse. Afterward, SPEC and the Councils had declared never again, never again would space travel be so dangerous, never again would so many perish. But, Boudicca had told me, they only changed what public outcry clamored for them to change, and when she tried to demand more, when she spoke up about what failures had led to the disaster, they had shunted her aside again and again, assigning her to routes a trainee could have flown, passing her over for higher positions and better ships, censuring her every time she spoke up. SPEC had made its point: they did not want her anymore. And without SPEC, without access to space, Boudicca had no reason to remain loyal to the Councils that had treated her so poorly.

All because of a single horrifying crash. Because she had wanted to keep it from happening again. Because she wanted those whose carelessness had lost lives to admit what they had done.

"She said there was—was it something wrong with the atmosphere filtration system?" I asked, trying to recall the details. "It made the crew sick, so they didn't notice the air was getting toxic, and they lost control? And it was some flammable gas?"

"I think so." Jas rubbed his hands over his face and inhaled sharply, as though trying to wake himself up. "I remember it now. They thought it was sabotage at first, because as far as anybody could tell there were never any alarms or warnings. The atmospheric control system was supposed to have an automatic limit for high levels of—I think it was carbon monoxide buildup. That's what incapacitated the crew. It wasn't sabotage after all. There was a glitch in the computers that had shut down the warning system and not restarted it."

"They asphyxiated before the fire started?" I asked.

"Probably. I don't think SPEC ever found out exactly what caused the fire. With high enough carbon monoxide concentrations, it wouldn't take much of a spark. They assumed it was in the cargo. There were construction supplies on board. Tools, fuel, that sort of thing."

"The point is, it burned everything, right? Can we do something like that?"

"They redesigned the carbon monoxide scrubbing system after the *Breton*," Jas said. "There's a fail-safe that restarts the active scrubbing no matter how it's shut down, plus the passive backups."

"So we use something else. Some other flammable gas."

"Maybe," he said. He called up an image on the screen: it was a schematic of the ship. He began flicking through the levels one by one, looking over them quickly. "There are multiple recyclers on every level. Not just for the living areas, but for the laboratories, for the medical bays, for the machine shops, for all of Dad's horticultural rooms. The system is designed so that every section can take care of itself in the emergency of a larger system failure."

"Okay," I said, following but not yet understanding.

"Their primary by-products of organic recycling are methane and ammonia, but they aren't kept as methane and ammonia for very long, because what the ship needs for power and propulsion is hydrogen. Hydrogen burns in air at low concentrations. And it burns hot."

My heart began to beat faster. "There must be safety mechanisms."

"There would be, normally," Jas said. "But my mother and the captain had to disable them. There wouldn't have been any other way to get the fire suppression system to swamp the entire ship while there were still people in every section."

"Will it be enough?" I asked.

Even as I spoke, I was thinking through the steps in my mind. Replace the breathable air with hydrogen in all of the ship's open spaces. Level by level. Chamber by chamber. For years I had been studying everything we could find about *House of Wisdom*, its schematics and systems, filling my head with knowledge in hopes that one day I would be able to spill it out, information flowing from my fingertips when we took control of the ship. I had never considered that all I had learned to make *House of Wisdom* shine would instead be used to turn it into an inferno.

Jas said nothing, so I answered my own question. "It will be enough. It has to be."

Much of what needed to be done could be done from the bridge or nearby systems command centers. Access this system, turn off that system. Malachi had removed all of the command restrictions. The medical monitor was able to tell us where nearly everybody aboard the ship had died, as well as where their bodies had ended up, and from that data we could identify every space that needed to be incinerated. Specks of light danced on the map before me. We opened doors and valves: the task was easy, once we knew how. We counted the dead by pairs, by threes, by scores. Four hundred and seventy-seven. We could not miss anybody.

I was focused on the task of closing the doors to protect the engine levels; there were no bodies farther aft than cargo. The radio transmissions from Orbital Control and *Pangong* had been a steady hum in the background of our work, welcome voices interrupting the ship's oppressive silence. The word *Homestead* caught my attention.

"Confirm course correction," a voice said.

Another voice rattled off a series of numbers and added, "Course correction confirmed. *Homestead* remains on course for Providence Station."

"They send out any more open broadcasts?"

A laugh. "Not yet."

"Keep an eye on them. At least they're headed where they said they'd go."

There was a quivering fear deep in my gut, tight and sickly and cold as ice.

"I need to try them again," I said. Jas gestured absently toward the radio, so I moved over a chair and opened the channel. "*Homestead*, this is *House of Wisdom*. This is Zahra. Please talk to me."

This time, the answer was immediate.

Adam appeared on the screen, scowling through streaks of muddy red. They had moved Orvar's body, but his blood remained splattered over the camera lens. Adam's expression twisted with surprise when he saw me.

"What do you want?"

"I need to talk to you about—"

Adam laughed. He actually laughed. Sitting in Orvar's blood-stained chair, his hands on the controls Orvar ought to be manning, pieces of Orvar's scalp and skull on the terminal before him, and he was laughing.

"You have nothing to say that I care to hear. I have more important things to do."

"Adam, please, listen—"

"Zahra, my child. You will be dead soon, or wish you were." His smile was thin. "If you live to be buried in a Councils prison, that will be better than you deserve for choosing to side with them. I only wish I could be there to see it."

That cold knot of dread tightened in my stomach. "What do you mean?"

"We are free," Adam said. "We are *free*. Do you understand? Can your small, scared animal mind comprehend that?"

I could scarcely breathe. "You're heading for Providence."

"We have our freedom. They tried to keep us from space, to keep us shackled to the ground, and we defied them. The whole world will remember us for it."

"You told them you're going to surrender. We heard the confirmation from Orbital Control."

Adam laughed again. I had never heard a more frightening sound. "The liars and deceivers will burn in their final moments."

"Adam, you can't, you can't—"

"I will be thinking of your betrayal until the end."

He ended the transmission. The navigation chart replaced his face on the display.

My heart was pounding. I began to tremble all over. I had hoped he would deny it. I had wanted to be wrong, to hear proof he could not be so cruel. I needed somebody aboard *Homestead* to listen. Somebody who could fly the ship to safety. Convince them to change their course and their minds. Convince them that what Adam planned was madness.

"What are they going to do?" Jas said.

His voice might have been coming from light-years away. I called for *Homestead* again. Again. I had to try. Again. There was no answer. The bloodstained bridge would be empty. Adam would be walking among the family. I knew his way: how he strolled, hands extended, smile soft, when he wanted to draw us all into a web around him. He would be reassuring them about the choice he had taken from their hands, and they would believe it was their own decision. He would be expounding upon how glorious their deaths would be, and they would be too frightened, or too overwhelmed, to disagree. I tried again. My voice cracked midway through the hail.

"Zahra," Jas said softly, "what are they going to do?"

"They . . ."

That scratch of breath, it was both my voice and not my voice. They will never let us be free, Adam would say, and the family would hear proof in SPEC's warnings. I know them better than they know themselves, he would say, and the chill of that knowledge would quell any dissent. It is the only way, he would say, and all would feel his despair. How very hopeless our hopes had been.

I said, "They're going to crash *Homestead* into Providence Station."

Jas opened his mouth, closed it. He looked toward the navigation display at the front of the bridge. He looked back to me.

"There are twenty thousand people living there," he said.

"I know," I said. "And three hundred on *Homestead*. Families. Children. My brother and sister. But Adam doesn't care. He won't change course."

"Are you—are you certain? Did you know that all along?"

My fear shattered into dismay. He had to believe me. I didn't know what to do, didn't know how to stop Adam, and I needed help. I had so little proof. Ten ruthless years. The firing of *Homestead*'s engines. Adam's smile behind a smear of blood.

"I didn't know," I said. Suspicions were not the same as knowing, worries not the same as proof. I had wanted so desperately to be wrong. "And yes. I am certain."

He stared at me for a moment longer, then reached in front of me to access the radio. "Fuck. *Fuck.* Okay. *Pangong*, this is *House of Wisdom*."

Captain Chavannes answered at once. "Mr. Bhattacharya, we

have been hailing you for nearly an hour! Why are you still aboard *House of Wisdom*? We are tracking the vessel *Brahmin*—" Then she blinked, and her gaze shifted. "You also said the hostile individuals had been neutralized. What's going on? Do you have demands to make, Ms. Dove Lago?"

I had not been called by that name since I had left my Councils secondary school ten years ago. It belonged to somebody else, a naive girl long vanished.

"She's not making demands," Jas said, impatience sharpening his words. "She's trying to warn you. *Homestead* isn't going to surrender. They intend to crash into Providence Station."

Captain Chavannes was skeptical. "They have indicated to us they intend a full and peaceful surrender," she said.

"Don't believe them. It's not slowing down, is it? They changed course but they aren't decelerating. Look at their trajectory. Is it right for docking? Shouldn't they be decelerating by now? It's still accelerating."

"We are tracking the ship's course," Chavannes said. "There is still time for—"

Jas rubbed his hands over his face in frustration. "And if they don't? They're going to *crash into Providence Station*."

Captain Chavannes's expression was pinched and unhappy. "Mr. Bhattacharya, as of right now—"

"I want to talk to my aunt again."

"What led you to this conclusion?"

"Let me talk to my aunt."

"Your aunt is currently unavailable. Her ship is—"

"She's not fucking unavailable. Let me talk to her."

"Mr. Bhattacharya, calm down. We know you are alarmed, but what you need to do is avoid any further rash decisions. You have already endangered your friends, and we are doing all we can to ensure *Homestead*'s safe surrender. You need to—"

"What can you do?" I said. "What can you do to stop *Homestead* if they don't stop themselves? Can you—can you fire something at it, or board it, or—what can you do?"

"Captain," Jas said. "You have to listen to her. She knows these people."

"I am listening, Mr. Bhattacharya," Chavannes said. "Ms. Dove Lago, despite what rumors would have you believe, SPEC does not actually have the ability to shoot down a passenger vessel at this orbit. We do, however, have a number of potential actions that can be adapted for a situation like this."

"Like what?" Jas said.

"We have been considering a boarding party since we first realized the nature of *Homestead*'s flight. We also have a number of industrial vessels in the vicinity that we can deploy as a deterrent."

"What kind of deterrent?" I asked. Putting other ships in danger would not deter Adam. It would only give him another chance to prove to the family that SPEC wanted to hurt them.

Chavannes looked as though she was considering her answer, but Jas spoke first. "You mean the ice-breaking fleet. The one at Tereshkova Shipyard."

"We are considering all resources and all actions," Chavannes said. "Including evacuating portions of the station. Do you know what manner of small vessels *Homestead* has aboard?"

"I—I don't know. I don't know if they have any," I said. "They are armed. Heavily armed. If you try to board—"

"I see. And emergency evacuation suits?"

"They have—I don't know. There will be some, but I don't know how many. There are more people aboard than the ship is rated for. There are more than a hundred children. They're only kids. They aren't—"

"We understand. In the meantime, I want both of you to stay put until we can retrieve you. We cannot spare the ships to chase after you and your friends at the same time. Is that clear, Mr. Bhattacharya?"

Jas answered, "We'll stay here."

"Thank you," said Captain Chavannes. "Please stand by, *House of Wisdom*. Keep your communications open. *Pangong* out."

Jas cut the radio connection from our end. He gripped the arms of his chair to push himself into the seat and looked at me. "What are their names? Your brother and sister?"

"Nadra and Anwar." It didn't seem like enough, names that meant so much to me but sounded so small compared to the void between us. "They're twins. They're fifteen. We were supposed to . . . we were supposed to be together here."

He didn't say he was sorry. He didn't say he understood. I neither needed nor wanted his pity. I only wanted him to know that there were lives aboard that ship that did not deserve to be snuffed out. They had never deserved anything that happened to them. They were not at fault for the fear and desperation and unfairness that pushed them into Adam's orbit.

"Will they be able to do anything?" I asked.

"I don't know. A passenger ship like *Homestead* should have a proximity buffer built into its navigation system, to keep it from getting too close to any other ship or station when it's not docking. Probably the first thing they'll try is to restart that remotely."

"Will they warn the station? Even if they don't believe us?"

"Yes, but they'll never be able to evacuate it," Jas said. "There are too many people. And there's the debris from the collision. The ice-breaking ships are supposed to be able to limit that, it's part of what they're designed to do, but they're not finished. They're not supposed to launch until later this year. Salvatore was going to work on them for his fellowship." A quick glance at me. "The man you shot on the shuttle."

I said nothing. He still carried the weapon I had handed over at his belt. I wondered if he had forgotten about it.

"I don't know what else they can do," he said. "There are no other ships nearby. *Pangong* is still too far."

We both looked at the navigation display. *House of Wisdom* and *Homestead* were as twins in a binary star, alone in a blank space amid all the lines and vectors and racing symbols. The isolation of *House of Wisdom*'s corner of space had been our security, when we made our plan. Now it was a terrible gulf too vast to cross.

I tried *Homestead* again. No answer.

"Every ship in orbit would be in danger, every orbital station, every spaceport, every space elevator and tether. Anything that eventually fell to Earth . . ." Jas rubbed his hand across his mouth and looked at the display again. "It would be the Collapse all over again, that much debris coming down. Exactly what we're trying to stop this fucking parasite from doing."

I tried again. *Homestead* remained silent.

"All ships have safeguards against that kind of thing," Jas went on. "Collision deterrence, proximity buffers, gravity-well avoidance."

"Adam will have disabled those."

"I know, I know. That's what I mean."

"You think SPEC will be able to stop *Homestead* after all?"

"No," he said.

Then he was quiet for a long, long time. On the radio, Orbital Control asked for another course and position verification from *Homestead*. They received no reply. The station master at Providence was requesting any and all vessels within the vicinity to report their position and capacity immediately. They had listened to my warning. It wouldn't be enough.

Jas said, "But I think we could."

I felt, for a second, my heart stop. "How?"

Jas looked at me, and he smiled an awful, bleak smile. "All we have to do is get in their way. We've got a ship big enough. We've got the only ship big enough."

*H*omestead's new course bent its trajectory inward so that it would miss *House of Wisdom* by a mere few thousand kilometers—a great span on Earth, but considered an unsafe distance by both Orbital Control, who were still pleading for an answer with growing alarm, and the ship's navigation computer. The display highlighted this close pass with a circle of red, a bloodshot eye in the center of the field of moving spheres, changing numbers, and shifting lines. The image was difficult to read, but Jas talked it through—not to explain it to me, I realized after an indignant moment, but to work it out for himself. He was more comfortable aboard a ship than I was, but he had no more experience piloting one. Our only chance of success lay in the fact that *House of Wisdom* had been designed to execute the commands of its crew smoothly and seamlessly, with as little room for human error as possible.

"We need to know where *Homestead* is going to be." Jas tapped at the navigation terminal, then tried something else. The display changed: numbers dropped out, orbital arcs faded, lines blinked away. "Oh. Okay. It's calculating the position automatically. Now for our potential courses, from orbital velocity . . . okay."

I made a guess at the new red numbers on the display. "That's the possible overlap zone?"

"Yeah, exactly. On a ship this size, with so much onboard computing power, it's designed to extrapolate potential collisions while it's in orbit. And lucky for us, right now that computing power isn't being used for anything else."

"So we aim for where it's telling us to avoid." I heard a hollow note in my own voice, an echo of faint disbelief. We were talking about *crashing the ships together* as though it were any other task, as simple as turning on the heat, changing the air pressure, using the radio.

As simple as replacing nitrogen and oxygen with hydrogen. Sparking a fire. The ship was primed and ready for that, but we had to deal with *Homestead* before we set that plan in motion.

"There's a range of possible collision points," Jas said. "Here. See that?"

On the screen the line that represented *Homestead*'s path toward Providence Station was highlighted in bright blue, and intersecting it was a narrow, pale green wedge with its point anchored at *House of Wisdom.*

"It's not a lot of room for error," I said. "Can we get there in time?"

"I hope so," he said, frowning in thought before sending a query to the ship's computer. "Mum designed the engines to be able to accelerate quickly, and we don't need to worry about conserving fuel or avoiding structural stresses. We can burn everything on board to get moving. *Homestead* might try to course correct once they realize what we're doing, so we'll have to watch it until—" It was the slightest hitch, that catch in his voice. "Until the end."

"Are we really going to . . ." Something almost like laughter burbled in my throat. I tried to swallow it down, but the wild edge of a giggle escaped as tears stung my eyes. "Are we really going to make them hit us? Are we really doing that?"

He sat back in the navigation chair and looked at me. "I'm kind of hoping that somebody notices and takes control of the ship before it happens. How likely is that?"

Every trace of hysterical laughter was snuffed out. I started to answer, stopped, tried again: "Adam isn't bluffing."

"We aren't either."

"But will it work?" I asked. "Are we *really* sure it will work? It's not going to mean two ships crashing into Providence instead of one?"

"*Homestead* is aiming toward the Earthside docking structure on the external face of the ring. I imagine that course is a feint, and they're really aiming for the outer edge of the ring. In any case, Providence is only seven hundred meters wide, so we only need to knock *Homestead*'s course downward by about half that. Force equals mass times acceleration, and we have several times the mass as *Homestead*, and much more powerful engines. We're not trying to stop them, just change their vector by about, I don't know, a degree."

"You sound like your mother," I said without thinking.

He gave me such a look of surprise that I almost laughed.

"From what I've seen," I said quickly. "In interviews."

"I . . . nobody has ever said that before," he said. "Mostly people tell me I'm not as smart as she was. And I'm not. I don't know for sure it will work. But even if we can get *Homestead* to scrape by Providence rather than a solid impact, it will save lives."

That, in the end, was all that mattered. But it did not change the fact that we were discussing *Homestead* as though it were a wrecking ball, when in fact it was a passenger vessel, one loaded past capacity and carrying innocent people. My people. All that was left of my families, both the one I was born into and the one I had chosen.

"Are you ready?" Jas said.

We could not stall any longer. I was ready.

"It's a big ship but it's going to be a huge kick of acceleration." Jas ran his finger along the edge of the console, a curiously sad smile on his face. "Mum always hated that nobody wanted to travel at more than 1 g. She wanted to show off what it could do. You might want to sit down."

I slid into one of the bridge chairs.

The sensation was slight at first, a subtle pressure from the chair beneath me pressing upward—then abrupt, marked by the loud thump of the corpses in the officers' room striking the floor all at once. Then I could feel it all over, the acceleration exerting its apparent gravity on every part of my body. It seemed to me impossible that I could have forgotten how it felt to carry weight on my shoulders, on my spine, with every limb and muscle.

After ten years of silence, *House of Wisdom* was under way.

I wished, with a sharpness that surprised me, there were windows on the ship's bridge. A view to the outside that was not filtered through computations and systems. A look at what was around us, and all that was not, stripped clean of the vectors and arrows, calculations and probabilities. I wanted to see Earth. I wanted to see the stars. I yearned for what I had imagined a thousand times: me and Anwar and Nadra, safe and warm, cuddled together as we watched the universe through the window. We would have seen in that darkness not death, not emptiness, not cruelty and fear, but possibilities. We would have been happy. I was sure of that. We could have been happy.

Jas said suddenly, "Where did the ship come from, anyway? *Homestead?*"

I was surprised by the question, but I replied, "They launched from Valle de México Spaceport."

"No, I mean, where did you get the ship? How did a bunch of North American separatists get their hands on a large passenger transport? How did you even get through the border checkpoints?"

There was no sense prevaricating now. "We have sympathizers in the Councils. I don't know who they are. There are ways through the borders if you have help on the other side and aren't trying to live as a Councils citizen. And one of the sympathizers maintains old SPEC ships for training use. It flew the Earth-Moon route for years, I think. Under a different name."

"And this person just . . . gave it to you," Jas said.

"Adam said—"

Adam had said a great many things, and most of them had been lies.

"I don't know who he was working with," I admitted. "Or why they helped."

Jas thought for a second, then said, "Adam doesn't sound North American. His accent. He's from somewhere in the Councils. Northern European, would be my guess."

"He left years ago." His own revelation, the first of many, he liked to say. I knew so little of Adam's past. He had never wanted it to matter. He had never wanted us to know.

"And he found somebody to provide a ship. And managed to get three hundred people to Valle de México, which is hundreds of kilometers from the border, without anybody noticing."

Adam had made it clear we were not to ask too many questions, lest we endanger our allies within the Councils. So I hadn't—but it was obvious now just how flimsy his explanations had been. How weak our plan had been. How many times we should have failed, if only somebody hadn't wanted us to succeed.

"Malachi said that someone in SPEC wanted us to come here," I said. "He didn't even know if his mission had been officially approved. He only knew what his superiors had told him."

"Who are his superiors?"

"I have no idea. Does it matter? He's dead. They spent ten years lying about what happened here, and Malachi is dead because of it."

"He was your friend?" Jas asked softly.

He was my friend. He was family. So was Panya. Dag. Boudicca.

Even Henke and Nico and Bao, in their way. But Malachi was the one I had brought into the family. None of this would have happened if he had not found the right crack in our defenses and slipped through. I had no energy left to be angry. Malachi was dead. I could not even look at him anymore, because there was nothing left to see but the ruined neck that no longer supported a head.

"Do you know what happened to my father?" I asked.

"I know what's in the Councils investigation records," Jas said, after a brief hesitation. "They don't say anything different from what's public. A security officer approached him at Presidio Station, and he died by suicide before he could be arrested."

"Do you believe that? Even knowing he wasn't responsible for the massacre?"

"I don't think the Councils assassinated him, if that's what you're asking. And he—he may have felt responsible."

I looked away, wishing I had not asked, and knowing I could not have avoided it. I didn't know how I had expected him to answer—how I had wanted him to answer. I didn't know what he could have said that would satisfy me. For ten years I had been thinking, *after they killed my father,* that terrible night as the dividing line between before and after, between the old life and the new.

"I remember him," Jas said. "Dr. Lago. I liked him. He was always laughing."

"Yes. He was." I stood up, feeling suddenly restless. The ship was traveling at 2 g or higher, and I wondered if the human body could feel every increasing tenth of a g, or if it was only my imagination that my limbs were becoming leaden weights as the minutes passed. "Everybody who knew him liked him. But they blamed him anyway."

Jas started to say something, then stopped, and said, "They'll know what happened now, with the data Baqir and Xiomara have. With my mum's message. They'll know he wasn't responsible."

"Do you think that will matter? You think the Councils will admit they lied? When have they *ever* admitted their lies? They claim to be better than the warlords and oligarchs from before the Collapse, but they're all the same. They only care about protecting themselves. They don't care—" I stopped. My voice was rising to a shout, echoing dully across the bridge. The anger, it seemed, had not burned itself out after all. "They don't care," I said quietly. "And you can't see that. You lied for them."

I turned away from him to pace around the bridge. It felt strange under increasing acceleration. Strange, but not impossible. I could have learned this, I thought, if we had made this ship our home. I could have learned to live when the engines were proving what Amita Bhattacharya had wanted them to prove. I could have grown used to the rapid changes from gravity to none, from being weighted to floating free.

A small black object on the floor caught my eye. It was a suppression weapon, the one Panya had tossed away in favor of her gun. I stepped over it to walk to the end of the curve of workstations, and turned to walk back.

"You're right," Jas said, after a long silence. "I did. At first because I was doing what they told me to do and I couldn't see anything but the walls of my hospital room, but later because . . . it was easier to let them speak for me. I kept hoping that if I just refused to ever talk about it, it would fade away." There was that quick, wry smile again. "It didn't exactly work out like that. Instead I've spent ten years thinking about little else."

Perhaps, I thought, perhaps this was an outcome he had foreseen from the first moment he set eyes on *House of Wisdom* through the shuttle window. Not Adam's cruelty, not SPEC's powerlessness, but the span of his life cut down to hours that could be counted on one hand, and this magnificent mausoleum, these dead, the same who had been with him all along, with him still, in these final moments. I had always hated the boy in the news reports for not crying at his parents' funerals, when I had felt like I would never be finished shedding tears of rage and grief for my father. But I had seen now what had been in that boy's mind. I wondered if anybody had ever told him it was not his fault he survived when so many hadn't.

I walked along the curve of the bridge again. I glanced over my shoulder. Jas was watching the display. I asked, "It's still working? The hydrogen?"

He answered without turning. "In the lower levels, at least, the concentration is well above where the fail-safes should be triggered, and the automatic filtering system hasn't switched itself back on."

He pointed to a display with a scrolling series of letters and numbers.

LV 0 H2 4% O2 18% N2 76%
LV 1 H2 5% O2 18% N2 75%
LV 2 H2 3% O2 20% N2 77%

"The concentrations are changing slowly now, but the recycling system is ramping up electrolysis," he said.

I bent to pick up the suppression weapon and tucked it into the back of my belt. "Good," I said.

"It's flammable at four percent," he went on. "We just have to hope nothing sparks early. Right now we should reach flammable concentrations on every level before—" His voice caught. "Impact."

He didn't sound relieved, or proud. Only tired.

"And this level will be last," I said.

I stopped behind his chair. I reached around to my back and took hold of the weapon. It wasn't the same design as the ones Adam's guards had used at the homestead, but it was similar enough that I understood the settings. Deter and subdue. Shock and sedation.

He sighed and ran his hand through his hair. "Yeah. By the time we open the doors, the whole ship will be ready to go up."

"Okay," I said. "Good."

I switched the weapon to Subdue and pressed it to the back of his neck. He sucked in a short, sharp breath, and every muscle in his body tensed. I pulled the trigger. The hum was quick, soft. Jas slapped his hand to his neck and twisted around to look up at me.

"What the fuck? What did you do?"

But already his words were slurring, his eyes fluttering.

"I'm sorry," I said. "I'll finish it."

He slumped in the chair. I caught him before he could fall. At this acceleration even the slightest bump on the head might cause injury. My hands were shaking.

I didn't know how long the sedative would keep him out. It wasn't hard to find the designated airlock for Level 10 evacuation, but because of the acceleration, I was sweating and breathless by the time I had dragged him that far. It was another struggle to get him into an evac suit. My thoughts were scattered, my motions hurried, and the effort of remaining upright grew harder with every passing minute.

The evacuation suit was considerably more advanced than those we'd donned aboard the shuttle. Those had been passive suits, nothing more, designed only to keep their wearers alive until rescue. This evac suit was equipped with thrusters that noted the speed and trajectory of the ship and fired to propel itself away; the goal was to counter the motion of the ship so that the evacuated person would be quickly jettisoned to safety.

At least, that was what was supposed to happen. I had no idea if I was doing it right. It was another item for the list of things I should have known. We had never seriously discussed evacuation, because we had never allowed ourselves to contemplate the possibility of failure. Adam had not allowed it. We had been so stupid to trust in his certainty to the point of burying our own doubts and fears.

I positioned Jas, still unconscious, in the airlock launch frame. I closed the hatch and depressurized the airlock. I launched the evac suit. From my point of view it happened so quickly: he was there, he was outside, he was gone. The system reported a successful launch and an active rescue beacon. It would have to be enough. They would bring him back to his aunt and his friends, to his research about quasars, to his twenty-six hours of telescope time, to his future. I had never meant to take a future away from any of our hostages, least of all from the one who had already suffered so much, but it didn't matter what I had intended. There is no nobility in regretting the violence you have done when it is too late.

I trudged back to the bridge slowly, slowly, every step an agony.

Alone on the bridge, I sat at the terminal to wait. The ship had already surpassed 5 g. Amita Bhattacharya's engines were a marvel. With every second *House of Wisdom* swung closer to its target.

The computer calculated time to impact as forty-two minutes. Not long enough for either ship to make a course correction wide enough to save them.

On the radio *Pangong* was calling for me and for *Homestead*. Orbital Control was hysterical, to put it mildly. On the navigation display I could see Providence Station, its evacuation vessels, the icebreakers moving too slowly into position. They would arrive in time to salvage what they could, no sooner. My head was throbbing and my shoulders ached. I looked for the emergency beacon of the evacuation suit on the screen. It was far from the ship, already left behind.

"... you hear us?"

A new voice came over the radio, quiet, wavering, but with an urgency that caught my attention.

"Can you hear us? Zahra?"

I sat forward quickly, my head spinning. I knew that voice. "Anwar!"

"Zahra!" My brother leaned toward the camera, peering at me through Orvar's blood. He was not alone. Nadra was behind him, her eyes wide with fear, and there were seven or eight others on the bridge as well. A couple of small children, two older women, and a few young men near the door. "Zahra, the ships are going to crash, and we don't know how to stop it. We can't change course. We can't change anything. Adam shot all the people who knew how to fly the ship." There were tears in Anwar's eyes and a catch in his throat, and I wanted more than anything to reach across space and take him in my arms. "Everybody's scared and the guards have guns and they won't tell us anything—"

"Anwar, listen to me. Nadra. Listen."

"But we—"

"Listen to me," I said, pleading. "You can still get away. There are evacuation suits on *Homestead*. Look for the evac airlock close to the bridge. You can—"

One of the men near the door stumbled backward with a shout of surprise, and the other lurched to catch him. The muzzle of a weapon appeared through the open doorway, then an arm, then the growl of a familiar voice telling them to move out of the way. One of the kids started crying. Nadra pulled Anwar away from the radio, and there was Adam.

My breath caught—how deeply those instincts sink into us, quivering fear in the face of familiar rage, that skittish animalistic cower—but the sensations, rather than growing, sank away, like water vanishing into parched soil. He could not hurt me now. He looked around, wild-eyed, until he saw me on their screen. He strode over to the console and slammed his hands into the panel as he leaned down.

"Do you think this changes anything?" he shouted, his voice thundering. His eyes were bloodshot, his hair unkempt, his face contorted with anger. There were sweat stains at his armpits and bloodstains on his sleeves. "Do you think you are accomplishing anything? You will *not* snatch our final victory from us."

"Victory?" I said. I wanted to draw upon my fear, my outrage, my horror at what he was doing, but I felt as though my heart had been set adrift in empty space, with nothing to knock against, nothing to fall into. I could hear shouts in the background, cries and screams of fear, a man bellowing for others to stay on the floor. The people aboard *Homestead* knew what was coming, and they were afraid. "This is not victory, Adam. You promised to protect the family, but you're killing them."

"We are ending our lives in defiance and strength," he retorted. "We are finally free of the crushing boot of the oppressors. We will be remembered forever as the only people courageous enough to defy the liars and deceivers. There was *never* going to be a way back from this. This is where we were always going to end."

Behind him one of the old women—Rosalinda, a kindly grandmother to everybody in the family—was shushing the weeping children.

"Do you even care about all the children who are going to die?" I asked.

"We make *sacrifices*," Adam spat, his pale face turning red. "Nobody has sacrificed more than I. You dare scold *me* about the hardships we have endured on our path to victory? *They would not have to die if you had done as you were told.*"

"No," I said, my voice drawing down as his shouts rang. "They would not have to die if you were anything more than a coward."

Adam scowled. "Your father was a weak slave of the Councils, and you are as weak as he was. You have always been weak. You have always cowered and groveled when a stronger person would have fought. You relished every chance I gave you to bend and kiss my feet."

"This is betrayal," I said. "This is worse than failure. Nobody will remember you as anything other than a monster. They will remember you exactly as you deserve."

"Your cowardice has never shown more than now," he said, his voice spiked with a disdain that would have crushed me only days ago.

"No," I said. He would not hear me, but I was not speaking to him. I was speaking to Nadra and Anwar, to Rosalinda and the others, to myself, if only to prove I still could, here at the end. "What you are doing is cowardice. I am only trying to keep you from hurting more people."

There was nothing more to say. There was no truth in Adam's orbit except what Adam decided truth to be, and that was as fickle as the weather, snapping from brilliant sunshine to deadly flash floods in the blink of an eye or the slap of an open hand. I could see now what Malachi had seen all along: that it was not a family but a spider's web, a trap that glistened so beautifully with morning dew, but at its center was Adam, a ravenous god in his own scrabbling creation, craving devotion, devouring praise, taking everything offered to him and giving nothing in return.

"You don't know anything of hurt!" Adam roared. "You don't—"

He broke off sharply. Nadra had launched herself at his back, and she hit him from behind with such force he doubled over with a grunt of surprise.

She took hold of his hair and slammed his head into the terminal. Then she dragged his head up and slammed it down again, again, and there were tears on her face, her breath was hitching with sobs, and I wanted to reach for her, wanted to pull her away, but it was Anwar who pulled her away. Adam's face was a wreckage of blood and shattered bone. Nadra let go with a gasp and shoved him to slump over the terminal.

Nadra stared down at her hands.

"Nadra, Anwar, listen to me," I said. My voice was shaking, but I needed their attention. "Rosalinda. All of you. You have thirty minutes. Get yourselves into evacuation suits and get away from the ship. Take as many people as you can. Anybody who will listen."

"You'll find us, won't you?" Nadra looked up at me and forced the words through her tears. "Even if SPEC arrests us? You'll find us?"

"They won't arrest you. Listen—they have proof that Dad didn't do what they said he did. They have proof that they got it all wrong. You have to make sure they don't hide that proof. Make sure they tell the truth. Do you understand?"

"How?" Anwar asked.

"Find Jaswinder Bhattacharya. Find his aunt, Councilor Bhattacharya."

"A Councilor?" Anwar said, incredulous. "But she'll—"

"They'll listen to you. Demand a meeting. You'll get it. You can make them tell the truth. I know you can." I reached out, aching to touch them. "I love you. Please go. Go as fast as you can."

They left the bridge quickly; Rosalinda had taken Adam's gun. When there was nobody, I ended the transmission.

I watched until the ship reported the sudden appearance of several emergency beacons in the vicinity of *Homestead*, and I exhaled. I had to believe Nadra and Anwar were among them. I had to believe they would be rescued. I had to believe they would not be held responsible for my crimes.

A red warning light began to flash on the screen: the hydrogen concentration in the lower five levels had surpassed 15 percent.

I reached for the radio again. I used the open emergency broadcast channel. I wanted everyone to know who those emergency evac suits were carrying. I needed them to understand.

I said what I had to say, and there were only minutes left. The stream of evac suits from *Homestead* had stopped. I had not counted them. There were more than a few, enough to form a bright cluster of stars on the navigation screen.

I entered the command to spark the fires, one level at a time. It would spread quickly.

I rose from the chair and opened the door of the bridge to let the deadly air in. Hydrogen gas has no odor, no color. It surrounded me, as invisible as desert wind twisting through a slot canyon. It felt like nothing at all. I staggered over to the officers' ready room and slid to the floor to lean against the glass wall. The parasites were still on the other side. I could see, in the tangle of corpses on the floor, a single plait of Panya's yellow hair.

My vision was dimming, marred by black spots, and my head ached. I didn't close my eyes. I wanted to keep looking at that constellation of bright stars on the screen, the proof that my sister and brother had survived, proof that there had been room for courage under the fearful oppression of Adam's madness. Proof that even the worst of us could not crush hope so thoroughly there was no way out of the darkness.

There was a roar of sound somewhere in the ship, like a storm rolling over distant peaks. The flash of light and heat, when it came, was as sudden and beautiful as the sun rising over the desert.

HOUSE OF WISDOM: This is . . . this is *House of Wisdom*. For anybody who can hear me. There are people evacuating from *Homestead*. I know your ships are tracking them. You need to know that those people mean you no harm. Some of them are children, and right now they need your help. Please do not blame them for what we've done. They only wanted a better life. They only wanted—and tell them I'm sorry. Nadra, Anwar, I'm so sorry. You deserve so much better. I want you to remember what Mama and Dad used to believe in. They used to believe in the Councils. Not the Councils as they are now, with their secret programs and closed borders and empty promises, but the Councils as they were meant to be. I remember Dad telling me about the First Council, when the people who survived the Collapse came together. The world was dying all around them, people were dying, they barely had food, they were living in a wasteland, the sky was falling, but they came together to promise each other humankind would never make the same mistakes again. They had no reason for hope, but they found it anyway. For a long time I've believed I would gladly condemn the Councils to the second Collapse they seem so determined to achieve. But Dad never wanted that. Dad liked to quote what Leung Ma-Lin had said: "The day we believe ourselves immune from the cruelties and atrocities of the past is the day we commit them again." He believed that. He wanted to prove that the people who had fled before the Collapse were wrong about humanity's fate. He would never, ever have done what he was accused of doing. Whatever his flaws, Gregory Lago believed in doing better than the past. The Councils can prove it now. SPEC can prove it. Don't let them hide the truth. Nadra, Anwar, I love you. I love you so much. Be safe.

I'm alone. I'm certain of it now. There's been no response from orbit for ten days [data corruption] so quickly up there. Even faster than here. There's nobody left except the dead. I'm going to try one last time to launch the craft remotely. I can only hope somebody receives this warning someday. They told us Earth was dying, but perhaps they were wrong. They told us we came into the darkness to save humanity from extinction, but perhaps that is somebody else's burden to bear. Whoever you are, whatever you have done to survive, this is *Mournful Evening Song*, and this is our final transmission. Our mission is over.

—FRAGMENT 7, *MOURNFUL EVENING SONG* VIA UC33-X

I woke in darkness, at the birth of the universe.

Everything we're made of came to be in the first moments of existence. There was the beginning, and so quickly thereafter, so brief a glimmer of time we can only conceive of it in millionths of a second, there was matter: electrons and quarks. Another glimmer and the quarks became protons and neutrons, dancing madly where only emptiness had been before. Ages passed— minutes, but when all of time is the hold of a breath, minutes are eons. Particles clumped into pairs. Time and space stretched, stretched, days, years, centuries, millennia rolling outward into the nothingness. Electrons organized themselves into flickering clouds of probability around the nuclei. The first atoms of hydrogen and helium were born. One million years, then two, time passing with no one to measure it, no memory to weigh it against, before gravity nudged those lonely atoms together into fierce burning lights to spot the darkness.

"And that," my mother said to me, "is where it gets interesting. Everything we are was born in the hearts of stars. Do you still think that's *boring*?"

My answer that day was a noncommittal shrug. I heard her tone as teasing and scolding. I was too young to recognize it as loving. I would not hear the love in her playful tutelage until years after she was gone. I had never thought her lessons boring, but I was afraid to admit interest to my mother, whose mind was so much faster than mine, whose well of knowledge was so much deeper. I wanted to learn things in my own time, even the lives and deaths of the stars.

"Are you sure you're my son?" my mother had asked, poking at my belly. "Maybe I picked up the wrong one at the maternity ward, because I know I asked for a child who doesn't find the universe *boring.*"

The space between a truthful memory and a story made true only in the repeated telling of it is smaller than we imagine, but I believe my mother was full of joy that day, the day Captain Ngahere announced that *House of Wisdom* was going to intercept UC33-X and bring it aboard for study.

We were floating together in my father's garden on Level 7. The ship was traveling at a steady velocity; within hours the propulsion drive would engage, and our feet would press to the floor, but that was yet to come. Around us the garden was an unending summer in vibrant hues of green, flowers fragrant and blooming. My mother had caught me skipping my lessons with the tutor to wander around the ship instead. Her punishment had been to bring me to the garden and teach me about the universe. Beyond the windows the stars were small, the sun behind us, the Earth tucked away on the other side of the solar system.

I remembered her laughter. The warmth of her arm around my shoulders. The pulse-skip of fear in my throat every time I thought about how far we were traveling. The answers I mumbled and excuses I offered when my mother noticed that I was not happy. I remembered her shoving me playfully when I rolled my eyes at her passionate biography of the universe, and the feeling of free fall that came with drifting toward the windows, as though there was nothing between me and the darkness, then a moment of panic, the kind of panic that claws at the throat and chills the blood, and I turned without thought, reaching for my mother, grasping for her hand and finding it out of reach, turning again, spinning out of control, and where my mother had been there was a pillar of fire in the darkness, and all at once, with the suddenness of a door slamming shut, a dream ending, a life snuffing out, my entire body shuddered with pain.

I cried out, a pathetic animal sound, the noise muffled in the helmet—

Helmet. Space suit.

Darkness, and light, and darkness again.

My vision was blurred, my head throbbing so powerfully I felt every heartbeat in my eyes, and my chest burned with a fiery agony that intensified with every breath. I was in a space suit and turning slowly—spinning, with nothing to grasp, nothing to reach for—and as I spun again, head over feet like the spokes of a wheel, I saw *House of Wisdom*, and smaller, so small, *Homestead*. The ships were tiny and distant and burning.

The collision had been indirect. An angled blow across *Homestead*'s nose had torn a great gash in the hull. Gases vented and the space around the ship was dotted with dust—

Not dust. Bodies.

I couldn't breathe. The dead were tumbling into space from the broken hull. I had killed them. They looked like specks from this distance. I had killed them. I couldn't breathe. As I turned again, the wheel going around, *Homestead* dropped out of sight, and there was the Earth, a small, cold marble, and the Moon, and the bright disk of Providence Station sliding out of view—and there were the ships again. Silent explosions, like lightning from far away, spewed blinding white light from every jagged wound along the hulls. They were so very far away.

I turned again, and there was nothing but darkness before me, and I moved without thinking, grasping although there was nothing to hold. Gathering spots overtook my vision. I thought I heard a beep—a voice—but it meant nothing, and I blacked out again. Somehow, somehow, even in the darkness, I knew I was spinning, and I knew I was falling away from the wreckage and the fire, and I knew I was alone.

S even hours." My aunt's voice, normally as polished as a gleaming blade, was ragged. "That's how long you were adrift."

I didn't remember all of it, but I remembered enough that I did not want to close my eyes, however exhausted I was by the effort of keeping them open. I remembered waking aboard *Pangong* in a quarantine tent with white-suited figures leaning over me, and waking again, still in quarantine, when a shuttle landed in Armstrong City, but the rest of the past few days were a blur of bright lights and looming doctors' faces. When I slept, I dreamed of fire and darkness.

The quarantine tent and biohazard suits were gone. The doctors were satisfied the parasite had not come with me. I wished I could find the same certainty. Reason told me that the parasite would have asserted itself by now, but every itch on my skin, every phantom sensation, felt to me like a silver worm slithering through my limbs.

Aunt Padmavati went on, "You weren't fitted into the evacuation suit quite right. That explains the bruising. Do you remember that?"

"No, but I didn't—" I said, tried to say, but a dry cough overtook the words.

She lifted a straw to my lips. "You didn't . . . ?"

The water was lukewarm. I gulped it greedily. "I didn't put myself into the suit. I wasn't awake. Zahra sedated me."

My aunt's eyes widened slightly. Too late I realized what I had revealed. I wanted to grab the words from the air and cram them back into my mouth, like a child hiding a cookie he should not have eaten.

But she had been sitting by my bedside when I awoke, every single time, even when the doctors and nurses were bustling through the room, and I was not going to lie to her. She seemed to me even smaller and more birdlike now. Her shoulders were thin, her graying hair escaping in wisps from the braid that wound over her shoulder. Every motion was deliberate in the way of somebody used to Earth's gravity now moving about on the Moon. She had never looked less like my mother.

"Jas?" my aunt said softly.

She touched my hand. Her skin was papery and dry but warm. I had forgotten what a warm touch felt like; it might have been the brand of a red-hot iron. I jerked my hand away, and my aunt withdrew hers. Her lips were pursed, her brow creased. I did not recognize this stranger who wore my aunt's face, a woman soft with concern where stern and unbending Councilor Padmavati Bhattacharya ought to have been, and I hated that she was not a stranger at all. She was who she had always been, now stripped of the armor she'd constructed over a lifetime.

"Baqir," I said. "Xiomara. Did they—are they—"

"They're fine," my aunt said. "They were retrieved by a SPEC ship."

"They're okay?"

"They were both moderately dehydrated and bruised, and

Baqir's shoulder is injured, but otherwise they are well. They have been cleared from quarantine. They will recover," Aunt Padmavati said.

Relief was a sharp pain in the center of my chest. She would not lie to me about that.

"Auntie, there's something—it's important. Dr. Lago didn't kill anybody," I said. "He had nothing to do with any of it. It wasn't even—"

"We know," Aunt Padmavati said, interrupting me gently. "Jas. We know. Everybody knows by now. His daughter made certain of that before she died."

I had not expected otherwise, but still I felt a pang upon confirmation of Zahra's death. She had apologized when she sedated me. Apologized, and promised to finish it. I had never meant to leave her to do it alone.

So sluggish were my thoughts that it took me a moment to ask, "What do you mean? What did she do?"

My aunt raised a single eyebrow, then reached for the panel beside the bed. Live news reports from across the world filled the wallscreen. *House of Wisdom. Homestead.* Dr. Lago. The man called Adam Light. A significant amount of debris had struck Providence, causing serious damage and seven fatalities. Of greater concern was the ongoing danger from the debris. Orbital Control had restricted space traffic while they monitored the possibility of a Kessler cascade. There were salvage crews working to clean up what they could.

"The man who was calling himself Adam Light was in truth a former Councils citizen named Jeffrey Kimball," my aunt said when an image of him appeared. "Twelve years ago he was convicted of assault. Rather than enter a counseling and service program, he fled to the desert."

I tried to decide if I cared about being right about that, that he had been a Councils criminal before he became overlord of his own scrabbling desert kingdom, but I felt nothing.

The news reports did not mention Malachi and SPEC's secret, forbidden mission. They did not mention the parasite. They were still referring to it as a bioengineered virus. The survivors from *Homestead* were receiving a great deal of attention.

As was Zahra.

"Listen," said my aunt as she called up a public audio file.

Zahra's voice filled the room. She sounded hoarse and tired. She was asking for help, not for herself but for her siblings, her family. For the memory of her father. She was saying goodbye.

I turned my head away, too late to hide my tears. To my right, tall windows looked over Armstrong City. There was no sunlight on the domes; Armstrong was somewhere in the middle of its long lunar night, as well as its artificially defined local night. Wispy clouds drifted over the city, twisting around the buildings and winding along rails and pathways. It was as close as Armstrong ever came to experiencing real weather, that fleeting formation and dissipation of moisture exhaled from the city's carefully maintained parks and farms. The buildings were mostly white, tinged with a silver gleam that faded into gray, with broad windows like flat blank eyes.

Zahra's message ended. My aunt moved in her chair but said nothing.

"How many people survived?" I asked.

"Eighty-three," she said.

Eighty-three out of three hundred. Eighty-three people who had believed they were leaving a life of hardship and misery for a gleaming home in the stars, for safety and comfort, for a dream of peace. They had so despaired of what Earth had to offer, having crashed so many times against walls they could not breach, they had followed a criminal narcissist on a hopeless voyage into space, and fewer than one-third of them had survived.

"Zahra had a brother and a sister," I said. "Twins. Teenagers."

"They survived. We're trying to locate their family. Their closest relation is a cousin, I believe. A researcher in one of the outer planets stations. None of the children will be punished for their part in what happened."

Some in the Councils would have suggested it. I knew that much without asking. There were always those who viewed the children of refugees and separatists not as victims but as pawns in a game in which the winners had been chosen long ago. I thought about the anger in Baqir's voice when he spoke about how his entire family had been denied citizenship because of the medicine his grandmother stole.

"And the others?" I asked. "The ones who aren't children?"

"That remains to be determined."

In the distance a train whipped along curving rails, darting between unseen stations. There was no color. No sound penetrated the walls and closed doors of the hospital room. Everything about the atmosphere and environment of Armstrong City was controlled, measured, balanced. There was a joke on Earth that a person could not cough on the Moon without triggering the city's viral filtration system. It was a marvel of environmental engineering.

All I could see was how delicate it was. How very easy it would be to destroy.

Don't let them make you lie, Malachi had said.

Already they were trying to erase him and all he had endured. Already they were doing exactly what he and Zahra had feared. I didn't even know if Malachi was his real name. If he had family, they would never know about the sacrifice he had made.

I was quiet for a moment, considering my words. "SPEC isn't going to admit their part in getting back aboard, are they? Is anybody even asking how three hundred people slipped through border checkpoints and stole a ship?"

"There are quite a lot of questions going officially unanswered."

"Will they tell people about the parasite? Or release the rest of the messages Dr. Lago recovered?"

"There are no plans to do so at this time," my aunt said. She was watching the screen, although I did not know that she was seeing it.

"Don't fuck around with me, Auntie." The words sounded more tired than angry, but it worked. She looked at me sharply, eyebrows raised. "I spent ten years lying to make things easier for them. If I'm expected to do it again, you should probably tell me what I'm supposed to lie about."

I could not guess what Aunt Padmavati saw when she looked at me then, but her expression was not one of shock or disapproval or disappointment. Instead of answering, she said thoughtfully, "I remember them, you know. Dr. Lago and Dr. Dove. I met them before he left for *House of Wisdom*. It was one of those tiresome ceremonial dinners. Everybody else was there because it was an obligation, but Gregory Lago was delighted. He took so much joy in his research, in sharing it, in hearing what others were doing. In what he might discover."

A pause, and she looked past me, turning her gaze to the view over Armstrong City.

"There have been a great many meetings lately about what the public does and does not need to know. I've not been invited to all of them," she said.

"But you don't think they're going to release the messages from *Mournful Evening Song*."

"No."

"They're going to keep saying it was a man-made virus. From Earth."

"Yes."

"And pretending to look for some anarchist or terrorist group to blame. Probably somebody in the wastelands. Somebody who can be blamed without anybody important being implicated."

"Not overtly, but yes, essentially."

"They're going to demand that I lie for them again. Baqir and Xiomara too. Are they threatening Baqir's citizenship? What do they have to hold over Xiomara?"

"I am not privy to those conversations."

"But you're letting them happen."

My aunt lifted one hand in a defeated gesture. "I don't know what you think my position entails, but I hardly have the power to unilaterally command the Councils' decisions. They've got quite a bit to argue about. Few people even believe they have the full story of what happened. The fire aboard *House of Wisdom*, followed by the collision, was so destructive it might be months before we recover anything useful. Zahra Dove Lago did quite a thorough job."

Her tone was so mild, so calm.

"Zahra had never even been in space before," I said.

My aunt did not reply. She was still not looking at me.

"It was my plan. Zahra helped, but I was the one who decided to destroy the alien parasite. I was the one who decided to deflect *Homestead* using *House of Wisdom*. I wasn't even sure it would work," I added. "But I did it anyway."

I faced my aunt as I spoke, and I did not turn away, even as the silence stretched, and stretched, and her eyes remained fixed on the gray city outside.

Finally, my aunt said, "Before you were born, Amita asked me if I would take care of you, should anything ever happen to her. I laughed when she asked. I knew nothing of children, but she was not asking in jest. I agreed because she wanted me to, and because I could not imagine anything would ever happen to her. I did not expect to ever have to raise a child. I always thought she would outlive me by decades."

"I know," I said quietly.

"No, Jas," she said, finally turning to face me, "I don't think you do. Do you want to know why I haven't been invited to very many Councils meetings over the last couple of days? It's a bit embarrassing, I'm afraid. I grew rather . . . heated in my response when Councilor Nyman suggested the doctors wake you prematurely to interrogate you."

I didn't know what to say, so I only said, "I've never liked him."

"He's a boorish, insufferable prick," my aunt said. "Jas, I did not think a young woman who's spent more than half her life on a desert homestead could have figured out how to revive the ship's engines and set such a carefully calculated course. I knew who had come up with the plan from the very moment it became clear."

"Mum's engines didn't need any help." My voice was hoarse. "They fired up like they'd never gone cold."

"Oh, of course they did," Aunt Padmavati said, with a breathy exhalation that was almost a laugh. "As though Amita would have accepted anything less. Do you know what they'll say about you, if the truth is revealed? If you become known as the one who destroyed humanity's first chance at communicating with alien life? Do you know what they'll say about your mother? Some people will understand, but others won't. Others will only see the destruction and the death. They won't see what was saved."

I sat up, ignoring the twinges of pain, and reached for her hand.

"Auntie, I knew exactly what I was doing. So did Mum."

She squeezed my hand and smiled sadly. "Jas . . ."

"And what happens if the Councils cover it up?" I asked. "They're going to search the wreck for everything they can. If any part of the parasite survives, and they aren't warned, it will happen again. There will be another massacre. They'll find somebody else to blame. And it might happen here in Armstrong, or down on Earth. We might not be able to stop it."

Her lips were a thin, worried line, but she did not deny it.

"I knew what I was doing," I said again. "We have to tell them. Release the data to the public. Let everyone know what happened and why."

"The Councils will never agree to that, but we—"

"So don't ask them! You've done it before! I know you weren't supposed to give me any of the ship's data when I was all of fourteen years old, but you did it anyway. You can—"

"Jaswinder," my aunt said calmly, the corners of her lips rising. "Please don't interrupt me. I was saying the Councils will never agree to that, but we don't have to ask their permission."

"Oh." I slumped back into my pillow. "No. We don't."

"I won't be able to shield you as I did before," my aunt said. "You're not a child anymore. You'll have to testify before the Councils. You'll be asked to tell your story over and over again. They won't allow you silence, not this time."

"I know," I said. "I don't want to be silent this time."

"If it is what you want . . ."

"It is."

My aunt hesitated for just a second, then she nodded and stood up. "Very well. I will take care of it. But for now, you are going to rest." She leaned over to kiss my forehead. "I love you, Jas. I'll come back tomorrow."

Only when she was gone did I think that was, perhaps, the first time she had said the words aloud—or perhaps the first time I had been able to hear them.

I wiped the tears from my eyes and watched the news for a while longer with the sound turned down low, but the dizzying blur of images and faces became overwhelming. They kept showing Zahra's picture: as she had been in her false SPEC identification, and as she had been as a child in a Councils school in Presidio Bay. So happy in the latter, so grim in the former. Ten years, a government's cowardly lies, the mesmerizing control of a narcissistic criminal, that's all it had taken to transform a smiling teenage girl into a notorious terrorist. And now she was gone. The damage could not be undone.

I shut off the wallscreen, and at once, without the distraction, a cold fear twisted through me. I felt like a person split in two, one who spoke the words of confidence and reassurance to my aunt, and another who curled up inside a raw wound of grief and fear and guilt. There were tears blurring my eyes and a dull pain throbbing in my chest.

I had meant what I said to Aunt Padmavati: People needed to know. I was not going to sink into silence again.

But in that moment, in that sterile room in the domed gray city, I was glad she had preserved the delicate peace around me for a short while longer. Eventually I fell asleep watching the clouds drift over Armstrong City.

The soft noise of the door sliding open woke me. The room was dark, as was the city outside. The mist had thickened, and the silver buildings were muted and gray. Local night again. I had slept through the day.

The chair beside my bed scraped. A hand touched mine.

"Sorry. I didn't mean to wake you."

Not a doctor or my aunt, but Baqir. He looked so much better than when I had last seen him. He was clean, rested, clear-eyed, with his brown hair falling over his face, dressed in a plain blue hospital robe and shuffling slippers. His left shoulder was encased in a healing brace; his prosthetic arm had been removed. The brace and bandages looked stiff and uncomfortable, but he did not seem to be in pain.

"Hi," he said. He wasn't smiling. I wanted to reach up to touch his face, trace my fingers along his jaw to his lips, to reassure myself that he was real, alive, here, but I did not move.

"Are you okay?" I asked.

He shrugged his good shoulder. "I'm fine. They're building me a new arm. Last one was unsalvageable."

"Oh." I didn't know what else to say, so I didn't say anything and we fell into an awkward silence. But we didn't have awkward silences, the two of us; that had never been our way. Baqir was fiddling with the belt of his hospital robe, and I could not stop looking at him.

"You know," he said, "I thought that smashing two fucking huge spaceships together was going to be the most insane thing your family did this week, but I think your aunt has outdone you."

"What? What did she . . ." Then I understood. I struggled to sit up. "She released the data from *House of Wisdom*."

"You knew she was going to?"

"It was my idea."

"I . . . don't think I am exactly surprised by that," he said. "For fuck's sake, Jas. They're going to be all over you. The investigators and journalists and—everybody. They're never going to leave you alone."

"I know," I said.

And I did. I did know, but even so, the prospect of having to tell the story—everything I would have to reveal—every accusation I would have to face—every warning I would have to give—it all began to drum at the medicated haze of my mind like the first dangerous rain of the monsoon. My breath was short, my heart fast, my thoughts suddenly racing.

"Hey, hey, don't do that," Baqir said. "Jas, come on, breathe. It'll be all right."

He took my hand and held on tight. I closed my eyes and focused on the touch of his hand, imagined that warmth spreading through me, melting an invisible frost that coated my veins and clung to my bones. He moved his hand and I thought he was leaving—already tired of my company, and I didn't have the energy to blame him—but he did not stand. He lifted my hand and kissed the palm softly. My eyes snapped open, and he pressed a second kiss to my hand, right where the fingers met the palm, then lowered our joined hands to the bed again.

He said, "If I hadn't been so fucked up, I would have realized what you were doing when you put us on that ship. I should have realized you never meant to follow us."

I held my breath for a moment—forced myself to let it out. My eyes felt hot but I did not look away. "I didn't want you to know."

"Yeah, I got that, but I should have anyway. I know you. I know everything about you." A pause. "Well. Almost everything."

I couldn't figure out what that tone meant, somewhere between sad and frustrated, amused and relieved. "I didn't want you to know," I said again.

"I know," Baqir said. "Because I know you're an idiot. And I'm really fucking angry about—about all of this. Everything. All of them, for what they did. And pretty angry at you too. But I'm also so fucking grateful that she didn't let you kill yourself."

I'm sorry, she had said. *I'll finish it.* I had assumed we would both die aboard *House of Wisdom*, Zahra with her guilt and I with mine. I had never been able to explain how it felt to be an empty shell of memory where a son ought to be, and how many times I had returned to *House of Wisdom* in my dreams, in my fears, in my nightmares. I had never been able to tell anybody how often I wished my mother had never sent me away at the end. Ten years I had been a ghost among the living. I didn't know how to be anything else.

I reached up to touch Baqir's face then, to brush his hair back from his forehead and feel the warmth as he leaned into my hand, but the motion made something pull in my side, and I gasped in pain.

"Okay, stop," Baqir said, sitting back. "You're hurt. Just—just rest."

"I'm not hurt. You sound like my aunt."

"I don't sound anything like your aunt and you know it."

"No. You don't." I settled for running my hand down his arm, grasping his hand again, feeling a small thrill when he didn't pull away. "What are they going to do to the survivors from *Homestead*? Not the kids. The adults."

"Who the fuck knows?" he said. "Turns out one of them is a Councils citizen, and she's sort of taken the lead in speaking for them. Probably because she's the only one anybody would listen to. You can ignore a bunch of desert-rat criminals, but you can't ignore a nice Councils grandmother who also happens to be a former professor of political science. If anything's been decided, they aren't saying."

"That doesn't seem good enough," I said, "just waiting for the Councils to decide."

Not for Zahra, who had only ever wanted a safe place to live. For her brother and sister. For the memory of their parents, whom the Councils had treated so cruelly. For the pilot who had tried to rescue the doomed crew of the *Breton*. For the young SPEC agent with the brown eyes and curly hair who had been sent on a mission doomed for failure.

Baqir did that awkward one-shouldered shrug again. "I doubt

anybody's bothered to ask them what they want. Or need. Or even why they were there in the first place. The Councils don't tend to like the answers, so they don't ask."

The bitterness in his voice had probably always been there, I thought, but I had always tried not to hear it.

"That's what Ariana wanted me to do, you know," he said. "For the project she was going to premiere at the Second Council. She was interviewing a bunch of people about—well, everything, people living all over the world and off it, but she wanted to talk to me about moving from the deserts to the Councils. I told her I'd think about it. It seemed like such a massive pain in the ass when she asked, and I didn't want my parents to see and think . . ." He smiled sadly. "Xiomara's going to try to get the project shown anyway, even unfinished. I think I might help her."

"I'm sorry," I said.

"Why? What for?"

"Everything. For . . . I don't know. Everything." My voice cracked on the last word, and there were tears stinging my eyes again. "I'm sorry we couldn't save Ariana. I'm sorry I never asked . . . I'm sorry."

"It's okay, Jas," Baqir said. Then, his voice little more than a whisper: "We'll be okay."

It overwhelmed me, how very much I yearned to believe him, to trust in the warmth of his hand holding tight to mine, his brown eyes warm and sad and knowing, and the reassurance that he was staying, staying beside me, staying close, and not leaving.

After a while he fell asleep with his head resting on the bed, a position that could not possibly be comfortable, but then Baqir had always been able to sleep anywhere. I watched him for a while, brushing my fingers gently through his dark hair, afraid to move too much lest I wake him. It seemed impossible that I could still be so tired, after doing almost nothing but sleeping for a couple of days, but my eyes kept slipping closed. Every time, every time, *House of Wisdom* was there, burning, and from the wounds in its side the dead drifted, alight as candles, and silver worms curled and crackled and whipped, and I could not grasp anything in the darkness. I had brought back an entirely new style of nightmare from *House of Wisdom*.

Eventually I gave up on sleep and turned on the wallscreen, without any sound, only to have something to stare at besides the gray city.

I was still staring blankly sometime later when the door opened. A nurse leaned into the room, and when he saw Baqir he rolled his eyes.

"There he is," the nurse said quietly. "Should've known. He's been asking about you nonstop for three days."

I didn't say anything, but whatever crossed my face made the man laugh softly. He came in to look over the medical monitors beside my bed. He had the tall, thin frame of somebody who had spent his life in low gravity, and he moved with the ease of a long-time Moon resident. When he saw the news on the wallscreen—they were showing images of the man called Adam Light and his top followers—he let out a breath and shook his head.

"Those people," he said, and I tensed, not wanting to hear what he was about to say. But he went on, "It's so heartbreaking. I can't imagine being so desperate that devoting myself to a monster like that seems like the only way out. But I suppose that's the problem, isn't it? I live in a great bloody bubble on the Moon. I've never had to imagine it."

The nurse caught me looking at him, and he smiled sheepishly.

"Sorry. You try to get some sleep too."

Then he was gone, and the room was silent again. I didn't sleep, but neither did the creeping nightmares return. I watched the news, and I watched Baqir sleep, and without shying away from where my mind wandered, without succumbing to despair or guilt or hopelessness, I let myself think. My aunt and I had a lot to talk about.

The Councils building in Armstrong City was a tall white structure of metal and glass, narrow as a blade, at the center of a broad plaza dotted by manicured spots of greenery. The lunar night was over, and Armstrong was once again welcoming the sunlight. The filtered light transformed the city, drawing people outside to fill the public spaces, casting rainbow prisms of color where there had been only white and gray before. Parks and gardens opened their roofs to reveal the life that was protected so carefully within.

Aunt Padmavati and I were waiting in a room on a high floor. Aside from a Councils page who peeked her head in every half hour to ask if we needed anything, we were alone. It was the first day of the Councils' preliminary meetings on the *House of Wisdom* incident. My aunt, due to her part in releasing the data from the ship, was to be questioned by her fellow Councilors. She seemed unconcerned. Though we had spent more time together and spoken more frankly to each other in the past fortnight than ever before, I still could not tell if her nonchalance was an act.

The page returned. "They've just finished hearing Dr. Sepulveda's statement now. You'll be called after a ten-minute break."

Over the page's shoulder, a quick glimpse down the hall revealed a woman with long steel-gray hair wound into plaits emerging from the meeting room. Dr. Rosalinda Sepulveda, one of the *Homestead* survivors, the Councils citizen and former professor who had emerged as their spokesperson. She had moved to the desert to be with her daughter and grandchildren when they joined Adam Light's family. The daughter had died aboard *Home-*

stead, after refusing to evacuate, but the three grandchildren had escaped.

The door closed again, and I tried to decide if what I had seen on Dr. Sepulveda's face in that instant was calm or fear. My palms were sweaty. I could not sit still. I could not stop thinking of Zahra's farewell, and how badly she had wanted a better life for her siblings, and how frightened and alone they must be at the center of so much attention. I knew my aunt had spoken to them while I was in the hospital, but for them, and for all the other survivors, nothing had been decided.

"What's going to happen to them?" I asked.

Aunt Padmavati put her hand on my knee to stop it from bouncing. It was not the first time she had done so. "I don't know any more than you do."

"Most of them didn't even *do* anything. Not much more than board a ship under knowingly false pretenses, and that's barely even a crime."

"I know, Jas. But the Councilors are also concerned with what the group as a whole attempted to do."

"None of them would have been there if they thought they had any other choice," I said. "They were desperate and afraid, and to them that man seemed like a better option than staying desperate and afraid."

"As I'm sure Dr. Sepulveda said to the investigation committee, in her own words, and will say again when they question her more thoroughly. Is this what you're worried about? It's unlikely they'll ask you about the survivors. I imagine they're rather more concerned with the parasite."

"Maybe they should ask me," I said. "Maybe they should ask everyone what they would do if given the choice between spending years and years trying to prove themselves worthy of the most basic fucking human decency or leaving it all behind."

"Jas," my aunt said gently, "it's not that simple."

"It's supposed to be," I countered. "The whole purpose of the Councils is supposed to be a way to stop using *it's not that simple* as an excuse to protect our own comfort while others suffer. That's what the Councils are trying to do, isn't it? They're trying to make it look like they're so fucking magnanimous for not blaming children for being raised in a poisoned wasteland, and hoping nobody will notice that they're ignoring all the people still there. All the people who are going to follow the next monster who comes along offering them something better. The Councils are supposed to *be* that something better. That was their whole fucking point, from the start. But it's like everybody's forgotten that."

My aunt gave me an assessing look. "You've given this a lot of thought."

I turned away, suddenly embarrassed, because the truth was I hadn't, not until I was forced to. I had spent my entire life not thinking about it. Not thinking about why Baqir banked his anger with deliberate calm when he talked about his childhood. Not thinking about how absurd it was that a world capable of building research outposts on moons hundreds of millions of kilometers away claimed it couldn't protect children from sickness if those children happened to be in the wrong place on the map. Not thinking about how insidiously easy it was to convince oneself that the burden of proving one's humanity rested entirely on the shoulders of those in need of help, and not on those who could help but chose not to.

"I'm thinking about it now," I said. "They're going to make me sit in there and justify trying to save humanity so, yes, I've been thinking about why it's worth saving."

Aunt Padmavati was smiling.

"What?" I said. "Do you think I'll just piss them off if I say something?"

She shook her head slightly. "I'm thinking about something Amita told me once, a long time ago," she said. "This was long before you were born, before she met Vinod. I had just returned home after a year in North America. I had been volunteering at an application processing camp. She was so excited about the work she was doing at university. Her mind was overflowing with ideas, so many brilliant thoughts she couldn't stop talking about them. They were only ideas then, before they became her Almora engine, but even then she knew she was going to put humanity back into deep space. She knew it. She had always been confident, but this was different. She knew she was going to build the engines that pushed humankind farther than it had ever traveled."

Aunt Padmavati paused, cleared her throat delicately. There were tears in her eyes, but her expression was one of warmth and fondness. This was not an unhappy memory for her, however much it must hurt to speak of my mother when she was young.

"She said she was going to fly so far away the sun was only a star like all the other stars. And I . . . well, I was not so arrogant as Amita, but I was quite a bit more self-righteous. And, yes"—and here my aunt's voice turned wry—"she was terribly arrogant. That she was right about how brilliant she was did not make her any less insufferable. But I had just come from the deserts, and I was certain I knew how to solve the North American problem, certain I knew how to convince all the separatists to join the Councils, so certain I could change it all.

"I asked Amita how she could be so cavalier about flying away when there were so many problems to solve on Earth. Wasn't it the same as the generation ships who left during the Collapse, I asked, all those wealthy and powerful people fleeing the consequences of the catastrophes they had created? Do you know what she said?

"She said she would be happy to leave, because she would be leaving me behind to keep the world safe while she was out finding new ones." Aunt Padmavati primly wiped her eyes and delicately blew her nose.

It was so easy to imagine Mum saying those words that, for a moment, I could almost hear them, in her bold and excited voice, her dark eyes glinting, in that way she had that always made my father smile fondly and tell her not to forget to eat supper when she went off to reinterpret the laws of physics this time. I missed them so much my heart ached with a deep, deep pain I did not think would ever entirely fade.

"That was fifty years ago. I think it's about time I start working on the challenge my sister set for me." Still smiling, my aunt went on, "Jas, there is no doubt you'll piss off the Councilors if you speak up in support of the survivors, which means you should absolutely say whatever you want to say."

"I'm glad you think so," I said, and I cleared my throat, "because I'm going to say I didn't save the fucking planet just so we can go on congratulating ourselves for not being barbarians anymore while we're still refusing to help people who need it. I'm going to say they should learn from what Zahra said about what her father believed."

"The world not as it is," Aunt Padmavati said quietly, "but as it is meant to be."

The door opened and the page leaned in. "They're ready for you, Councilor Bhattacharya, Mr. Bhattacharya. Right this way, please."

We stood, Aunt Padmavati and I side by side. She reached up to adjust my collar, picked an invisible speck from my shirt.

"Ready?" she said.

"I'm ready."

Together we followed the page from the room. Sunlight shone through high windows, and voices rang from the room where the Councilors had gathered. They sounded angry, impatient, talking over and past each other, accents and languages from all over the world, too much noise for too close a space. My aunt gestured for me to enter first. I hesitated, letting myself look out over the city, transforming beneath the vast domes and rising light, and all of it so very fragile, so delicate in its beauty. The universe was larger now, and more terrifying, but the same mistakes lingered, and the same truths remained. Everything built by human hands could be destroyed. Everything dreamed by human minds could be preserved. There were trees blossoming in rooftop gardens across the city.

The Councilors fell silent as I stepped into the room. My hands were not shaking anymore.